# THE HORSE AT THE GATES

## A POLITICAL THRILLER

### DC ALDEN

## ALSO BY DC ALDEN

*Invasion*

*Invasion - The Lost Chapters*

*The Angola Deception*

*Fortress*

Join my **VIP Reader Team** for news, updates, bonus material and special discounts:

**Sign Up!**

*This hollow fabric either must inclose, Within its blind recess, our secret foes;*
*Or 't is an engine rais'd above the town,*
*T' o'erlook the walls, and then to batter down. Somewhat is sure design'd, by fraud or force: Trust not their presents, nor admit the horse*

**Virgil's Aeneid**

# PROLOGUE

'Tell me, what will happen after the bomb, after the chaos that will follow?'

The young student whispered the question as he leaned across the restaurant table, careful to shield his mouth with the palm of his hand as he'd been taught. His contact, Javed Raza, a burly field operative with Pakistan's intelligence agency, waved the boy back into his seat and summoned a waiter with a snap of his fingers. He'd arrived at the popular Islamabad restaurant only moments ago and understandably the boy was eager to press him for information, but the meeting had to appear casual, just two friends enjoying lunch. Raza made sure he sat facing the street and draped his crumpled suit jacket over the back of the chair.

'All in good time, Abbas.'

He scooped up a menu. Raza saw the boy frown as the waiter delivered a carafe of water to the table. Ah, the impatience of youth; he knew the feeling, the thrill of a forthcoming operation, the excitement as details of the target unfolded. He should be feeling the same but today he wasn't himself. Maybe it was the weather; it was damned hot, the sky a clear blue, the sun a relentless white orb baking the city. He poured a tall glass of water and raised it to his mouth, his lips barely moving. 'Be patient. Eat. Then we talk.'

The waiter took their order and hurried away. Raza fanned his sweating face with a folded newspaper and watched the street. Their table was outside on the pavement, set deep in the shadows of the Haleem Cafe's striped awning that offered some protection from the midday sun. Nearby, the lunchtime crowds squeezed through the bazaar's narrow streets. Businessmen jostled for space alongside burqa-clad women, while street vendors lounged outside garish shops and ramshackle stalls, smoking cigarettes and touting their wares with monotonous mantras. The noise was incessant as voices battled with each other, with the taxis and motorbikes that revved and honked their way through the human tide. Laughing children ducked and dodged through it all, oblivious to the crowds, mocking the curses that followed them, ignorant of the hardships the future held for them—if they survived, Raza observed.

His dark eyes narrowed as a passing military foot patrol cut a path through the throng, weapons held across their chests, suspicious eyes peering beneath helmet rims. Islamabad had barely been touched by the violence spreading around the country yet there was nervousness in the soldiers' movements, a sense of urgency that fuelled their swift passage through the narrow confines of the bazaar. Raza watched the crocodile of green helmets bobbing through the crowd until they were lost in the distance.

The food arrived in short order, delivered to the table in steaming bowls; spicy lamb biryanis with alu subzi potatoes, taftan bread and chapattis, with a side order of shami kebab for the boy. They ate in relative silence, watching the ebb and flow of the bazaar as the tables around them filled with lunch goers. Raza could only manage a few mouthfuls then pushed his plate away, the nausea that had plagued him all morning robbing him of his appetite. Finally the table was cleared and the carafe refreshed. Raza produced a small white tablet from a pillbox and slipped it under his tongue, washing it down with a glass of water as the waiter delivered a pot of coffee to the table.

'You are unwell?' Abbas asked, pouring them both a cup.

'It's nothing. The heat.'

'It's barely thirty-five degrees.'

Raza ignored the observation. He pushed his coffee cup to one side and leaned forward, his thick, hairy arms folded on the table. 'So,' he began, his voice low, his eyes scanning the other diners, the passers-by, the street vendors, 'you are prepared?' Although both men spoke fluent Punjabi, they slipped easily into Arabic.

'Yes,' replied Abbas, burping loudly as he drained his cup. 'I have made my peace.'

Raza noticed that the boy's green eyes shone brightly and his hands shook in anticipation, like a fighter seconds before the opening bell, energised, powerful, a machine of violence waiting to be unleashed. He'd seen this before, in others, those that had been chosen for missions from which there would be no return. This operation was different though; this time there could be no fasting, no ritual ablutions, and this had troubled the boy. But security was paramount.

'Your courage is an inspiration to others. Your family will honour your name.'

Raza watched the boy stroke his thick beard and lower

his eyes. He stared at the tablecloth for a moment, then looked up and said, 'They have no knowledge of this.'

'Have no fear,' Raza assured him, 'they will be informed.'

'They are poor. I am their only son.'

'Arrangements have been made. They will be compensated handsomely.'

The boy's eyes closed momentarily, the guilt lifted from his shoulders. It was only right. The parents were farmers, scratching out a living from the stubborn soil of the Siran Valley. Like most parents they nurtured a hope that their young son, blessed with an aptitude uncommon for his lineage, would support them during their advancing years. It was not to be, the boy drawn to the cause in his first semester at the University of Engineering & Technology in Khuzdar. There he'd been marked for interest, cultivated, schooled in the necessity for global Jihad. Normally such an intelligent asset would not be wasted on a single operation, but today was different.

'Tell me, Mister Javed, after the bomb. What will happen?'

Raza spoke quietly, his eyes watchful. 'It will not be as you imagine, my young friend. The armies of Allah will advance without weapons and the battles will be bloodless, fought in the polling booths and government chambers of the west. It is true, many will die today.' Raza paused, studying the boy before him. 'You are untroubled by this.'

'The cause is worthwhile, is it not?'

'More than you realise.'

'Then it is not for me to pass judgement, only to execute the mission.'

Raza leaned back in his chair and regarded Abbas with a satisfied eye. The candidate was much more gifted than the usual batch of ignorant goat herders and mental cases that rarely hesitated to sacrifice their young lives for Allah.

'Where is the vehicle?'

The boy pointed a slender finger towards the eastern end of the bazaar. 'Some distance away, as you instructed.'

'Let's walk.'

The bill was settled and the men left the restaurant, plunging into the river of bodies, allowing the swirling current of humanity to carry them along yet disconnected from the herd. The boy walked slightly ahead, subtly shouldering a path through the crowd. He was acting like a bodyguard Raza realised, protecting his master from the worst of the throng. None challenged his sharp elbows, his garb and purposeful movement brooking no argument. Despite the waves of nausea, Raza smiled with satisfaction. The boy would not disappoint.

They left the bazaar behind them, and Raza was thankful to be free of the stifling press of humanity. He held his jacket over his arm as the afternoon sun beat the earth, hammering the asphalt roads and dusty pavements. He took a crumpled handkerchief from his pocket and mopped his clammy brow, wincing as a sharp pain shot up his arm and pierced his neck. He tried to ignore it, following the boy as he turned off the main road and into a shady side street where the battered Toyota pickup waited. Raza almost sighed with relief.

They climbed inside, Raza fumbling with the air conditioning as the boy coaxed the engine into life. The dark blue pickup threaded its way through quiet back streets and out onto Jinnah Avenue, where it merged with the heavy eastbound traffic. As the Toyota cruised along in the nearside lane, Raza watched the passing landscape, the roadside advertising hoardings, the flame trees that lined the busy avenue, the looming towers of the city's financial district, glass and steel facades sparkling beneath the hot sun.

'Look around you, Abbas, look how our country tries to mimic the west, how our leaders crave their acceptance, how they flood our markets with western goods, undermining the laws of sharia with their twisted values.'

'Traitors,' the boy spat, his eyes glued to the road.

'Europe is another matter,' Raza continued in a low voice, massaging the ache in his left arm. 'Their governments and institutions are slaves to political correctness. Their leaders are wary of our growing power, our willingness to defend our beliefs with violence, but are too shackled by their liberal ways to challenge us. Instead, they appease us with weak words and fear in their eyes.'

Ahead, through the dirt-streaked windshield, Raza saw the Aiwan-e-Sadr, Islamabad's Presidential Palace, squatting majestically between the Parliament and the National Assembly buildings. For a moment, Raza ignored the numbness in his hands. For the average citizen, the regal cluster of modern architecture represented absolute power and authority in Pakistan, yet for Raza it offered nothing more than a charade of stability, the corrupt politicians that lurked inside seeking to paper over the cracks of Pakistan's fractious existence, to smother its deep religious and political divisions. Raza despised them.

'A house of cards,' he hissed through his teeth, 'ready to fall.' He pointed through the windshield. 'Turn here.'

The boy yanked the wheel to the left and soon the Toyota was cruising the shaded streets of the Markaz district, less than a mile from the Presidential Palace. At Raza's instruction he turned again, pulling the vehicle up onto the driveway of a residential property. It was nondescript, a whitewashed bungalow set back from the road, the door and windows secured behind steel grills, the type of dwelling fancied by a senior government worker or moderately successful businessman. Raza looked up and down the street, shielding his eyes from the glare of the sun. Nothing moved, not even a stray dog. He climbed out of the pickup and headed towards the shade of the arched portico, a set of keys in his hand. He unlocked the steel security gate, then the front door, and led the boy inside. He flicked on the lights, revealing a large, open living area, whitewashed walls and a red tiled floor. Every window was boarded with thick sheets of plywood, and there was no furniture to speak of. They passed a kitchen, empty cupboards left open like mouths waiting to be fed. A short hallway led them to a rear bedroom and Raza unlocked the door with a thick brass key. Inside, the room was in darkness, the window sealed with another sheet of plywood. There was no bed, only a table, barely visible in the gloom, an indistinct lump on its surface. Raza ran his hand around the wall and found the light switch. An overhead strip light hummed and blinked into life, washing the room in its harsh industrial glare. A green military rucksack occupied the table top. A very large rucksack.

'How many people does it take to create chaos?' asked Raza rhetorically, checking the snap-locks on the rucksack for signs of tampering. 'Long ago, nineteen martyrs armed with box cutters crippled the world's largest superpower in a matter of hours. London and Madrid suffered similar chaos when a mere handful of our soldiers—'

Raza's words caught in his throat. His head swam, then his stomach lurched violently. 'Wait here,' he commanded. He walked quickly along the corridor to the bathroom, where he performed two tasks. The first was to throw up, his knuckles white as his hands grasped the cool rim of the sink. After his exertions he let the water run, splashing his face and neck. He stood upright and looked in the mirror. Not good, he realised. His brown skin had taken on a grey pallor, the rings beneath his eyes darker than usual. His shirt was soaked, the thick hair on his chest visible through the damp material. He didn't have much time.

The wave of nausea temporarily sated, he moved on to task number two, which required him to stand on the toilet seat and reach up into the small roof space above. From the dark recess he retrieved a thin aluminium briefcase and headed back to the bedroom.

'You are unwell,' the boy said. This time it wasn't a question.

'It does not matter.' Raza placed the briefcase on the table and snapped open the locks. Inside, cushioned within thick foam compartments, lay two brushed-steel tubes with distinctive red caps. 'You recognise these?' he asked. The boy snorted, almost indignantly, Raza noticed. Such confidence. He spun the briefcase around and the boy ran a finger along the grey foam, lifting out the bridge wire detonators from their compartments and inspecting them with a practised eye. He nestled them carefully back inside the foam then turned his attention to the rucksack.

'It is not as I expected.'

'These things rarely are.'

The boy unzipped a fastener around the outside of the rucksack and removed a green nylon flap. Behind it was a panel, the writing on its green casing clearly Urdu. 'One of ours,' he remarked.

Raza nodded. 'Based on the Russian RA-One One Five tactical model. This one was originally intended to take out the Indian naval base at Karwar. The design is crude. No timing mechanism, no remote detonation—'

'A martyr's weapon,' the boy finished. He embraced the rucksack in his arms and dragged it towards him. He unfastened the top snap locks and rolled the nylon material down, partly revealing the smooth metallic tube inside. He peeled away several Velcro flaps until the inspection and access panels were visible, then stood back. Raza watched him run a hand along the metal casing of the warhead. 'It is a thing of beauty,' the boy whispered.

Raza stepped forward and lifted the foam panel containing the detonators out of the briefcase, revealing a comprehensive and sophisticated set of screwdrivers and a pair of small electronic devices that he didn't even pretend to understand. He pushed the case towards the boy.

'You have all you need?'

Abbas ran a finger over the screwdrivers then removed the devices, checking power levels and nodding approvingly. 'Everything.'

The older man mopped his sweating face and neck with his handkerchief. 'Good. Then I must leave.' He checked the digital Timex on his wrist. 'The President will begin his address to Parliament in one hour and twelve minutes. You should detonate the device at exactly two forty-five.'

The boy checked his own watch and nodded. Already Raza could see his mind was elsewhere as he laid his tools carefully on the table in a precise and specific order. There would be no cries of *Allahu Akbar* here today, no other jihadi proclamations or exhortations of violence. They were both professionals, men of faith to be sure, but professionals first and foremost. He left the boy alone, closing the bedroom door behind him.

Raza secured the front of the house, re-locking the security gate. He backed the Toyota off the driveway, idling by the pavement as he searched the street for inquisitive eyes, for waiting army trucks or hovering helicopters. There were none. He jammed the vehicle into gear and headed north, towards the Pir Sohawa Road, the winding, twisting route that would take him up over the Margalla Hills and beyond the range of the blast.

He'd travelled less than two miles when the pain gripped him, his chest constricting as if a steel wire had been curled around his torso and violently tightened. He cried out and swerved the Toyota off the road, the front tyres bouncing over the kerb as it slewed to a halt in a cloud of red dust by the roadside. He clutched his chest, arms wrapped around his body, then turned and vomited onto the passenger seat. He finished retching after several moments, cuffing silvery strands of bile from his mouth as sweat poured down his face. He needed help, fast. Cars drove by him on the road, oblivious to his plight, the pickup stalled deep in the shade of a stand of eucalyptus trees. He considered calling an ambulance, but that was pointless. The hospital was less than a mile from where the boy now laboured.

No, he had to get away.

He pulled himself upright and leaned back in his seat, moaning softly, willing the pain to pass. Through the wind-shield his eyes searched the densely wooded hills before him, seeking the road that would lead him to safety in the valley beyond. Another wave of pain jolted him sideways, pulling him down onto the passenger seat, his body settling into the puddle of bile and barely-digested lumps of food already congealing on the cracked leather. With a trembling right hand he reached into his trouser pocket, his thick fingers desperately seeking the familiar shape of his pillbox. He withdrew it, flicking open the lid as another knife of pain stabbed his chest. He fumbled the box, spilling the contents into the foot well below him. He panted heavily, his lungs labouring under the strain, his damp face resting on the hot leather of the door panel, a thin string of saliva dangling from his lower lip. He stared down at them, a constellation of heart pills scattered across the rubber matting, as distant as the Milky Way itself. The sound of the nearby traffic faded to a distant hum as he stared up through the windshield, the blue sky barely visible between the dark leaves of the eucalyptus. The thick overhead covering swayed back and forth, the branches bowing and waving before a gentle afternoon breeze. The motion seemed to calm him and the pain gradually subsided, his damaged heart slowing its frantic, erratic rhythms. His breathing retuned to something like normality, yet still he could not move. Instead, he lay still, staring at the shifting trees until they blurred, then faded from view...

His eyes snapped open, his heart quickening. His breath came in ragged gasps and, once again, he felt the first ripples of pain fanning out around his body. Something was wrong. He was still alive. With dangerous effort he dragged his left arm from beneath his body. The blue LCD display pulsed before his eyes: 14:43. He let his arm drop, moaning in temporary relief. The pain ebbed and flowed across his chest, getting sharper with each wave, building towards its deadly finale. Raza settled onto his back and waited for it to be over, briefly wondering what Paradise would be like. He hoped it would be as he'd been taught, that the rewards for martyrdom would be as described, that his heart would be whole and strong once more. He hoped it would be all of that.

Through the windshield the branches ceased their rhythmic swaying as the breeze suddenly faded, then died. Everything became still. With his good arm Raza tried to shield his eyes as the sky overhead suddenly brightened, turning from blue to a dazzling, burning, searing white.

The leaves vanished.

The trees, vaporised.

THE TWO-MEGATON DETONATION wiped the administrative heart of Islamabad off the face of the earth, killing the President, the Senate, all of the National Assembly, plus every other living organism within a two-mile radius. Beyond that, roads melted and tall buildings were levelled, the blast wave rolling across the flat plain to the west and destroying everything in its deadly path. Thousands died in an instant, thousands more were buried, blackened and burnt.

High above the earth, in the cold vacuum of space, orbiting satellites and remote sensor platforms recorded the light pulse and the resulting heat bloom, downloading real-time images and digital data to frantic controllers in scores of monitoring stations across a dozen countries. World leaders were woken, or interrupted, or whisked to emergency facilities, depending on their proximity to the ruins of Islamabad. The Indian government was first to denounce the ghastly event, immediately denying any involvement while ordering their armed forces to go to full nuclear alert. The world held its breath and waited.

While the radioactive fallout drifted on the wind and settled across the Pothohar plateau, the political fallout was carried around the world. Governments squabbled, diplomacy failed.

Pakistan disintegrated, and descended into violent darkness.

## HEATHROW, MIDDLESEX

'Eight minutes out, Prime Minister.'

Gabriel Bryce cursed silently, gripping the tan leather armrests a little tighter as the pilot's voice hissed inside the soundproofed cabin. Around him the sleek executive helicopter continued to buck and dip as it headed west, buffeted by a strong head wind and violent rain squalls. He glanced at the two close protection officers opposite, noting the tension in their bodies as the helicopter chopped through the deteriorating weather. He took small comfort in the fact that he wasn't the only one trying to conceal his anxiety.

Timing could be a real bastard, Bryce observed. His first helicopter trip in weeks just happened to coincide with a major storm front sweeping in from the Atlantic. Devon and Cornwall had already taken a battering and soon it would be London's turn. The experts said the worst was due in about six hours, which offered Bryce a sliver of optimism. By then he should be safely back in Downing Street, tucked up inside the warmth of his apartment.

The helicopter dropped suddenly, the soundproofing in

the passenger cabin failing to smother the roar of the engines overhead as the pilots fought to correct the stomach-churning plunge. Bryce's mouth was dry, his heart thumping in his chest. He knew he was in capable hands, that the pilots were experienced, that the state-of-the-art helicopter was fitted with every safety device imaginable; yet still he felt powerless, exposed – scared, if the truth be told.

It was the fear of crashing, of course. Not the impact itself, but those terrible moments, sometimes minutes, before an aircraft hit the ground, when the crescendo of human howls competed with the ear-splitting scream of the engines, the bone-rattling vibration of a failing airframe, the abject terror on the faces of the passengers. He'd imagined it many times, visually aided by his fascination for air crash investigation programmes. Why he did it, he didn't know, but he regretted watching them every time he boarded an aircraft.

He recalled the collision near Heathrow, almost twenty years ago now, between a British Airways triple seven and a Qantas airbus, one of the big double-decked ones. Both planes had a full passenger manifest, the airbus loaded with jet fuel after take-off a minute or so before. The collision had lit up the night sky, the burning wreckage raining down across the town of Windsor. Bryce recalled a number of charred corpses had the audacity to land within the grounds of the Royal castle, an event that generated almost as much official outrage as the circumstances of the collision itself.

Yet it had changed things completely, the third runway scrapped, the plans for a new airport dusted off and speedily implemented. Now, London International strad-dled the Thames estuary, a billion over budget and four years overdue, but an example of what could be done if the political will and the necessity were there. Bryce smiled wryly; all it took was a tragedy on an unimaginable scale for it to happen.

The helicopter shuddered and lurched to the left and Bryce strangled the armrests once again. He felt a hand on the sleeve of his overcoat.

'Almost there,' soothed Ella. His Downing Street Chief of Staff sat in the seat beside him, completely unruffled, bundled up in a black North Face parka, her blond hair tied back in a loose pony tail, her deep brown eyes blinking rapidly behind rimless designer glasses. Bryce could tell she was faintly amused by his aversion to flying, so he focussed his mind on other matters instead.

'What's the latest from NASA?'

Ella fished inside her parka and produced her phone. She massaged the touch-screen with practised ease. 'Still no contact. Right now they're saying it could be a software failure with the communications code package, either on the craft itself or at the deep space site in Mojave.'

'Poor bastards,' Bryce muttered, 'all that way and we don't even know if they survived the trip.' The thought put Bryce's own fear of flying into perspective. The first manned mission to the moon in over half a century, the three-man crew still orbiting that distant, barren rock, all contact with the craft lost, the deadline for mission failure—an astronomically expensive mission—fast approaching. It made Bryce question how such an achievement was accomplished so easily all those years ago. 'We'd better prepare something, just in case.'

'I've got Sam working on it.'

'Good. Anything else?'

Ella scrolled down the screen, flicking each line of news feed with a soberly painted fingernail. 'The storm is hogging the domestic headlines. Floods and wind damage down in Cornwall, channel crossings cancelled, etcetera. Nothing else worth mentioning.'

Bryce grunted an acknowledgement. Their journey tonight had been a clandestine one, descending into the tunnels beneath Whitehall, their footsteps echoing along dimly-lit subterranean chambers until they emerged into the pouring rain outside the old Admiralty building on the Mall. The car that idled by the pavement whisked them unescorted through the streets of Victoria and across the river to Battersea power station. In the shadow of the massive structure the executive helicopter waited, rotors already turning. Within a few minutes Bryce could feel the strength of the approaching storm as the aircraft battled through the sky across west London. At least it's dark, he thought. He didn't care to see the towering wall of black clouds as they headed towards them.

'One minute,' announced the pilot over the intercom, and Bryce began to relax a little as the aircraft dropped lower and the turbulence subsided. Chain-link fencing flashed beneath them, then a jumbled collection of flat rooftops. The nose of the helicopter tilted upwards as it flared for landing opposite a single-storey building, cloaked in darkness and fronted by a tarmac apron. Bryce glimpsed a solitary figure sheltering beneath the overhanging canopy, then he was lost in a storm of spray as the aircraft settled onto the tarmac. The bodyguards were already unbuckling their belts and Bryce saw the tension in their faces, glimpsed the ugly black weapons concealed beneath their raincoats. There was a pause as the rotors wound down and Bryce saw the figure by the building head towards the helicopter, umbrella held like a shield against the weather.

The bodyguards piled out and stood guard on either

side of the door, their eyes probing the night, raincoats flapping in the wind. Cold air rushed in, snatching the warmth of the cabin away as the man with the umbrella waited by the open door. His thin face had a well-worn look about it, the eyes sunk deep into their sockets, dark hollows under the cheekbones. The corduroy collar of his Barbour was turned up around his ears and a fine sheen of raindrops clung to its waxy surface. He held the umbrella aloft, his hands wrapped in black leather gloves, his eyes squinting against the rain. He had to shout to make himself heard.

'Welcome to Heathrow, Prime Minister. I'm Brian Davies, Chief of Operations.' He nodded to Ella. 'Follow me, please.'

Bryce stepped out of the aircraft. Silver sheets of rain swept across the tarmac, driven on by the relentless wind. He buttoned his coat to the neck and thrust his hands in his pockets, following Davies toward the unlit building where they huddled beneath the canopy. Overhead, one of its metal panels had worked loose and was banging a demented tattoo in the wind. Davies held open a filthy glass door and gestured them all inside. Bryce stamped his wet shoes on the floor, the sound echoing around the darkness. Should've worn something a bit sturdier, he realised.

Davies stooped to pick up a large flashlight by the door and swept its powerful beam around the immediate area. Bryce saw they were in an abandoned terminal building, the floor a mixture of cracked tiles and threadbare carpet. Most of the external windows were boarded up, the surrounding walls heavily stained by water damage. Overhead, rain hammered on the roof and buckets lay scattered around the floor, catching the leaks from above. The place was derelict, an unused concrete shell located at the far edge of what was once the world's busiest airport.

'This is Security Station Four. It used to be the old VIP terminal,' explained Davies. 'We've had one or two snoopers since we opened for business, but they never get further than the fences.'

He led them through the building, the cone of light bouncing in the darkness, until they reached a heavy-looking grey door emblazoned with a black stick figure being zapped by a large bolt of electricity. The words beneath read, *Danger of Death – No Entry To Unauthorised Personnel*. Davies tapped the sign and smiled. 'More subterfuge.' He produced a swipe card and the door clicked open. 'Please follow me.'

'Wait here,' Bryce ordered the policemen. He ushered Ella through the door and closed it behind him. The smell of decay and damp was gone, replaced by warm air and a low electronic hum. Davies led them into another dimly lit corridor, a glass partition running along its length. Behind the glass was a high-tech control room, dozens of monitors and coloured lights glowing in the darkness. Bryce counted a dozen or so people scattered around the windowless walls, dressed in civilian clothes and monitoring banks of surveillance screens.

'Don't worry, they can't see you,' Davies informed them. He tapped the glass with a knuckle as they headed towards yet another security door. 'All this is one way. The operators in there are monitoring the accommodation areas on the old runways.'

Bryce paused behind the glass. The first thing he noticed was the lack of activity on the screens, no doubt due to the late hour and the terrible weather. The camera angles were varied; interior shots of brightly lit public rooms and long, empty dormitory corridors. There were night vision images in shades of grey and ghostly green, probing dark and muddy alleyways and deserted open areas. Litter seemed a common feature in almost every shot, spilling out of plastic bins, piled in corners or tumbling through the barren dreamscape. A sudden movement caught Bryce's eye, a distant camera capturing a man ducking out of an accommodation block, a burqa-clad woman trailing behind him. The man unfurled a striped umbrella then hurried out into the night, the woman already soaked as she trailed obediently after him.

'What a charmer,' observed Ella.

They followed Davies up a metal staircase to his first floor office, originally an observation deck the operations chief explained. A single desk occupied a space near the far wall, alongside two metal filing cabinets. The other walls were decorated with a multitude of large-scale maps of the Heathrow site, apart from one wall that looked out over the runways. That one was made of a single sheet of glass and Bryce was drawn to it, Ella falling in beside him.

'Jesus,' she breathed, shaking off her coat.

It had been just over eighteen months since Bryce had last visited the site, almost two years since Islamabad was destroyed by the nuke. Back then he'd given a short speech over at Terminal Five, emphasising the need to give aid and comfort to the refugees who'd travelled so far and suffered so terribly. Thirty prefabricated temporary accommodation blocks had been erected, clustered around the old taxiways and aircraft stands of the terminal, each housing two hundred people. He'd welcomed the new arrivals, drank coffee, posed for photographs and then returned to London, his duty done. It was supposed to be a temporary arrangement, a short-term fix; no one had expected the civil war in Pakistan to last long. Yet it had, the violence spreading across the country, the refugees continuing to flee westwards, transiting through the Gulf States to Egypt, where over a million people still languished in desert camps outside the cities. From his elevated vantage point, Gabriel Bryce stared out across the expanse of Heathrow and shook his head; it was hard to imagine that an airport once existed here at all.

Beyond the waiting helicopter, beyond the double chain-link fence that surrounded the terminal building, the Heathrow Relocation Centre sprawled into the distance, a seemingly endless landscape of two-storey structures that marched towards the dark horizon. The disused runways, the aprons and taxiways, the grass verges, most of it had disappeared, swallowed by the prefabricated city. Halogen lamps clustered on steel towers glowed above the rooftops, rain sweeping through their bright shafts of light. The nearest accommodation blocks were five hundred yards away, curving into the distance in line with the well-lit perimeter fence. Rubbish piled against the chain link and strands of material fluttered in the wind, caught in the crown of razor wire that topped the boundary. Distant lights glowed in the old terminal buildings.

Bryce turned away from the window, pulling off his overcoat. He was dressed casually, grey slacks and a black turtleneck sweater. 'Quite a sight when you see it up close,' he remarked.

Davies hung the coat on a stand behind the door. 'You should see it in daylight.' He took a seat behind his desk, inviting Bryce and Ella into empty chairs opposite.

'Looks deserted out there,' Bryce observed.

'Friday's a busy day for the population here. There're prayers of course, followed by all sorts of meetings and sit-downs. The main arrivals hall in Terminal Five is being used a mosque, as are the ones in the other terminals, plus there are several more scattered around the site. They're all full to bursting on Fridays.'

There was a tap on the door and an Asian man entered, a tray of coffee and biscuits held before him. He wore a navy Border Force fleece zipped up to the chin, partly obscuring his wispy beard. He nodded politely, while Davies cleared a space on his untidy desk. Bryce shot a look at Ella as the man backed out of the room. Davies caught the exchange as he passed around the mugs.

'Taj is my right-hand here. Very high clearance.' The security chief leaned back in his chair. 'Well, you can see the operation has grown immeasurably since you were last here. As I explained on the phone, we're struggling to cope.'

Bryce sipped at the steaming coffee as he registered the untidy mess of papers on Davies' desk. Behind him, a high spec printer beeped continuously, spitting out sheets of paper. 'I was aware of a certain level of pressure on resources here, Mister Davies, but nothing like you described during our conversation.'

'The place is falling apart, Prime Minister. To all intents and purposes we've lost control.' Davies unlocked a desk drawer and removed a single sheet of paper. He handed it to Bryce. 'This is why I couldn't talk on the phone.'

Bryce gave Davies a puzzled look, and began to read:

---

CONFIDENTIAL SECURITY INCIDENT REVIEW. NOT FOR CIRCULATION. EYES ONLY:—

12-01: 661/541: Female stoned to death by large crowd of male assailants between blocks 227 & 228, sector 14.

11-02: 1025/445: Two security officers seriously assaulted in sector 09 during routine patrol. Personal protection equipment, swipe cards and radios stolen.

29-03: 256/091: Teenage girl doused with flammable liquid and set on fire outside maternity unit at Terminal 2.

27-05: 199/472: Male killed during large disturbance at wedding ceremony in Terminal 4.

22-08: 088/190: Two males found hanged in washroom in block 17, sector 3. Murdered by unknown assailants for alleged homosexual activities.

---

BRYCE LOOKED UP, his face pale. 'These incidents happened here?'

Davies crunched on a biscuit and nodded. 'All in the last eight months. I assumed you knew because detailed reports of each incident were sent to both my own superiors and to Minister Saeed. He ordered a blanket censorship.'

*Tariq.*

Bryce held up the sheet of paper between his thumb and forefinger, as if the contents were somehow contagious. 'What about the suspects? The witnesses?'

'Some of the incidents were captured on CCTV, but Minister Saeed had the footage seized. He promised an internal inquiry but it's yet to happen. The casualties have been explained away as accidents, suicides, that sort of thing.'

'He's covered this up?'

Davies hesitated. 'Well, that sort of accusation is above my pay grade, Prime Minister. However, I can tell you that Minister Saeed's office makes very little attempt to liaise with Operations these days, unless it's to restrict our effectiveness in some way. I've raised concerns with my own chain of command, but I've been told in no uncertain terms to shut up and crack on.'

Bryce handed the sheet of paper back to Davies. 'This is unacceptable.'

Davies locked the report away and swept a hand towards the window. 'The simple truth is, out there beyond the wire the rule of law is an imported one. They have their own leadership hierarchy, operate a working Sharia court system, manage their own disputes, and so on. One by one our integration programmes have been scrapped and my staff no longer patrol the accommodation blocks or any of the public areas.'

'Why?'

Davies looked pained. 'Minister Saeed believes our presence intimidates the refugees.'

Bryce got up and went to the window. Rain continued to lash the camp, urged on by the strengthening wind. The roof above creaked before its power, but Bryce was oblivious to the fast approaching storm. 'You've spoken to the minister directly about your concerns?'

'I managed to get a moment with him a few weeks ago. He told me in no uncertain terms that the running of the camp must not be interfered with.' Davies leaned back in his chair. 'I'm not sure if you're aware of the influence he holds here, Prime Minister. He gave a speech in Terminal

Five when he was last here. You could hear the roar of the crowd from this office.'

Bryce pointed to Davies' computer screen. 'Show me the footage.'

The security chief shook his head. 'All monitoring systems in the terminal buildings are disabled when Minister Saeed visits. Privacy issues.'

Bryce stared across the dark expanse of Heathrow. This was getting worse by the minute. 'You were right to contact me directly, Mister Davies.'

The chief of operations took a sip of coffee. 'There are other concerns, Prime Minister.' He put his mug down and began ticking them off on his fingers. 'We have a rising birth rate that our medical facilities cannot cope with, we're seeing disease outbreaks, we've got tribal and family disputes, many ending in some form of violence. And we're losing refugees too, a thousand in the last six months, just disappearing into the night. Some we pick up outside the wire, most we don't. I haven't got the resources to combat it.'

Bryce thought he'd misheard. 'Escaping?'

'Every day. We can't cope.'

Bryce was finding it hard to take it all in. Control of the site had been lost, that much was clear, and Tariq had allowed it to happen. Worse, he appeared to be actively encouraging it. Behind him, Davies took advantage of the Prime Minister's silence.

'It's like another country out there, a country of over one hundred thousand. And rising.' Davies lowered his voice and Bryce had to face him to hear what he said. 'The fact is, it doesn't feel like a humanitarian effort anymore. It feels more like a siege.'

'That's dangerous language, Mister Davies.'

The security chief didn't blink. 'It's the truth.'

Bryce turned back to the window. So, the monthly brief he'd been receiving from Tariq's office was deliberately evasive, a smoke screen to hide the true nature of what was happening here. But why? He marched back to his chair and pulled his coat on, helping Ella into hers.

'I want a detailed dossier on what you've just told me. Include everything, Mister Davies. Media files, departmental communications, minutes of meetings, the lot. I'm putting a stop to this shambles.'

Davies hesitated, his hands folded nervously on the table. 'You're shutting us down?'

Bryce nodded. 'That's why you contacted my office, isn't it?'

'Sir, with all due respect, I'll need some assurances. Being a whistle-blower doesn't exactly look good on one's CV. I've got financial commitments, a pension to consider—'

Bryce cut him short, snapping the collar of his coat around his ears. 'You'll be taken care of, Mister Davies, you have my word. It's your superiors who'll be seeking new employment opportunities.'

Davies rose from behind his desk, clearly relieved. 'I appreciate that, Sir.'

'As soon as possible, Mister Davies.'

Outside, helicopter rotor blades beat the air, whipping clouds of spray across the tarmac. Thirty seconds later they were airborne, the nose of the helicopter dipping as it cleared the boundary fence. As they climbed higher, Bryce settled back in his seat. The whole relocation programme was experiencing a fundamental breakdown and refugees were still arriving, hundreds every day. Bryce felt a mixture of emotions: anger, confusion and a lingering sense of unease. Davies had painted a picture of growing lawlessness, sanctioned by Tariq himself. *Murders, for God's sake.* Something had to be done.

Next to him, Ella said, 'you're kidding, right? About shutting down the programme?'

'Does it sound like I'm kidding?'

Behind her designer frames, Ella's eyes widened. 'You can't do that. Brussels won't allow it, and besides, EU immigration laws prevent us from excluding members of extended families already settled here in Britain. We're legally bound to accept them. We'd be overruled, Gabe. Worse, the press will hang you out to dry.'

'To hell with the press,' Bryce seethed. 'People have been killed back there, Ella. This is exactly the sort of ammunition I need to block Cairo.'

The Chief of Staff's face paled in the dim cabin. 'You're what?'

'Look, if we can't deal with a few hundred thousand refugees, what d'you think will happen if we ratify Cairo?'

'Jesus, think about what you're saying, Gabe. Anyway, you can't block it,' she warned, 'you've already signed off on the framework document. The wheels are in motion. They're building the stage as we speak, for Christ's sake. It's too late.'

'Without my signature the treaty is a no go,' Bryce reminded her.

'But we need that deal. Egypt is sitting on top of some of the biggest shale gas fields the region has ever seen, not to mention the oil finds; they're practically giving it away compared to our existing deals with Russia and the Gulf states. Accession is a small price to pay in comparison. We have to be realistic, Gabe.'

Bryce's nostrils flared. 'It's not the prospect of Egypt

joining the EU that bothers me; it's the millions of refugees they're trying to unload on the rest of us.'

'Oh, please. Now you're beginning to sound like your own hate mail.'

'Rubbish.' Bryce found it difficult to filter the frustration out of his voice. 'Look, we've already given leave to stay to over four hundred thousand refugees, plus the hundred thousand back there at Heathrow still waiting to be processed, and tonight we've discovered that the whole place is a complete and utter shambles. No,' he declared, chopping the air with his hand, 'there'll be no more refugees. And no treaty, not until we get our own house in order.'

Ella took a moment to remove her glasses, polishing the lenses with the cuff of her sweater. 'And when are you thinking of dropping this bombshell?'

'As soon as Davies delivers that dossier. Then we can push some temporary legislation through parliament.'

Ella slipped the glasses back on her face. 'Gabe, you need to think about things very carefully. All this could play straight into the hands of the far-right, not to mention the opposition.'

'And what about the murders, Ella? The security breaches? If that gets out before we get a chance to denounce it we'll look even worse.'

'Maybe you should talk to Oliver first, before you take this any further.'

'He already knows.'

Oliver Massey was a former party treasurer, major financial contributor and political mentor. In the early days he'd helped Bryce in his bid to become MP, the wealthy textile magnate subsequently backing Bryce's campaign for party leadership and later donating a large percentage of his election-winning war chest. Massey was his closest friend, albeit a distant one, a very private figure who preferred the sunnier climes of the Caribbean to the wind-swept shores of Britain. Looking beyond the rain-streaked window Bryce didn't blame him. 'It's not just you I confide in, Ella. Oliver is aware of my doubts about Cairo, and shares them. He's prepared to back me whatever decision I make.'

'But you just can't—'

'Enough,' he scowled. 'I won't be swayed on this. Your job is to keep on top of Davies, make sure that dossier shores up my decision. We need to spin it aggressively, so when we do go public people fully understand the scale of the problem.'

Ella stayed quiet, knowing better than to argue when he had the bit between his teeth. His premiership had been a tough one, born on the back of a serious economic downturn and a failing power infrastructure. Ella was right, the country needed Cairo, but at what price? Super-cheap energy would certainly boost the economy, but if they couldn't cope with the long-term effects then the whole exercise was pointless. And there were other, darker repercussions to consider. Violence had begun to rear its ugly head, a spate of attacks that bore all the hallmarks of religious intolerance: two churches burnt down in Lancashire, Jewish cemeteries desecrated, shops firebombed. Bryce had ordered a media blackout in an effort to quash any escalation but the warning signals were clear. There could be no more refugees, no Treaty of Cairo, until the situation had been brought firmly under control. The electorate, and Brussels, would understand.

Ahead, the sparkling towers of London shimmered in the night as the helicopter began its descent. 'When does Tariq get back from Istanbul?'

'Next week.' Ella reached for her phone. 'You want me to pull him out of the conference now?'

Bryce shook his head. 'No. The Islamic Congress will kick up a stink if we yank one of their guest speakers.'

'So, how do you want to play this?'

'We keep it to ourselves,' Bryce ordered. 'Just you, me, and Davies. When the dossier's ready we go public.'

Ella turned the phone over in her hand. It was a nervous gesture, Bryce knew. 'What about Cabinet? You'll have to brief them.'

'No. I can't afford any leaks on this one.'

'That's a risky game, Gabe.'

'I'll chance it. I'm fed up with off-the-record briefings making the front pages.'

'And Tariq?'

'Screw Tariq,' Bryce snapped. 'This whole mess could sink us thanks to that idiot. As soon as we've got that dossier Tariq is out. Finished.'

Below, the ghostly luminance of Battersea's chimneys swept into view as the helicopter circled the power station to land. Bryce unbuckled his seat belt as the aircraft settled on the glowing pad. It was only after he'd stepped out into the rain swept darkness, as he settled into the back seat of the waiting car, that he realised he hadn't noticed the turbulence of the return journey at all.

# 2

## LONDON

THE MAN SLIPPED PAST THE SHAVEN-HEADED BOUNCER and yanked open the heavy wooden door, careful to grasp the worn metal handle with only two fingers. The door swung shut behind him and he wiped his fingers on the leg of his jeans. The King's Head public house was, as expected, a shithole. Situated at the heart of the Longhill estate in north-west London, the single-storey concrete block sported mesh-covered windows, graffiti-daubed walls and a chalk notice board that promised satellite TV and home-cooked meals. The only thing cooked around here was heroin, the man speculated. In any case, the King's Head was a focal point of dubious entertainment for the residents who occupied the surrounding concrete towers, and it was here he'd find the man he sought.

The inside was gloomy, the narrow windows set high around the walls beaming thin shafts of milky daylight across the floor. The man clamped his mobile phone to his ear, faking a conversation while his eyes adjusted to the shadows. The bar was directly in front of him, enveloped in a layer of blue fog. Smoking laws were unenforceable here, a pointless and potentially dangerous exercise for any local official who might be bothered to try.

To his left, along a short corridor, a dimly lit pool room stretched towards the rear of the building. More smoke swirled over the tables, a heady mix of tobacco and cannabis leaking along the corridor. Young men drifted in and out of the table lights, feral street roughs with pale chins jutting beneath baseball caps and hooded sweatshirts. Pool balls cracked noisily, the air punctuated by harsh laughter and coarse language. The man looked away, careful not to make eye contact with the players. To his right several tables and chairs were clustered together, their occupants bathed in the light of a huge TV. A cry went up, cruel encouragement for the horses that galloped across its high-def surface.

He made his way to the bar, his trainers rasping noisily on the tacky floor. He finished his bogus conversation and slipped the phone back into his pocket. The landlord, a middle-aged, flat-nosed rough with tattooed arms, glanced up from his newspaper.

'Yeah?'

'Lager. Small one,' he said, pinching his finger and thumb together. He paid with the coins in his pocket and retired to a quiet corner where he unfurled a Racing Post, sensing his presence had slid back into welcome obscurity.

Thirty minutes passed. The man relaxed a little more, confident he was now a part of this miserable landscape. A casual glance in his direction would confirm that he was just another of life's hard-luck stories, crushed by the system, his only solace a few cheap beers and an afternoon watching the races. Still, it paid to be vigilant. Observation was his tradecraft, a skill he had honed over many years.

Ten more minutes passed. Another groan went up from the horse-fanciers. One unlucky punter ripped up his betting slip and tossed the scraps onto the floor. He pushed his chair back and sauntered towards the toilets. It was him, the man decided, recognising the target from the surveillance photographs: Daniel Morris Whelan, thirty-eight years old, medium height, slim build, shoulder-length brown hair, a faded St. George's cross in blue ink tattooed below his left ear.

It was time.

The man left his newspaper on the table and casually followed Whelan into the gents, careful to push the door open with his shoulder. It was a foul-smelling convenience, the walls an urban collage of graffiti and right-wing political stickers, the single toilet stall to his right blocked and caked with excrement. Flies hopped and flitted across a thin barred window high on the wall and water dripped noisily, the sound echoing off the once-white tiles. The smell was overpowering. He held his breath and moved past the toilet stall. Whelan was in the far corner, urinating freely, his body swaying slightly as the overflow from the urinal splashed around his worn sports shoes. The other two receptacles were filled with cigarette ends, tissue paper and gobbets of phlegm. He saw Whelan turn, saw him register his unwillingness to use the blocked facilities.

'Cleaner's on holiday again,' Whelan quipped. He zipped his fly and wandered over to the sinks, where a stain-less-steel wall tile served as a mirror. He didn't wash his hands. Instead, he pulled a comb from the pocket of his jeans, scraping his long hair back off his forehead and smoothing it down with his other hand.

The man stepped gingerly across the puddled floor and

unzipped his fly. 'Bloody disgusting,' he muttered with unrehearsed venom. He saw Whelan study him in the mirror, taking in the jeans and the old combat jacket, the dark hair, cut short and neat.

'You must be new round here,' Whelan chuckled.

'Just passing through,' the man replied, his urine splashing loudly. 'Met a mate on the high street, got me a bit of work. Just as well, coz I need the money bad. Still on parole, see.'

He saw Whelan's eyebrow arch with interest. 'Really? Where were you banged up?'

'Winchester. Fourteen months. Violent Disorder, GBH.'

'Oh yeah?' Whelan rinsed his comb under a tap and slipped it into his back pocket. 'Well, you're in good company. Lot of ex-cons round here.'

The man zipped his fly and stood at the sink next to Whelan. No soap of course, or hot water. He rubbed his hands vigorously under the cold tap. 'That's what you get when you defend your country, stand up for what's right.' He shook his hands dry and leaned on the sink, hoping his outburst would have the desired effect.

'A patriot, eh? Like I said, you're in good company. What's your name?'

'Eddie.'

Whelan held out an unwashed hand. 'I'm Danny. Fancy a drink?'

THEY HUDDLED TOGETHER in a gloomy corner, away from the TV screen and the luckless punters, the table cluttered with empty glasses. Whelan cleared a space and rolled a cigarette, carefully sprinkling a few shards of cannabis resin along its length. He fired it up, tilting his head and blowing out a long plume of smoke.

'Fourteen months, yeah? That's harsh.'

'I was stitched-up,' grumbled Eddie. 'Long story short, this Pakistani firm was running gear on the estate, heroin mostly. That shocked me at first because they're Muslims. You know, supposed to be religious and that.'

'All part of the jihad,' Whelan observed, sucking on his cigarette. 'It's not just about bombs and bullets. They're playing the long game.'

Eddie nodded, his meticulously rehearsed story flowing easily off his lips. 'Anyway, they were grooming my mate's sister, got her hooked on the gear, pimping her out to minicab drivers and that. So me and him went round to the flat where she was staying with one of them. We knocked on the door, and I could see the geezer behind the glass, right?' Eddie leapt to his feet, a muscular arm pitching forward. 'Bang! I heaved a lump of concrete through the door, caught him right in the face. Next minute we're inside, giving the fat bastard a good pasting—'

'Sweet.'

'—then two others come running out into the hallway, so my mate does both of 'em with the pepper spray.'

'Beautiful. Burn their fucking eyes out,' purred Whelan.

Eddie's devilish grin faded. He slumped back down into his seat, deflated. 'That was it,' he sighed. 'Police turned up, we got nicked. Didn't want to hear our side of the story, didn't give a monkey's about my mate's sister. Hate crime, pure and simple. Feet never touched the ground.'

Whelan pinched the end of his cigarette, balancing it carefully on the lip of the ashtray. 'This country's had it.'

He waved a nicotine-stained finger between them. 'See, the government don't give a shit about people like me and you, don't care about real English people. We don't fit in to their bullshit, multicultural experiment. That's why we've got to stick together, know what I mean?'

Whelan rolled up the sleeve of his faded grey sweat-shirt. 'Check that out,' he whispered. The three lions *passant* were tattooed on the inside of Whelan's left bicep. Unlike the blue smudge on his neck, this tattoo had been expertly drawn, the colours bold and vivid, the mediaeval lions a clear and exact representation of early English heraldry, the initials *EFM* in angular black type beneath.

'Jesus, that's beautiful,' breathed Eddie. 'English Freedom Movement, yeah? Hard core, that mob.'

'Used to be, before the ban,' Whelan sighed, rolling his sleeve back down. He lifted his glass and saluted a small shield sporting the same three lions fixed above the bar.

Eddie hadn't noticed it earlier, barely visible amongst the faded Union Jack bunting that ran across the dark wood panelling near the ceiling. He took another sip of lager and snorted. 'There's me going on about my troubles and here I am, sitting with a proper patriot.'

Whelan smiled, clearly enjoying the respect Eddie was showing. 'Don't worry about it. We all do our bit. You've spilt blood, done your bird. Me, I've had run-ins too.'

Eddie nodded sympathetically. He already knew about Whelan's brushes with authority; a drink-driving offence whilst employed by the civil service, his subsequent dismissal, public disorder fines for the distribution of offensive literature. His CV wasn't the most extensive he'd seen, but it contained three essential ingredients: military service, a police record and connections to racist organisations.

'Don't matter what we do or say, government just does what it wants,' Eddie moaned. 'Take Bryce, for instance—'

'Fucking traitor.'

'—letting all them refugees come over here, giving them benefits and houses. Take a walk around Brent Cross these days and you'd think you're in Karachi or wherever. All the supermarkets, all the takeaways, they've all gone Halal you know.'

'You wait. When they sign that Cairo treaty the flood-gates will really open,' Whelan complained. He drained his glass. 'Fancy another?'

Eddie nodded. 'Why not.'

Whelan ambled across to the bar, returning a minute later with two more glasses of cheap lager in his fists. He sat down and raised his glass. 'Here's to England. What's left of it.'

They lapsed into silence. Whelan shoved his glass aside and began rolling another cigarette. 'You said your mate got you some work. Doing what?'

'Nothing much,' Eddie shrugged. He rummaged in the front pocket of his jeans and pulled out a scrap of paper. 'He works for an employment agency. They don't hire ex-cons, but he's offered me a job off the books. All cash in hand.' Eddie smoothed the paper out on the table. 'That's the number, some sort of refrigeration company. They want me to make a delivery, big fridge or something.'

Whelan lifted the glass to his lips. 'What's it paying?'

'Five hundred quid.'

Whelan choked on his lager, coughing foamy droplets across the table. He cuffed his wet chin. 'For delivering a fridge?' he rasped. 'Bullshit.'

'Straight up. My mate reckons something's not kosher but five hundred for a day's work is a nice chunk.'

'A right result,' agreed Whelan, clearing his throat. 'Your mate at the agency, is he looking for anyone else? I used to drive for the civil service, important documents, that sort of stuff. I drive HGV too. Learned in the army.'

Eddie ignored him, rubbed his unshaven jaw. 'The thing is, I'm not sure if I want to do it.'

Whelan brightened. 'Why not?'

'It's risky, me being on license and that. If I get caught I'll be back in Winchester in a heartbeat.'

'True. Five hundred doesn't sound much when you weigh it up.'

'I'll sleep on it, decide in the morning.' Eddie rose from the table. 'Another drink?'

'Sweet,' Whelan grumbled.

'Alright. I'm off for a dump first. Back in five, yeah?'

DANNY WHELAN's bitterness bubbled to the surface as he watched Eddie lope towards the toilet. *Five hundred quid*; some people had all the luck. What little cash Danny made on the side usually disappeared quicker than a fart in the wind. The horses didn't help, or the dogs. They bled him dry, along with the lottery and a bit of puff. His dole money was normally gone by the end of the week, sucked back into the system that supported both him and his Dad in their twelfth-floor flat near the King's Head. He'd worked a bit, in the army of course, then the government job. He'd still be there if it wasn't for that piss-up after work. And the breathalyser on Chelsea Bridge.

He thought his luck would change when he joined the English Freedom Movement. They were a proud organisation, patriots one and all. True, there were a few boneheads amongst them, but mostly they were decent folk who wanted to see the UK's borders tightened, an end to Britain's membership of the EU, a revival of British values and customs. Danny had felt at home amongst its ranks and then, a few short months after he joined, they passed the Hate Crime legislation and overnight the English Freedom Movement became a banned organisation. All meetings were cancelled, its members scattered to the four winds under threat of prosecution and imprisonment. *They didn't even put up a fight,* Danny recalled.

He'd been promised so much. The Movement was an impressive network of patriots who didn't want foreigners laying their patios or painting their houses. For new members like Danny the jobs were supposed to come flooding in, all cash, the taxman be damned. The Movement was supposed to be better than the Masons, guaranteed to find work for their own. But now it was gone, over, and once again Danny was left to fend for himself. Typical.

*Not like that lucky bastard Eddie.*

Danny glanced towards the toilets. He was still in there, doing his business. Who was this Eddie anyway? He wasn't a local, just a jailbird with a friend in the right place. Danny used to be in the Movement; where were his friends? Where were his connections?

Danny toyed with the scrap of paper, a ticket to an easy five hundred quid pinned beneath the ashtray. He swallowed hard. What if he just took it? Okay, Eddie was a big bloke, with rough hands and lumpy knuckles, a fighter's hands. If he caught him he'd probably batter Danny without breaking sweat. Yet Danny's gut feeling told him Eddie wasn't going to risk it. That being the case, five hundred quid would go begging, and Danny would gamble a kicking for that.

He shot another look at the toilets, pocketed the scrap of paper and headed quickly for the pub door.

Locked inside the toilet stall, Eddie had to concentrate hard to stop himself from gagging. He'd tried to flush the toilet clean but the pathetic trickle of water from the cistern barely touched the sides. So he waited.

He checked his watch. Ten minutes had passed, enough for Whelan to take the bait. He exited the stall, took a moment to compose himself, and walked out of the toilet. He crossed to the bar, glancing over his shoulder. Whelan was nowhere to be seen. He ordered a bag of peanuts and went back to the table, taking his time to leaf through the Racing Post. When he was certain Whelan was long gone he stood up and made his way outside, blinking in the daylight as he left the King's Head in his wake.

He walked briskly through the estate and headed toward the park that formed its western border. He gave a wide berth to a gang of hooded youths baiting two vicious-looking dogs and cut through a stand of trees towards the main road. He headed north towards Wembley, dumping the combat jacket into a rubbish bin along the pavement.

The car was where he'd left it, a VW Golf, parked in a supermarket car park over a mile from the Longhill. He started the engine, slipped it into gear and pulled out onto the main road. He wrinkled his nose, the stink of the King's Head still wrapped around him, the taste of cheap alcohol in his mouth. He popped a mint and powered down the window, his fingers drumming the steering wheel as he crawled through the traffic. Now that the pieces were in play he felt excited at the thought of what was to come. There was much at stake, he knew that, but personally he cared little for politics. It was a game, always had been. What truly motivated him was money, and after this job he'd be set up for life.

Still, he was intrigued to see how it would all play out.

The Minister, in his own poetic way, had described it best; he'd likened Europe to a piece of fruit, ripened by the sun, dangling seductively from a thin branch.

Soon it would be picked.

## 3

## GUILDFORD, SURREY

His close protection officers kept a discreet distance as Bryce stood by the grave, the smooth white marble and splash of colourful flowers distinguishing it from its moss-covered neighbours. Still fresh too, noted Bryce. That would be Jules, Lizzie's green-fingered sister who lived a few miles from the cemetery. He never brought flowers himself, mindful of his wife's hay fever and the discomfort it had brought her. Jules was a decent woman, but Bryce had never really clicked with the rest of her family, the pressure of his work and their strong Conservative values denying them the common ground that neither party had really sought.

Lizzie had been different, a rebel of the clan, an art history student when they'd first met at Cambridge. It was Lizzie who'd introduced him to Oliver Massey, who'd wined and dined the multi-millionaire until he was convinced that Bryce was the real deal, helping to secure the financial backing that had launched his political career. His wife's inability to conceive meant that Lizzie was a permanent fixture at Bryce's side, even after that routine physical which was anything but. She'd fought hard – and privately at first - but the fight was one sided, the cancer taking her eight months before the general election. Bryce had been swept into Downing Street on a tide of sympathy, but the truth was that the devastation he felt was not the pain of loss but of crushing guilt. He wished Lizzie were here now, standing before him, so he could assuage some of that guilt. But she wasn't.

He squatted down and tidied the grave, brushing away the twigs and fingering wet mulch from the recessed inscription. The marble was cold to the touch, a sensation that Bryce always found mildly unsettling, a reminder of the frozen eternity of death, of the pale bones that lay beneath his fingers. He withdrew his hand and stood, his knees cracking in protest. He sat down on a nearby bench, pulling his overcoat around him and thrusting his hands deep into its pockets. Despite the cold it was a beautiful day. A late September sun shone in the sky, and closer to earth, songbirds flitted across an untidy mix of tilting head-stones and cheerless stone angels. He could cope with visiting on days like this. Winter was a different story, the cemetery ringed by lifeless trees, damp soil and death under leaden skies. How he wished that Lizzie had opted for cremation.

At the end of the row his security people stood ready to turn others away, selfishly guarding Bryce's quiet reflections from the public. Sometimes it made him feel a little guilty, but not today. Today he was enjoying the peace it offered.

As if on cue he watched a woman being turned away. She was wrapped in a pale green overcoat, her grey hair cut short. Bryce watched her through guilty eyes as she waited patiently, a posy of flowers clutched to her chest, a large handbag held in the crook of her elbow. He waved at the bodyguard to let her through.

After the indignity of a bag search and a pat down, she stopped in front of a nearby grave and changed the flowers that wilted in a small vase. The memorial was a basic arrangement, a simple weather-beaten headstone, a border of white gravel littered with dead leaves. A small Union Jack planted at the base trembled in the breeze, and a photograph in a silver frame lay propped against the stone, the soldier's proud pose faded by time and the elements. She glanced over her shoulder and Bryce nodded politely.

He looked down the hill, the graves marching away in solemn ranks toward a distant line of poplars. Dozens more flags caught his eye, adorning the headstones of soldiers killed in Afghanistan. He shivered, burying his chin deep inside the cashmere folds of his overcoat. What had it all been for, anyway? After the pullout the Afghanis had returned to their feudal existence, the Mullahs once again ruling from the ruins of Kabul, the provinces carved up amongst the warlords, the poppy fields thriving. And the drugs continued to pour into the west, an unstoppable tide of misery that plagued Europe. It was just one more problem to be tackled, a growing list that was rapidly piling up outside Bryce's door. A drum began to beat behind his eyes and Bryce pinched the bridge of his nose to stem the sudden headache.

He glanced to his right where the woman had retired to the next bench, handbag resting on her lap. Bryce got to his feet and approached her, hovering a short distance away. The woman saw him, raised a hand to shade her eyes from the sunlight.

'Good morning.' Bryce gestured to the bench. 'Do you mind?'

'Please,' the woman replied, inching further along.

He perched himself on the edge of the bench and extended his hand. 'Gabriel Bryce.'

She took it, her grip surprisingly firm. 'I know who you are.'

She was well spoken, and didn't offer her own name, which Bryce thought unusual. She seemed unfazed by his company, which was a rare experience for the Prime Minister. Meetings with the public were carefully managed, and typically with pre-screened supporters or loyal party members. This woman was different, and Bryce was intrigued by the randomness of the encounter. On closer inspection she was younger than Bryce first assumed, her brown eyes bright and intelligent. She was probably in her mid-fifties but looked ten years older. Perhaps it was bereavement that had aged her. Bryce knew all about that.

He pointed to the nearby headstone. 'Your son?'

'Gavin. An only child.' The smile never made it to her eyes.

The faded picture propped against the headstone showed a young man wearing full dress uniform, his back ram rod straight, his hands placed stiffly on his knees, chin tilted upward towards the camera. His face was frozen in that serious boy soldier expression, pride and vulnerability all in one, his eyes barely visible beneath the gleaming peak of his service cap. Bryce raised an eyebrow. 'Afghanistan?'

The woman nodded. 'Such a waste, don't you think? It pains me to see politicians fawning all over those Taliban creatures. Such a betrayal.'

Bryce squirmed, recalling last year's visit to Downing Street by the robed and turbaned delegation from the Islamic Emirate of Afghanistan. 'I know it sounds harsh madam, but that's the reality of politics. Every conflict ends with dialogue and compromise, if only to prevent more loss of life.'

The woman stiffened. 'I'm not a fool, Mister Bryce. I understand the way the world works. But to see you and others shaking hands with the very people who maimed and killed our boys, well, quite frankly it disgusts me.'

Bryce shifted on the bench. This wasn't going the way he expected. Before he could muster a suitable response the mobile in his pocket began to vibrate. 'Excuse me.' He glanced at the screen, then up the hill towards the cemetery access road where Ella stood watching him. She held up her arm and tapped her wrist. Bryce waved and got to his feet.

'I'm afraid I have to go.'

The woman looked away. 'Of course.'

'I'm sorry for your loss.'

'And I for yours.'

Bryce thought she meant it. He offered her a smile and headed back towards his waiting car.

'Do you despise your country, Mister Bryce?'

He stopped, turned around. 'Excuse me?'

'Our culture, our values. Do you despise them? If you intend to sign that Cairo treaty then you must.'

'Why do you say that?'

'Because it's the truth.' The woman nodded towards her son's grave. 'That's a temporary headstone, the second this year. The others were smashed, Gavin's picture torn up, the flags trampled on. I'm not the only one.' She waved a hand around the cemetery. 'Most of the other soldiers' graves have been vandalised too, and the Jewish ones. The police say it's kids, but everyone knows it's not.'

Bryce shrugged his shoulders, unsure how to respond. 'I'm afraid I don't have—'

'Jihad, Mister Bryce. That's right, and I don't mind

saying it, although most people are either too blind or too stupid to see it. Our cities are changing every day, slowly but surely, and Cairo will be the final nail in the coffin.' The woman regarded him as Bryce struggled for an answer. 'I've offended your socialist sensibilities, haven't I? The truth has a habit of doing that.'

It was strange to hear such uncomfortable language from a respectable-looking woman, but despite that her words resonated with him. He remained silent as she produced a tissue from the sleeve of her coat and dabbed at her nose.

'Politicians always make the mistake of confusing opinions with facts, and facts can be so politically inconvenient, can't they? It's no wonder people are leaving.'

'Leaving?'

'Yes, leaving. Emigrating. Two families in our street have already gone. People are fearful of the future, that's why they're moving away. Our border controls are a shambles, people's movements unrecorded for years, successive governments turning a blind eye.'

'I wouldn't believe everything you read in the Daily Mail,' Bryce blustered.

The woman's face flushed, her hands twisting the straps of her handbag. 'Don't patronise me, Mister Bryce. You people believe you're better than the rest of us, treating the electorate with contempt while you dismantle our democracy piece by tiny piece. But you've gone too far this time. Those refugees camped in the Egyptian desert will have the right to become EU citizens if that terrible treaty is signed, and we both know where most of them will be headed.'

'Well, that's not strictly-'

'I'm a Christian, Mister Bryce. I believe in charity, in helping those less fortunate than us, but where does it stop?

Our public services, our institutions, they just won't be able to cope. If you sign that treaty it will mark the beginning of the end.'

Her eyes bored into him, her lower lip trembling. Bryce could feel her anger and was momentarily lost for words. It had been a long time since a member of the public had lectured him, certainly not since his days as a young MP. He glanced again towards the grave she visited, her only child, laying dead beneath the soil, her words echoing his own misgivings. Was it any wonder she was angry? He needed to disengage, walk away. He shuffled his feet, looked up the hill.

'These are complex issues, Madam—'

'Yes, of course. Stupid of me to think I could possibly understand them.' She got up and walked to her son's grave, kissing her fingertips and laying them gently on the headstone. She stepped back onto the path, turned and faced him. 'Besides, I'm just a law-abiding taxpayer whose family has lived here for centuries. On what planet would someone like you ever have the interests of someone like me at heart?' Before Bryce could reply the woman turned on her heel and walked briskly away.

He watched her go, unable to muster a response. The encounter had unsettled him, exposed the raw nerve that was Cairo. This wasn't a briefing document or a think tank report; this was a person, with a life and a voice, and a dead son that gave her the moral authority to confront him. This was real.

Ella appeared at his side, jabbering away into her mobile phone, the breeze whipping at her hair, at the faux fur collar of her beige overcoat. 'Who was that?' she asked, following his gaze.

'Nobody.' He could feel Ella's eyes on him.

'Are you alright, Gabe?'

'Of course. Why'd you ask?'

Ella shrugged her shoulders. 'Nothing. You look a bit pale.'

The woman was distant now, a small figure glimpsed between the landscape of headstones. Then she was gone. 'I'm fine. Let's go.'

The ministerial convoy waited along the access road, engines purring. Doors swung open as Bryce approached. He was about to duck inside his BMW limousine when he heard a faint chant carried on the wind. A large group of people had gathered at the main gates of the cemetery, placards held high. Policemen lined the road, herding them towards the opposite pavement.

'Who are they?'

'Student rent-a-mob,' explained Ella. 'They arrived in a coach a little while ago. They're well organised, a camera crew, nicely printed placards etcetera. Someone's tipped them off.'

'No bloody privacy anymore,' Bryce fumed. He ushered Ella inside the BMW and wriggled out of his overcoat. Ella raised the glass partition, sealing the rear passenger compartment with a soft *thunk*.

'I've issued a D-Notice,' she announced. 'They can't use any footage of you within the cemetery grounds.'

'Good.' Bryce watched the Range Rover in front move off, then the smooth power of the BMW kicked in as it accelerated after it. They approached the main gates at speed, the ranks of headstones on either side a grey blur, the faces of the curious flashing by. Then the BMW was through the gates, turning past the police motorcyclists that blocked the road, past the chants of the protestors, their placards dancing an angry jig above the police cordon – *No More Borders! Justice for Refugees! Yes to Cairo!*

'You think they know something's in the wind?'

'Not a chance,' Ella replied. 'If they did there'd be thousands of them.'

Ten minutes later the convoy curled up the slip road and onto the A3 motorway towards London. Bryce stared out of the window, watching the traffic flash by as the convoy ate up the miles towards the capital.

'Tell me about tomorrow.'

'The press conference is scheduled for five-forty five,' Ella informed him, 'followed by the Cabinet meeting at six-fifteen. I've laid on a few extra bodies for the communications office, too. We're going to get steamrolled.' Ella paused, toying with the phone in her hand. 'There's still time, Gabe. We can justify the Heathrow suspension, but stopping Cairo is going to be a bloody hard sell. If you brief Cabinet beforehand they'll be more inclined to support your decision. Cutting them out of the loop like this will just piss them off.'

Bryce shook his head. 'My mind's made up, Ella. This way the Heathrow dossier will have maximum impact, both here and in Brussels. If we get public opinion on our side Cabinet will be swayed more easily. Then we can push it through parliament.'

'You'll be undermining their authority, Gabe. I'm getting a ton of calls already, demanding to know what the press conference is about. There's a lot of frustration out there.'

'Once we go public they'll understand. Which brings me onto my next question: how are you and Milo getting on these days?'

'We're good. Why do you ask?'

'I see he's running *The Observer* now.'

'Correct. Worked bloody hard for it too.'

'Maybe you two shouldn't have got divorced.'

Ella glanced at the back of the driver's head, slipped her hand over Bryce's. 'It was inevitable. I met someone else.' Bryce pulled his hand away. 'I'm sorry, Gabe. That was inappropriate.'

'You think Milo might help us?'

Ella shrugged, the awkward moment already behind her. 'Maybe. He's not your biggest fan but he's a player now. What were you thinking?'

'Give him the inside track, off record briefings, help him shape the narrative. There'll be a lot of negative press, much of it from our own side. If we can get our message out there, engage public opinion, we can turn this around.'

Ella lowered her voice. 'Have you actually thought about the repercussions, Gabe? I mean really thought about them?'

'I've thought of nothing else this past week.'

'DuPont will go absolutely ballistic when this breaks, as will the other Euro leaders. We're not the only ones who need that gas and oil. Most EU economies are depending on it.'

'I know that,' Bryce snapped. He took a breath. 'Look, all we're talking about here is delaying the treaty, not scrapping it. We need assurances, guarantees. The same applies to the relocation programme. Milo could really help us with this. Will you talk to him?'

'Of course I will. Thankfully he still adores me.'

'Good. Sooner rather than later, please Ella.' He was silent for a moment, then he said, 'What about Tariq?'

His Chief of Staff tapped her phone. 'I've scheduled five minutes in your office just before the press conference.'

'It won't take that long.'

Ella frowned. 'Strange, he's barely been seen since he returned from Istanbul. Even Rana's being cagey about his movements.'

A police motorcyclist shot past Bryce's window, square jaw jutting beneath his black visor. 'She's his deputy. She'd lay down in traffic for him. Anyway, it's irrelevant. Tariq's history.'

'The next few weeks are going to be hell,' Ella muttered.

This time it was Bryce who reached out. He gave her hand a reassuring squeeze. 'Don't worry, we're doing the right thing. People will see that.'

Ella looked away. 'I hope to God you're right Gabe, I really do.'

Bryce saw her reflection in the glass and knew she was worried. He was too, but there was no going back now.

The convoy continued northwards, the outriders carving a path through the afternoon traffic. Bryce took advantage of the silence, staring out of the window as he contemplated firing Tariq. He'd once been a trusted comrade, rallying Britain's Muslim community behind Bryce's election campaign, intelligent, loyal, a dependable mouthpiece. He was passionate, a team player, and Bryce had rewarded him with Security and Immigration. Yet the minister had become distant in recent months, and made no secret of his increasing engagement with the Islamic Congress of Europe. It was out of his remit but understandable; Tariq was seen as a major conduit of Islamic influence and opinion in Bryce's government, something Bryce had encouraged for his own political purposes, yet somehow it had led to the debacle at Heathrow. Despite the betrayal, he would miss Tariq's powerful cultural influence. He'd be a hard man to replace. Something else he had to work on.

Outside, the green fields of Surrey yielded to the urban sprawl of the south London suburbs. Raindrops tapped the window, slithering across the thick glass like mercury. He thought of the woman back at the cemetery, her emotive words, her warnings. Whatever her politics, she was right: the Treaty of Cairo had to be stopped. The question was, for how long?

Sirens wailed as the convoy slowed and the traffic thickened. Bryce looked beyond the warehouses, beyond the industrial units and the suburban rooftops that lined the road to where the sky met the earth.

In the distance, far to the east, storm clouds gathered on the horizon.

# 4

## LUTON

THIRTY-FOUR MILES TO THE NORTH, DANNY WHELAN swung the truck around the car park and stamped heavily on the brakes. He crunched the gear lever into reverse, the warning signal beeping loudly, and backed towards the covered loading bay. He watched his wing mirror carefully, as one of the mosque staff waved him backwards. A loading bay, for Christ's sake; how big was this place? Too bloody big, he decided. Still, he had a job to do.

The text message had woken him long before dawn. The truck was a fairly new and unmarked Ford Cargo, parked on the edge of an industrial estate near Kings Cross. The estate itself had been deserted, the surrounding businesses barred and shuttered, the morning sun still loitering beyond the horizon. Danny had waited in the shadows, half expecting to see an enraged Eddie pacing around the truck, but there was no one about. He'd found the keys behind the fuel tank, the envelope with ten crisp fifty pound notes tucked inside in the glove box. Danny's heart sank when he'd inspected the paperwork, briefly tempted to take the money and run, but common sense prevailed. If he played his cards right it could be the start of a regular gig and, besides, all he had to do was deliver a fridge to a mosque. No one had to know.

Danny didn't really think about it on the journey north, humming away to the radio as the truck rumbled along the M1. It was only when he turned off the motorway and saw the distant gold dome dominating the skyline that his mood changed. The Luton Central Mosque was huge, almost as big as the one being built in the east end of London. Danny remembered complaining about that one, an afternoon of drunk-dialling Stratford council to voice his protest, every do-gooder he spoke to singing its praises, about serving the needs of a diverse community, the celebration of different faiths and all their other bullshit. He remembered raging inside the public phone booth, remembered the warnings about recorded calls and prosecution. Who cared about his opinion anyway? Opinions weren't allowed anymore.

He engaged the handbrake with a sharp hiss of compressed air and jumped down from the cab. Danny's eyes were drawn upwards, where the golden dome and minarets thrust upwards into the sky, visible for miles around as they towered above the surrounding suburbs. For a moment Danny just stood there, quietly impressed by the sheer scale of the construction. He remembered seeing the grand opening on the news, Bryce and his entourage padding around in their socks, waffling on about diversity and equality while the PM's female staff were forced to wait in a separate wing, polite smiles fixed on their faces. Fucking hypocrites. But there was no doubt about it, the Luton mosque was huge, and as buildings went, a pretty impressive sight. And there were lots of CCTV cameras, he noticed.

He clambered up onto the loading bay, dusting off his jeans as the mosque worker in a white robe stepped forward, hand outstretched.

'I am Imran. You have paperwork?'

Danny pulled a printout from his back pocket. 'That's all I've got, bruv.' He scraped his hair back and removed a self-rolled cigarette from behind his ear. It had just a little touch in it, enough to give him a buzz, but not enough to get him nicked. He searched his pockets for a lighter until he realised the bloke was staring at him.

'Smoking is forbidden.'

Danny removed the cigarette from his lips and replaced it behind his ear. Normally he wouldn't swallow shit from someone like him, but he needed this job to go smooth and, besides, the bloke was a big lump, head like a coconut, shovels for hands and a wide set of shoulders straining at the stupid dress he was wearing. Best not to wind him up.

Imran pointed at the truck. 'Open, please.'

Danny poked a fat green button and a battered metal tailgate lowered itself onto the loading bay with a loud whine. He threw the shutter up and stepped back.

'There you go, Abdul.' Danny waved a hand at the industrial freezer strapped to the side of the truck's interior. It was big, woven in clear plastic shrink-wrapping like a giant insect cocooned in a spider's web. Danny was glad he didn't have to shift the thing himself.

Imran glanced at the unit then turned to Danny. 'Please, you help? No one here.' He waved an arm around the deserted loading bay.

Danny glanced at the cars parked nearby; someone was here all right, they just didn't want to get their paws dirty. Well, he needed the money more than the grief. Danny nodded. 'Come on then, Abdul. Let's make it quick.'

He released the restraining straps and pushed the unit towards the tailgate, relieved the thing was on wheels but surprised by the weight. Empty fridges were normally pretty light, he assumed. This one weighed a ton. Imran stood immobile as Danny struggled to manoeuvre the wheels over the lip of the tailgate. Lazy bastard. He braced his arms and pushed with all of his strength.

'Watch your toes!' warned Danny as the unit rumbled onto the loading bay. Imran saw it coming and stepped deftly out of the way. 'Really moves when you get your weight behind it, eh?' The man said nothing, steering the front end towards a set of large double doors.

Despite himself, Danny was intrigued. He'd never been inside a mosque and he wasn't sure what to expect. He knew there was a main hall where everyone prayed, but that was—

'Stop!' barked Imran as they crossed the threshold. He pointed at Danny's scruffy white trainers. 'Please remove. Forbidden.'

'Yeah, yeah,' moaned Danny, hopping around on each leg as he slipped off his trainers, his socks making damp footprints on the concrete. He placed his shoes on the tailgate then glanced up, straight into the lens of a CCTV camera. The rest of them were probably watching him right now, laughing their beards off at the stupid Infidel. 'Keep me socks on, can I?' he sniped. He focused on the money and together they steered the unit inside. Danny's eyes swivelled left and right as he puffed and grunted along the corridor, stealing a glance inside the rooms along the way. They passed a large kitchen, deserted, only the cold light of a flycatcher filling the room with its electric blue glow, a bare storeroom, empty shelving fixed to its walls. In fact, the place had an air of desertion about it, Danny realised. It was quiet, almost silent, like a proper church. Imran called a halt and Danny straightened up.

'I think I've slipped a disc,' he grumbled, rubbing his back. 'You sure there's not a couple of bodies in there?'

The big Muslim ignored his banter. 'In here,' he commanded.

Danny sighed and heaved his end around, wheeling the unit into another storeroom. This one was also empty.

Imran held a finger to his lips. 'Quiet. Prayers,' he whispered, pointing at the wall. Danny listened carefully. He could hear it now, the low drone of voices coming from the other side of the grey cinderblock partition. Must be the main prayer hall. Together they lined the unit up along the wall. Danny dusted off his hands.

'There you go, Abdul. All sorted.' Then he looked down, frowned. 'Hang on, there's no power outlet along that wall.' He tugged the unit away from the cinderblock and crouched down. Nothing. Then he studied the unit itself, running his hands over the thick plastic. 'That's weird. Doesn't seem to be a power cable.'

'Leave it.' Imran waved Danny towards the door.

Puzzled, Danny knelt down, peering beneath the unit. 'No compressors. How come it's so heavy then?' He straightened up and studied the other walls. 'You got no power sockets in here at all. How you going to juice the thing up?'

'You are fridge expert?' Imran hissed, ushering Danny out of the room.

'Just trying to help, bruv.' *Ungrateful bastard.* Anyway, the job was done. He scribbled a finger on the air. 'I suppose I should get your autograph, Abdul. You know, a signature or something?'

'Wait here.'

Imran entered a room further along the corridor. Danny followed him, peering through the narrow glass window. Abdul was hunched over a desk, scribbling on the delivery docket, while another couple of beardies were packing several large crates with files and computer stuff. Across the room, someone else was clearing out a bookshelf. Imran's face filled the window and the door swung open. Danny stepped back, a wry grin on his face.

'Moving out already?' he teased. 'What's up, Abdul? Not paid the rent?'

Imran's hand shot out and grabbed Danny's shirt, yanking him towards his large barrel chest. The other shoved the signed invoice roughly into his shirt pocket. Danny recoiled as Imran's hot breath wafted in his face, the stench of garlic filling his nostrils.

'My name is Imran. *Im-ran*,' he growled. He shoved Danny away, then waved his hand dismissively. 'Take truck and go.'

Crimson-faced, Danny swivelled on his stockinged feet and marched out to the loading bay. He fumbled with his trainers, cursing under his breath as he squeezed them on. He tried to fasten his crumpled shirt until he realised two of the buttons were missing. Taking a deep breath and summoning up as much dignity as his boiling emotions would allow, Danny hopped down from the loading bay and climbed behind the wheel of the truck. Thirty seconds later he was steering the vehicle beyond the gates of the mosque and out onto the main road, deliberately forcing a minibus full of worshippers to swerve out of his way.

*Fat bastard,* he raged silently, *laying his filthy paws on me.* He panted heavily, his thin face still flushed with anger as he gunned the truck through busy traffic. He gripped the steering wheel hard as he imagined his bloodied fists pummelling Abdul's face, raining blow after blow as the bastard pleaded for mercy through split lips and broken teeth. No one messes with Danny Whelan.

But he knew that's all it would ever be, a violent fantasy. He wasn't like the other blokes, the hard cases that went looking for trouble, orchestrating violence against ethnic gangs and left wing rent-a-mobs. Even in his youth he wasn't much of a fighter, more of a periphery sort of geezer, someone who got a few boots in after the others had taken the victim down. Like a jackal, in one of them wildlife TV shows he liked so much.

*Coward,* his inner voice mocked. And it was true. Danny knew blokes who would've cracked Abdul the minute he got stroppy, the sort of people who would never back down, even if it meant ending up in intensive care. There were some like that in the army, a couple in the King's Head, rough fuckers with short fuses, always ready to take offence, even quicker to unleash a whirlwind of fists and kicks. Or a knife. Danny kept well clear, circling them like they had leprosy. Nutters. But at least they could hold their heads up high. Not like him. Fucking church mouse.

He fired up his cigarette, the tobacco and narcotic mix assuaging his anger and numbing the shame of his rough treatment at the hands of an immigrant. Concentrate on the money, he advised himself. Five hundred quid was a lot of dough. He had to use it wisely, not waste it on gear or gambling. Well maybe a little, as a reward to himself.

As the traffic thinned and the miles rolled beneath the nose of the truck, Danny saw the blue sign for the M1 motorway and headed south. He'd be back in London in an hour, home in two. I'll give Carlos a bell, he decided, score a quarter of the grade A gear, the real mellow stuff that filtered out all the bullshit. He'd wash it down with a few pints at the Kings, maybe shoot the shit with the boys, spend a little of that hard-earned dough.

After the day he'd had, he'd certainly earned it.

## 5

# DOWNING STREET

The shutter rattled upwards, the warehouse beyond cloaked in darkness. The silver Ford emerged almost silently, lights extinguished, the driver a vague shadow behind the wheel. In his rear-view mirror he saw the shutter lowered behind him. He shifted in his seat and concentrated on the road ahead, steering the vehicle through the narrow backstreets of Waterloo. He cruised past empty industrial units and scruffy local authority tenements, past brightly lit convenience stores and busy pubs, until he reached the roundabout at the southern end of Waterloo Bridge. From there he headed north across the river Thames.

He looked to his left, where the lights along the embankment were strung like pearls, curving towards the Palace of Westminster and the seat of power in Britain.

'Are we ready?'

'Almost.'

Bryce buttoned the front of his suit jacket, checking the

Tag Heuer Monaco on his wrist as he adjusted the stiff cuffs of his shirt. It was almost time. Normally he enjoyed the speeches, the attention of a large audience. When it went well it was empowering, exhilarating. Today would be very different. There would be a storm of criticism following his statement, and for a moment his nerve faltered. He was about to turn into a road he'd never travelled before, with no way of knowing where it would lead him. He refocused his thoughts as Ella fussed around him.

'Your speech has been uploaded into the teleprompter and these are your notes, just in case.' She handed over a thin sheaf of white cards. 'The press are waiting. Most of the Cabinet are here, too.'

Bryce raised an eyebrow. 'What about Tariq?'

'Running late.'

Bryce shook his head. He leafed through the neat stacks of folders and documents piled on his desk. 'Where the hell did I put that Heathrow dossier?'

Ella pointed to the opposite wall. 'In your safe.'

'So I did. Where's Davies now?'

'I've got him squirrelled away downstairs. Sam's briefing him. Poor man's terrified.'

'He'll live.'

Bryce crossed to the wall safe. His private study was situated on the first floor, tucked away at the rear of the building, a quiet bolt hole where he would often escape the demands of office. He liked its size and its light, its lack of formality. It was modestly furnished with a mahogany writing desk and a red leather Chesterfield sofa along one book-lined wall. The opposite wall boasted three large French windows that overlooked the rose garden below, and in the depths of winter a fire crackled in the grate at Bryce's feet.

The wall safe was mounted inside the chimney breast, hidden behind a hinged replica of Aivazovsky's 'The Ninth Wave'. Bryce had a fascination for seascapes, stemming from the sailing holidays of his youth and his all too brief flirtation with offshore racing during university. There was never any time for it now and he often missed it. He studied the painting for a moment, the castaways clinging to a broken mast, helpless as the sea threatened to engulf them; today, he thought he understood how those poor people felt. He punched the keypad and the thick hatch swung open. Bryce turned around. Rana Hassani's tiny figure stood in the study doorway.

'The relocation programme is to be suspended?'

Bryce shot a glance at Ella, who immediately moved to intercept Tariq's Deputy. 'I'm afraid the Prime Minister can't see you right now, Rana. If you would—'

'Well?' Hassani demanded, dodging Ella's outstretched arm.

Bryce retrieved the dossier and closed the safe door. 'Where did you hear that?'

'So, the rumours are true.'

Bryce struggled to keep his own temper in check. 'Rana, I don't have time for this.'

The diminutive minister stood her ground. 'Prime Minister, with respect, I don't think you've thought this through.'

'Really?' he bristled, waving the dossier in the air. 'I think when you've heard the contents of this report you may reconsider that opinion. Now, if you'll excuse us.'

Hassani didn't move. 'I'd like a moment of your time.' She tilted her veiled head respectfully. 'Please.'

Behind Hassani, Ella shook her head. Bryce ignored her. 'You've got one minute.' He stood by the French doors, arms folded. Outside the sun had already set, the sky a palette of deepening blues, the clouds brushed with streaks of pink and red. Beyond the perimeter wall, groups of tourists gathered in small knots on Horseguards Parade. The historic square seemed quiet, subdued.

*Two families in our village have already gone...*

'Prime Minister,' Hassani began in a quiet voice behind him. 'The relocation programme is a humanitarian effort on an unprecedented scale, a challenge that we here in Britain have met with resounding success.'

Bryce turned to face her. 'I'm afraid that's not the case—'

'Let me finish,' Hassani commanded, holding up her hand. 'Suspending the program is not only illegal, it will also damage international relationships, especially across the Islamic world. Furthermore, it will cause great distress amongst Muslim voters right here in Britain, and I needn't remind you how important their vote is. To even suggest such a course of action is unethical, unconstitutional and, quite simply, unacceptable.' Her voice had risen steadily as she spoke, the last word delivered just short of a bark. Before Bryce could answer, the deputy minister continued her lecture.

'Both Britain and Pakistan have enjoyed a long history together and many of the refugees see Britain as a spiritual home. To deny them the opportunity to come here is an abuse of their human rights. The programme must continue. It is our duty to—'

'A duty we can ill afford,' Bryce cut in. He took a deep breath, knowing he had to tread carefully. 'Rana, I sympathise with your argument, but the fact is those same refugees have travelled through some extraordinarily prosperous countries to arrive at the gates of Europe. You should know that I intend to pursue agreements with the Gulf States, encourage them to accept a share of the burden until the situation in Pakistan is resolved.'

Hassani's eyes bored into him. 'The refugees are a burden to you?'

Bryce chewed his lip; this debate was going nowhere. He glanced at his watch. 'Time's up I'm afraid.'

'I strongly advise you to reconsider,' Hassani urged, wagging a slender finger at the ceiling. 'Much hatred has been directed towards the refugees and this suspension will only fuel such loathing. You will bear that responsibility, Prime Minister.'

Ella stepped between them. 'I think you've made your point, Rana. Now, if you don't mind, the PM has a press conference to attend.' She glared at Ella then left the room, leaving the door wide open. Ella swung it closed behind her.

Bryce spread his hands. 'How the hell did she find out?'

'It wasn't you or me. Must be someone at Heathrow, one of Davies' team.'

'I warned him, no leaks.'

'If Rana knows, then so does Tariq.'

'It doesn't matter. In a few minutes everyone will know.'

'She's right about one thing,' Ella warned. 'The Muslim community will see this as a bad day for them.'

'Which reminds me...' Bryce produced a piece of paper from his pocket. 'A shortlist, for Tariq's replacement. Go over it, would you? Let me have your thoughts?'

'I will.' Ella stood in front of Bryce. She reached out, smoothing the lapels of his jacket. 'You look very nice,' she smiled. 'Very handsome.'

'Ella—'

'Don't panic, Gabe. I'm not about to force myself on

you.' Her eyes flicked towards the Chesterfield. 'Although it wouldn't be the first time, would it?' Bryce said nothing as she picked a thread of lint from his tie. 'I'm here for you, Gabe. Whenever you're ready. We can start again.'

'We should never have started in the first place.'

'We fell in love, Gabe. It wasn't planned. Lizzie never knew. No one did.'

Bryce took a step back. 'It was wrong.'

'That's the guilt talking. It didn't feel wrong when Lizzie was alive, healthy.' Ella closed the gap, took his hands in hers. 'I miss her too, but I miss us more. I know somewhere deep inside, you feel the same.'

A faint smile touched the corners of his mouth. He squeezed her hands. 'You're persistent, I'll give you that.'

'I'm in love. That's never going to change.'

She let go, brushed the shoulders of his jacket. Behind the glasses her brown eyes sparkled, and Bryce felt those long buried emotions stirring. Maybe one day, when the guilt no longer ate him, when the timing was right, they could be together again.

Ella gave him a final once over. 'Ready to face the mob?'

Bryce nodded. 'As I'll ever be.'

They left the room, striding past Bryce's apologetic private secretary. As he followed Ella down the Grand Staircase he paused beside his photographic portrait, hung alongside previous Downing Street incumbents. It was a moody black and white study of sincere statesmanship, his thick grey hair swept back off his suntanned forehead, the sharp lines of his tailored suit more Vanity Fair than the Labour Review. Bryce studied the photograph intently, unsure if he recognised the man who held his gaze with such confident ease. He felt a sudden bout of anxiety and headed quickly downstairs.

His Chief of Staff carved a path through the expectant faces packed into the corridor outside the State Dining Room. Most were familiar: Cabinet ministers, their expressions ranging from curiosity to indignation, anxious advisors glued to their phones, and a sprinkling of Downing Street staff, all drawn by the mystery of the moment. They pressed against the walls to facilitate the Prime Minister's smooth passage, a few quiet words of greeting and encouragement following him along the corridor. Ahead, the bright glare of the press conference beckoned, the buzz from the assembled media rising as they neared the room.

Ella peeled away at the threshold and the chatter died away. 'Good luck,' she whispered. Bryce, dossier held by his side, took a deep breath and stepped into the glare of the TV lights.

THE SILVER FORD circled Parliament Square and turned into Whitehall. The driver slowed just before Downing Street, where a large crowd had gathered outside the black steel gates. They were mostly tourists, attracted by the history, by the ebb and flow of ministerial cars and the rows of high-tech satellite broadcast vans lining the pavement outside the Foreign and Commonwealth Office. Armed police officers in black body armour eyed the van as the driver stopped for the obligatory security checks. He powered down the window and held up his ID card for inspection, the policeman giving a thumbs-up to an operator behind the bomb-proof glass of the control booth. The anti-vehicle trap was lowered and the black gates swung open. The driver nodded and drove into Downing Street. He had no reason to fear the security checks or any other inspection, his familiar face, valid ID and the van with the imposing black crest of the Government Mail Service emblazoned on its sides ensuring a trouble-free passage into the most famous cul-de-sac in the world.

'Good afternoon,' announced Bryce, settling behind the lectern. There was an enthusiastic chorus of replies from the press corps packed within the State Dining Room's wood-panelled walls, pens poised above notepads, recording devices held expectantly. He took a sip of water and cleared his throat, blinking into the TV lights arranged across the back of the room. He glimpsed his reflection in the teleprompter, the light catching the expensive sheen of his grey Hugo Boss suit and the rich red of his perfectly knotted silk tie. He looked every inch the European statesman he was, and today he would prove how seriously he took that role. Words glowed on the teleprompter, scrolling slowly upwards.

'For some months now the focus of this government has been centred on divisions in international relations. As I speak here today, the civil war in Pakistan still devastates the country, US and Chinese warships eye each other suspiciously in the South China Sea as the troubling military build-up continues and closer to home, Polish terrorists persist in their attacks on Russian interests as the Kremlin orders more and more tanks toward their western frontier. In short, the world is witnessing worrying divisions. Along with my colleagues in Brussels and the United Nations, I have spent many months attempting to pull people round to a common position. Today, that is still the goal of this government, the search for peace and greater understanding amongst the international community, under the guidance and governance of the European Union and the United Nations.'

Bryce took a moment to allow the weight of his words to percolate amongst the journalists around the room.

'But the quest for peace should begin at home, for how can we lecture others when the concept is an alien one for some of our own citizens?' He glanced down, flicking over the cover of the dossier. He frowned, his eyes scanning the words uncomprehendingly. A low murmur filled the room, banishing the awkward silence.

Bryce held up a hand. 'I'm sorry, there seems to be a slight problem...' His voice trailed away. He was looking at an intelligence-briefing document, not the Heathrow dossier. He'd picked up the wrong bloody report. He saw Ella striding towards him. He clamped a hand over the microphone as the chatter increased around them.

'I've picked up the wrong report.'

'I'll go get it.'

Bryce shook his head. 'It's in the safe. I'll only be a minute.'

'Go. Quickly.' Ella summoned one of Bryce's press officers to the lectern with a curt hand gesture.

Bryce leaned into the microphone. 'My apologies, ladies and gentlemen. We'll continue in a moment.' He scooped up the erroneous document and strode from the room, a buzz of confusion trailing in their wake. He paused in the lobby. 'Wait here,' he ordered Ella.

He took the stairs two at a time, heading towards his private study.

ALONG DOWNING STREET'S narrow confines, shadows

deepened and lights began to glow as the warble of evening birdsong competed with the steady throb of the city. Government workers hurried purposefully up and down the cul-de-sac, the door to Number Ten opening and closing with industrious regularity. A police officer stood guard outside, and the press corps gathered behind steel barriers across the street, camera lenses trained on the Prime Minister's residence. They chatted quietly, the banter often punctuated by a peal of laughter or the chirp of a mobile phone. The silver Ford glided by them all, camouflaged by its banality, a regular fixture in Downing Street's landscape. It reached the end of the cul-de-sac, swinging around to face the Chief Whip's office in Number Twelve before reversing, then heading back up the street. It purred to a halt outside Number Ten, the driver obscured by tinted glass, his lips moving in quiet prayer.

Bryce closed the study door behind him and marched across the floor to the wall safe, angry with himself. He should've checked, made sure. Still, he'd only be a moment and the press corps was clearly intrigued by his forthcoming announcement. The safe beeped and the door swung open. He extracted the Heathrow dossier, thumbing through the pages to check its contents. Satisfied, he placed the intelligence brief back inside the grey metal womb and sealed the door.

He swung the Aivazovsky back in place. He made a sudden promise to himself: when all this was over he would make time to take to the sea, to hear the snap of a wind-filled sail, to feel the shifting deck beneath his feet, to taste the salty air on his tongue. No excuses, no postponements. A day out, someday soon, to ride the swell of the sea.

He pushed the painting home, feeling the click of the

magnetic catch, then turned to leave the room, the Heathrow dossier clutched in his hand.

AT THE TOP of Downing Street the tourists still gathered behind the security gates, posing for photographs as commuters hurried past them, eager to return home after another busy day. Across Parliament Square, the quarter bells of Big Ben heralded the approaching hour as the giant minute hand crept towards its summit. Many people heard the first chime of the great bell, its familiar peal ringing out over London, announcing the hour of six o'clock.

No one heard the second.

The sudden pulse of white light was brighter than a thousand suns. Microseconds later, a tremendous detonation ripped through the air, the pressure wave punching its way through the walls of Downing Street, through the Cabinet and Foreign Ministry buildings, hurling concrete, metal and flesh before it. Debris was thrown hundreds of feet into the sky, chased by a roiling ball of flame that reached high above the rooftops. Buildings shook and windows were blown out for hundreds of yards. As the earth trembled, a choking cloud of smoke and dust rolled across Whitehall, enveloping everything in a yellow fog, blinding and suffocating as it spilled across the roads and pavements. In the dreaded lull that followed, a rainstorm of twisted steel and stone crashed to earth, showering the streets with deadly wreckage.

Alarm klaxons wailed into life across central London, filling the air with their chilling moan. In Downing Street, an enormous crater, several yards deep and filling rapidly with water from a cracked main, marked the spot where the silver Ford had parked only a moment before. Building facades on both sides of the street had been ripped away, exposing shattered interiors where fires glowed, and a snow-storm of paper drifted on the dust-filled air.

High above the rooftops, thousands of startled birds wheeled above the carnage in a black, screeching cloud.

# 6

## AFTERMATH

Bryce's vision wavered between darkness and a strange, blurred world he didn't recognise. He preferred the darkness. It was strangely comforting, but a pounding ache in his lower jaw denied him the beckoning shadows. He opened his eyes, cuffing away the dust that clogged them. The first thing he saw were his hands, black with soot and cut in a dozen places. He felt dizzy and nauseous, and everything sounded muffled, as if his ears were blocked. He realised he was lying on his back on the floor of his study. What was left of the ceiling above was scarred and pitted, wires and cables dangling like jungle vines. His books were scattered around him, covered in dust and filth, competing for space with jagged floorboards and splintered furniture.

He lifted his head. The French windows had been punched out and a gentle breeze swirled dust and soot around the remains of his study. Through the blanket of partial deafness he heard the sound of roof tiles slithering and scraping above, then watched them sail past the windows before crashing onto the patio below. And he could smell gas. That wasn't good. As his ears began to clear his first lucid thought was a gas blast. He tried to move, but couldn't. His leg was trapped.

He struggled against a rising tide of panic. He was half-buried in debris, his Hugo Boss shredded and coated in dust and blood. He took a deep breath that caught in his lungs and he coughed violently. He moved his arms slowly, shrugging off the plaster and timber until he could move his upper body. He moved his right leg, drawing his knee up. No pain, good. The other leg wouldn't move, pinned beneath a jumble of debris. The ache in his face persisted and he found his jaw, feeling carefully for damage. His fingers came away slick with blood. He spat several times, trying to clear his mouth. He probed his gums, his tongue slipping between the gaps of his broken teeth. No wonder his whole head was splitting in pain.

He called for help, his throat thick with dust. He doubted anyone more than six feet away could hear him. He searched for his secretary, saw her desk overturned, debris piled against a crumbling wall as if swept there by a giant's broom. He thought he saw something pale amongst the carnage, a limb perhaps. He forced himself up into a sitting position, an inch at a time, the pain shooting through his chest. He lifted his chin, peering over the piles of rubble across the floor of his study—

Beyond the remains of his private office, Number Ten was gone, the front of the building ripped away. Across the void the wall of the Foreign Office lay similarly exposed, its blackened rooms and broken furniture resembling a macabre doll's house. As Bryce watched, a section of floor groaned and gave way, crashing to the street in a cloud of dust.

Closer, the staircase inside Number Ten marched up towards the sky, balustrades dangling like broken teeth, the roof above gone. He felt weak and slumped backwards. Everyone had been downstairs; Ella, the Cabinet, the press, Downing Street staff. Why couldn't he hear their cries for help, for God's sake? *Am I the only one left?* He heard more sirens but they seemed distant. Where were the emergency services? Minutes had passed, maybe more. It was dark, he was alone, trapped, with no way of—

He fumbled inside his jacket, his fingers tugging at the mobile phone buried in his pocket. The screen was cracked but the device still worked. He thumbed the contacts button, saw the name of the only minister he knew for sure hadn't been in the building. He tapped the screen, lifted the device to his ear. A click, a hiss, then the wonderful sound of a distant ringing tone.

Tariq Saeed, surrounded by an entourage of police and security personnel, entered the lobby of Millbank Tower. Despite the wailing sirens, the constant squawk of police radios and frantic shouts echoing around the marble atrium, he heard the soft warble of his mobile phone. He pulled it out of his pocket, checked the screen.

He stopped in his tracks.

Around him the scrum of policemen braked sharply, boots squeaking on the polished floor. *Alive?* Saeed bit his lip. He should be dead, incinerated in the blast. Someone else, perhaps? Unlikely. Then Bryce had somehow survived. Remarkable, yet he was reassured by the fact that the number was being monitored. He turned to the senior police officer beside him, waved the device in the man's face.

'The networks, should they still be operating?'

The policeman shook his head. 'Transmitter towers are being shut down as we speak. Takes a little time, sir.'

'Then make it happen faster.'

The Minister for Security and Immigration headed towards the elevator.

CALL ENDED.

Bryce fumbled the handset. It dropped through a gap in the rubble, the screen glowing in the dark of a small crevasse. He fished for it, scraping the flesh of his fingers, until he'd scooped it back onto his lap. He checked the screen; *No Service.* He tried the number again but the network was down. Maybe it wasn't a gas blast, Bryce reasoned. In the event of a terrorist attack it was standard procedure to cut the public mobile networks. Is that what this was? His blood ran cold. He tried calling for help several times but his voice was weak, his breath coming in painful gasps. For the first time since he'd regained consciousness, Bryce thought he might die before he could be rescued.

He wasn't sure how many minutes had passed when he heard someone crunching through the rubble below. He raised himself up, shouting until his voice croaked painfully. A head bobbed into view over a pile of bricks. It was a man, wearing civilian clothes.

'Where are you?'

Bryce raised his arm 'Over here!'

The man veered towards him, scrambling over shattered bricks and splintered timbers.

'Thank God,' Bryce gasped.

'Don't move.'

Bryce obeyed, the stranger's manner immediately

authoritative. In the fading light Bryce saw he was in his late thirties, his short hair flecked with grey, the pale line of an old scar curving beneath his right eye. He wore a black fleece and khaki trousers, the ones with pockets down the legs. An intricate tattoo covered his left forearm and a black digital watch glowed on his wrist. He produced a torch from a small rucksack, waving it around the debris.

'It's my leg,' Bryce moaned, 'It's trapped.'

'Be quiet!'

A sudden avalanche of debris thundered close by. Dust billowed up from the remains of the lobby, filling the room with choking black filth. The torch dimmed, the man momentarily lost.

'I'm sorry,' Bryce coughed.

'Shut up!'

He heard the man stumbling around. As the air cleared he saw him heaving a thick timber from the rubble. He hefted it in his hands and scrambled back to Bryce's side.

A sudden roar filled the air and a helicopter appeared overhead, whipping up another storm of dust and debris. The searing shaft of a searchlight lanced through the building, the Sky logo clearly visible on the side of the chopper. The pain was suddenly forgotten. Bryce waved frantically.

'Over here!' he shouted. 'Help us!'

The stranger turned away, shielding his face from the dust storm. He pulled a baseball cap from his pocket and tugged it over his head.

Something behind him caught Bryce's eye, something bright that drifted past the shattered roof, darting beneath the blackened rafters. A burning ember, dancing on an updraft, quickly joined by several others. Bryce stared in horror at the mountain of dry timbers, the piles of books that surrounded him. 'Jesus Christ, the place is on fire.'

The stranger didn't say a word, just jammed the stave beneath the timber trapping Bryce's leg. It shifted, but not enough. More glowing embers began to swirl through the building, a swarm of deadly fireflies that tumbled through the debris, settling on the dry kindling that lay all around. Bryce's eyes widened in fear. He was going to burn to death on live TV.

'For Christ's sake, hurry up!'

## MILLBANK

HE STOOD BY THE FLOOR TO CEILING WINDOW ON THE twenty-second floor of Millbank Tower, watching the pall of dense black smoke rolling above the rooftops of White-hall. Despite the chaos and panic around him, Tariq Saeed remained markedly unruffled. As usual his black hair was neatly parted to the side, his beard trimmed close, immaculate in a navy blue pinstripe suit and a pale blue tie that perfectly matched the colour of his eyes, as if he'd chosen it for that very reason. He hadn't, of course. The blue eyes were a reminder that somewhere in his distant past, an ancestor – a woman, no doubt – had disgraced herself by lying with a foreigner. Or perhaps she'd been raped, a common enough occurrence during Europe's sordid colonial escapades, but a disgrace nonetheless. Honour decreed that death should have followed, and yet somehow the infected gene had survived, passing down through the generations and bestowing on Saeed a childhood of playground bullying, an adolescence of female interest, an adulthood of envy and suspicion. He stood out from the crowd, both physically and intellectually, had married a beautiful woman, siring three healthy boys, all blessed with their mother's dark brown eyes. If they were old enough to understand what was in his heart, they would feel pride in their father's achievements.

Behind Saeed, the Emergency Management Centre was packed with dozens of high-ranking officials; bureaucrats from the Civil Contingencies Secretariat, a cabal of senior police and fire officers, MPs and Ministry of Defence personnel, suits and uniforms, gathered in tense groups as they regarded the solitary figure by the window. Saeed sensed their sympathy, but it was more than that. There was also respect, for Tariq Saeed, Minister for Security and Immigration, was now one of only three surviving senior government officials. As for the other two, one was already on his way to Millbank. The other was blackened and bloodied, his frantic waving from the rubble of Number Ten now being broadcast on the bank of TV monitors behind him.

*The best laid plans of mice and men,* Saeed mused, balling his fists behind his back. His eyes wandered across the dark skyline. He could make out Big Ben and Westminster Abbey, a triumvirate of famous spires jutting upwards through the haze, but beyond Parliament Square, beyond the hundreds of emergency vehicles choking the streets, smoke and dust blanketed everything. Deep in that fog, flames glowed like angry coals in the darkness as night crept across the city.

Saeed inched closer to the glass and looked down. Far below, twirling strands of blue and white tape had been strung across the surrounding streets. Across the Thames the south bank was closed to traffic as thousands of civilians streamed away from the area, All modes of transport had been shut down – trains, tubes, buses, everything. London was at a standstill.

Saeed glanced over his shoulder. The senior emergency service personnel were standing in a loose half-circle behind him, locked in discussion. As Saeed opened his mouth to speak, another distant boom rumbled across the city. He turned in time to see a fireball rolling skyward over White-hall. The uniforms surged towards the windows, crowding around Saeed. He bristled at the physical proximity.

'That looks like the Foreign Office,' the Fire Brigade's Director of Operations warned. 'Could be a fuel tank erupt-ing, or a gas main letting go.'

'Gas supplies to the whole area have been shut off,' confirmed another voice.

'Residual fumes in the pipes, then. Or maybe storage tanks. Has anyone any idea how many fuel storage tanks there are in government buildings?'

'Isn't that your responsibility?' sniffed the Metropolitan Police Commissioner. 'Surely you have inventories for this sort of thing?'

The fire chief turned on him. 'Of course we do. I just don't have them to hand—'

Saeed welcomed the squabble, the dithering and uncer-tainty. The Commissioner was a typical choice for the Met's top job, a political appointee rather than a policeman, a Common Purpose graduate whose nomination had been guaranteed by Saeed and others in return for unswerving loyalty. There were many like him in positions of power, both in this room and across the country. He turned away from the window.

'Is the Prime Minister safe yet?' His voice was smooth, his accent polished and eloquent, the result of private schooling and a Cambridge degree that had long since buried all traces of his immigrant upbringing.

'We're sending in another team now,' the fire chief confirmed. The first team had sustained casualties, broken limbs and severe head injuries, when a section of Downing Street's facade has collapsed on them. The collapse was fortuitous; perhaps Bryce would die in the rubble after all.

The doors to the room flew open and the imposing bulk of Nigel Hooper, Secretary of State for Defence, swept into the room, his entourage of advisors trailing behind him like pilot fish. His grey suit was covered in dust, his shoes scuffed and dirty. He came to a halt in the middle of the room, waving a document above his head.

'This is more than just an isolated incident,' he bellowed. The voices in the room died away. 'There's been another bomb, a few minutes ago. At the Luton Central Mosque.'

All eyes turned toward the bank of TV monitors, where a Breaking News ticker tape scrolled across the lower half of the screen. There was no footage as yet, but that would soon change. Hooper approached Saeed. He shook his large, balding head, and laid a meaty paw on the Minister's shoulder. His words dripped with sympathy. 'It's terrible news for your community, Tariq. For us all,' he added quickly.

Saeed cupped a theatrical hand over his mouth. 'Friday prayers. The mosque would've been packed.'

'We must brace ourselves for many casualties,' Hooper soothed. He turned to face the room, the document once again raised above his head, brandished like a religious artefact before devoted worshippers. 'Mobile phone conversations, intercepted less than six hours ago. They refer to a *spectacular*, quote unquote. There's also direct reference to this afternoon's press conference.' He slapped the folder into the chest of a loitering assistant. 'This is a truly horrendous day. We must act swiftly and decisively.'

Saeed almost laughed. It was clear from Hooper's expression that he had no idea what to do next. He steered the Defence Minister away from his entourage. 'Are you alright, Nigel?'

Hooper swallowed hard and nodded. Tiny grains of dust from his head drifted towards the carpet. 'Thank God you called when you did. Another few minutes and I would've been in Downing Street. Makes me sweat just thinking about it.' He patted the dust from the sleeves of his jacket.

Saeed took a step closer. No one was watching, or listening.

'We need to talk, Nigel.'

THE DARKNESS WAS ALMOST COMPLETE, the smoke thicker, the glow of the fire visible beyond the shell of the study wall. Bryce coughed and spluttered, holding a handkerchief over his nose and mouth. He could hear voices, frantic and unintelligible, in the shattered remains of Downing Street. The helicopter hovered somewhere above them, the searchlight still picking them out in the debris. All the while the stranger grunted with effort at the timber trapping Bryce's leg.

The evening wind shifted, drawing smoke up through the building like a chimney. Bryce glimpsed a tongue of flame through the gaping brickwork. Then another. He was going to burn to death, like an accused witch, the flames igniting his clothes, scorching his flesh—

'Hurry, it's getting closer.' He was tugging his own leg, ignoring the pain, the shortness of breath. The stranger worked his stave deep into the debris. Suddenly Bryce felt the timbers shift around his leg, the blood suddenly flowing into his limb.

'That's it. Keep going!'

The stranger pushed down again, using his body weight, levering the debris upwards. Bryce reached down, pulling his knee towards him, his calf scraping across wooden splinters and rusted nails. He ignored the pain, the tearing of flesh. He was out, free.

'Move!' the man bellowed. He dragged Bryce across the wreckage of the study. Bryce stumbled, reaching out to break the fall, sinking to the elbow in broken plaster, wood, glass and nails. He was yanked up by his collar, dragged towards the staircase. His shoe was missing, the sock wet with blood. He didn't feel the pain, only the heat from the fire, roaring up from the lobby, curling hungrily beneath the first floor landing. He threw an arm up over his face.

'Prime Minister!'

Two men ran up towards them, their clothes blackened and shredded. Bryce didn't recognise either of them, and his rescuer ordered them all down the shattered staircase. Broken glass crunched under Bryce's feet. Former Prime Ministers stared back at him, their faces lit by a hellish glow. The fire was now a living thing, consuming what remained of the lobby, roaring up towards the roofless sky. Timbers cooked and splintered, cracking in the heat. Bryce glanced toward the interior of the building, where corridors and staterooms once existed, now a dark grotto of unspeakable devastation. Smoke and flames belched from within.

The familiar black and white tiles of the lobby were submerged under a sea of rubble. He felt a hand on his collar and then he was being dragged again, the heat of the flames pushing him onwards until he'd stumbled out into

Downing Street itself. He caught himself on the edge of a deep crater. He was rooted to the spot, shocked by its enormity. *A bomb. No doubt.*

The stranger steered him around the crater, manhandling him over hillocks of brick and rubble, helped by the other two survivors. On the other side of the street the Foreign Office was an inferno.

They were trapped inside a cathedral of destruction, the flames all around, towering towards the night sky.

THE ROOM WAS QUIETER NOW. Hooper's entourage loitered nearby, deep in discussion. Every phone in the room was in use, glued to the ear of a pale-faced official, their voices strained, urgent. Civil Contingency people and assorted government workers crowded around a conference table, heads huddled together, voices laced with the whisper of uncertainty, tapping furiously on electronic tablets. Police officers crowded around a map of London that covered a whole wall. Others came and went, low-level flunkeys and secretaries, seeking purpose, craving the leadership, the stability that had been so suddenly and so violently snatched from them. Saeed could see the fear, the unspoken pleas for help in their eyes as they snatched glances towards the two most senior members of government still walking and talking.

He guided Hooper towards the window. The power had been cut to Whitehall. Big Ben was now a tall shadow in the distance, shrouded behind a veil of smoke. Beyond, the sky glowed a deep red, as if a meteorite had crashed to earth.

'There's no constitutional model for an event like this,' Saeed began. 'We must pray that Gabriel makes it out alive, but in any event the continuity of government must be maintained. We have no Cabinet, but thankfully we still have a parliament and both Houses. Constitutional experts will be consulted of course, and the Royal Household will need to assert it's prerogative, but the Solicitor General and Lord Justices have made it clear that interim authority be passed to you to act on the Prime Minister's behalf until the situation is clarified. As your most senior minister, you will of course have my full support.'

Saeed watched Hooper as he struggled with the enormity of events. He stroked his heavy jowls with fat fingers, his bulbous eyes flicking left and right, darting beneath bushy brows. He truly was an ugly man, Saeed concluded. And predictable.

'This is all legal?'

'Of course. Parliamentary sovereignty and the rule of law demand it. Your authority will not be questioned. In the meantime several floors here at Millbank will temporarily house your new administration. Security measures mean that the surrounding streets and the embankment will be restricted areas. The Tate Gallery will have to close, I'm afraid.'

Hooper's gaze was fixed on the destruction in Whitehall. 'I'll need your help during this transition, Tariq. The perpetrators of these hideous acts must be caught quickly. Tensions will be running high across the country, particularly in your own community. I want you to be my second in command. My Deputy Prime Minister, as it were.'

Saeed nodded. 'Of course, Nigel. You can count on me.'

THE FLAMES TOWERED ABOVE THEM. Bryce's skin prickled with the heat, his body pierced with a thousand daggers of pain. He no longer had any control over his own body, his arm draped around the stranger's shoulder, his feet fragging through the rubble. His other two rescuers cleared a path ahead, stumbling, shouting, waving.

And then they were clear.

The cauldron of heat was finally behind them.

Bryce slipped from the stranger's grasp and fell to the ground. Hands grabbed at his arms, pulled him to his feet. His eyes struggled to comprehend the scale of the damage. Whitehall was covered in debris, the asphalt road barely visible under a carpet of wreckage; huge chunks of masonry, twisted metal, a sea of shattered glass glinting in the fire-light. Vehicles lay abandoned in the street, their doors flung open in haste, the nearest ones overturned and engulfed in flames. Bodies littered the scene like piles of sackcloth, some limbless, some half-buried, their clothes torn and shredded, bags, footwear, scattered everywhere – the detritus of instant carnage wreaked upon an unsuspecting populace surrounded them. Even the street lamps had been decapitated by the blast.

Thick smoke swirled and eddied on the evening breeze, the air tainted with the stench of burning rubber. Bryce could taste it in his mouth, on his tongue. He heard a shout, footsteps pounding. Sirens wailed close by.

'Keep moving!' the stranger shouted.

'Which way?'

The smoke seemed to be getting thicker, a choking black ceiling above them. Bryce felt himself being dragged forward again. He had no strength left, his legs like iron, his lungs devoid of oxygen. His head swam. He couldn't go on, couldn't take another step. Then suddenly the smoke parted like a curtain before them.

A sea of blue and red lights stretched across Whitehall,

filling Parliament Square. Dozens of figures raced towards them, the sound of their running feet rising to a crescendo, a stampede of salvation. Bryce sank to his knees, exhausted, the relief almost palpable. He felt a hand on his shoulder and looked up. The stranger's cap was covered with filth, his face streaked with soot.

'Your name,' Bryce gasped. 'I need to know your name.'

'It's Mac,' the stranger panted.

'You saved my life, Mac. Thank you.'

The words caught in his throat. Tears streaked through the dirt on his face, and then his saviour was lost behind a wall of uniforms. Urgent hands reached down for him, lifting him off the ground. His senses were assaulted, the acrid smell of burning, the garbled chatter of radio transmissions, the multitude of voices jabbering in an unintelligible chorus around him. Sirens wailed and helicopters clattered somewhere above. He felt claustrophobic, hemmed in by a scrum of uniforms, medical green and police black, the cold contact of their clothing abrasive against his raw flesh. Some held Perspex shields overhead, protecting him from further assault, like a cohort of Roman Legionnaires surrounding their wounded General. Bryce was a rag doll in their hands. His head lolled back and he stared upwards, beyond the helmets and visors, to where a faint dusting of stars glittered in the night sky. He thought it was the most beautiful thing he'd ever seen.

He was lowered onto a stretcher, then lifted into an ambulance. Doors slammed and paramedics in masks and gloves loomed over him, slicing the clothes from his body. They wiped and swabbed, checking pressures and pupils and beats per minute. They swayed in unison as the vehicle moved at speed, sirens clearing the way. He stared up at the ceiling, at the alien beings that surrounded him, peering, probing, puncturing his skin with drips and needles.

He'd live, of that much he was certain. He was sliced and diced, battered and bruised, but he sensed there was nothing immediately life threatening. The paramedics, in their cold and impersonal language, confirmed it. He let the motion of the ambulance calm his shattered nerves.

He'd survived.

THE SUDDEN SHOUT STARTLED SAEED.

'They've got him! The Prime Minister's alive!'

Reaction to the news rippled around the Emergency Management Centre, greeted with smiles and sobs, handshakes and embraces. A smattering of hesitant applause quickly died away. Some of the women hugged each other, others dabbing moist eyes with balled-up tissues. Saeed stifled his own frustration. 'What's his condition?' he snapped.

The Speaker of the House broke away from a gaggle of senior police officers and scurried across to where Saeed and Hooper waited. 'He's not out of the woods. It's serious, multiple injuries. They're taking him to King Edward the Seventh. It'll be a while before we know any more.'

'Any other survivors?' Hooper inquired.

'The rescue teams are in there now. It's too early to tell.'

The Met Commissioner crossed the room and joined them. 'There's more,' he announced. He handed a folder to Hooper. 'Our first breakthrough.'

Hooper arched a bushy eyebrow. 'Already?' He leafed through the folder, the thick sheaf of camera stills within.

The Commissioner nodded. 'This man was captured on surveillance cameras at the Luton mosque yesterday morning. He delivered a large container, an industrial refrigeration unit we think.'

'I thought the mosque was destroyed,' Hooper said.

'The security cameras were backed-up off site. CCTV and ANPR tracked the vehicle to the Kings Cross area. We're trawling the local authority cameras right now, and every officer in London is now looking for that truck. We'll find it.'

Saeed peered over Hooper's shoulder. Daniel Morris Whelan had been captured from several angles, the high definition images well-defined and extremely detailed. 'That tattoo on his neck looks distinctive. Do we know who he is?'

'We're running the images. Nothing yet.'

'What about the Downing Street bomb?'

The policeman frowned. 'Judging by the aerial footage the crater suggests a vehicular IED. We're pulling all the Downing Street feeds as we speak. Again, it's a matter of time.'

'An inside job,' Saeed concluded.

The Commissioner gave a curt nod. 'Without doubt.'

Hooper passed the folder back to the policeman. 'Use every available resource you have, Commissioner. I want these bastards flushed out.'

The atmosphere in the room had changed dramatically, the news of Bryce's survival injecting the air with the hum of quiet optimism. Human traffic in and out of the room gathered apace as messengers made up for the lack of mobile phone coverage. Saeed's mind drifted, still perplexed by Bryce's survival. The van's floor and side panels had been packed with military grade explosive, every nook and crevice, every void and space, the vehicle's suspension specially modified to take the extra weight, the driver a

Christian convert who'd yearned for Paradise. The van was directly outside when it detonated. Despite the years of structural strengthening and fortifications, Number Ten had folded like a house of cards. Circumnavigating Parliament Square at the precise moment, even Saeed had been momentarily unnerved by the sheer force of the blast, the shock wave that had rocked his official car, the debris that had rained on the roof, the rolling dust cloud that engulfed Parliament Square. Bryce had survived all that. Saeed shook his head.

He studied the faces around him, the streams of officials that continued to press into the Emergency Management Centre. The room was now filled with yet more senior officials; government and judiciary, emergency services, defence, media people, all drawn to the new hub of power in Britain. He watched Hooper acknowledge the late arrivals, saw his eyes register the size and importance of this growing audience. He leaned into the Defence Minister's ear. 'Nigel, you should say something.'

'You're right.'

Hooper buttoned his jacket, brushing the dust from its flanks and lapels. Saeed gestured for the heavy wooden doors to be closed and the chatter in the room faded to silence as Hooper cleared his throat.

'Ladies and gentlemen, we are in the grip of a crisis as unique as it is terrifying. Whitehall has been decimated by a bomb, as has the Luton central mosque.' Saeed studied their faces, expressions that ranged from fear and uncertainty to lingering shock. 'Casualties are unknown at this time,' continued Hooper, 'but the death toll is expected to be considerable.'

A troubled murmur rippled around the room. Hooper acknowledged it with a grim nod.

'I can tell you now that evidence is already beginning to emerge. We have a face, and a vehicle, and soon we will have a name. Clearly the intention was to decapitate the government and spark civil unrest. They have failed on the first count and we must work hard on the second to ensure that our communities are protected, that the ambitions of these murderous bigots are thwarted and each and every one of them is brought swiftly to justice.' Hooper paused for a moment, as if searching for the right words. Saeed sensed the building tension, the recent fear shifting towards quiet determination.

'We have to protect what remains of our government,' Hooper continued. 'In light of the severity of the situation and the undetermined condition of Prime Minister Bryce, the relevant constitutional authorities have endorsed my temporary status as head of government until the situation becomes clearer. It will be a heavy burden indeed, and I hope I can count on each and every one of you.'

Saeed watched the back of Hooper's head, the folds of flesh pressing together as his polished dome swept the room, his suspicious eyes already seeking out possible dissenters. There were none. He watched Anna Morgan, the Solicitor General, break ranks and approach Hooper. She was a tall woman, thin, with collar-length black hair and a severe fringe. Her boss was missing somewhere amongst the rubble of Downing Street, which technically made her the acting Attorney General. Saeed knew that for many in the room the crisis also had its upside, a sudden promotion being the obvious and immediate benefit.

'Nigel, I think I speak on behalf of the room when I say that you have our full and unequivocal support,' gushed Morgan.

'Thank you, Anna,' Hooper smiled, shaking her outstretched hand.

'Thank you, Prime Minister.'

The words hung in the air, like an unfamiliar, yet not unpleasant odour. Saeed watched the crowd for a reaction but there was no obvious one. A camera flashed, the handshake a visual metaphor for the transition of power, captured for immediate dissemination by the media. Saeed almost smiled; there was tomorrow's front-page right there. And by the time the sun rose, Bryce's head might just as well have been found in a gutter. The King was dead, long live the King.

And there was something else too. In less than an hour Millbank had become a nexus of power, the new administrative heart of the country, an evolution of huge psychological significance for those around him. Soon there would be a scramble for desk space, with whole floors being hastily rearranged, while the security cordon tightened its grip on the surrounding streets. Whitehall had been emptied, a sinking ship whose passengers sought the comfort and security of Millbank, desperate to be a part of the new government that was taking shape in front of Saeed's eyes.

Elsewhere, today's events would be met with great joy. Behind closed doors in Ankara, in marbled halls across the Middle East, the men of power would talk favourably of Saeed and what he'd accomplished so far. There was still a long way to go, many years in fact before the plan came to full fruition, and Saeed hoped that he'd see it in his own lifetime. His heart almost sang at the thought of it, of the pride his children would feel, the esteem his name would be held in throughout the *Ummah.*

Only Bryce remained a problem. A sudden recovery, the resumption of power, the continued opposition to the

Treaty of Cairo, all could tip the scales in the wrong direction. Bryce had to be sidelined, hindered, his name and reputation devalued. It had to be done carefully, subtlety, so that the name of Gabriel Bryce became an uncomfortable and embarrassing topic of discussion. The trick was to convince Hooper, who stood a few feet away, pumping hands and revelling in his newfound status.

Saeed finally allowed himself a careful smile. Power was such a corrupting influence, a drug that, once savoured, demanded to be fed. Hooper was already a junkie. Saeed felt it too, yet his rise to power had been engineered for a much higher purpose, a divine quest that rose above the sins of vanity and personal gain.

And Bryce stood in the way of that.

But not for long.

## 8

## LONDON

DANNY WHELAN STOOD IN THE DOORWAY OF THE kitchen, watching his father tackle a stack of dirty dishes. Like most of the other rooms in the twelfth-floor apartment the kitchen was small, yet spotlessly clean. Danny glanced at the wall calendar beneath the clock, September's image of a turreted castle, the flag of St. George fluttering above its ramparts, grey stone walls framed by snow-capped peaks. Beneath the stirring image, the text read: *Scenes of England, reproduced with kind permission for the English Freedom Movement.* The bitterness welled inside him, a reminder of the legacy that the Movement had bestowed on him; a tattoo he usually kept covered and a calendar that would soon be out of date. But right now, those were the least of his problems.

The old man was hunched over the sink, thin arms covered in soapsuds as he worked his way through soiled plates and saucepans. His white cotton vest hung loosely off his bony shoulders, his baggy sweatpants gathered in grey folds around the worn carpet slippers.

'Thanks for dinner, Dad.'

The old man didn't look up, his attention focused on cleaning a large, greasy pot. 'My pleasure, son. Nice to have a decent bit of steak for a change.' His voice was scratchy, a lingering symptom of the chest infection he'd recently suffered. Danny tutted and held out a well-worn sweatshirt.

'Put your top on. You'll catch your bloody death again.' The old man wiped his hands on a tea towel and wrestled the sweatshirt over his head. Danny moved to help him, pulling it down around his waist. 'There you go, pops.'

'I can manage.' He plunged his hands back into the soapy water. 'What are you up to then?'

Danny shrugged. 'I was thinking of going out for a while. Find out what's going on.'

'It's all over the news.'

'I mean on the street.' Danny tugged a wedge of cash out of his pocket. He peeled off several notes and laid them on the counter.

'What's this?'

'For food and stuff. Bit towards the bills, too.'

The old man dried his hands on the tea towel. 'What was the job again?'

'I told you, a delivery.'

'What sort of delivery?'

'A fridge. Big bloody thing it was too, one of them industrial ones.'

'Where to?'

'Eh?' Danny felt the blood rushing to his cheeks, the sudden pounding of his heart.

'The fridge; where did you deliver it to?'

He remembered Abdul's dirty breath, the hands that twisted his shirt. He remembered the news bulletins, seen through a haze of blue smoke and chemically dulled senses, the shattered dome, the white sheets lined along the pavement, the wailing relatives. He swallowed hard. 'Some place out west. Near Reading.'

The old man scooped up the money. 'Well, I can't say we don't need it.' He pocketed the cash and used the tea towel to wipe the worktop. 'So, where are you off to then?'

'The Kings, I guess.'

He peered out of the kitchen window. Beyond the tower blocks the city sparkled under the night sky, the view one of the rare benefits of living on the Longhill Estate. Up here they couldn't smell the rubbish-strewn alleyways or see the graffiti on the walls. Instead, the signs of social deprivation were audible, the bickering families, the jumbled drone of televisions and sound systems, the pitiful whine of housebound dogs. For the last forty-eight hours Danny had filtered it all out, had smoked enough resin to flatten a bull elephant, but the nightmares had penetrated the fog of drugs, the blanket of sleep that had wrapped itself around his body. Last night he'd thrown up in his bedroom, as the news from Luton grew more terrible with each passing hour.

They would come for him, sooner rather than later.

He could hand himself in right now, tonight, tell them everything, but would they believe him? He'd be arrested, interviewed, remanded in a high-security prison while they investigated his story; a bloke called Eddie with no last name, a cash in hand job, a mobile phone that was now disconnected, the lorry covered in his DNA. Anyone with half a brain would know something was dodgy. And there was Downing Street too, the bomb going off at exactly the same time as Luton. Whoever went down for this would go away forever. The thought chilled his bones.

'You all right, son?'

Danny turned away from the window, saw the troubled

look in his dad's eyes. 'I'm fine,' he lied. 'It's just this stuff on TV.'

'You get yourself wound up, Danny. All the bitterness, the hate, it'll eat you up. You should be making the most of your life. If your mum were alive she'd tell you the same.'

Danny felt a sudden wave of emotion. The confession lingered behind his lips, like caged birds waiting to be released in an explosion of wings. He turned away, unable to look his own father in the face.

'You're right, dad. I'm pretty bloody useless.'

He felt the old man's hand on his shoulder. 'No you're not. You've had your problems, a bit of bad luck, that's all. There's still plenty of time to turn your life around.'

'Sure.'

'You go out and enjoy yourself. Try not to think about things too much.'

'Okay, pops.'

Danny slipped on his coat and grabbed a tatty baseball cap off the hook by the front door. He paused for a moment, watching the old man settle down in front of the TV, the light flickering off the wall, the canned laughter. He stared at the door to his bedroom, where the rucksack waited beneath his bed, stuffed with clean clothes and a wash kit, money and passport. The letter to his dad lay in a drawer, stained with tears of guilt and drug-induced self-pity. He stood there a moment longer, then closed the front door behind him. He couldn't leave, not yet. He'd give it another night, a few more hours to weigh up his options, make a decision.

*Run...*

He shook off the thought as he trotted down the stairs, past the terminally broken elevators in the lobby and out into the night. He pulled the baseball cap low over his brow, navigating the concrete alleyways of the estate, fading in and out of the street lamps.

He heard it before he saw it, the low hum of propellers, then the blink of a red collision light as the nose crept into view above the nearest tower block. He kept his head down as the unmanned airship drifted overhead, its platform of surveillance cameras scanning the streets below, the ghostly white letters that read 'POLICE' clearly visible on its smooth black flanks. Danny ducked inside an unlit lobby until it had moved away.

*Run, Danny...*

He turned the corner towards the small parade of shops and ducked inside the King's Head, nodding to the bouncer in the doorway. The pub was busier than usual, the lights dimmed low, the ambience seemingly warm and welcoming, which was unusual for the Kings. Danny loitered near the door. There was no discernible tension in the air, no strangers lurking. Music thumped quietly in the background. He scanned the heaving crowd, hoping that Eddie might be there, knowing he wouldn't.

He sauntered over to the bar, squeezing between the drinkers. The landlord nodded.

'Alright Dan? Usual?'

'Sweet.'

The landlord pushed a pint of lager in front of Danny, leaving a wet trail across the bar. 'Cheers.' He handed over a ten-pound note and sipped the froth. The scene reminded him of a distant New Years Eve, during his one and only tour of Afghanistan, most of the camp bedded down for the night, the tent lit by a small lantern. He could still see the grinning faces of his mates around the card table, the clink of bottles as they saw the New Year in, cocooned within the confines of the camp, the warm embrace of their friendship.

He missed those times, those friends. 'Decent crowd this evening.'

'Yeah, funny that,' observed the landlord, scanning the note under a reader. 'Something about a national crisis I suppose.'

'Reminds me of when I was in Afghanistan,' Danny began, warming to the theme. 'It was New Years Eve. Me and some of the lads, we'd managed to—'

The landlord had already drifted away to serve another punter. *Ignorant bastard*. Still, Danny's job tonight was to keep his ear to the ground, see if anyone had been nosing around the estate. He found a table, pulled off his coat, sat down. He found half a spliff in his pocket and debated whether to spark it up or not, his resolve already crumbling as he smoothed the spliff between his fingers. He was supposed to stay alert, not get stoned. Besides, hadn't he had enough lately? Then again it would help him relax, calm his frayed nerves. He clamped it between his lips. Fuck it, why not? He lit it, exhaling slowly and rocking back in his chair, enjoying that familiar buzz and yet hating himself at the same time.

He swallowed his lager in deep, shameful gulps. What a loser he'd turned out to be, his discipline gone to shit, a mere shadow of the man he once was, all those years ago when he'd taken the oath and worn the uniform. He closed his eyes and again the memories returned, the smell of the dry Afghan air, the taste of jet fuel in his mouth, the roar of the helicopters as they—

Overhead lights blazed into life. A groan echoed around the bar.

'Special announcement on the news,' explained the landlord, pointing to the TV on the wall. The sudden change of vibe only worsened Danny's mood.

'Turn it up,' a voice yelled.

The landlord stabbed at the remote control with his thick fingers. 'Hang on, for Christ's sake.'

The familiar logo of the BBC filled the screen, the theme tune growing louder as the landlord toyed with the remote.

Danny finished his smoke and dropped the butt on the floor, crushing it beneath his trainer. The stopwatch graphic reached zero and the music finished on a long, piercing scrape of strings that Danny found slightly unnerving. His heart began to beat a little faster. He looked over his shoulder. The roughnecks from the back room had drifted into the main bar, baseball caps and hoods pulled low over glowering faces. He looked away as a sterile newsroom filled the screen, a suited and suitably sombre man on one side, a Hijab-wearing female on the other.

'Good evening,' the man opened, 'and welcome to BBC London News. We now being you a special bulletin.'

'Still can't hear it,' someone behind Danny shouted.

The landlord barked for quiet, thumbing the volume button to the max.

The Muslim woman adjusted her glasses, the navy-blue veil framing her oval face. 'At Europe House this afternoon, interim Prime Minister Nigel Hooper met with European Union President Michel Dupont and representatives from the Islamic Congress of Europe to discuss the ongoing threat to Muslim communities across the continent. In a statement issued this evening, both the President and the Prime Minister have pledged to tackle rising Islamophobia, and are considering amendments to existing hate crime legislation, a move welcomed by—'

A storm of abuse drowned out the newsreader. For once Danny stayed quiet.

'Keep it down,' growled the landlord, thumping the bar with his fist. Once again the newsreader's voice filled the room.

'...extended session in the European Parliament, during which Turkish MEPs called on the British government to continue with the Treaty of Cairo ratification process as a gesture of reconciliation and greater European harmony. In London, Deputy Prime Minister Tariq Saeed welcomed the Turkish statement and declared that Britain's fledgling government was dedicated to the European Union's policy of expansion and peaceful integration. Later, Minister Saeed and several other senior figures visited the King Edward the Seventh hospital in Marylebone, where Gabriel Bryce is undergoing treatment for injuries sustained in the terror attack. A hospital spokeswoman announced his condition as serious but stable...'

*Peaceful integration;* what a joke, Danny grumbled silently. He shoved back his chair and headed to the lavatory. He stood at the urinal, a familiar vein of anger replacing the fear and apprehension that had plagued him since Luton. More laws, more legislation; Freedom was fast becoming a thing of the past. He wandered over to the sink, checked his reflection. He looked tired, dark circles framing his bloodshot eyes. That would be a lack of sleep and too much dope. His hair needed a cut and a shave wouldn't go amiss either. Maybe tomorrow. It would probably be a good move anyway, smarten his act up, change his appearance a little, just in case. He yanked the lavatory door open. The bar was silent, the TV booming.

'...A powerful compound used almost exclusively in military applications, according to forensic experts. The vehicle used to transport the device to the Luton mosque was found early this morning on an industrial estate in north London...'

Danny froze by the wall, fear gripping his insides like a cold vice. The shattered remains of the Luton Mosque filled the screen, its walls reduced to piles of smoking rubble, the dome tilted at a jarring angle. He looked around the bar. Everyone was riveted to the news bulletin.

*Run, Danny...*

On the screen the image changed to an aerial shot of Whitehall, the road clogged with police vehicles, ambulances and digging equipment. The Foreign and Cabinet Offices were reduced to piles of blackened rubble and ant-like figures scurried over the debris that was once Downing Street. Only a few walls remained, the teetering brickwork propped with steel supports. In the daylight, the size of the bomb crater and the sheer scale of the devastation brought a gasp from the punters around the bar.

'...More than forty of the dead were Egyptian tourists who'd travelled to Luton from their hotel in London. That brings the combined death toll to almost three hundred, including many serving Cabinet members and other senior government officials. Police have just issued an image of a man wanted in connection with the attack. Thirty-eight year old Daniel Whelan, from London, was captured on CCTV cameras at the Luton Mosque shortly before...'

*NO!*

Danny was horrified to see his picture flash up behind the newsreader. He dragged his eyes away from the TV, saw the drinkers around the bar looking at each other in disbelief.

'Was that Danny?'

'Can't be.'

'Is that his last name? Whelan?'

'They've made a mistake, bruv.'

'He was here a second ago.'

Danny was already moving towards the main door, head low, legs like jelly, squeezing behind the punters still glued to the news broadcast. He glimpsed the landlord's puzzled face, the eyes that registered the empty table, the jacket over the chair, the glass of unfinished lager, the roughnecks with their pool cues. The bar was quiet, the mood of the crowd still doubtful, yet Danny knew that wouldn't last. He reached the main door, pushed it open, moving past the oblivious bouncer as the newsreader's words chased him from the premises.

'...Member of a banned organisation, with a string of previous convictions. The Metropolitan Police has offered a substantial reward for information leading to Whelan's arrest. Meanwhile, tributes to the victims of the Luton attack continue to pour in from across the Islamic world...'

*Run, Danny.*

*RUN!*

Cold fear snapped at his heels. He sprinted across the estate, arms and legs pumping, heart pounding. He reached his block in less than two minutes, yanking open the security door and staggering against the wall inside, his chest heaving.

Then he heard them.

The rumble of feet on the pavement, the whoops of excitement echoing around the towers. They were coming for him, knew where he lived. He was trapped.

He stared through the mesh-covered door, saw the roughnecks coming hard and fast, pool cues in their hands. He ducked beneath the stairs, held his breath in the darkness as the roughnecks stormed the building. They ignored the broken lifts and headed up the stairs, their chilling howls echoing through the building. The stampede receded, their cries fading as they climbed higher up the stairwell. Young and reasonably fit they may be, but twelve floors was an effort for anyone.

Danny crept out from the recess and headed back out onto the estate. He felt sick with fear, with shame at the thought of his leaving his dad at the mercy of the pack. *Coward!* his inner voice screamed, but Danny forced it from his mind. He had to get away fast.

He dropped down a flight of stairs into an underground car park, a black, rubbish-strewn chamber, a graveyard of stripped-down, burnt-out vehicles. He hesitated only for a second, then moved through it quickly, bounding up another concrete staircase at the far end. Another alleyway, then he was lost in the darkness of the park, loping across the open space and into the trees on the other side. He stopped, crouching in the bushes, his breath coming in painful heaves. He heard more shouts, saw another posse hunting him, flashlights probing around the tower blocks, sweeping across the park for signs of flight. Danny edged further back into the undergrowth, watching their frantic movements as they charged along balconies and thundered down staircases, their cries of frustration echoing across the estate, desperate villagers armed with flaming torches, seeking out the monster in their midst.

He'd seen enough. He turned his back on them, on the Longhill estate and the life he knew, and disappeared into the trees.

# 9

# KING EDWARD THE SEVENTH HOSPITAL, LONDON

SOMEWHERE IN THE DARKNESS BRYCE HEARD A NOISE. It was an indistinct sound at first, a low murmur lurking somewhere on the outer edges of his consciousness. Then he heard another sound, rather like the first, but pitched slightly higher. Voices. Yes, that was it, voices, out there in the shifting shadows. He felt himself moving towards them, the blackness slowly turning to grey, then a milky whiteness. He saw two dark shapes, directly ahead, very close. They spoke quietly, almost whispering, and Bryce still couldn't make out what they were saying. Other indistinct objects suddenly morphed into familiar forms. He saw a large TV, a picture frame on the wall, an empty chair by the window. The voices fell silent. Bryce slowly turned his head, heard the familiar metallic clatter of his chart at the end of the bed, caught a glimpse of a man leaving the room, the door closing with a soft click. He rubbed his eyes and blinked several times as he finally returned to the land of the living.

Which was funny, because he didn't feel alive. In fact, since he'd been in hospital he'd felt disconnected from the real world, drifting in and out of consciousness, a sensation rather like an out of body experience, he imagined. He felt no pain, only fatigue. Lately he couldn't stay awake longer than an hour or two. He was told he needed to rest, the cocktail of drugs that seeped into his veins fighting the infections, bolstering his immune system, feeding his battered body. Rest, the consultant ordered, rest the nurse insisted, rest the orderly advised. All he did was rest.

He turned towards the window, where the view was distinctly uninspiring; a windowless building blocking out most of the natural light, the brickwork streaked with rain patches, the thin sliver of sky grey and forbidding. The room itself was comfortable enough, if a little too warm, with all the trappings a private hospital offered. There was a wall-mounted TV opposite his bed, a sofa and two chairs for visitors, a fridge, and a well-appointed private bathroom near the door to his right. Tasteful artwork adorned the walls, a mixture of Edwardian landscapes and eclectic post-modern pieces, and an abundance of flowers from well-wishers filled vases on every shelf and sideboard. A luxury dressing gown with a royal crest embroidered onto the breast pocket hung from a hook behind the door. Bryce yearned for the strength to stand upright, to wrap the garment around his body and venture outside his heavily-guarded room. If only he had the strength.

He'd lain immobile for over a week, wired up to IV drips, meters, monitors and God knew what else. He had a needle feeding fluids into a fat vein in his left hand, while a crescent of tiny suckers clamped to his chest monitored his heart. A catheter was inserted into his penis and a large dressing covered the wound to his thigh. To the left of the bed, an impressive bank of electronic equipment displayed a confusing array of information that Bryce didn't even pretend to understand. Despite all of that, he was thankful to be alive.

He'd seen the images on TV, the devastation of Downing Street, the horror of Luton. It was worse for them, the worshippers at the mosque. Politicians were targets, he accepted that, but to destroy a mosque, a holy place, was unthinkable. How people could ever contemplate such an act was beyond Bryce's comprehension.

He'd seen Nigel Hooper on the news, his legally and constitutionally appointed successor. Bryce wasn't a huge fan but he was grateful someone from Cabinet had survived. Yet it was Tariq's presence at his side that bothered him. He'd dodged a bullet over Heathrow and now there he was, Deputy Prime Minister. It was wrong.

Bryce chastised himself. He should be rejoicing that his old comrade had survived. And the new Cabinet, well, there were some good choices and some strange ones. Clearly changes would have to be made when he was back on his feet.

The door opened and his personal orderly, Sully, breezed in, wheeling a trolley beside Bryce's bed.

'Good morning,' he beamed in a cheery London accent. He wore a maroon tunic and black trousers, a plastic name badge pinned above his left breast pocket. Bryce guessed that he took part in some kind of recreational sport, the wide shoulders and muscular arms testament to a regime of intensive physical activity. He really should ask him about it, after all Sully seemed to be a permanent fixture in his room these days. Setting the brake on the trolley, the younger man tilted his head to one side and gave a small bow. 'Breakfast is served.' He removed the stainless steel plate cover with a flourish, a small ring of steam rolling up towards the ceiling. 'Porridge, scrambled egg, juice. No hot beverages, I'm afraid. Doctor's orders.'

'Lovely,' Bryce replied without enthusiasm. The drowsiness and the protective gum guard combined to slur his words. He plucked the guard from his mouth. 'Sully, someone was in here a minute ago, doctors I think. Who were they?'

The orderly frowned. He glanced around the room, as if the people Bryce referred to could still be present. 'In here?'

'Yes. Perhaps you passed them in the corridor?'

The orderly shook his closely cropped head. 'I don't think so. There's only me and nurse Orla on duty today.'

'What about the policeman outside? He must have seen them.'

'There's no one out there. Shift change, probably.'

'Well, *someone* was here.'

Sully said nothing. Instead he pumped up the pillows behind Bryce's shoulders and placed the breakfast tray across his lap.

Bryce toyed with the food, forcing himself to swallow several mouthfuls. He just wasn't very hungry. What he really wanted was a strong pot of coffee to blast away the fog of fatigue. He needed to wake up, get a little fresh air, maybe some exercise. Any exercise, in fact.

He pushed the tray away as Sully fussed around the room, emptying the wastepaper basket and tidying the magazines on the coffee table. Fatigue aside, Bryce was certainly on the mend. The pain that had wracked his body had been reduced to a few minor aches, the excruciating sensitivity of his missing teeth soothed by the remedial dental repairs. His ribs no longer hurt, the broken nose would soon be reconstructed, and he could move his leg a little more each day. The cuts and lacerations across his body had all been cleaned and dressed many times. He was healing nicely, he'd been told. Before too long he'd be back in charge, sitting behind his new desk on the twenty-sixth floor of Millbank Tower. He was looking forward to that day, although things were never going to be the same.

There'd been so much death, friends, colleagues, and Downing Street staff. He'd caught Rana Hassani's funeral on the news, the streets of Slough thronged with mourners, the outpouring of grief and rage that had resulted in clashes with the police. There'd be more funerals to come, a public service to commemorate the deceased, a day of national mourning.

He thought again of Ella, lying in her own personal hell. Incredibly she'd been found alive, buried under a mountain of rubble, one of only a handful of survivors from Downing Street. She was still in a coma at St. Thomas', her injuries extensive, not least those to her spine, yet against the odds they'd both survived. Perhaps a higher power was at work, sparing them both when so many others had perished. He desperately wanted to see her but he wasn't ready yet, either physically or emotionally. It would be a long, hard road back for Ella. With a healthy Gabe by her side, maybe it wouldn't be quite the ordeal she might imagine.

The door opened and nurse Orla marched into the room. She wore a uniform of light blue, a crisp double-buttoned tunic and trousers that strained against her heavy frame, her hair knotted in a tight auburn bun at the nape of her neck. Bryce didn't care for her too much. He thought her attitude a little stern, and she didn't utter a single word as she inspected the monitors by his bed.

'Well, nurse Orla, what's the prognosis?' Bryce began, hoping to stir up a little banter. She didn't answer. Bryce glanced at Sully, who ignored them both, rearranging the flowers in their vases. 'Nurse,' Bryce repeated, injecting a little authority into his voice.

She turned towards him. Her wide, freckled face seemed locked in a permanent frown and she seemed irritated at the interruption. She picked up his temporary dental work perched on the sideboard, inspecting the dentures closely. 'They've done a grand job, haven't they just?' Her accent was Irish, not the harsh vowel sounds of the province, but the gentle cadence of the far south.

'Nurse Orla.'

Her head swivelled towards him. 'What is it?'

'I had a couple of visitors a few minutes ago. Who were they?'

'Visitors?' She seemed as puzzled as Sully at the suggestion. 'You've had no visitors since the day before yesterday. Prime Minister Hooper and Minister Saeed stopped by. Quite a day that was, I can tell you.'

'Doctors, then. Consultants. They were looking at my chart.'

Orla straightened up, hands on her wide hips. 'No, you've made a mistake. Access to this room is strictly controlled. Sure, I'd know if anyone had been in here.'

'I saw them,' Bryce insisted. 'They left when I woke up.'

She glanced at the fob watch dangling from her tunic. 'You were asleep?'

'I'm always bloody asleep!' he snapped. Orla stared at him like an aggrieved schoolmistress. Bryce took a deep breath. 'I'm sorry about that. A little frustration, that's all. I feel so doped up I can barely stay awake.'

'It's called the healing process,' Orla reminded him, patting his arm as if he were a child. She turned her attention back to the monitors as Sully sprayed glass cleaner on the windows in short puffs of mist.

Bryce spoke to her ample backside. 'You said Ministers Hooper and Saeed were here?'

'Yes. And the photographer.'

Bryce jerked upright. Orange juice slopped across the tray. 'Please tell me they didn't take any pictures.'

Orla shrugged her shoulders. 'Of course she did. The Prime Minister said the country had a right to—'

'I'm the Prime Minister, for God's sake!'

'Well, in any case, they wanted to send a message to the terrorists, that they'd failed.' She removed the tray from his lap and placed it back on the trolley. 'Although they didn't print the most flattering picture of you, I must say. You looked quite ill.'

How dare they publish his picture without permission, Bryce fumed. What the bloody hell was Nigel playing at? 'Why don't I have a phone in here? Bring me a phone, would you? I need to make a call.'

Orla shook her head. 'I don't have that authority.'

'Well find me someone who has!' Bryce barked.

'Try not to get yourself excited.' Before Bryce could retort, Orla spun on her heel and headed towards the door. 'I'll see what I can do,' she said over her shoulder.

Bryce's head swam, the world shifting on its axis. He clamped his eyes shut until the giddiness faded. His heart thumped in his chest as his pulse quickened, banishing the fatigue. It felt good. Beside the bed, the monitors flashed and beeped their disapproval. Sully remained diplomatically silent, using a long feather duster to clean the TV.

'Turn that on, would you, Sully?' The Turk complied. 'Were you here when they were taking pictures?'

Sully shook his head. 'I was downstairs with the other staff. There were lots of very important people here, lots of police too. All the streets were blocked off outside.'

Bryce waved a hand for silence. On the TV a reporter stood outside the Houses of Parliament, a large umbrella held aloft as rain and sleet lanced across Parliament Square. The historic building was ringed with huge slabs of concrete and razor wire. Armed police stood guard behind the barricades, black uniforms and assault rifles glistening in the rain.

'...In parliament behind me, where the Egyptian delegation is meeting behind closed doors with government officials to finalise details of the energy bill, expected to come into force when Prime Minister Hooper endorses the Treaty of Cairo. Deputy Prime Minister Tariq Saeed said earlier today that he was hopeful Britain would soon announce its intention, particularly in light of the recent attempts by Far Right demonstrators to...'

'Tariq,' Bryce whispered.

'Excuse me, sir?'

'Nothing.' Bryce pointed to the screen. 'Tell me, Sully, what do you think of this treaty?'

The Turk studied the reporter huddled beneath his umbrella as he tapped the feather duster lightly in his hand. 'I think people are fed up with being scared. People want stability, they want the economy to pick up. I think Cairo's a good thing.'

'What about the refugees in Egypt?' Bryce said. 'Aren't people worried about the numbers, the potential strain on public services?' He lowered his voice. 'The tensions it could cause?'

Sully shook his head. 'My mum and dad came over when I was a boy, knuckled down, paid their bills. Where I live most people are from different parts of the world, and everyone gets along. You once said that this was a country of immigrants, remember that, sir? Well, you're right.

There're no British anymore. We're all in it together,' he grinned.

'So you support the treaty then?'

'Of course. Oh, I nearly forgot.' He bustled over to the trolley, retrieving a parcel from the lower shelf. He handed it to Bryce. 'Arrived yesterday.'

He'd received a mountain of get well gifts since the attack; a veritable forest of plants and flowers, video messages from world leaders and media personalities, and a ton of mail from ordinary people. He'd barely had a chance to look at any of it. This would be the first one he'd unwrapped himself and it was a welcome distraction. The package was quite heavy, the thick padded envelope unceremoniously ripped open at the top and marked with a 'SCANNED' security stamp in bold red letters. He withdrew the contents.

It was a book, a beautifully bound volume with a dark blue spine inscribed with gold lettering. Bryce turned it over: *Chasing the Rainbow – A History of Around the World Ocean Voyages*. The cover showed the bow of a yacht, buried deep in the trough of a huge grey wave, black storm clouds pressing down above the mast. It was a powerful image, frightening even, and Bryce guessed it was somewhere in the Southern Ocean. He thumbed through the glossy pages and something dropped into his lap. It was a small card, the words on it handwritten in a neat block of text. It read:

---

*Hello Prime Minister,*

*Tried to hand you this in person but apparently I don't have the necessary clearance. In any case I hope you're recovering well. They ran your bio on the news the other day and I noticed you were once a keen sailor, so I thought I'd leave this book with you. It seems we both have something else in common, as well as surviving a major terrorist attack! Anyway, it's a cracking read and maybe when you're feeling better you'll come and visit. I'd be happy to take you out on the water again, get a bit of sea air. Always works wonders for me.*

*Get well, good luck.*

*Mac*

---

HE TURNED THE CARD OVER. The logo on the front was a clear outline of a yacht, the words *Mike McGann - Boat Delivery Specialists* beneath, a website link, email address and a telephone number. Bryce read the message again, deeply moved by the gesture. The first call he made would be to Mac, not only to thank him for the book but for his life too. He hadn't had the chance to do that yet and it bothered him greatly. Without Mac he wouldn't be here.

Nurse Orla swept back into the room. She paused at the foot of Bryce's bed and cleared her throat, her hands folded in front of her. 'I'm afraid I can't get hold of anyone right now, Sir. Your call will have to wait.'

'It can't,' Bryce said. 'Let me have your mobile phone. I'll cover any cost.'

Orla frowned. 'I don't—'

Bryce held out his hand. 'Don't be ridiculous. Your phone. Please.' He saw Orla glance at Sully, as if she were seeking permission. Bryce frowned. 'Why are you looking at him?' He turned to the Turk. 'Sully, let me have your phone.'

The Turk shook his head. 'Nurse Orla is right, she doesn't have the authority and neither does the hospital.' He waved her away and Orla hurried from the room. Sully put down his duster and came over to Bryce's bed, squeezing his muscular frame into a chair. He leaned back, crossing one leg over the other. Bryce was confused.

'What's going on? And since when does an orderly give orders to a staff nurse?'

The Turk smiled. Rain drummed on the window.

'Minister Saeed has expressly forbidden any contact with the outside world. For now.'

Bryce thought he'd misheard. 'He's what?'

'It's about your personal safety, sir. We've had threatening phone calls, here at the hospital. A security guard has been arrested, as well as a kitchen porter. We're monitoring suspicious activity in the apartment block across the street.' Sully leaned forward, shoulders bulging beneath his purple tunic. The chirpiness had disappeared, replaced by a voice that was measured, serious. Authoritative. 'Minister Saeed believes that an infiltration exercise is in progress. That another attempt might be made on your life.'

Bryce's eyes narrowed. 'Who are you, Sully?'

The orderly glanced at the door, kept his voice low. 'I've been sent here to watch over you, on Minister Saeed's orders. He insisted you be looked after.'

'I want to speak to him.'

'He's coming here, very soon.'

'You're looking out for me?' Sully nodded. 'Then who were the two people checking my chart when I woke up? Why did they run off?'

The Turk pushed himself out of his chair and pressed

the call button next to Bryce's bed. 'You sure you weren't dreaming? An after-effect of your medication?'

'Don't patronise me. I know what I saw.'

Sully ignored him as Nurse Orla reappeared. 'Let's get him settled.'

As Orla busied herself next to the bed, the Turk took the card from Bryce's fingers and replaced it inside the book. 'I'll put this with your personal effects. Let me know when you want it.'

'What I want is to make a bloody phone call.'

'Not possible.'

'I'm not asking. Don't forget, I'm the Prime Minister.'

'Well, technically that title now belongs to Nigel Hooper.' Sully shrugged his shoulders and smiled. 'Hey, don't shoot the messenger. I'm following orders, that's all. Now, Minister Saeed will be here in the next few days, so I suggest you rest until he gets here. Then you can talk.'

'No, I want my phone call, dammit. Are you... you... can you...'

The words trailed away. His mouth felt thick, his tongue heavy. He turned his head, saw Nurse Orla regulating the drip chamber. Sully turned off the TV and gathered his cleaning materials, placing them on the trolley. Orla pulled the sheets over Bryce's chest and slipped the mouth guard over his upper gum.

'Get some rest, now.'

Sully looked down at him. 'Don't worry, Gabe. I'll be watching your back.'

He heard them chuckle, the voices sounding distant, as if he were at the bottom of a deep well, two dark silhouettes far above him. He opened his mouth, tried to speak, but his body failed him.

The lights dimmed and he heard the wheels of the

trolley squeaking out of the door. They left silence in their wake, only the distant patter of the rain on the window registering in his dulled senses. His eyes closed once, then twice, those familiar waves of fatigue once again pounding the shoreline of his consciousness.

Then the world turned black.

# 10

## HERTFORDSHIRE

Danny emerged from a stand of trees by the side of the road as the approaching bus slowed for the stop. He wore a high-visibility orange raincoat with a *Network Rail* logo on the back, the collar turned up against the early morning drizzle, a black beanie hat pulled low. The bus rattled to a halt and the doors hissed open.

'How far you going?' he asked the driver, a chubby young Asian man with spiky gelled hair and a gold ear stud. The driver pointed above his head, his hands wrapped in black fingerless leather gloves.

'It's on the front, mate. Watford general.'

'Right.' Danny fished the travel card from his pocket and tapped the reader as the bus pulled away. He found an empty seat at the back and sat down, relieved to be out of the bone-chilling cold. There were several other passengers scattered throughout the bus, most wearing uniforms of one sort or another. Early hospital shift, Danny assumed. They paid him no attention, most absorbed by their phones or the passing countryside. He rubbed a hand across the dark growth on his face, over his severe and uneven haircut. No one would recognise him in a hurry. He shifted lower in his seat, digging his chin below the collar his coat and stretching out his legs. He yawned, the warmth enveloping him, his mind replaying the events that had led him to this point.

Sheer panic had fuelled his flight from the Longhill. He'd run for more than a mile when exhaustion forced him to stop, to think. He'd checked his surrounding, the deserted street, the chain link fence, the warning signs. He'd scaled the fence, scrambling up the embankment, the railway line deserted, the occasional train carefully avoided. He'd kept to the shadows. Sirens wailed across the city.

The crew hut had been occupied when he'd first encountered it, a large single-storey portacabin just past the station at Neasden. He'd waited in the undergrowth, listening to the muffled voices, watching the flickering light of a TV beyond the mesh-covered windows. After a while, several orange-clad workmen piled outside and boarded a small engine. With a loud clanking and a flash of electrical discharge, it headed off into the darkness.

Danny crept inside. The TV was off, the cabin silent. There was a range cooker and a microwave in the large kitchen, a couple of battered sofas and a table piled with newspapers. He rummaged through the drawers, found a pair of scissors, and went to work on his hair in the adjacent washroom. He stole a pair of navy blue overalls and changed into them, stuffing his jeans into a waste bin. He drank coffee and helped himself to food from the fridge. He turned off the lights and sat in the darkness. He weighed up his options.

Cheated out of their prize, someone on the Longhill would've called the police. The estate would be crawling, his dad's flat torn apart. The guilt had choked him, but he had no choice; the longer he stayed on the run, the more chance the real terrorists would be caught. The cabin was isolated, far from the streets, a source of warmth, food and fresh water. It was worth the risk.

A fine drizzle fell that first night. Danny took an orange work coat off a rack by the door. Behind the cabin was a thick copse of birch and ferns. Deep amongst the trees he found what he was looking for, a pile of rotting railway sleepers choked with vegetation. He made a crawl space underneath, where he could keep dry, where the thermal imaging cameras couldn't penetrate. He found some discarded sackcloth and made a bed inside. Returning to the portacabin, he helped himself to newspapers, a plastic bottle of water and a toilet roll.

One night turned into two, then four. During the day he stayed hidden beneath the sleepers. He kept his mobile switched off, knowing someone, somewhere would be waiting for its signal to appear on the grid, for his position to be triangulated and targeted by men with dogs and guns. He dozed in his den, like a fox waiting for the world outside to darken, hoping that each passing hour would see the hunt slacken, the investigation move in a different direction. But the newspapers told a different story.

He read an article in the Guardian about himself, the photo a sneering police mug shot, his unremarkable education, his service with the Logistics Corp, his sacking from the civil service, his arrest for banned literature. The article depressed him. It painted a picture so bitter, so angry and vengeful, that even Danny believed it. He'd wept when he read about his father's arrest.

As the sun set on day five, Danny realised they'd never stop searching for him. He had to run, get away as far as possible. To do that, he would need help.

He broke camp and stocked up with a final raid on the portacabin. He took water, food, a pair of cutters, a pre-pay travel card and a couple of twenty pound notes from two separate wallets. He headed north again, tramping along the stones by the side of the tracks, the orange raincoat turned inside out. After a mile or so he dumped his mobile phone in a deep rabbit hole along the embankment. Keeping it was pointless.

The night was quiet, the sky clear and littered with stars. He left the lights of the city behind as the track wound its way northwards through fields and woods. Lights shone to the left and right, isolated farms, industrial estates. The only living things he saw were foxes and darting bats.

Ten miles beyond Neasden exhaustion overcame him. He curled up in the undergrowth of a large embankment and slept until a weak sun broke the horizon. An hour later he'd climbed the fence just south of Radlett station. He couldn't walk much further, his feet were blistered and he was freezing cold. The bus was a risk, but one he was prepared to take. He was just another early morning commuter. No one was looking for a rail worker.

He sat in silence at the back of the bus, watching the countryside pass by. In the distance, the sprawl of Watford loomed. He wasn't that far away now, his destination about eight miles on the other side of town. A short time later the bus turned into Watford General Hospital.

Danny got off and weaved through the car park towards the bicycle shelters. It wasn't long before he found a suitable ride, a well-used and unremarkable mountain bike. The cheap chain proved tougher than it looked, the stolen cutters slipping in his hands, but after a few anxious moments he'd stolen his first bike. He pedalled away from the hospital, heading for the edge of town.

He crossed the Grand Union canal, then the bridge over the M25 London orbital, relieved to be swallowed up by the countryside again. As the sun climbed into the morning sky Danny navigated a succession of empty lanes, knowing the house he sought wasn't far away. He'd googled it many times, had read about the political gatherings and the lavish social events that were once held there. He'd even rented a car once, driving up here just to see it, captivated by the high black gates, the gravel driveway that curved towards the secluded Georgian mansion. He hoped – no, prayed – the man was still there.

He cycled through the village of Marshbrook. A tractor rumbled past in the opposite direction, the driver waving cheerfully. Danny kept his head down, pedalling past the few shops, the thatched roofed pub, a row of pastel painted cottages, before the village surrendered to fields and hedgerows once again. The lane he sought was the last turning on the left, just beyond the edge of the settlement.

The tarmac gave way to a well-worn dirt lane. There was an open field to the right and several large houses to the left, partly hidden by walls and trees. Danny felt like a trespasser.

At the end of the lane, a set of high black gates barred any further passage. Danny climbed off the bike, sweating from his exertions. Beyond the gates, thick banks of rhododendron bushes lined the gravel driveway towards a stand of tall cedars. He could just make out the roof of the distant house.

A sudden breeze made Danny shiver. What if the man had moved? What if the new owners recognised him? And yet he had no choice other than to push the intercom button set into the high wall.

'State your business,' ordered a voice from the tinny speaker.

Summoning all his courage, Danny pulled off his coat and lifted the sleeve of his t-shirt, revealing his tattoo for the camera above the gate. There was silence for several long moments, then the same voice said, 'wait.'

The minutes crawled passed. A dog appeared behind the gates, a German Shepherd, its paws slapping the gravel as it bounded towards him. It skidded to a stop, its brown eyes locked on Danny, a low growl rumbling in its throat. Danny took a step back. The dog bared its yellow teeth. Not once did it bark. This was a well-trained animal, Danny realised, not like the snapping ghetto breeds paraded by their idiot owners back on the Longhill.

Suddenly, to Danny's horror, the gates hummed and swung inwards.

'Inside. Be quick about it.'

A man emerged from the rhododendrons. He looked a little younger than Danny, his fair hair cut short, a British Army camouflage jacket over jeans and green wellingtons. In his arms he cradled a military-style black shotgun. The voice, bearing a slight West Country twang, was the voice on the intercom.

'Don't worry about Nelson, he won't harm you as long as you do as you're told.'

Danny wheeled the bike through the gates, keeping it between him and the loping Alsatian. Nelson darted away, back around the curve of the driveway. Danny followed his escort through well-kept grounds, the grass neatly trimmed, the dead leaves raked into wet piles. The smell of wood smoke hung on the air. Around the walls, ranks of evergreens screened the estate from prying eyes.

The house loomed ahead. Danny thought it was amazing, like a footballer's house, or a film star's. It had big double doors, a porch with white columns and a huge glass lantern. It was old – *period,* Danny corrected himself – but it had been beautifully restored, the window frames painted white, the walls a shade of soft green that blended in with the surrounding grounds. At a right angle to the main house, two cars were parked in the shadow of a large carport, a white Bentley Continental and a more practical Nissan pickup. Danny was impressed, and not a little intimidated. He continued across the drive, wheeling the bike towards the main door.

'Not that way, round the back. And leave the bike.'

They skirted the side of the building, following a landscaped path to the terrace at the rear. Garden furniture was stacked in neat piles and tropical plants ringed the terrace like a Mediterranean hotel. A flight of wide steps led down to another terrace and a covered swimming pool. Further away, the ground sloped towards a shallow valley and the distant, sun-dappled Hertfordshire countryside. From the rear of the house there wasn't a single dwelling as far as the eye could see. For the first time in a long time, Danny felt safe.

'Twenty-four acres, in case you're wondering.'

He turned. A man sat at a wrought iron table, beckoning him. He was a big man, bald, tanned, his eyes shaded by designer sunglasses, his impressive bulk wrapped in a navy blue Barbour jacket. He didn't get up as Danny approached, the remnants of a hearty breakfast scattered across the table in front of him. In his fist he held a large cigar, the smoke whipped away by the wind. Danny's armed escort whispered in the man's ear while Nelson settled down beside his chair, head between its paws, relaxed but watchful.

'Get rid of the bike, please Joe,' the man ordered. His London accent was harsh, his voice deep. 'And that God-awful jacket.'

Danny tugged the raincoat off and handed it over. Joe trudged back around the side of the house.

'Joe's my sister's boy. She's fucking useless, heroin addict, but he's a smart lad. Ex-army, like you. Three tours in Afghanistan.'

He waved Danny into a chair. Danny sat down on the cold metal seat, his thin body shivering in the wind.

'I didn't mean to disturb you like this, Mister Carver. I didn't know where else to go.'

Raymond Carver, former chairman and founder of the English Freedom Movement, laid a reassuring hand on Danny's arm. Danny noted the thick, well-manicured fingers that patted his goose-pimpled skin, the heavy gold Rolex, the chunky gold necklace that nestled in the dark hair beneath his open neck shirt. He'd only ever seen the man once before, from a distance, at a rally in a field in Kent. Ray Carver was a big man in the flesh, a hard man, a street fighter in his younger days, a businessman, politician, and self-made millionaire. Danny had never been more intimidated.

'That's alright, Danny. Can I call you Danny?'

'Sure, Mister Carver.'

'Let's cut the formal bullshit, shall we? Ray or Raymond, whichever you like.' Carver rescued his dying cigar with several large puffs. 'No-one knows you're here, right Danny? You didn't tell anyone you were coming? Anyone at all?'

Danny shook his head earnestly. 'Not a soul.'

'That's good.'

Carver held out his hand. 'I need your mobile phone.'

'I dumped it.'

'Where?'

Danny told him. Carver nodded, satisfied. 'How did you get here, son?'

'I walked, mostly.'

Carver took off his glasses and stared at him. His grey eyes were like pebbles, cold, hard. 'Bullshit.'

'I swear, Mister Carver. I followed the train lines for most of the way. Took a bus into Watford.'

Carver leaned forward, tapping the embers of his cigar into a cut-glass ashtray. 'The police have got every transport hub in the country covered.'

'It was a rural bus. I got off at the hospital.'

The older man balanced his cigar in the ashtray and dragged his chair closer to the table. He produced a small notepad and pen from his pocket, flipping it open to a blank page. 'Okay, Danny; I want to know what happened from the moment you decided to run. Every route you took, people you saw, where you slept, ate, took a shit, everything. From the beginning.'

Danny told him, his thin arms wrapped around his body. He was freezing, the sharp breeze gusting across the terrace, cutting through his t-shirt and filthy overalls. Carver seemed oblivious to his distress, to the tremble in his voice, scribbling away on the pad as he recorded every detail of the escape. He's a careful man, Danny reminded himself, knowing the interrogation was necessary. Because that's what this was, an interrogation. Carver went back over the same questions several times, forcing Danny to repeat himself through chattering teeth. For thirty minutes Danny talked, with as much detail as he could remember.

Eventually Carver put down his pen. 'You're sure that's everything?'

'Positive,' Danny chattered, his arms tucked inside the bib of his overalls. 'They've got me bang to rights, Ray. I've been stitched up.'

Carver shrugged, shoving the notepad in his pocket. He slipped his sunglasses back on. 'You're an easy target, son.'

'The people on my estate, they were hunting me like a dog.'

'Every one of 'em a fucking Judas. You can't go back there, anyway.'

'Mind your blood pressure, Raymond,' cackled a voice from the French doors.

Danny saw an older woman step out onto the terrace and waddle towards them, her silver hair cut fashionably short, a heavy parka wrapped around her voluminous frame. Like Ray she was suntanned, her ready smile dazzlingly white.

Carver smiled. 'Danny, this is my wife, Tess.'

'Missus Carver,' trembled Danny.

'Tess will do just fine.' In one hand she held a black puffer jacket, the other shading her eyes from the sun. The bangles on her wrists chimed as she moved.

'Where're your shades?' Carver said. 'All that squinting will make your lines worse.'

She pulled a face at Danny. 'He's such a flatterer, isn't he? Here, you must be freezing.'

Danny almost snatched the jacket from her outstretched hand. He pulled it on and sat back down, tucking his chin deep inside its warm folds.

'Well, it's nice to meet you, Danny,' Tess said. 'Love the new look, by the way.'

Danny ran his hand across his stubbly head. 'It was a rush job.'

'Don't worry, I'll tidy that up for you. I used to cut hair

for a living. That's how I met Ray. Course, he had some back then.' She gave her husband's dome an affectionate stroke.

'Any news?' Carver asked his wife.

Her smile disappeared. 'It's all about Cairo now.'

Carver snorted, clamping his teeth around the soggy end of his cigar and firing it up with a gold lighter. 'And so it begins,' he growled. 'What about our guest?'

'Cairo's knocked him off the top slot.'

'That's good. What else?'

'Joe's taken the pickup, gone to have a look around the village and beyond for any unusual traffic.'

'I want him to go into Watford, check the hospital. Danny got off a bus there, nicked a bike. The police will be all over that place if they've got a sniff.'

Tess pulled a mobile from her pocket. 'I'll ring him now.'

Carver shook his head. 'No phones, love. Tell him when he comes back.' He turned to Danny, exhaling a thick swirl of smoke. 'You'll stay here for now, Danny. We'll keep you out of sight.'

'I'll go and sort out some clothes for you, ' Tess said. She kissed Carver's head and waddled back to the house. Danny thought he could still hear her bangles even after the door had closed.

Carver stubbed out the cigar and checked his Rolex. 'Come on, I'll show you to your room.' He got to his feet, hitching the waistband of his jeans up beneath the bulge of his belly. He followed Carver around the house and across the courtyard. Beneath the carport, Carver stopped outside a large wooden door. He unlocked it and led Danny inside, pushing the sunglasses on top of his head. They climbed a narrow flight of stairs.

'This is the guest apartment. You'll be comfortable here.'

Danny looked around the self-contained accommodation, impressed by the modern furniture, the spacious kitchen, the neat bedroom with a view that overlooked the rambling grounds. 'Are you sure, Ray? I don't want to put you to any trouble.'

'Keep it clean, that's all I ask. There's a phone in the kitchen with a pre-programmed number for the house. Don't use it unless it's an emergency, and for fuck's sake don't call anyone, understand?' Danny nodded. 'Good lad. As you can see you've got a TV, plus a few books on the shelf. I'll get some food sent over later. Tomorrow we'll go for a walk around the estate, stretch our legs. Get to know each other.'

Danny stared at his own reflection in the TV screen. Coming here had solved his immediate problem but it suddenly dawned on him how much danger he was putting his hosts in. So what if he'd been a member of the Movement? Did that give him the right to just turn up, impose on people who clearly felt a duty to help?

'Are you sure about this, Ray? You could all go to prison if they find me here.'

Carver shook his head. 'They won't.'

'They know I was in the Movement, Ray. They might come here, question you and Tess.'

Carver shrugged his large shoulders. 'So what? I disbanded the Movement a long time ago. You must remember that, Danny.'

Danny stared at the carpet. 'I remember.'

'You think I was a traitor too, right son?'

'I didn't know what to think, Ray. I was gutted, I remember that much. I'd not long joined.'

Carver sighed. 'It was only a matter of time before they shut us down. I resigned my chairmanship, took a legal position. I protected myself, Danny, sang from their poisonous hymn sheet. I even made a donation to the Pakistan Relief Fund. D'you know how much that hurt?' He smiled suddenly, slapped Danny on the back. 'Don't worry, it's not all doom and gloom. I've got friends out there Danny, influential people in authority. I'd soon find out if the law started looking this way.'

Danny nodded, forced a smile. 'That's a relief.'

They heard footsteps on the stairs and Tess puffed into the room, a stack of neatly pressed laundry tucked beneath her numerous chins. 'These are for you, Danny. Some of Joe's old clothes.' She loaded the pile into Danny's arms. They smelt of lavender. 'There's a plastic bag under the sink in the kitchen. Bag up those rags you're wearing and leave it downstairs. It'll all go on the bonfire.'

Carver nodded. 'Grab a shower and get some rest, son. We'll talk in the morning.'

As he turned to leave, Danny said, 'Are you really retired, Ray? Is the Movement really dead?'

Carver stopped and turned around. He stared at Danny for several moments then tapped his wide chest. 'You can't turn off what's in your heart, right Danny?'

He couldn't help himself. Danny beamed. 'I knew it! So where will all this end?'

'It won't, as long as there're people like you and me. You've managed to elude one of the biggest manhunts this country has ever seen, make it all the way up here without being caught. You're smart, a quick thinker. In fact, when I look at you I see a bit of myself there.' He slipped the sunglasses back over his eyes. 'Personally, I think you're a bloody hero, son. Now, get yourself some rest. You've earned it.'

Carver stamped down the stairs and slammed the door behind him. Exhausted, Danny peeled off his socks and collapsed onto the sofa. He'd been called a lot of things in his life, but never a hero. Better yet, the Movement still lived and breathed, and that meant Danny wasn't alone anymore.

As he listened to Carver's footsteps crunching across the courtyard, Danny stretched along the deep cushions, a smile creasing his bearded face.

11

---

CHEQUERS

Wrapped in a full-length white robe, Tariq Saeed stood at the bedroom window, the curtains parted, the room still in darkness. Below him the valley sloped away to the south, cloaked in mist and bordered by shadowy woods. To the east, the sky paled before the rise of the sun. It was time.

He knelt down on the prayer mat and closed his eyes, clearing his mind of all distractions. He breathed deeply, preparing himself for *Salat,* the first of his five daily prayers. His lips began to utter the quiet litany, his forehead brushing the mat as his mind, body and soul united in worship. He felt it then, as he did every day, the connection to his fellow Brothers, knowing that across the country they too were performing their own rituals. Only today that feeling was stronger, considerably so. For Saeed, this new dawn promised so much more.

Mentally and spiritually prepared, he dressed himself in a black sweater and corduroy trousers and made his way downstairs to breakfast. A hovering steward took his order of toast and fruit juice and he ate alone, the daily papers spread across the table before him. Cairo dominated the front pages, a compliant media taking up the Treaty torch with impressive gusto. Saeed made a mental note to thank those editors personally.

He took coffee in the library next door, where a log fire roared in the grate. He sat in a wing-backed chair by the window, watching the sun climb above the woods, the mist rolling back before its watery rays. A dog barked, the sound muffled through the thick glass, and a black shape darted from behind the walled garden, streaking out into the field beyond. Hooper followed a moment later, looking every inch the country gent in a green Barbour and matching wellington boots. Saeed finished his coffee and went to fetch his coat.

Outside the air was brisk, scented with morning dew and damp earth. Saeed wrinkled his nose as he trudged after Hooper. He hated the countryside, with its rank odours and cloying dirt. Hooper, on the other hand, was a man in his element. Saeed watched him striding across the field ahead, a walking stick in his hand, calling to his lunatic animal that darted and panted and chased all manner of unknown tormentors. Hooper's bodyguards trailed a short distance behind, coats open, hands free. One of them saw Saeed and called to Hooper. Saeed braced himself as the Labrador spotted his approach and scuttled towards him, legs pumping through the grass, tongue lolling from the side of its mouth. He cringed as the animal reared up on its hind legs and attempted to greet Saeed with its slavering mouth.

'Buster! Get down!' Hooper bellowed. The animal complied, spotting another unseen quarry and sprinting across the field. 'Sorry about that,' Hooper grinned. 'He tends to get a little excited in the morning. Millie used to walk him around the park at home, always on a leash of course. Out here he goes wild, absolutely loves it.'

Saeed fell into step beside Hooper, wet grass clinging to his boots. The policemen kept a discreet distance behind them. 'You've made quite a home up here, Nigel.'

Hooper's face was flushed pink by the sharp air, by the brisk pace he set across the field. 'Do I detect a note of disapproval, Tariq?'

'Of course not.'

'Bullshit. I've heard the whispers. Well, maybe Chequers isn't the most convenient place from which to govern the country but spending more time here was your idea, remember? More secure, you said. More opportunity to get things done.'

'I stand by that.'

'Then squash the bloody gossip.'

Hooper was right, the move had indeed been Saeed's suggestion, reinforced by the manufactured security briefs and the chaos of Millbank. The pressure had got to Hooper, and he'd leapt at Saeed's suggestion of splitting his time between Chequers and London. Hooper could no more resist the temptation of ruling the country from his own private estate than an alcoholic with money in his pocket could walk past a convenience store. Meanwhile Saeed worked behind the scenes, both supporting and quietly discrediting Hooper in equal measure.

And the man had certainly become accustomed to life at the Buckinghamshire estate, as Saeed had anticipated. Hooper was born of country stock, his elderly father still presiding over several dozen acres of Lincolnshire country-side. It was where Hooper had grown up, cementing his love of all things outdoors, a love that took him into the armed forces where he'd enjoyed an unspectacular career in the Logistics Corps, rising to the rank of lieutenant-colonel. Politics followed, the move to London permanent after he met his future wife at a party in Chelsea. Saeed had discovered that the woman was as nakedly ambitious as Hooper and equally at home in the country.

And Chequers certainly fitted their bill, an estate of historical import and period elegance, of manicured grounds and attentive staff. It offered status, and Hooper's wife had taken to the role of First Lady like a duck to water, the transition from modest terraced house in Putney to the impressive Buckinghamshire pile made with an ease of entitlement that surprised even Saeed. He'd heard her sharp voice several times around the house during his visits, either berating staff or acting as an unofficial tour guide to her envious London friends.

Saeed glanced over his shoulder. The policemen were some way back, the house shrinking into the distance as Hooper continued his morning constitutional. The demented dog flew between them once again, yapping and panting, before sprinting out toward the tree line.

'Buster!' Hooper bellowed after the fleeing animal. He tutted and turned to Saeed. 'So, what's this latest theory, Tariq?'

'The rumour is, Gabriel was planning to use the press conference to announce his resignation.'

Hooper arched a bushy eyebrow. 'Seriously? Who's the source?'

Saeed ignored the question. 'We know that he'd been troubled for some time. There were gaps in his diary, cancelled engagements. Then there was the visit to his wife's grave the day before. Not unusual but significant, given the timing.'

'Has Gabriel mentioned something?'

'You've seen him, Nigel. He's in no fit state to communicate coherently. We'll probably discover the truth eventually but right now it's not important. The narrative fits. I think we should consider using it.'

Hooper frowned. 'It's all very strange. The unscheduled visit to Heathrow, that Border Force guy killed in Downing Street. What the hell was *he* doing there?'

'Coincidence, perhaps. As far as the media is concerned I think we should run with the resignation line.'

'What about Gabriel's friends? They may reject the theory.'

'True. And perhaps they have theories of their own. For example, this mysterious press conference was to announce a snap reshuffle that would've seen you pushed out.'

Hooper came to a sudden halt. 'There's no evidence of that.'

'That's my point, Nigel. There's no evidence of anything. We must give them something, otherwise rumours will continue to circulate around Westminster. People will keep digging.'

'Can we get away with it? The resignation thing?'

'We have friends who are willing to go on record. Managed carefully, and with significant media coverage, it'll work.'

'Run with it then.' He resumed his brisk pace and Saeed had to trot to catch up. 'What about this Whelan character? Any news there?'

'He's disappeared. CCTV caught him jogging past a petrol station in northwest London a couple of days after the bomb but since then, nothing. Either he's gone to ground, or he's managed to flee the country. Whatever the case, he'll be caught eventually.' A flurry of birds took to the air, exploding noisily above the tree line. The dog's manic barking echoed across the fields. 'We need to talk about Cairo, Nigel. You're stalling, and concern is mounting. What's the problem?'

Hooper grunted a vague reply. He brooded for several moments before coming to a sudden halt. 'The truth? Cairo's the bloody problem.' He thrashed at the long grass with his walking stick, cutting through the wet stalks like a scythe.

'I don't follow.'

'It's going to clash with the Washington thing. I'm in a real bloody quandary.'

'We've already decided, the Ambassador will attend that event on your behalf.'

'Yes, but Britain's fingerprints are all over that ridiculous moon project. I really think I should be there.'

Saeed knew why, of course. Hector Vargas, the American President, had organised a lavish memorial service and a series of events to commemorate the three astronauts, now officially declared dead, in the same week as the ceremony in Cairo. The charismatic Vargas would be attending those events, along with senior US politicians, foreign dignitaries, NASA officials, former astronauts and a sprinkling of movie and media personalities. As well as the memorial service at Arlington there was to be a reception dinner at the White House, followed by a Hollywood-produced extravaganza at Cape Canaveral in Florida designed to celebrate the astronauts' lives and mankind's achievements in space. Saeed had dangled the itinerary in front of Hooper like a worm on a hook and predictably he'd taken the bait, drawn to the much-anticipated display of glitz and power like a moth to a flame. Saeed brought him back to earth with a shake of his head.

'No, I don't think that's possible. You'll be the only EU head of state missing from Cairo.'

Hooper flicked an irritated hand. 'So what? The whole thing's symbolic, for God's sake. The deal's been done. It's a signature on a document, followed by fireworks and drinks. There's nothing to stop you deputising for me, Tariq. Besides, British firms provided components for the craft's communications package, no? According to NASA that's one of several points of mission failure.'

The man had done his homework, Saeed mused. He remained silent, pretending to consider Hooper's argument. After a few moments he said, 'Granted, there is some truth to that statement. Your attendance would certainly say much about your character and political responsibilities, and if Vargas could be persuaded to publicly support your attendance, it could also reap additional diplomatic rewards right here in Europe.'

Hooper shifted from foot to foot, as if he was about to break into a jig. 'So you're saying it's doable? What about Dupont and the Commission? I can't afford to piss them off.'

The PM shuffled impatiently as Saeed performed a master class of contemplation. 'I doubt he'd object if we spin it right. I could beef up British culpability in connection to the tragedy, let President Dupont know that Vargas' people are quietly leaning you on to make a significant diplomatic gesture. He'd understand I'm sure.'

'And you've no objection to standing in for me?'

Saeed nodded. 'It would be an honour.'

Hooper beamed. 'Wonderful.' His eyes took on a faraway look. 'You know, I've only ever been to Washington once, and that was as a tourist. Boiling hot summer, just after we got married. Millie and I took photos outside the

White House. Jesus Christ, she's going to wet herself when I tell her.' He turned on his heel and headed towards the house. 'We should start back, Tariq. You've got lots to do.'

Saeed didn't move. 'There's something else. About Gabriel.'

Hooper's satisfied smile melted. He retraced his steps slowly, like a man navigating a minefield, until he stood facing Saeed. 'Well? What is it?'

The Deputy PM kept his voice low. 'Physically, he's recovering well. If he's declared fit sometime in the near future, there's nothing to stop him retaking office.'

Hooper's eyes widened. 'Excuse me?' He stepped closer, jabbing a finger at the shorter man's chest. 'You said he was incoherent. You promised me he'd be out of the picture for months.'

'The situation has changed. The fact is, any sudden revival and Gabriel resumes power. If that happens he might spike Cairo.

'He wouldn't dare,' growled Hooper. 'It's been through parliament. A declaration of intent has been signed, billions of Euros spent. We can't go back.'

'He could stall it. Legally he'd have that power. As Prime Minister.'

Hooper's face darkened. 'I'm the bloody Prime Minister.' He stole a glance over his shoulder at the loitering police officers. 'Can he do that? Constitutionally, I mean?'

'Of course he can. He could demand a reshuffle, seek a vote of confidence from the parliamentary party. The country would marvel at his recovery of course, and he would use that emotion for political leverage. You've seen him, Nigel. If anything, Gabriel Bryce is a pro.'

Hooper's jowls flapped from side to side. 'No, Brussels would overrule him.'

'Constitutional processes enshrined in British law must be allowed to run their course before the Commission could influence matters. Gabriel could do a lot of damage before then.' Saeed paused, allowing the scenario to take firm root in Hooper's imagination. 'The Washington trip would be cancelled of course.'

'Fuck!' Hooper lashed the grass with his stick, decapitated flower heads tumbling through the air.

Saeed let him stew for a while. Hooper turned towards the distant house, clearly contemplating a life without the privilege, without the prestige and the power he'd become accustomed to. 'There must be something we can do. Some clause, a legal precedent perhaps?'

Saeed shook his head. 'I've spoken to the Attorney General. If Bryce passes a physiological examination and is declared fit, all this goes away.' He swept an arm around the estate. Hooper looked as if he were about to burst into tears.

'But we've worked so hard, made significant political progress. Surely it can't be undone as easily as that?'

'It can,' Saeed assured him. 'Your appointment is a temporary one, remember? Gabriel is recovering quicker than expected. If he continues to do so, well, it's over.'

Hooper's shoulders sagged. He leaned on his stick and stared at the ground, crushed. The animal trotted back to its master and sat at his feet, tail wagging, eyes pleading. Hooper nuzzled the dog's neck. 'It's alright, boy.'

They stood alone in the field, the policemen loitering some way off, stamping their feet. Saeed leaned closer. 'There is another way, Nigel. Another option.'

Hooper lifted his head. 'What are you talking about?'

'The scene outside the King Edward remains the same, does it not? Most of the news crews have gone but every week the hospital administration releases a statement and fresh flowers decorate the railings. And the media continue to mention Gabriel of course, his condition, speculation on his future, a general assumption that things will get better.'

Hooper nodded. 'Go on.'

'What if another attempt was made on his life? Something that might jeopardise the safety of staff and patients, something that would keep the threat of terrorism firmly entrenched in the public consciousness?'

Hooper's eyes narrowed. 'Are you talking about a false flag operation?'

'Yes. Staged correctly a botched attack on an infirm Gabriel Bryce will not only make front-page news, it would give us the legal and moral authority to move him, and by default *remove* him from the public consciousness. No one gets hurt, the flowers outside would wilt and die, and the hospital administration would breathe a huge sigh of relief. Life would go on and Gabriel Bryce would fade into obscurity like a retired politician. Out of sight, out of mind.'

Hooper's tongue darted lizard-like between his moist lips. 'And move him where?'

'A secure psychiatric facility.'

The PM's eyes widened. 'You want to shove him in a loony bin? Are you mad?'

'An *undisclosed secure location* will be the official phrasing. Think, Nigel. If you transfer him to another private hospital the problem remains the same. Bryce will continue to recover while your political aspirations wither on the vine. The moment he's able to sit up and hold a coherent conversation our vision for the future, and your travel plans, will simply melt away.'

Hooper shook his head. 'We'll never get away with it.'

'Of course we will. Gabriel Bryce's security and well-being are paramount. He'll be housed in a private wing, be given around the clock medical care, guarded carefully. No one would dare challenge the decision once it's made.'

'No, I don't suppose they would,' Hooper muttered. 'This is all very Machiavellian, Tariq. I can't say I feel totally comfortable with it.'

'Would you feel more comfortable back at Defence?'

'Good point. This nut house you mentioned, have you somewhere in mind?'

'Yes, a facility in Hampshire. It's scheduled for decommissioning and the land to be sold to developers. Most of the patients have already been transferred elsewhere. It's secluded and highly secure. A private suite has been made available. The chief administrator there is an old university friend of yours, I'm told. Duncan Parry?'

Hooper raised his eyebrows. 'Duncan? Really? Good God, I haven't seen him for years.'

'Mister Parry has been made aware of the many opportunities that exist in the NHS executive in return for his cooperation and discretion. I've arranged for him to visit you here, for a private dinner.'

'What about Gabriel? You think *he'll* cooperate? Be discrete?'

'The level of threat he faces will be explicitly impressed upon him. Survival is a powerful instinct. He'll be compliant, at least for the short term.'

Hooper was silent, clearly struggling with his options. It was a pointless exercise, Saeed knew; Hooper, like the other players, was wholly predictable. They'd all been specifically targeted, studied for extended periods, their lives disassembled, their psychological processes broken down and analysed. They'd been followed, photographed, monitored, their homes and vehicles bugged, their financial and medical records obtained, their psychoanalytic and social cognitive patterns deconstructed, the layers peeled away to reveal the psychological buttons that could be so easily pushed.

Duncan Parry was a case in point. To his colleagues he was a capable manager of a secure mental health facility with a stable home life and modest ambitions. The reality was somewhat different. Parry was deeply embittered, his career floundering in the wake of his peers, a functioning alcoholic who detested his wife and spent too much time on some extremely dubious websites. Restless and consumed by inadequacy, Parry would leap at the chance to improve his circumstances.

And there was Hooper himself, ambitious but wholly unqualified for the highest of offices. Initially there wasn't much to go on in his personal life. He had no obvious vices, his two privately educated young sons consuming a large chunk of his income and modest investments. The boys' recent move from a little-known boarder in Shropshire to the gothic spires of Charterhouse was in keeping with Hooper's new found status, and therein lay his Achilles heel. Hooper's life was all about prestige, whether earned or bestowed, it did not matter. He was a social climber, driven by a harridan of a wife who relentlessly goaded Hooper about the material worlds of her friends and their successful husbands. The Downing Street bomb had been a fortuitous event for both of them. Saeed himself had heard the voice recording, the whispered intimacy after a short and rare bout of sex, the witch's words dripping in Hooper's ear; *this is your moment, Nigel. Don't screw it up, for God's sake. You'll never get another opportunity like this...*

Hooper had responded accordingly and power had been seized, ambitions fulfilled by the blood of others. Now all that remained was this crucial piece of the jigsaw. Once that was in place, the picture would be almost complete. It was time for a decision.

'Well, Nigel?'

The words snapped Hooper out of his reverie. 'Yes?'

'What would you like me to do?'

The PM stepped closer. 'How long will he be in this facility?'

'Not long. Once Cairo is signed there can be no going back. Afterwards, well, Gabriel can return to the land of the living and we can continue our work. There's a new continent to shape, Nigel, new partners to nurture and support, with you providing the necessary leadership.' Saeed smiled. 'And there's the small matter of the Prime Minister's new residence. You'd have final approval of the interior design, of course. Or would that be Millie?'

Hooper tried and failed to stifle a wide grin. 'You're right, what's past is past. Gabriel Bryce was a competent leader, but the world has turned. It's time to move on.' He clapped his hands and rubbed them briskly together. The dog got to its feet, tail wagging furiously. 'Set it all up, Tariq. Let's get this thing moving.'

'I'll need your authorisation. I have good contacts at Thames House. Discreet operatives will need to be sourced.'

Hooper waved a dismissive hand. 'You deal with it. Draft the papers and I'll sign them.' He turned to face the sun, a milky white disc that gave little warmth but flooded the field in golden light. 'This is a new start for us, Tariq, a new start for Britain. We'll remember this day for a long time to come.'

Saeed shielded his eyes from the light as the jigsaw piece slotted neatly into place. 'I'm sure we will, Nigel.'

# 12

## KING EDWARD THE SEVENTH
## HOSPITAL, LONDON

THE SHOUTING INVADED HIS DREAMLESS OBLIVION, THE screams rising only to fade again, before rising once more. It was an anguished wailing, both familiar and disturbing. The darkness turned to grey, then to bright white as he drifted upwards through the layers of fatigue. The room swam into view. The screaming was louder now, yet still Bryce found it difficult to focus.

He knew his condition wasn't normal. November was almost upon them, his wounds almost healed, and yet some days he felt as weak as when he'd first arrived. It was the drugs, he suspected. At first he welcomed them, numbing the pain of his wounds, the loss of so many friends and colleagues. Now it was different. His body was healing but his mind was still clouded, his thought processes often vague and confused. He wanted to shout at the consultants as they pored over his charts, at the nurses who cleaned and dressed his wounds, at Orla, who tampered with his drip as Bryce watched her through heavy-lidded eyes. But he didn't have the strength. He wasn't getting better, he was getting worse. And the screaming was getting louder.

*Sirens.*

The door to his room flew open. Overhead lights snapped on and a group of people marched in, doctors, nurses, armed policemen in black body armour. One of them yanked the curtains closed, shutting out the night. Bodies crowded around his bed.

'What's going on?' he mumbled. Medical staff pressed in from all sides. The bed covers were stripped off, his body unplugged from the tubes and monitors. 'Someone talk to me, please.'

He saw a familiar face lingering behind the medics, talking earnestly to a helmeted policeman.

'Sully?'

The orderly glanced at him then looked away. The uniform was gone, replaced by a dark roll neck sweater and winter jacket. Then Bryce smelt something burning and suddenly everything made sense; the building was on fire.

The doctors loomed over him, tugging at his eyelids, blinding him with pen torches, checking his vision with waving fingers. Bryce could see the hairs in their nostrils, caught the whiff of breath mints and tobacco. A trolley was wheeled next to the bed and firm hands gripped his limbs.

*One, two, three, lift...*

Smoke drifted across the ceiling, faint wisps of white and grey. A blanket was thrown over him, a pillow placed beneath his head, transport straps secured around his chest and legs. Orla appeared at his side, a raincoat over her uniform. They were going outside, a fire assembly point. Bryce almost smiled. At last he'd feel the cold night air on his face, in his lungs. The doctors, gathered around the trolley like a stone-faced jury, nodded their consent. Responsibility was passed, commands issued in harsh voices. The trolley was set in motion. He looked up. Sully leaned over him, grunting with effort, guiding Bryce out of the room and into the corridor outside. He felt like cheering.

Corridor lights flashed overhead like white lines on a road. Black helmets bobbed in and out of his vision and he caught a glimpse at the clock on the wall behind the nurses' station: 02:14. Orla looked down at him several times, concern knotting her brow. They entered an elevator with walls of brushed metal and recessed lighting. The doors rumbled closed, the bedlam left behind. Sully on one side, Orla on the other, two policemen by his feet, weapons clasped to their chests, silent as the elevator traveled downwards. It jerked to a halt and the doors swished open. A digitised female voice announced their arrival in the basement. Cold air filled the elevator and the trolley shuddered as Bryce was backed over the threshold. The two police officers remained inside, one of them stabbing a button with a gloved finger. The doors closed and they were gone, taking the light with them.

Bryce lay there, alone in the gloom. He saw a low concrete ceiling overhead, festooned with metal pipes. He could smell petrol fumes and the stale odour of cigarette smoke. He twisted his head. He was on a raised loading bay that overlooked a large underground car park. Sully leaned over him.

'You need to wear these. Don't worry, it's just a precaution.' He pulled a blue paper head cover over Bryce's hair, a surgical mask over his nose and mouth. Finally, he slipped a pair of clear plastic glasses over Bryce's darting eyes.

'What's happening?' There was still a faint slur to his speech and his voice sounded muffled behind the thin mask.

'Relax. It'll soon be over.'

'What will?'

Sully held a finger to his lips. 'No talking.'

He turned away and Bryce saw the flare of a match. Orla stood next to Sully, bundled in her raincoat and smoking a cigarette. Neither seemed concerned about Bryce's health, and that both reassured and troubled him at the same time. He heard footsteps, the echo of voices. Bryce couldn't work out what was being said. Footsteps clacked across concrete and doors slammed. An engine started up, then another. Blue lights swept the concrete walls, the ceiling. Bryce strained his neck, saw a police vehicle drive off, followed by an ambulance, then another police vehicle. They disappeared up a ramp, sirens screaming into life.

'Let's go.'

It was Sully's voice. The brake was released and Bryce felt the trolley rumble down a shallow slope. A vehicle backed towards the ramp. It wasn't an ambulance, more like a commercial van. Bryce was confused.

'Sully, what's happening? Where are we going?'

'Somewhere safe.'

Another man appeared, wearing overalls and a baseball cap, helping Sully and Orla to lift the trolley into the van. They climbed in behind him, locking the trolley wheels and fussing over a tangled web of nylon cargo straps. Bryce noticed that the inside of the vehicle was empty. The rear doors slammed shut and Sully positioned his backside on a wheel arch. The driver squeezed past the trolley and into the driver's cab and a moment later the van's engine rumbled into life. Orla leaned over him, adjusting the blanket up beneath his chin. She nodded at Sully.

'Let's get the heaters on. It's cold back here.'

Sully banged his fist on the wall of the van. 'Move it.'

Orla stumbled as the van started rolling, then she disappeared into the front cab. Bryce felt the vehicle power up the underground ramp and out onto the street. Sirens filled the air, much louder now, the van's interior lit by emergency lights. He heard urgent voices outside and someone rapped the side of the van twice. They moved forward again, then slowed and stopped. More voices, the crackle of radios. He heard Orla talking, her voice pressing, authoritative. He glanced at Sully, who seemed oblivious to the external dialogue, his arms folded across his chest, his legs stretched out before him. Beyond Bryce's exposed and pale feet, the rear doors had no windows, the outside world a vacuum of visual references.

The van moved off again, accelerating cleanly this time, the chatter from the driver's cabin more relaxed. Shafts of yellow light drifted across the van's roof with soothing regularity. Sully stood up and removed the articles from Bryce's head, dumping them on his lap.

'You'll need them later,' he announced, his body swaying with the motion of the van.

Bryce ignored the comment. 'Where are we going?'

'We have a situation. You're being moved, as a precaution.'

'Where to?'

'Somewhere safe.'

'A security situation?'

'Correct. Now get some rest.'

Bryce snorted. 'That's all I ever do. Tell me where we're going.'

Sully ignored him, and Bryce felt strangely unsettled by the man's behaviour. Sully had always treated Bryce with courtesy and respect. Now he seemed indifferent, impertinent even. Maybe it was the stress, the late hour, but Bryce suspected it was more than that; it was a shift of priorities. After all, it was Nigel who now ran the country, who dominated the political headlines. Bryce was no longer Prime

Minister, something he'd come to accept, but he'd always believed that that was a temporary state of affairs. Soon he'd be well enough to retake office, or so he kept telling himself. But lately he'd begun to question that particular future.

The cold truth was, things were much different now. The mood of the public had changed, influenced by an enthusiastic media who had thrown their weight behind Nigel's fledgling government and the Treaty of Cairo. Opinion polls reflected the same, a growing optimism for the future. For Bryce, a return to power could be a hard sell.

As the van travelled through the night, he reflected on the campaign being waged against his political past. The tragedy of the relocation programme remained buried beneath the rubble of Downing Street, replaced by a media smorgasbord of Cabinet tussles, of dead wives and imminent resignations. Bryce had once been a master of media manipulation, had used it many times to further his own cause. Now it was being directed at his premiership, his policies, and lately his mental state. He'd been subtly replaced in the public consciousness, no longer a world leader, just a broken man who invoked nothing more than pity.

The ticking of the indicator interrupted his dark reflections. He felt the van drift to the left and the rhythmic thump of rumble strips beneath the tyres: they were leaving a motorway, Bryce figured. A few minutes later the van stopped.

He strained to catch the quiet discussion in the driver's cab. A door opened, then slammed. Footsteps outside faded to nothing. Orla loomed over him.

'How is he?'

'Okay,' Sully said.

'Please don't talk like I'm not here,' Bryce huffed.

Sully chuckled. 'Well, officially you're not.' He slapped Orla's ample backside. 'Let's go. And keep it under fifty.'

Bryce twisted his neck. 'What's happening?'

'You'll find out soon enough. Just relax.'

The vehicle swung around and Bryce suspected they'd rejoined the motorway. Outside he could hear the sound of vehicles moving at high speed. Sully spoke in the dark.

'Not far now, Gabe. D'you mind if I call you Gabe?'

Bryce turned, saw the defiance in Sully's eyes. 'Something tells me you're going to anyway.'

'You're catching on fast,' Sully grinned. 'They found a device, back at the hospital. It went off in the room directly below yours. Apparently it didn't detonate properly, just caused a fire. That's why you're being moved.'

'What sort of device?'

'The sort that goes bang.' He leaned back against the side panel and yawned.

'So, where are we going?'

'Another facility. More secure.'

'Don't treat me like a bloody child, Sully.'

'Relax. You're going to be well looked after.'

Bryce turned away and stared at the ceiling. He was travelling on a motorway in the dead of night, in an empty van with no medical equipment and no police escort, to an undisclosed location. That told him one thing, at least; he was healing well. And this sudden journey, while unsettling, was invigorating him. He still felt woozy, though not nearly as bad as before, and probably because he wasn't on that God-awful drip. He turned his head. 'I want to speak to the head consultant when we get to wherever we're going,' Bryce announced.

Sully murmured in the gloom. 'Sure. It'll be a while, yet.'

The journey passed slowly for Bryce. He stared at the roof, the intermittent wash of headlights sweeping above him, the hum of the tyres. He dozed several times, the gentle sway of the vehicle lulling him into a shallow slumber.

Once again the ticking indicator focused his attention, waking him from a restless sleep. They left the motorway, Bryce registering every bump in the road, every turn. The roads were getting narrower, the world outside more remote, the occasional brush of a hedgerow along the van's flanks.

'Almost there,' Orla suddenly called from the driver's cab.

Sully yawned and stretched, balling his fists and rubbing his eyes. 'How long?'

'Five minutes.'

'Shit.' He sprang to his feet, looming over Bryce and yanking his restraining straps. Bryce felt his arms pinned, his chest suddenly constricted.

'Jesus Christ,' he wheezed, 'what the hell are you doing?'

'It's for your own safety.'

Sully pulled the head cover back on, the surgical mask and glasses over Bryce's face. Bryce began to panic, his heart rate accelerating. 'Listen to me, Sully; I'm ordering you to release me and tell me what the hell is going on.'

'I can see the gate,' Orla shouted.

'Slow down.'

Sully reached into his pocket and took out a fat silver pen. Not a pen, Bryce saw, something else. Cold fear gripped him as Sully's hand twisted his head to one side. 'Hold still,' he ordered, 'it's just a sedative.'

'No more drugs,' Bryce pleaded through Sully's fingers.

'Please—' A bee sting pierced his neck. Sully let go, watching Bryce closely. 'For God's sake, Sully. I need to... need to...'

And then he couldn't speak, couldn't move his tongue. Icy fingers travelled across his body. He felt his feet twitch violently, then they too froze. All he could do was move his eyeballs. He was immobile.

*Paralysed.*

His mind screamed but no sound came from his mouth. He could hear himself breathing, the respirations loud inside his head, could hear the gentle beat of his heart as the drug calmed him, dispelling the terror, the anxiety.

Sully stood over him, patted his cheek. 'He's deep. We're good.'

He heard the engine slow, the chatter of the nurse, a man's laugh. Something hummed and whirred, a metal gate rattling open. The van purred slowly for a minute, turning one corner, then another, finally coming to a halt with a gentle squeal of the brakes. The engine shut off.

They'd arrived.

For a moment there was silence. Then Sully moved and the rear doors of the van opened, inviting an icy blast inside. Bryce could feel it on his lips, inside his mouth: the rest of his body had shut down, like a slab of dead meat. His head lolled from side to side as the folding wheels of the trolley hit the ground. He stared up at a building, a dark, Victorian edifice where the darkened windows were covered with steel bars. A prison? Then he was on the move again.

Rubber doors flapped open. Brightness blinded him, neon strip lights, passing overhead. A strong smell of antiseptic invaded his nostrils. Sully and Orla guided the trolley into an elevator. It travelled upwards, humming quietly.

Outside there were more ceilings, more lights. A door opened, a shadowy room beyond.

'You're here. Good.' It was a man, a voice he didn't recognise. 'It's all over the news, you know.' A figure loomed over him, thinning grey hair, heavy framed glasses, a worrying tinge of alcohol on his breath. 'What's the prognosis?'

'Ischemic stroke, caused by the stress of the incident. He's had a max dose of Heparin, his vitals are strong and he's responding well.'

'Good.' The man moved out of sight. 'The wing is fully prepared. We can move him now or leave him here for the night.'

'Let's move him after breakfast,' Sully said.

'What about the other staff?' Orla this time.

'This whole block has been mothballed. It's empty. As far as anyone else is concerned you're a clinical decontamination team from London. I'll issue your ID's tomorrow. In the meantime I'll show you to your accommodations.'

Bryce heard them shuffle from the room and the light snapped off. He heard Orla laugh outside, the sound brittle, eerie in the dark. His mind reeled, fear and confusion tumbling together like clothes in a washing machine. Where the hell was he? He'd expected a hospital but this felt more like a prison. Or perhaps a mixture of the two? What kind of—

He felt his eyes widen, his throat constricting as fear flooded his consciousness.

*A psychiatric facility*.

How was that possible? A mistake had been made, a horrifying mix-up—

No. He'd been kidnapped. Sully and Orla, others most certainly, had used the fire as cover to snatch him from the hospital. He'd been driven in the dead of night to this terrible place, left alone, abandoned.

Terror stalked him, lurking in the shadows, threatening to engulf him.

He closed his eyes, shutting out the nightmare.

A distant scream echoed through the wing.

## 13

## HERTFORDSHIRE

Danny swung the axe and brought it down sharply, splitting the thick log into two neat halves. He tossed them into the back of the Nissan pickup, deciding he'd chopped enough to stock Ray's woodpile for another week. He swung the axe again, burying the blade into the ancient tree stump, then slapped the dirt from his hands. A chill wind gusted through the woods, scattering noisy waves of dead leaves before it. Overhead, skeletal treetops creaked and swayed, the blue sky above paling before the approaching rain front. Danny secured the tailgate and climbed inside the cab.

The sweat on his body began to cool and he pulled a green fleece over his t-shirt. He scratched his face and neck, still unused to the sensation of a full beard. Ray seemed pleased with its progress though, the dark hair just about thick enough to partially cover the tattoo on his neck, helping to—what was the word Ray used? —oh yeah, *culti-vate* a new image. The walkie-talkie on the seat beside him crackled into life.

'You out there, son?'

'Go ahead.' Ray was careful. No names on the radio.

'Come up to the house. Quick as you can.'

'On my way.'

Danny hopped out of the pickup and worked the axe from the stump. He was about to throw it in the back when a movement caught his eye. It was Joe, moving through the trees about fifty yards away, the black shotgun slung over his shoulder. Nelson bounded ahead of him, a flash of brown and black fur darting through the woods. Danny had already decided that he didn't like Joe. He was a miserable bastard, and had practically ignored Danny since he'd arrived. There was something not quite right about him.

Danny put it down to jealousy. After all, Ray had taken Danny under his wing, put him in the guest apartment, and invited him to dinner in the main house a few times. Ray often sought out Danny's company, spending hours walking and talking, getting to know each other, becoming friends. It was different for Joe: Ray treated him more like a gopher, a dogs body. So Danny had decided that that was the man's beef. Joe was simply a big, jealous, miserable twat. And he never took that combat jacket off either. Chill out bruv, the war's over.

Danny remained hidden behind the tailgate until Joe was out of sight, wondering where he'd been. The path he was on led from the house down to the lower wood—the plantation, he'd heard Ray call it—a thick forest just beyond the firebreak. Danny had never been down there; in fact, it was the only part of the estate that Danny had never explored.

He made a snap decision; Ray was waiting for him up at the house and Joe was headed in that general direction. Maybe this was his chance to take a quick look. He set off through the woods and joined the path. The ground sloped gently down towards the valley and presently the trees gave way to a wide firebreak. Danny froze, watching, listening. The wood was silent, the air thick and leaden.

Across the firebreak, tightly packed ranks of mature firs marched up the opposite slope towards the estate's distant southern boundary. Danny scratched his head. There was nothing here, no tracks, no outbuildings, nothing. Suddenly a rabbit broke cover and hopped out into the firebreak. It sat on its haunches, oblivious, its tiny nose twitching as it inspected the air. Danny made a clicking sound with his tongue and the rabbit darted back across the break. He watched it scoot between the trees, losing sight of its bobbing white tail as it hopped past the shovel.

Danny frowned. He stepped across the firebreak and into the plantation on the other side, the ground beneath his feet carpeted with dead needles. He swatted branches away from his face until he found himself in a small clearing. Here the air was dead, the ground cold and wet, a place where the overhead cover filtered out the daylight, creating pools of deep shadow.

The shovel was planted in the damp brown earth, its worn red handle conspicuous against nature's backdrop. Propped against a nearby tree was a pick, and a long handled entrenching tool. Danny took a step forward then stopped. The ground didn't look right. He knelt down and looked closer. Small metal pegs ringed the clearing, pinning a dark green tarpaulin to the ground. He loosened a few of the pegs and threw back the sheet in a cloud of pine needles.

The hole had been cut into a rough rectangle, about six feet long and three feet wide. It was deep too, and dank water had collected at the bottom, its oily surface reflecting Danny's looming shadow. It was a trench. He stroked his beard, wondering why someone, Joe probably, would dig a trench in such a remote spot. He looked again. No, not a trench, it was more like a—

Danny swallowed hard and took a hasty step back. A grave. There was no other explanation. The clearing was dark, the ground soft, the tools left behind to finish the job. Someone had dug a grave. Why?

A bird shrilled close by, startling Danny. He threw the tarpaulin back, pegged it, then camouflaged it as before. He headed back to the Nissan at speed, sliding behind the wheel as he caught his breath. He fired the engine into life and headed back to the house. As he curved around the driveway he saw Ray waiting on the porch.

'About time. What kept you?' He wore a grey turtleneck sweater and matching sweat pants, a pair of gold-rimmed spectacles hanging on a chain around his neck.

'Sorry,' Danny mumbled, slamming the Nissan's door. He cocked a thumb over his shoulder. 'I've got the firewood.'

'Never mind that. Come inside. I'd like you to meet a couple of friends.'

Danny hesitated. 'Friends?'

Ray chuckled. 'Don't panic, son. All will become clear.'

He followed Ray into the main reception room. The walls were decorated with a series of Old English oils and a fire crackled in the grate. Two men occupied one of four large sofas clustered around a huge glass coffee table. One wore an oversized rugby shirt with the collar turned up, the material straining against his potbelly and falling over designer jeans. The other man was older, mid-fifties, his long sandy hair tied back into a ponytail. He wore jeans too, and a black t-shirt with 'Cannes Film Festival' in faded lettering on the left breast. Neither of the men stood.

'Danny, I'd like you to meet two very good friends of mine, Marcus and Tom.'

They exchanged handshakes. The fat one, Marcus, had a strong grip, almost challenging. With Tom it was like squeezing a dead jellyfish. Danny took a seat on the opposite couch next to Ray.

'The famous Danny Whelan,' Marcus beamed. 'A real pleasure.' He waved a hand around the room. 'How are you finding life at Chez Carver? Not too uncomfortable, I hope?'

'Ray's been very kind.'

His host patted him on the knee. 'Giving shelter to a patriot in need, that's all.'

All eyes turned towards the door as a rhythmic jingle announced the arrival of Tess. She sashayed between the sofas in a capacious mint-coloured frock, the thin material struggling to contain her ample, bra-less bosom. Danny looked away, embarrassed.

'Refreshments,' she announced brightly, placing a tray of tea, coffee and biscuits on the table between them. She glanced at Ray. 'Got everything you need?'

'Yes, my love.'

As she passed behind Danny she pinched a tuft of hair between her fingers at the nape of his neck. 'That'll need a little trim. Can't have you looking all scruffy again, can we? Someone might recognise you.'

'Course not,' Danny replied, rubbing his neck. He noticed Marcus smiling as he stared at Tess's breasts. 'Let me know when it's convenient.'

'We'll do it today. Before your picture.'

Danny frowned. 'My what?'

Tess smiled and jangled out of the room. Ray poured coffee and settled back into the sofa. 'I wanted you to meet these two gentlemen, Danny, not only because they're good friends of mine, but also because they can help you.'

'Okay,' Danny mumbled.

Ray took a loud sip of coffee. 'Tom and Marcus are men of influence and skill respectively. Highly valuable commodities in these troubled times.'

Marcus dunked a biscuit in his drink, a chocolate finger, waving the soggy digit in the air. 'Think of us as magicians, Danny. Now you see him, now you don't.' He popped the biscuit into his mouth.

'We're artists,' Tom added. He spoke with a Midlands accent, flat, monotone.

Danny smiled self-consciously. 'You boys are starting to freak me out.'

'Take it easy,' Ray laughed. 'There's no need to be nervous. They're here to help set you up. For your new life.'

'My new life?'

'That's right. For example, Marcus takes care of a lot of outsourcing contracts for the government. In this case the printing of biometric passports.'

Marcus raised an eyebrow. 'You left yours behind, is that right Danny? Don't worry, we'll get you a new one. New face, new passport. It's not a problem,'

Danny found himself stroking his beard. 'Really?'

'Sure. We'll record all the relevant details today, including your photograph. Before that, Tom needs to do a little prep work. Tom?'

'That's right, Danny.' The older man tapped a large silver flight case clamped between his calves. It was the first time Danny had noticed it. 'What we're going to do today is to subtly change your appearance. Now, I can see that the lifestyle here has improved your complexion, and added a little volume to your facial bone structure.'

Danny frowned. 'Are you a plastic surgeon or something?'

Marcus laughed, popping another biscuit into his mouth. 'Plastic surgeon, that's a good one.'

'I work in the movie business,' Tom explained. 'Make up and prosthetics, to be specific.' He tapped the flight case between his legs. 'I've got a range of products, coloured contacts, hair dyes, a little latex to change the shape of your nose, skin crèmes that will cover your tattoos. Applied professionally we can alter your appearance quite significantly.'

Marcus polished off the last of the biscuits and wiped his mouth with a napkin. 'Then we take your picture. In a couple of weeks, boom! No more Danny Whelan.'

'You'll be able to come and go as you please,' Ray smiled, slapping Danny's knee again. 'Travel around, even leave the country. Not bad, eh?'

Danny said nothing at first. He stared at the flight case, at the men opposite. Then he shrugged. 'I guess.'

Ray's smile faded. 'Gents, why don't you get set up in the study while I have a quick chat with Danny?'

'Sure.' Marcus heaved himself out of the chair and led Tom from the room. Ray turned, his eyes narrowing.

'Something's wrong.'

'It's nothing,' Danny mumbled, studying his dirty fingernails. A shadow crossed the room, the dying sunlight finally yielding before the approaching storm. The rain announced its arrival, drumming against the windows.

'C'mon, son. Out with it.'

Danny got to his feet. He thrust his hands in his pockets and stood by the window, watching the storm front sweep across the hills behind the house, opaque sheets of rain drifting beneath steel grey clouds. The window frame rattled as the wind gusted around the building.

'You've been good to me, Ray. You took me in, put a roof over my head, food in my belly. I owe you so much already. And now this?'

'What?'

'This. A new passport, professional make-up; I'm not stupid, all that costs a fortune. Look, I try and pull my weight around here, but I'm hardly a professional handy-man, am I? So why are you going to all this trouble, Ray? What good am I to you?'

'You're in the Movement. We look out for our own.'

Danny stared out of the window. 'The Movement's dead.'

Ray got to his feet. He laid a hand on Danny's shoulder, squeezing it with strong fingers. 'I told you before, as long as people like me and you live and breathe, the struggle continues.'

'But I can't pay you back, Ray. For any of this.'

The big man studied him for a moment, his grey eyes unblinking. 'Look, I'll be straight with you, Danny. You can't stay cooped up here forever, we both know that. And the authorities will never stop looking. Your only hope is a new life, far away from this country.' Ray paused. 'I was thinking New Zealand.'

Danny winced. 'New Zealand?'

Ray stepped closer. His breath reeked of stale coffee and cigars. 'Like you said, you're not stupid. You'll need more than a bit of makeup and a new passport to stay in the UK. We can't manufacture medical records or bank accounts, that sort of stuff. Sooner or later you'll fall foul of some bloody busybody and that'll be it. But what I *can* offer you is a chance to get out.'

Danny watched the rain lash across the patio outside. 'With all due respect Ray, how the hell do I get to the other side of the world? And what would I do if I got there? I don't know shit about New Zealand.'

Ray held up a hand. 'You're right, you can't travel by normal routes, even with a new passport. It's too risky. But there is another way, a tried and tested method.' He lowered his voice, as if there was someone else in the room. 'There's a place on the Kent coast, a small fishing port. I've got a friend with a boat there. He can get you where you need to be, smack bang in the middle of the international shipping lanes. Busiest in the world, the English Channel. Anyway, every few months a boat comes through, a big Norwegian container ship, goes all over the world. The owner's a very good friend of mine, the crew completely trustworthy. It's due to transit the Channel just after Christmas. In a couple of months you could be starting a new life in New Zealand.'

Danny was silent for a while, staring at his feet, trying to imagine living on the other side of the world. This was all moving too fast. 'I don't know anyone over there.'

'I do, Danny. I've got good friends, powerful friends. Setting you up will be far easier than here. Not so strict with their checks and regulations, see. As I said, a man could get lost down there, live a good life. This country's finished, anyway.'

*Maybe Ray's right, maybe I could get lost,* Danny thought. There was nothing here for him, anyway. Well, almost nothing.

'What about my dad? I can't leave him.'

Ray hesitated, then rummaged in his pocket and produced a folded piece of paper. 'The authorities had him moved to this address in Battersea.'

Danny snatched it from Ray's fingers. 'Why? He didn't do anything.'

'People were making life difficult for him on the estate. He'd become a target. They thought it best to move him.'

'Jesus Christ, poor dad.'

'We can get him out, same way as you, but it'll be after you've gone. He can start again too. You can both live your lives in peace.'

Danny covered his mouth, the guilt threatening to choke him. Dad had lost his home, a place where Danny had grown up, where they'd all been happy once, the rooms filled with memories of a long-dead wife and mother. Now his dad had been evicted, bundled away in the dead of night to a strange place. He'd be alone, traumatised, and it was all Danny's fault. He had to get him out, get them both out, and start their lives again. It was up to Danny now.

'Tell me something, Ray; this new life, for me and my dad. How much is it going to cost?'

Ray toyed with the Rolex on his wrist. 'It's not a case of money. Our currency of trade is loyalty, Danny. It's about devotion to the cause. Patriotism.'

'I'm loyal, Ray. And I'm a patriot, you know that.'

'I believe you Danny, but a man should be judged by his deeds, not words.'

Danny squared his shoulders and held out his hand. 'You can count on me, Ray. Whatever you need, I'll do it.'

Ray gripped Danny's hand and shook it, his tanned face breaking into a bright, beaming smile.

'Thanks, Danny. I was hoping you'd say that.'

# 14

---

# CAIRO

'COME ON, GABE, UP YOU GET. THE SHOW'S ABOUT TO start.'

Bryce peered over the edge of the covers. Sully stood in the doorway, beckoning. He rolled over, tugging the thin quilt up beneath his chin. 'I'm not coming.'

Sully shook his head and marched across the room. He was dressed in a green tunic and trousers, his muscled arms bulging beneath short sleeves, an extendable baton in his hand. Bryce winced as Sully racked the weapon out with a loud *crack!* He tapped the baton on the metal bedstead. 'Get up.'

Bryce threw off the quilt, rubbing his eyes. 'I'm tired. Don't want to watch TV.' His stomach churned with excitement, and he fought the urge to leap out of bed. Instead he remained immobile, staring at his feet.

Sully collapsed the baton and placed it back in the holder beneath his tunic. 'We all have to do things we don't want to, Gabe. I don't want to drive down here twice a week to babysit you but orders are orders. So now I'm giving you one. Get up.'

Bryce had pushed him far enough. He swung his legs onto the cold floor.

'Good boy. Get yourself cleaned up. I'll be back in a bit.'

Sully left the room, his sneakers squeaking on the grey linoleum. He heard the jangle of keys then the metallic *clang* of the security gate as it slammed home. He was alone.

He stood up and stretched, his bones cracking, then stepped into his slippers. He shook out his arms and dropped to the floor, pushing out a dozen press-ups. Then he walked back and forth across the room, swinging his arms, rolling his shoulders, getting his heart rate up. It wasn't the best workout in the world, but it was the only way that Bryce could maintain a modicum of fitness. Later, after Sully had retired for the night, he would march up and down the corridor for an hour, gradually increasing the pace until his lungs heaved and his body ran with sweat. If he were caught he'd be in serious trouble. No one wanted him to get well.

He thought back to when he'd first arrived. The paralysis had eventually worn off, but not before he'd soiled himself. He'd been ferried to a deserted top floor wing and dumped on a bed. He'd lain in his own filth for most of that first day, alone and terrified. He'd felt fear before, in the rubble of Downing Street, but this was different. This was something darker, more terrifying.

His initial fears of kidnap had quickly faded. There had been no demands, no talk of a ransom. Sully had often repeated that his isolation was all in the name of security, but as the weeks had passed even he had given up the pretence. They both knew the truth; Bryce was simply a prisoner.

He understood the concept of torture all too well now.

His stark surroundings, the solitary confinement, the unknown drugs that Orla fed him all combined to induce a frightening cocktail of fear, of varying states of disorientation and lethargy. The food was barely edible, there were no exercise facilities or even the chance of fresh air. Bryce had never received a single visitor, or phone call, or even seen a newspaper. He'd been deliberately cut off from the world outside. Then there was the physical abuse, a punch here, a slap there, and in a recent act of degradation, Sully had forced him to strip naked, ordering him to crouch in the corner of his room while Orla photographed him from various angles. Such was his life now.

His accommodations were no better. A large unheated room, a single iron-posted bed, a nightstand, his few books stacked neatly on the shelf beneath. A large wooden locker stood against the far wall, his hospital clothes hung neatly within, alongside a small desk and a single metal chair. The walls were padded up to a height of maybe eight feet, the once white material now grey and stained. The paintwork was cracked and peeling, and the overhead strip lights had been removed except the ones above Bryce's bed. Sometimes, Sully left those on at night.

He'd become accustomed to the cold, the radiators beneath the windows lifeless. The windows themselves were huge, four of them, ten feet high at least, partially sealed on the inside with thick sheets of obscured plastic. When it was quiet Bryce would often carry the table across the room and stand on it, peering over the plastic sheeting. Beyond the rusted bars the view outside was one of open grass, of a double chain link fence topped with coils of razor wire, of the woods beyond that shielded the facility from the outside world. Bryce would stand there as long as possible, watching the clouds drift across the sky, the trees bending in the wind. But mostly he watched the main gate.

He was in Hampshire, near the town of Alton. He assumed that because some of the commercial delivery vans had that name on their side panels. Pedestrian traffic came and went via electronic gates adjacent to the security post. From his restricted view point it didn't appear to be a large facility, just four dark and decrepit Victorian buildings including the one he was in. Two of them were empty, surrounded by temporary hoardings and empty rubbish skips. The facility was being wound down, Bryce presumed. Much like his own life.

In the corridor outside his room, past the washroom and toilets, past the heavily secured steel mesh gate, existed another world, a world of oppressive silence, occasionally punctuated with unintelligible shouts and tortured screams. Bryce had added his own, but no one ever came. Those pitiful cries had ceased some time ago. The only voices he heard, the only people he saw now, were Sully and nurse Orla.

When they were around Bryce acted dumb, often forgetful, popping his medication when ordered. He'd stopped asking questions, making demands, had allowed his physical appearance to deteriorate. He was no longer any bother, just another medicated shadow in a facility full of them. Outside the world turned, life went on. Inside, Gabriel Bryce was fading from view.

He pulled on a threadbare dressing gown and shuffled down the corridor to the washroom. He stared at his reflection in the mirror. How he'd changed since his arrival. The thick grey hair was gone, regularly shaved by Sully into a tight crop, the scars of Downing Street pale and prominent. The lines around his eyes had deepened and his broken nose remained uncorrected. Grey stubble bristled around his chin and hollowed cheeks, his shaves rare and always supervised by the watchful Sully. The poor diet and lack of any grooming had taken their toll; he'd lost twenty pounds and aged ten years. The former Prime Minster of Great Britain was virtually unrecognisable.

He splashed tepid water around his face and neck, shivering in the chill of the washroom, then towelled himself dry. He heard the security gate open and wrapped the dressing gown around his body. Sully waited outside.

'Let's go.'

Bryce was elated to be finally leaving the wing. He shuffled behind Sully, head down, the urge to run and shout, to rejoice, almost overwhelming. But he checked those emotions, his eyes roaming the desolate corridors, the empty noticeboards and vacant stairwells. His suspicions were correct; the building had been abandoned. The knowledge frightened him, but he remained silent as he trailed obediently behind his minder.

They passed through three more padlocked security gates before stopping in front of a wood-panelled door that bore the faded legend 'TV LOUNGE'. He followed Sully into a windowless room. Like the rest of the building the paint was peeling off the walls and everything smelled of damp. A dozen easy chairs were arranged in a loose semi-circle in front of a dated TV.

'Take a seat,' Sully ordered. 'Tonight's a big night.'

'Why?' Bryce muttered the words, feigning disinterest as he flopped into the chair.

'You'll see.'

Sully picked up the remote and settled into the seat next to Bryce, his legs splayed out before him. He started flicking through the channels then settled on the BBC, the screen filled by a low-angled aerial shot, slowly panning across a flat landscape of palm trees and ancient monuments, where dazzling lights and piercing laser beams lit up the evening sky, where a heaving multitude thronged before a giant, red-carpeted stage that was filled with suited and robed dignitaries. Bryce fought hard to keep his expression neutral as he stared at the screen, the camera flashes that lit up the night like a cosmic storm, the long line of limousines, the smart ranks of ceremonial troops, the camera zooming in towards the historic document that rested on its purpose-built plinth, waiting to be signed.

Bryce's heart sank. The world, and his place in it, had indeed passed him by.

Cairo had begun.

THE CEREMONY WAS HELD in the shadows of the Great Pyramids of Giza. The sun had already set when the first European leaders arrived, their air-conditioned limousines whisking them from the centre of Cairo to the giant stage beneath the towering Pyramid of Cheops.

Saeed's limousine was one of the last to arrive. He stepped out of the vehicle into a storm of camera flashes, the dazzling lights reflecting the gold embroidery of his knee-length black Sherwani jacket and silk trousers. Dozens more cameras tracked his graceful passage up a flight of red-carpeted stairs where he was greeted by waiting European heads of state. Below the stage, hundreds of European politicians, dignitaries and legislators gave him a standing ovation. Saeed took his place in the front row, absorbing the atmosphere of the spectacle about to unfold.

'Impressive, isn't it?' remarked the German Chancellor seated alongside him.

'Amazing.'

And Saeed meant it. The elevated stage was dressed like a movie set, two terraced rows of luxury seats fashioned like the thrones of the early Pharaohs. Forming the backdrop was a stand of massive columns resembling those at the ancient site of Karnak, decorated with intricate hieroglyphics and flanked by two huge sphinx-like statues with flaming torches set between their massive paws. The Pyramid of Cheops towered behind, a man-made mountain of stone bathed in a magnificent display of light that changed colour as the sky darkened, while the gentle strains of the Berlin Philharmonic Orchestra drifted on the sultry air. The Egyptians had outdone themselves, Saeed decided.

He looked out across the desert, where an estimated crowd of two hundred thousand stood behind temporary barriers under the watchful eye of the Egyptian army. Above them he noticed a red light blinking in the night sky, the media blimp drifting silently overhead, its multiple cameras beaming the images to a waiting continent. A continent about to change forever.

'The gown,' observed the Chancellor. 'A nice touch. And so representative of modern Britain.'

Saeed smiled alongside the German. The Chancellor may have been born in Hamburg but his loyalty would always lie with his Turkish roots. 'Thank you, brother.'

'I see things have settled down at home.'

'The new administration has provided the stability that Britain so desperately craved.'

'And how is the Prime Minister?'

'You've seen the news. The trip goes badly for him. The media senses blood in the water. The opportunity to move against him may present itself sooner than planned.'

'Proceed with caution, my friend. Many eyes are watching now.'

An aide approached and handed the Chancellor a slip of paper. He read it, then sat a little straighter, adjusting the cuffs of his crisp white shirt.

Saeed raised an eyebrow. 'All is well, I trust?'

'They're on their way.'

SULLY ELBOWED Bryce on the arm. 'Recognise a few faces there, Gabe?'

Bryce shrugged, feigning disinterest. He'd noted the exotically dressed Tariq and the German Chancellor in the front row. There were many other personalities gathered there in Cairo; the leaders of Turkey, France, the Netherlands, Egypt, Spain, Italy, and others. Significantly the Irish and Danish luminaries were seated at the back, punishment no doubt for once sharing Bryce's misgivings about the treaty. Yet there was one leader so obviously missing from the lineup: Nigel Hooper. Even the commentary hadn't yet mentioned him.

The picture cut to an aerial shot of a convoy moving swiftly through the suburbs of Giza. The palm-lined highway was swept clear of traffic, police outriders shadowing the fleet of black Mercedes limousines in a dance of blue lights.

'Here they come,' Sully announced brightly. 'The show's about to begin.'

THE RIPPLE of applause grew louder, like an approaching rainstorm, the sound rolling across the desert floor in steady waves and crashing against the strings of the orchestra's energetic concerto. Limousines snaked their way towards the pyramids, headlights blazing along the blacktop. Cameras began to flash as the orchestra shifted gear from the delicacy of Handel to Beethoven's rousing Symphony number Nine.

*Impressive*, Saeed mused. Egyptian ceremonial troops surrounding the stage came to attention as one, their weapons held stiffly before them. The symphony built towards its thunderous climax, the applause of the multitude rising like the sound of the ocean into the Egyptian night. Saeed got to his feet.

The Presidents of Europe and Egypt had arrived, their limousines sweeping around to stop at the bottom of the steps in perfect symmetry.

DANNY WATCHED from the window as darkness settled across the Hertfordshire countryside. It had become something of a ritual at the end of the day, a cup of tea and a biscuit as he watched the shadows stretch across the fields behind the house, the crisp air punctuated by the call of evening birdsong, the cautious appearance of white-tailed rabbits and other wildlife. As he sipped his brew Danny saw a firework explode somewhere over the rolling hills towards Watford. Then another.

Everyone would be getting pissed tonight, and Danny briefly wondered what was going on back at the King's Head, then decided he couldn't care less. He was glad to be away from that shithole. The law might still be hunting him, but here, behind the walls of the estate, the air was clean and the view a vast improvement. For the first time in many years, Danny felt useful, a part of something. Despite everything, he was happy. Soon, him and dad would be gone, free to start their lives over. He'd done some research, even watched those Lord of the Rings films a few times. New Zealand was a beautiful place. He was actually looking forward to it.

The phone rang, startling him. He picked it up off the kitchen counter. 'Hello?'

'Come and join the party, son.'

In the background Danny could hear music, laughter, the buzz of conversation. 'Are you sure, Ray? I'm supposed to be in hiding.'

'I've invited a few close friends to the house. You couldn't be in safer company. Tidy up and get over here.'

Twenty minutes later Danny let himself in through the kitchen door wearing a pair of beige chinos and a freshly pressed white polo shirt. He checked his appearance in the entrance hall mirror. His hair had grown a fraction, allowing Tess to tidy it and sweep in a side parting. The beard was neatly trimmed and his complexion had that healthy outdoors look. All in all, he felt no one would recognise him from his mug shot and that gave him a bit more confidence. Still, the thought of meeting new people was a little intimidating.

'Very handsome.'

Danny turned and saw Ray in the doorway of the main reception room. 'Come on, son. Everyone's waiting.'

Danny swallowed nervously and followed him inside. There were maybe twenty people scattered around the dimly-lit room, all well-dressed and clearly moneyed, the ladies in party dresses and sparkling jewellery, the men in jackets and trousers. Danny felt distinctly underdressed. Music played softly in the background and the large TV in the corner had been muted, the channel tuned to the event in Cairo. The atmosphere was relaxed, hospitable, which

Danny thought was weird, considering the ceremony playing on the TV.

Ray swept a meaty arm around his shoulders and led him into the centre of the room.

'Can I have everyone's attention for a moment?'

The chatter died away and Danny felt his cheeks redden as the gathering studied him, curious expressions on their faces. He saw one woman on the sofa whisper something to a heavily made-up blond beside her and both women giggled softly, ramping up Danny's embarrassment. Some edged closer to him, while others lingered around the walls, their faces lost in the shadows. Danny felt like a specimen in a glass box. Ray's strong fingers squeezed his shoulder.

'Friends, I'd like you to meet Danny Whelan. As some of you know, Danny has been a guest of mine for a while now and I'd like to think in that time we've become friends, right Danny?'

Danny's cheeks burned a deep crimson. Thank God for the beard. 'Er, yeah, of course Ray.'

Laughter cackled around the room. Ray held up his hand for silence.

'When Danny went on the run he used his wits to evade capture, to keep himself fed and dry. He used guile and ingenuity at every turn, hiding by day, moving like a fox through the night, his one aim to make it here, to my door, unmolested. And, more importantly, undetected.' Tess appeared next to Ray and handed him a champagne flute. 'You've all read Danny's story. You've all read the lies, the distortions, the government propaganda. The Danny Whelan I know is nothing like that. He's intelligent, loyal, and like all of us here tonight, cares passionately about the future of this country. If anyone encapsulates what it means to be a patriot today, it's this man here. Ladies and gentle-men, I give you Danny Whelan.'

'Danny Whelan,' the room echoed, raising their glasses. Danny felt his chest puff with pride, his misgivings, his embarrassment, banished. He saw the respect in people's eyes, and stood a little straighter. As usual Ray was right; he was *somebody*.

He watched the big man empty his champagne glass in one hit. 'That's enough from me. Let's get pissed.'

As laughter rippled around the room, Ray steered Danny towards the buffet tables set against the wall. The white linen tablecloths were decorated with champagne buckets, with neat rows of tall crystal flutes, and an impressive feast of hot and cold foods. Ray studied Danny's face as he set his glass down.

'See?' he laughed, 'Told you they wouldn't bite.'

'I appreciate what you said, Ray.'

'I meant every word. You're a symbol of hope for all of us.' Ray leaned over the table, selected a large prawn from a carefully arranged display, and popped it into his mouth. 'Every day you wake up a free man, every minute you evade the clutches of the state, that's another small victory for us.' Ray sucked his fingers clean, picked up another glass of champagne and chugged it back. He handed a full one to Danny.

'Cheers, Ray.' He took a careful sip, enjoying the cold crispness on his tongue. 'Can I ask you something?'

'Shoot.'

'If the treaty's so bad, why have a party?'

Ray burped softly, fish breath wafting under Danny's nose. He tapped the side of his head with a greasy finger.

'It's all about mental attitude, son. Every setback must be viewed as an opportunity to do things differently, to reassess one's strategy. The Movement's threatened? Shut it down and go in a different direction. You thought it was dead, right? Take a look around you. Everyone in this room is a committed patriot, even more so now.'

'What do you mean?'

Ray looked pained. 'I mean The Treaty of Cairo. By midnight tonight it'll be signed into European law without a single referendum in any EU country. You think that's democracy? Course it isn't, it's nothing but a filthy, stinking lie. This bullshit on TV is a call to arms for patriots everywhere. It's given us the incentive to develop a new strategy. One that people will take notice of.'

Danny took another sip of champagne. Ray seemed agitated, his voice a little louder. Around the room, eyes turned towards them.

'Think about it, son. After midnight, anyone can waltz into Egypt and claim asylum under European law. And once they do, they won't wait around in that flyblown shithole. No, they'll continue west, into old Europe, where Muslim enclaves sprout like weeds, where maternity wings are bursting with foreign litters, where liberal governments bend over backwards to fill the begging bowls. The relocation programme was the start of it all. I mean, does anyone seriously believe that those refugees will up sticks and go home once the war ends? Walk away from free health care, internal plumbing, a benefits system that asks no questions? What fucking idiot would do that?'

Ray chugged another flute of champagne then wiped his mouth with a napkin. His mood had darkened, his eyes flicking toward the TV screen. It was a side of the man Danny had never seen before, and it made him nervous. Around the room people were watching, listening.

'We're under attack,' Ray fumed, 'have been for

centuries. Europe might party tonight but the hangover's going to be a bitch. The media will spin it of course, and deluded liberals will justify the need for unchecked immigration in case our feeble little country falls into ruin. I give it ten years, maybe less, before the tipping point is reached. When that happens they won't bother to hide it anymore. They'll demand Sharia Law and Europe will sink slowly into anarchy. I'm talking ethnic violence, religious bloodletting, our culture destroyed, cities in flames; it'll be the end of everything.'

Ray's voice trailed away as he stared into the middle distance, Danny belted back his champagne, feeling depressed and a little uneasy by Ray's bleak vision. He might even be right, but Danny took comfort from the fact that him and dad would be on the other side of the world, watching it all on the news.

'Nice speech.'

Danny turned around. Marcus had sidled up behind them, a wide smile on his chubby face. 'Lovely spread as usual, Mister Chairman.'

The cheery interruption snapped Ray out of his morbid trance. He waved a hand across the well-stocked tables. 'Help yourself, Marcus.'

'Way ahead of you, Raymondo.' He patted his pot belly, his hand moving to the breast pocket of his shirt. 'Got something for you, Danny. A present.'

'Not here,' Ray snapped. He led them out of the room to the study across the hallway, closing the door behind them.

Danny cocked a thumb over his shoulder. 'I thought they were all friends.'

'Need to know basis,' Ray grumbled. He slipped on a pair of glasses and held out his hand. 'Let's see it.' Marcus handed over a crisp new passport that Ray inspected for several moments. 'Very nice,' he said, offering it to Danny.

Danny flicked through the stiff pages, running a thumb over his subtly altered image, his new date of birth, the name 'EDUARD ZALA'.

A brand new, legit passport; Danny was impressed.

'Well, what d'you think, son?'

'It's perfect, Ray.'

'All legal and above board,' Marcus assured him. 'That's a Slovak name. You could pass for a foreigner with your new look.'

'Cheers,' Danny replied, feeling faintly insulted. He studied his picture again. 'Does this mean I'm leaving soon?'

Ray snatched the passport from Danny's hand and slipped it into his pocket. 'Not just yet. Remember what I said about deeds not words?' Danny nodded. 'Good, because an opportunity has presented itself to us, something that will upset the party mood in Brussels.'

Marcus stared at him and smiled. Danny's throat suddenly felt very dry.

'Really? What's that then?'

Ray turned away and held the door open. The sound of laughter drifted across the hallway. 'All in good time, Danny boy. Let's get back to the party, shall we?'

Marcus smiled and winked. He clapped Danny on the back and ushered him from the room.


Deputy Prime Minister Saeed flicked the embroidered vents of his tunic and gratefully re-took his seat, easing himself into the deep red cushion. It was the twelfth standing ovation since the ceremony had begun and his legs were beginning to tire. A short distance away, EU President Michel Dupont stood behind a bloom of microphones as he delivered a carefully worded address that spoke of peace and unity, of economic progress and the free movement of peoples that would sweep away all borders from the face of Europe. Saeed smiled; if only he realised the gravity of the mistake he was making.

He looked around him, at the other leaders who clapped and cheered their own demise, and felt nothing but contempt for them. At the podium, the President concluded his speech to thunderous applause. One by one, the assembled heads of government stepped forward and signed the Treaty of Cairo, the line of suited dignitaries winding across the stage as the orchestra played softly in the background. As the minutes went by, each signatory stood in front of the marble plinth and made his or her mark on the treaty document, then gathered at the side of the stage. Congratulations were exchanged, hands shaken, backs slapped and cheeks kissed as the signatures on the treaty slowly filled the page. History was being made, and they were all part of it.

Then it was Saeed's turn.

He stepped forward as a cosmic storm of camera flashes lit up the night, twinkling like stars across the desert. He stood behind the plinth for a moment, admiring the rich texture of the treaty document, the rows of swirling signatures, the declaration at its head that would mark a new stage in Europe's long and bloody history. An aide waited, the uniquely crafted Mont Blanc pen held in an outstretched hand. Saeed took it, then scratched his signature across the page next to his printed name. He straightened up and shook the loitering President's hand.

'Congratulations,' beamed Dupont.

'Allahu Akbar,' Saeed murmured in reply.

He saw the President's smile slip a fraction. Any reply,

if one was forthcoming, was lost as fireworks exploded above them, lighting up the night sky in a thunderous storm of noise and colour.

It was a glorious sight. Saeed's senses drank in the celebrations and the smile that creased his face was a genuine one, a triumphant one. The years of hard work, the political deal brokering, the sacrifices of his brothers and sisters, had all amounted to this night.

President Dupont was the first to leave, gliding back towards the air-conditioned comfort of the Egyptian premiere's palace in his black Mercedes limousine. Saeed joined the other leaders as they filed slowly towards the steps at the side of the stage, pressing flesh with many of his colleagues on the way, fawning words dripping in his ears. At the top of the staircase he couldn't help himself; he waved to the ecstatic crowds, energised by their excitement. It was truly an amazing sight.

As he turned to step down he noticed something else that thrilled him. The sight made his heart beat faster, his skin tingle, the hairs on the back of his neck stand on end. Beyond the pillars of the magnificent stage, the flags of every European Union nation hung limply from a forest of flagpoles, teased into occasional life by a sluggish night breeze. It was briefly lit by the last of the fireworks and lost again in the darkness, but Saeed's eye caught it nonetheless. It wasn't there earlier and Saeed assumed that it wouldn't be there much longer, but to those that recognised its significance the point had been made. He smiled.

As he watched, the wind picked up again and the flag unfurled, snapping open to reveal the white *Shahada* inscription emblazoned across a black background. For that briefest of moments, the flag of the *Khilafah*, the global

Islamic state, flew above the unwitting heads of Europe's elite.

Saeed descended the stairs and climbed into his waiting limousine, the smile on his face a little wider.

'WELL GABE, what did you think of that?' Sully got to his feet, stretching his muscular frame.

Bryce shrugged, inspecting his fingernails. Inside, his mind was a whirlwind; Hooper was still across the Atlantic, Tariq in Cairo, the treaty now written into European law; things were happening so fast that Bryce found it hard to focus. He kept one eye on the news ticker at the bottom of the screen. The markets had clearly welcomed the treaty, and the cities of Europe were celebrating events on a breathtaking scale. In London the streets were mobbed and fireworks rippled across the night sky. In a relatively short space of time Britain had been transformed from a land plagued by social division and economic uncertainty to a nation filled with hope. No wonder he was yesterday's man. He'd been banished, in every possible—

'—Gabriel Bryce, who clearly couldn't be here tonight.'

Bryce stiffened, his eyes flicking back to the TV, a studio panel of political commentators grouped around a circular table.

'Yes, unfortunate for the former PM, but our current leader Nigel Hooper chose the memorial service in Washington over one of the most important nights in Europe's history. An inexplicable decision by any standard.'

'What about his live link address?'

'Well, I think that did more to highlight the torrid time he's had in America, rather than show support to the treaty itself. I think it calls into question his political judgment.'

'Another British Prime Minister undone by Cairo?' invited the BBC anchor.

The smug expressions around the table made Bryce twist his fingers in anger. He took a deep breath, aware that Sully was watching him. On TV the debate continued.

'It's now generally accepted that Gabriel Bryce was going to announce his retirement prior to the Downing Street bomb. His continued doubts about the treaty had made him deeply unpopular in the party—'

'Not something a politician likes to hear,' Sully tutted, shaking his head.

Bryce was about to offer a vague answer when a voice on the TV said, '—in light of his recent stroke. Although the security around him remains tight, the reports coming out of Millbank are suggesting that Bryce has suffered considerable mental deterioration.'

'That's right, Jonathon. His weekly blog had become increasingly rambling, sparking concern from several mental health charities over its continued publication.'

Bryce stared at the pundits around the table, the expressions of regret, the shaking heads. *What bloody blog?*

'Yes, it's all quite tragic. Our thoughts and prayers are with him tonight. Now, if we can shift focus back to Cairo, our viewers have been voting throughout the evening on the treaty and Deputy Prime Minister Saeed's performance in Cairo, both given seemingly overwhelming approval. We'll be sharing those results and getting his own reaction to tonight's historic events from the man himself, who'll be joining us live in the next hour—'

The words no longer registered. It all made sense now, a sudden flash of light that banished the shadows of doubt from his mind. Now he knew. The pieces had been swept from the board until only one remained.

*Tariq.*

Tonight he'd witnessed a coronation in all but name.

The TV blinked off. Bryce was rooted to his seat, his legs numb, his eyes fixed to the black screen. He saw his reflection there, a frail shadow he barely recognised. Sully's dark silhouette stood close by, looming over him like an angel of death.

A chill crept up Bryce's spine.

*Death.* That's what Sully represented, what this place had in store for him. He could see it now, as if a map had been rolled out before him. It all seemed so clear, so obvious, that Bryce felt like screaming in frustration. But he didn't. Instead he took a deep breath, his eyes fixed on the lifeless TV. He let the muscles in his face relax, his jaw slacken.

'Gabe?'

Bryce turned his head. 'Did they say my name?'

'Yes,' Sully confirmed. 'You had a stroke, Gabe. The first night, remember?'

Bryce frowned. 'I couldn't move.'

'That's right.' Sully patted him on the arm. 'We're going to get you more pills, Gabe, stronger ones. Make you feel better.'

'A stroke,' Bryce mumbled.

'A bad one. Come on, let's go.' He let Sully help him up and followed him back to the wing. Bryce shuffled along the empty corridors, his hands thrust into the pockets of his dressing gown, slippered feet slapping against the cold linoleum. Sully walked ahead, keys jangling in his hand as he whistled tunelessly. *Dead man walking* – the phrase came to Bryce then, the realisation that his isolated wing had in fact become death row, that he would never again see the outside world. A debilitating stroke followed by significant mental deterioration – they were setting the scene, softening the blow for the day it was officially announced; *former Prime Minister Gabriel Bryce died this morning as a result of a second, massive stroke...*

He cupped a hand over his mouth as the bile bubbled up his throat. Sully grabbed his arm and yanked him into a utility room. Bryce folded over a sink, retching into the basin. He turned the tap, rinsing his mouth as another wave of nausea gripped his stomach and he vomited loudly.

'That's it, get it all out.' Sully took a few paces out into the corridor and tapped his mobile phone. Bryce came up for breath. As he leaned on the sink, his watery eyes roamed the shelves above. There were a few boxes there, brown cartons all clearly labeled; latex gloves, sterile syringes, antiseptic wipes. Instinctively he reached up and rummaged inside, quickly shoving the item into his pocket. He bent over the sink and forced himself to retch again, an ear cocked for the termination of Sully's phone call. When it did he splashed his face with cold water and straightened up. The panic had subsided, the fear momentarily banished, replaced by a clarity of thought that Bryce hadn't experienced in quite some time. A coup had taken place, a coup so obvious that the public were simply blind to it.

'Ready?'

'Something I ate,' Bryce mumbled, rubbing a damp hand around his neck. 'I feel tired.'

Sully led him back to his wing. He locked the gate behind Bryce and spoke to him through the rusted mesh. 'Get some sleep. Nurse will get you started on those new tablets tomorrow.'

Doors slammed and footsteps faded as Sully disappeared into the night. Bryce made straight for his bed, burying himself beneath the thin quilt. He didn't have long, that much was clear, his deterioration now public knowledge. Soon the order would be given, and his life would probably end in this soulless, wretched room. A certificate of death would be issued, arrangements made for a private funeral. Nothing would be questioned, the loose ends taken care of. It had been done before, removing people who threatened covert agendas; a weapons inspector killed in an empty wood, or an RAF Chinook slamming into a Scottish hillside, the end result was always the same. Nothing could be proved, a copious use of the word 'conspiracy' effectively discrediting any meaningful investigation. The dead were mourned and the world moved on.

And who would mourn for Gabriel Bryce? He had no siblings, no parents or children, and if he believed his own theory, Ella would now be a victim too. The flowers on his grave would wilt and die and the moss would creep across the stone to eventually obscure his name. He would be quickly forgotten, a page in history, his legacy one of failure.

He felt the hand of Tariq Saeed on his back, pushing him towards his impending doom. How much he knew, how many others were involved, Bryce could only speculate. The scale of the conspiracy was almost impossible to accept, yet the wheels of state would grind on, the lives crushed beneath its giant cogs of no concern to a population disconnected from the cold realities of modern politics.

With Hooper seemingly discredited it was only a matter of time before Tariq made a move for the premiership, of that Bryce was certain. Before then, the field of play would have to be cleared. Soon the order would be passed, the security gate opened for the final time, Sully's footsteps along the corridor, the angel of death hovering at the foot of his bed. Bryce felt a mixture of emotions: fear initially, then despair, and finally anger. No, he wouldn't make it easy for them, wouldn't allow them to dictate the time and place of his own demise. If it were to be his final act, then at least he would have control over its execution.

Under the covers of his bedding Bryce eased the hypodermic needle and syringe from its shrink-wrapped packaging and secreted them inside the frayed lining of his mattress.

## 15

## LONDON

The Gulfstream descended rapidly through the clouds to reveal a miserable landscape of steel grey seas and dark, oppressive skies. The aircraft banked into a steep turn, skimming above the white horses that galloped across the sea below.

Tariq Saeed watched from the window as the plane levelled out, effortlessly gliding along its priority-landing path towards London International. He was always impressed by the feat of engineering that straddled the Thames Estuary, a glass and steel city of lights sprinkled across the cold waters of the North Sea like a modern day Atlantis. He pulled his seat belt a little tighter, careful not to crease his shirt. He was dressed more conservatively than recent appearances in Egypt; a charcoal grey suit, white shirt and a dark blue tie. Serious, sober, assured; that was the impression he chose to convey today.

Beneath him he felt the landing gear thump into place, saw rolling waves exploding into white spray against the giant rocks of the outer breakwater. He closed his eyes for a moment, his pulse quickening as he contemplated the morning ahead.

He'd enjoyed three days of private meetings and spiritual contemplation in Cairo, hidden behind a smokescreen of diplomacy and trade talks, purposely delaying his return to the UK. In his absence, Nigel Hooper had been forced to weather the storm of his disastrous transatlantic trip alone. The cancer of political failure had already taken its toll; advisors had jumped ship, his Chief Press Officer resigning for 'personal reasons', his handpicked team of sycophants overwhelmed by the relentless pressure of the media.

Hooper had called Saeed in Cairo, at first demanding, then practically begging him to come home, but Saeed had stalled. The tactic had worked, his informants reporting a series of bad-tempered meetings, of expletive-riddled phone calls and hurled objects. Hooper was cracking fast, and while the man who would be king paced the floor of his office in Millbank, Hooper's rattled wife was under similar siege, door-stepped at every opportunity by a persistent press. Saeed smiled; it was all coming apart so graphically, so predictably. The Hoopers had been elevated far above their station, but now they'd served their purpose it was time to bring them crashing down.

The Gulfstream returned to earth with a gentle bump, rolling along the slick black tarmac and taxiing to a halt outside the VIP terminal building that glowed in the half-light of a cold December morning. His BMW limousine waited on the apron, flanked by several black Range Rovers and police cars manned by heavily armed officers. Saeed buttoned his jacket as he trotted down the steps, the memory of Cairo's balmy climate snatched away by a stiff northwesterly. The estuary wind whipped across the tarmac, bringing with it the roar of an Emirates Airbus taking off from a nearby runway. Saeed paused for a moment, watching the double-decked airliner tilt skywards, clawing its way through the grey ceiling above, no doubt headed for the warmth of the Gulf. Saeed felt a pang of envy.

He ducked inside the BMW's soundproofed interior and moments later the convoy was headed at speed towards the causeway road and the distant Kentish shoreline. Saeed pressed the intercom button.

'How long?'

'Forty minutes,' his driver replied. 'Traffic's a little heavy this morning.'

'Take your time.'

He glanced out of the window as the convoy hummed along the wide causeway. Far beyond the guardrail a legion of offshore wind turbines spun steadily, and sea birds wheeled in the sky above. A miserable day, Saeed mused, for Hooper at least. And it was about to get a lot worse.

The journey by car was designed to increase the Prime Minister's frustration, his sense of isolation. As if on cue, the mobile in Saeed's hand vibrated with a new message; Hooper had erupted behind the doors of his office, a loud and abusive exchange with the wife—excellent news. Moments later the phone rang, and Saeed saw it was Hooper. He let the call ring out, and the two subsequent calls, knowing it would send the man's blood pressure sky rocketing. Saeed then made several calls himself, to the Privy Council, the Supreme Court, the Attorney General's office and others. Everything was prepared.

The cavalcade hissed along the Whitechapel Road, sirens clearing a noisy path into the city. Curious faces lined the route, early morning commuters, market vendors and shopkeepers, drawn by the spectacle of a powerful, fast moving convoy. Saeed stared back; so much had changed in Britain, and particularly here in London's East End. The faces he saw were like his own, the shops a colourful mixture of food markets and takeaways, electronic goods stores and clothing emporiums, the signs in Bengali, Urdu and Arabic. Bunting crisscrossed the street, a leftover from the celebrations of last week.

As they passed a side street Saeed caught a glint of the dome above the new East London mosque. He craned his neck, catching it again as they slowed for a busy intersection. He thought it looked splendid, the burnished gold metal reflecting ambient light even on such a grey day, the minarets dominating the local skyline. As they should.

Soon the suburbs were left behind, the convoy snaking through the city and into Whitehall, gliding past the bomb damaged Ministry of Defence and Richmond House buildings that were still undergoing refurbishment. However it was the opposite view that gave Saeed the most satisfaction. Behind the fences, surrounded by men in hard hats and heavy equipment, what little remained of Downing Street was held upright by an intricate mesh of scaffold tubes and steel supports, blanketed in white plastic sheeting like a sick patient wrapped in bandages. The surrounding Cabinet and Foreign Office buildings had been partially demolished, creating unobstructed views across St. James Park. Some said the bomb had ripped the very heart out of London. Saeed preferred to think of it as surgery, intrusive and painful, yet ultimately necessary.

Outside Millbank the BMW glided to a halt, advisors scurrying towards Saeed's car, umbrellas braced against the wind and rain. The Deputy Prime Minister climbed out and they moved en-masse towards the building, crossing the lobby in a damp procession. Saeed headed straight to his office on the twenty-fifth floor and closed the door. He ordered coffee and a Danish, flicking through the TV channels until he settled on the BBC's Middle East roundup. He'd been watching for less than three minutes when the phone rang. Saeed muted the TV.

'Yes?'

'Sir, I have the Prime Minister on line one.'

'Put him through.'

A click, then Hooper's voice, sharp, edgy. 'Tariq?'

'Good morning, Nigel.'

'I need you up here. Now.'

'On my way.'

Saeed replaced the receiver and leaned back in his chair, savouring his first coffee of the day. Five minutes became ten, then fifteen. The phone rang again but Saeed ignored it. Instead, he used a key to open his desk drawer and extracted the folder that had been placed there while he was in Cairo. He flicked through its contents, satisfied that everything was in order. It was time.

He took the elevator to the twenty-sixth floor. The first desks he saw were empty, papers scattered in disarray across them, the phones pulsing and warbling, calls unanswered. Only one or two of the Prime Minister's personal staff were at their desks, their faces drawn with fatigue, phones clamped to their ears, talking in hushed tones. He glanced towards the kitchen, where a group of men and women huddled together behind the glass wall, seemingly locked in heated discussion. Saeed recognised several of them, key advisors from Domestic Policy, Communications, and the European Secretariat. One of them saw Saeed and the others turned, their expressions startled, embarrassed, scattering from the kitchen like frightened mice. There was a sense of panic in the air, of desperation. Saeed likened it to the last days of the Third Reich, the rats buried in their hole, nervously awaiting the end.

Hooper's secretary stood behind her desk, chattering on a phone. Behind her he could hear Hooper's muffled voice through the thick mahogany doors of his private office. On seeing him the secretary quickly ended her call, smoothing her skirt and blouse as he approached. She stood smiling in front of him, hands clasped together.

'Welcome back, sir.'

'Thank you, Polly.'

'Congratulations on your trip to Cairo,' she gushed, chestnut ringlets bobbing like springs around her face.

'A great day for Europe.'

'And for you.'

'How is he?'

Polly lowered her voice. 'Losing control. His personal numbers and email addresses were leaked as instructed, as well as Millie's diary. Since then the press has been relentless. He's no longer taking calls from anyone, except you. He's been trying to contact you since you landed.' She glanced toward the double doors. 'He's drinking too. Nothing excessive, but the signs are there.'

Saeed nodded. 'Okay Polly, I'll take it from here. We'll need complete privacy. No interruptions at all.'

'Yes, sir.'

Saeed paused outside Hooper's office. 'And get a message out, would you? I expect to see people working, not gossiping around the water cooler. There's still a country to be run.'

'Of course.'

Saeed rapped on the PM's door and stepped inside.

It was a huge office, an executive corner suite with a private bathroom that offered stunning views across an impressive swathe of London skyline. Nigel Hooper stood with his back to the room, staring out through the glass wall, shirtsleeves rolled to the elbows, his hands thrust into his pockets. He wore wide spotted braces over a heavily creased blue shirt, the armpits already damp with sweat. He turned his bald dome towards the door and Saeed noted the perspiration on his brow, the tie dragged from the neck, the open shirt collar. The man was a mess.

'Well, well, the prodigal son returns.'

Saeed said nothing. He took a seat in front of the Prime Minister's desk, an enormous teak affair piled high with reports, ministerial papers and folders, with discarded sweet wrappers and dirty coffee cups, with a plethora of Polly's hand written post-it notes demanding decisions and actions. Across the room was a large conference table, littered with a dozen broadsheets. For Hooper, none of them held good news. A bank of TV screens mounted on an aluminium pole stood in the corner of the room like a high-tech coat stand, each tuned to a different news channel. Saeed saw himself in Cairo, signing the treaty and waving to jubilant crowds. In glaring contrast he saw Hooper and his wife on another, puffing up the steps of a British Airways Dreamliner, not leaving the shores of the United States with statesmanlike dignity but rather as fugitives, undercover of night. Then there was Whelan, his stark mug shot superimposed over patrolling policemen at ports and airports. The screens resembled a living chessboard, all the pieces still in play, the game converging towards its predictable conclusion.

'Where the hell have you been?'

Saeed turned away from the TV. 'Good to see you, Nigel. How are you?'

Hooper flopped into the heavy black leather chair

behind his desk, the tortured mechanism squealing in protest.

'Cut the bullshit, Tariq. Where have you been?'

Saeed shrugged. 'Cairo.'

Hooper banged his fist on the desk. 'Don't be bloody facetious. You should've been here. I need you.'

'And I needed time to think.'

Hooper threw his arms up in the air. 'Think? Really? Well, join the bloody club. That's all I've been doing for the past week while you've been basking in glory.' He rubbed his face in exhaustion, breathing heavily. When he spoke again his voice had lost some of its edge.

'I'm sorry, Tariq. That was uncalled for.' He grabbed the desk and pulled himself in, toppling a stack of papers onto the floor. He didn't seem to notice at all. 'All this shit is getting on top of me. Those bastard journalists won't leave me alone, and I've lost half my team through resignations or sickness, which is bullshit, fucking cowards. I'm like a fucking leper here.'

He peeled a post-it note from his computer, read it, then crushed it in his hand.

'This is all because of Washington. What a stupid, stupid idea that was. Jesus Christ.' Hooper rubbed his temples, as if he could physically massage the memory from his mind. 'A monumental fuck-up from the moment I got there. I assume you're familiar with the details?' Saeed pulled an uncertain face. 'Well, it wasn't pleasant, I can tell you. They seated us a dozen rows back during the memorial service, wedged between the Croatian Ambassador and some tin pot general from Zambia who spent half the service leering at Millie. The fucking Yanks kept calling me Prime Minister *Hopper,* and to cap it all Vargas refused a private audience, even after I'd sent the Ambassador to petition him on my behalf. I nearly choked on the humiliation. As for Millie, well, the less said the better.'

Hooper banged his fist on the desk, sending more papers spilling onto the carpet. 'They're calling me star-struck, arrogant, and now the media are blaming me for souring the Special Relationship. I should've concentrated on Cairo, made that my focus. Why did I bother with Washington? Why?'

The Prime Minister shoved his chair back and crossed to the window. He stood there for several moments, watching rain flurries lash against the glass. Saeed waited in silence, his fingers tracing the edge of the folder in his lap.

'I've been thinking about the treaty,' Hooper said eventually. 'I want to tap into its success, exercise some damage limitation. There's work to do on the trade talks, yes?'

'Some low level stuff,' confirmed Saeed.

Hooper waved the observation away. 'I want you to organise a trip to Cairo, arrange something with Bakari, throw in a speech or two, a photo-op around the pyramids. You know the drill.'

Saeed almost laughed. Hooper's naivety was breathtaking. 'That's a bad idea, Nigel. The moment has passed, the stage dismantled. Besides, President Bakari is embarking on a tour of the Gulf States next week. There'll be no one at home.'

'Shit!' Hooper fumed. 'Okay, we'll organise something else, a state dinner perhaps, right here in London; Egyptian Ambassador, EU delegates, all the players. You can open with a few remarks about Cairo, then big up my role in its ratification. I know you did a lot of the leg work Tariq, but that was your job, right?'

Saeed said nothing, allowing Hooper to indulge his fantasies.

'I'll start with a few words about Washington, gloss over the diplomatic fuck-ups, emphasise the fact that I wasn't acting in self-interest. That I spoke to you every night when you were in Cairo.'

'But you didn't,' Saeed pointed out.

Hooper's eyes narrowed. 'I know that. Play along.'

'Why would I do that?'

The wind buffeted the glass, driving the rain before it. Hooper's large frame stood silhouetted against the window, hands on hips, legs apart. Saeed thought he looked ridiculous, like a West End player about to break into an absurd dance routine. There was a look of disbelief on his face, too, as if he hadn't heard properly.

'Why?' Hooper marched across the room towards the conference table, snatching up a newspaper in his large hands. He spread it wide so Saeed could read the headline: *Hooper we have a problem: PM misses NASA tribute as plane suffers technical fault.*

'No? Still not getting it?' Hooper flung the paper away, its sheets scattering across the carpet. 'How about this one?' *Hooper implicated in veteran compensation scandal*, the headline screamed. 'How the fuck did they get hold of that story?'

Saeed had already seen it, the leaked tariff reduction emails, Hooper's unguarded comments about legless squaddies demanding lottery-sized payouts causing particular offence amongst the Armed Forces and the public in general.

'Actually, it was me who leaked that particular piece.'

Hooper's face reddened. 'You did what?'

'There'll be others too, unless you do the right thing.'

Saeed opened the folder on his lap and handed Hooper a cream-coloured envelope.

'What's this?'

'Your resignation letter. Please read and sign at the pencil mark.'

Hooper didn't speak for several seconds, his eyes flicking between Saeed and the envelope. He sat down behind his desk, tore it open and read the contents. He peered over the top of the page. 'Is this some sort of joke?'

'No joke,' confirmed Saeed. 'Please sign where indicated.'

He watched Hooper re-read the letter, the carefully worded text on rich cream paper bearing the Prime Minister's seal, his full title clearly displayed below the small pencil cross. The letter gave no specific reasons for the resignation, only that the decision hadn't been taken lightly and was to be effective immediately. Hooper dropped the letter as if it were coated in poison.

'You're out of your tiny mind.'

'This isn't up for discussion, Nigel. Sign it and go now, today. It's in your own interests. And in the interests of the country, of course.'

Hooper leaned over his desk. Saeed noted the thick, hairy forearms, the huge dome of a head, the hair spilling out of the collar of his shirt. He was like an ape, Saeed observed, a sweaty, uneducated ape. He caught the odour of stale coffee as Hooper barked at him.

'Who the hell do you think you are, Tariq? You think your little song and dance in Cairo has given you the balls to challenge me? How fucking dare you.'

'You're out of your depth, Nigel. Everyone knows it except you. Go now and you'll get to keep your pension, walk away with whatever dignity you have left. Fight me on this and you're finished.'

'Fuck you!'

Hooper swept the desk clear with a furious hand, scattering folders and papers onto the carpet. Saeed turned towards the door, towards the frosted glass where the opaque circle of Polly's face was frozen outside the room.

'I suggest you calm down, Nigel.'

Hooper scooped up the resignation letter and stuffed it back into its envelope. He skimmed it across the desk and it dropped to the floor. 'Change of plan; I want your resignation, you jumped-up little shit.'

Saeed took a deep breath and sighed. He'd been expecting this, the anger, the desperation. He knew Hooper wouldn't go willingly, so now it was time to up the ante. He got to his feet, extracting several documents from the folder, and laid them carefully across the recently cleared space on Hooper's desk. The Prime Minister frowned, the boiling anger suddenly tempered by confusion.

'What's this?' he growled.

Saeed laid the final item down, a large envelope, then spread his hands across the table, like a magician presenting his opening illusion. 'It's a road map, a route you will travel if you refuse to go quietly.'

Hooper snatched up the first document as Saeed explained. 'That one is the order to have Gabriel Bryce removed to an NHS psychiatric facility, signed and dated by you. Attached is a printout of the confidential email ordering me to begin the process.' Saeed's finger traced over the documents along the desk.

'This is a printout of the visitor's log at Chequers, recording Duncan Parry's stay.'

'Duncan?'

'That's right. He's signed an affidavit, stating that you forced him to circumvent admission procedures and accept Bryce as a patient in the name of national security. I've done the same, expressing my deep disquiet as to your motives and my concern for Gabriel Bryce's health. These documents were drafted and lodged with the Attorney General's office at the time. They will remain in her possession, sealed, as long as you announce your resignation today.'

Hooper's face had turned from puce to ash white in less than a minute. He picked up the papers one by one, his disbelieving eyes scanning their contents, turning them over in his sweaty hands as if careful scrutiny would reveal them to be forgeries. Finished, he let them fall to the table. 'All this was your idea, Tariq. The only way to guarantee Cairo, you said. Take the country forward.'

'If you recall, you were more concerned about Washington than Cairo, which was why a message was conveyed to President Vargas before your visit.'

'What message?'

'It was felt that the White House should be given the opportunity to distance itself from any potential scandal. Your humiliation in Washington is proof that they took that opportunity.'

Hooper's face boiled. 'You fucking snake. You think I'll just bend over, let you fuck me up the arse? I'll bring you down with me, smear you with enough shit to—'

He stopped suddenly, a sneer twisting his mouth. 'I get it now; Prime Minister Saeed, eh? You think that's got a nice ring to it? You like the look of this office?' He jabbed a finger towards Saeed's chest. 'The bright lights of Cairo have fried your brain, Minister. You think I'm going to make way for you? Think again.'

Saeed retook his seat. There were only two ways this could go and clearly Hooper wasn't going to take the easy route. 'I'm sorry you feel that way. This country has suffered a lot of turmoil since the terror attacks and Cairo has given us all much hope for the future. You don't figure in that future, Nigel. Your reputation is in the toilet, you've lost the confidence of the party and the people. Even your own staff are jumping ship.'

Saeed shifted in his seat and crossed his legs, brushing a speck of imaginary dust from his trousers. 'Consultations with the Privy Council's office and the Parliamentary Party are complete and unequivocal; Nigel Hooper is a political liability and must be replaced. This afternoon I will issue a statement in the House calling for a vote of no confidence. And I'll get it, Nigel, because the deep disquiet felt by many in regard to your stewardship will not go away. The country has lost faith in your abilities to carry it forward and many European leaders have expressed a reluctance to work with you. As for your international reputation, well, that speaks for itself. But there's more.'

Saeed waved a hand towards the large envelope on Hooper's desk. 'That contains further evidence against you, Nigel, evidence of more nefarious activities carried out in your name.'

Hooper snatched it up and tore it open, the photographs spilling out over the desk. Hooper spread them out and picked one up, his eyes narrowing, then widening as he finally grasped what he was looking at.

'Jesus Christ, is that—?'

'Gabriel Bryce, yes. Evidence of the treatment you condemned him to, his graphic deterioration in that awful facility. It's all there, all engineered by you.'

Hooper let it slip from his fingers. It skimmed the desk and landed by the heel of Saeed's immaculately polished brogue, a disturbing image of Gabriel Bryce, stripped naked and crouched in the dark corner of a padded room, bony arms wrapped around his knees, his eyes pleading, haunted. Even Saeed was shocked when he first saw it.

'Jesus Christ,' Hooper whispered, 'what sort of person are you?'

'There's something else.' Saeed indicated another photograph on the desk. 'You remember this occasion?'

Hooper scooped it up and studied it. 'My last tour of Afghanistan.'

'Correct, taken just before you resigned your commission. An interesting composition, don't you think?'

On the surface the photograph was unremarkable as military photographs went, a couple of dozen soldiers in desert fatigues grouped in front of a large truck, smiling faces, eyes squinting in the harsh Afghan sunlight. Hooper was at the front, overweight even then, arms clasped stiffly behind his back, puffy face glowing in the heat.

'Where did you get this?'

'Millie.'

Hooper's eyes narrowed. 'Excuse me?'

'Your wife has been most co-operative. Washington has made her a laughing stock amongst her peers. She's a very defensive woman, very bitter. And she blames you, of course. I have it on good authority that she's been in contact with a very reputable firm in Lincoln's Inn that specialises in divorce.'

Hooper reacted like he'd been punched. 'She what?'

'Don't be naive, Nigel. We both know that status is the cement that binds your marriage together. That's crumbled now, and Millie is keen to distance herself from your collapse.'

'Selfish fucking bitch,' Hooper growled. 'So she gave you a photo, so what?'

'As I said, an interesting composition; the man at the back, fourth from the left; do you recognise him?'

Hooper shook his head. 'No. Should I?'

'Yes, you should. That's Daniel Whelan.'

Hooper's mouth dropped open. 'Jesus Christ, so it is. I'll be damned.'

'Correct. The photograph connects you to Whelan, to the horror of Luton and Downing Street.'

'Don't be ridiculous,' Hooper snorted.

'Hard to believe, I know, but let's look at the facts. You both served in Afghanistan at the same time—'

'So what?' exploded Hooper, flapping the photograph in the air. 'This was taken at Kandahar. There were thousands of troops there, how the hell am I supposed to remember every man under my command? Especially a fucking private!'

'Coincidentally your careers in Whitehall overlapped too. In fact at one point you both worked in the same building. You see the link now? Somehow access was gained to the government vehicle used in the attack for an extended period of time, which proves Whelan had an accomplice with significant security clearance. The explosive material was military grade, and you have extensive contacts throughout the armed forces in your previous roles as Defence Minister and your service in the Logistics Corps. You avoided the blast itself—'

'Because you called me!'

'—and conveniently assumed authority. Since then, the hunt for the bombers has stalled and Whelan remains at large. A dossier has been compiled. There are grounds for a criminal investigation.'

Hooper dropped heavily into his chair. He looked shell-shocked, defeated. 'This is an outrage. You can't prove a thing.'

Saeed laughed. 'What's the quote, Nigel? *A lie can travel the world while the truth is still tying its shoes?* The truth doesn't matter. Proof doesn't matter. Your reputation is already holed below the waterline and if this goes public you'll sink without trace. The police will want to interview you under caution. With your name already in tatters, the stain of suspicion would be hard to erase, whatever the real truth may be.'

Hooper buried his face in his hands, his breath coming in small gasps. At first Saeed thought he was crying, then changed his assessment to panic. The fight had certainly left him, he could see that now. Still, it wouldn't hurt to turn the screw a little more, just to be sure.

'But it's not just about you, is it Nigel? There are your two young sons to consider, both nicely settled in their new school. Charterhouse, is that right? An outstanding school, however the board will frown upon any association with the Hooper family name and its stench of failure and disgrace. Not a good example for the rest of their young charges, and I'm sure the other parents will have something to say, too. A shame really, and all because their father refused to co-operate for the good of the country.'

Saeed reached down and picked up the resignation letter at his feet. He smoothed it out and passed it across the desk. 'This doesn't have to be messy, Nigel. Sign the letter and leave now, today. Arrangements will be made. You'll be comfortable. Nothing extravagant.'

'What about my boys?'

'They'll stay at Charterhouse, as long as you do as you're told. After all, why should the sons be punished for the sins of the father? Unless, of course, the father decides to open his mouth, in which case their little feet won't touch the ground.'

Hooper slumped further down his chair, like a boxer on his stool, bloodied, beaten, unable to continue the fight. His face was a sickly grey colour, his eyes fixed on the landscape beyond the window. Confusion, disbelief, anger, denial, acceptance; Saeed had seen them all today and in a relatively short space of time. Hooper was a predictable animal and he'd played his role perfectly, but now it was time for the principal to leave the stage. Saeed slipped his mobile from his pocket and punched a number.

'Come up now,' he ordered, ending the call.

Hooper lifted his head. 'Who was that?'

'I have a small team downstairs. Time is of the essence, Nigel, the continuity of government paramount. The office of the Prime Minister is to be reorganised.'

'What happens now?'

'You'll sign the letter, and a car will take you to Chequers. You'll have three days to vacate the premises, after which I suggest a long holiday. Perhaps you'll be able to save your marriage, perhaps not, but you'll talk to no one. A security team will be assigned to you to make sure you keep your mouth shut. Some time in the future you'll be assessed, and maybe a suitable position will be found, strictly supervised of course, but you'll get used to it. The alternative will be much worse, I can assure you.'

Saeed got to his feet and gathered his evidence.

Hooper looked up at him and said, 'Why, Tariq? Why set me up, threaten me, threaten my children? What did I ever do to you?'

Saeed leaned over the desk. He kept his voice low, conscious of the people gathered outside the room. 'The truth is you disgust me, Nigel. For you, the office of Prime

Minister represents nothing more than power and prestige. You're right, I do want this job, but for entirely different reasons than your own.'

Saeed glanced towards the door, The vision never failed to excite him, the opportunity to share it a rare occasion and only in the company of those that strove towards it. He decided to offer Hooper a glimpse before he had him removed from public life. He leaned in close, his voice a whisper.

'Europe is heading in a new direction, Nigel, and this country needs a leader who understands that vision. Not the bureaucratic hallucination that DuPont and those fools in Brussels cling to but something far greater, a historical concept that has fired the imaginations of men for centuries. You think I care about this office and its responsibilities? I couldn't care less. It's nothing but a tool to be used to dismantle the arrogance of the west, to pave the way for something magnificent, a creed that was born in the sands of Arabia and will one day come to rule the world, *Insha'Allah.*'

Saeed straightened up, flushed with righteous contempt for the creature before him and all he represented. 'You're stupid man, Hooper, stupid and arrogant, and now you've served your purpose.' He tapped the resignation letter on the desk. 'Sign it and embrace the obscurity you have been offered.'

Hooper hung his head, arms dangling over the rests of his chair. If he was beaten before, he was well and truly crushed now, Saeed knew. He'd get no more trouble from him.

Hooper raised his tired, bloodshot eyes. 'Give me a couple of minutes, would you Tariq? Allow me to compose myself?'

Saeed glanced at his watch. 'You've got five.'

There were a dozen people settling behind desks in the outer office, all handpicked to take over the running of the Prime Minister's office. Most were communications staff that would disseminate the news of Hooper's resignation to a waiting world. The broadcast would not come as a shock, Saeed knew, because Hooper had performed so badly, and with Christmas around the corner people would soon be preoccupied with their own indulgences. The timing was perfect. Polly moved towards him.

'How is he?'

Saeed smiled. 'Nigel will be leaving us shortly.'

'Leaving?'

'Nigel will tell you himself, I'm sure.'

Polly put a hand to her mouth. 'He's resigning?'

Saeed kept his face neutral. 'Let's just hear what he has to say, shall we?'

He turned towards the door, saw Hooper's bulk hovering behind the frosted panel. Then he heard the lock being thrown. Saeed stepped forward and twisted the brass knob. He turned to Polly. 'Get security up here now.'

There were several thumps from inside the room. Saeed hammered on the thick wood.

'Nigel, open the door. Nigel!'

There was no answer, only several more thumps, each one progressively louder. What was this, some sort of last minute tantrum? Whatever dignity Hooper might've possessed he'd now clearly discarded. Saeed had a mental image of him being led out into the street in handcuffs. Or maybe even a restraining jacket. Perfect.

The loud crash of glass startled everyone.

'Everybody out! Clear the room!' Saeed ordered. Two

security guards appeared, dark suited, wide shouldered. Saeed pointed to the thick double doors. 'Break it down.'

The men set about the task with relish, taking turns to aim ferocious kicks against the brass mechanism. Within thirty seconds both men were sweating, a minute, panting for breath, their faces twisted in anger. Then the wood splintered, cracking like a pistol shot. Another well-aimed foot and the doors flew inward, crashing against the wall. The guards bundled into the room, Saeed behind them.

Everybody froze.

Hooper stood by the broken glass wall as a cold wind barrelled around the room, snatching at newspapers and documents. Saeed noticed Hooper's heavy leather chair was gone, no doubt lying in the street below. Hooper's shoes were inches from the edge, his gaze off towards the distant horizon. Saeed turned to the security guards and ordered them out, to run and fetch help. He took a few paces towards Hooper and stopped. They were alone.

'The police are on their way, ' he said quietly. 'You'll be arrested now. Finished.'

Hooper turned, his eyes brimming with tears of self-pity. Saeed studied him carefully. The psychologists had missed this flaw in Hooper's profile, a defect suddenly so tantalising for its potential. There was real despair in those bloodshot eyes, the prospect of a life without meaning, a life lived alone and in disgrace, at the outer fringes of obscurity. Saeed heard the muffled thump of boots on carpet, the rattle of equipment in the outer office. He waved the police officers back and took a step closer. Hooper's eyes shifted, locking with Saeed's, searching for something, for hope perhaps, or forgiveness, and finding none. Saeed's lips moved, the words uttered softly.

'Do it.'

Hooper's eyes shifted to the uniforms that filled the outer office and a sob caught in his throat. His shirt soaked by the invading rain, his tie flapping wildly in the wind, Nigel Hooper closed his eyes, took a sharp breath, and stepped over the window ledge.

# 16

## HERTFORDSHIRE

DANNY'S FINGERS TRACED THE GREEN PLASTIC CABLE, probing the prickly branches of the Christmas tree – an imported Norway spruce, according to Ray – until he found the offending bulb. Its tiny filament was burnt out, so he replaced it with another and threw the switch. The room now bathed in the soft glow of decorative lights, Danny stood back to admire his handiwork. All he had to do now was hang a few baubles, put the fairy on top, then hoover up the two million needles that had fallen off while he fixed the stupid lights.

Real trees were a pain in the arse. Danny smiled as he remembered a drunken Christmas a few years ago, the spontaneous purchase of a genuine fir outside the Kings Head, the trail of dead needles as he dragged the thing back to the flat. Dad had roared with laughter, and they'd made a valiant attempt to decorate the sorry-looking tree as it stood almost naked in the living room. That had been a good Christmas. Danny tried to recall exactly what year that was but failed, the annual celebrations now jumbled into a confusing mix of fleeting memories, most of them spent stoned and pissed in the King's Head. But this year would be different, he was sure of that.

He positioned the golden angel at the top of the tree and turned off the rest of the lights around the room. Danny smiled. Now it felt like Christmas.

Behind him, Tess poked her head around the door.

'Danny love, can you – oh wow!'

She swished into the room, bundled up inside a green parka and a white roll-neck sweater. Her cheeks were flushed red, her eyes fixed on the glowing, sparkling evergreen that reached majestically towards the high ceiling. 'Oh Danny, that's beautiful, really lovely. You've done a wonderful job.'

'Cheers, Tess.'

'Ray's useless at that sort of thing,' she said, making her own delicate adjustments to the decorations. 'You've got a real eye for it, though.'

'Took me ages,' Danny confessed. 'To tell you the truth I had a spot of bother with—'

'Jesus, look at the mess on my good carpet.'

'Well, it's a real tree, Tess.'

'I know what it is, Danny. Just get it cleaned up, before Ray sees it. And when you're done, the pickup needs unloading.'

'Sure.'

Danny shook his head behind Tess' departing back. Scolded like a bloody footman, for Christ's sake. And it wasn't the first time. Tess had been really nice from day one, but since the party she'd cooled towards him. Ray too. Something wasn't right.

It took ten minutes with the Dyson before Danny was satisfied the carpet was needle-free. Outside, the light was fading fast and the freezing rain threatened to turn to sleet.

The rear of the Nissan was filled with carrier bags bulging with groceries, and it took several trips before he'd piled everything onto the kitchen's impressive centre island.

'There, all done,' he puffed.

'Thanks,' Tess mumbled, tapping away at her mobile phone. 'Put the meat away, would you, love?'

'Sure.' He rummaged through the bags, found several packs of fresh chicken breast. 'Fridge or freezer?'

'Pop 'em in the freezer, please. Ray's organised a couple of turkeys for Christmas Day.'

Danny stacked them neatly inside the icy compartment and closed the door. 'You expecting many this year?'

Tess shook herself out of her parka and began putting the groceries away. 'There'll be eight of us on Christmas Day and about twenty for the party on Boxing Day.'

'Nice,' Danny smiled. 'My dad usually does Christmas dinner, but he's not the best cook in the world. He usually sleeps all afternoon too, so I'm sort of on me own. It'll be different this year. I'm looking forward to it.'

Tess paused as she emptied another bag on the counter. 'I don't think you'll be joining us, Danny. Sorry, love.'

Danny felt it again, a strange tension between them. 'Oh,' was all he could manage to say.

Outside the security light blazed into life and Ray stepped in through the back door, his Barbour jacket and Bushman hat spotted with raindrops. 'Jesus, it's freezing out there.' He slammed the door behind him and pecked his wife on the cheek. 'Did you get everything?'

Tess smiled. 'Pretty much. Shops are nightmare busy.'

'Must be Christmas,' Ray teased.

'I told Danny he wouldn't be joining us this year.'

Danny caught the look between them and began to feel uneasy. Ray steered him towards the back door. 'I think it's time me and Danny had that little chat,' he told Tess. 'Would you give Joe a buzz, ask him to join us in the garage?'

Danny followed Ray around the side of the house, snapping the collar of his jacket up as another belt of rain swept overhead, lashing the driveway in cold sheets. He didn't feel cold, just apprehensive. *A little chat.* People only said that when they had bad news. Something was coming his way.

The garage was hidden behind a neat row of conifers that swayed and hissed in the wind. It was a single-storey construction, its corrugated metal roof slick with rain. Danny had never been inside. Ray used a key to unlock the large sliding door and yanked it open. He ducked to his left as an urgent beeping echoed around the darkness. Danny stepped out of the rain, his boots echoing on the concrete floor, as Ray disabled the alarm system. Despite the gloom he could see a vehicle covered with a tarpaulin.

'That's a Vauxhall under there,' Ray said.

A figure loomed in the doorway and Joe appeared, wet hair plastered to his head, dressed in his usual combat jacket and jeans, the Mossberg slung across his back.

'Get the door, please Joe.'

Fluorescent lights overhead buzzed and blinked into life. Danny thought the garage looked pretty normal. The cinderblock walls were lined with Jerry cans, oil drums, agricultural equipment and various motor spares. To his left a workbench ran the length of the wall, covered in a mess of technical manuals, tools, various sprays and tins of paint, and the obligatory oily rags. Normal, Danny thought. Yet something wasn't right. And what was Joe doing here?

Ray slapped his hat down on the workbench, gripped one end with both hands and pulled it outwards. That was when Danny noticed the hinged end section, the wheels disguised in the thick legs; very clever. Ray squatted down near the wall and lifted out a large cutaway built into the concrete floor. He rummaged inside the recess, then laid two items on the bench's chipped and oily surface. The first was clearly a pistol, its undeniable shape wrapped in a faded green cloth. The second was a black plastic shock-proof case. He brushed his hands on the legs of his corduroy trousers.

'This is it, Danny. This is what it's all been about.'

Danny stared at the cloth. 'What's the gun for, Ray?'

'I'll get to that.'

He brushed past Danny and dragged the tarpaulin off the car. It was a Vauxhall as Ray had said, a modest four-door estate, dark blue, the type used by families with small children.

'You driven one of these before?'

Danny shrugged. 'Sure.'

'This one is clean, registered to a British born Slovakian called Eduard Zala, the name in your new passport.' He fumbled in the pocket of his Barbour and handed the document to Danny. 'There you go. You'll need that. Right now the real Eduard Zala— who incidentally shares a credible likeness with you—has taken his family back to the mother country for Christmas to see his folks. Which means that for a short window, you can be Eduard.' He rapped his knuckles on the bonnet. 'This vehicle has been modified with hidden storage compartments, one under here, the other beneath the steering wheel. That one's for the gun, just in case you need to get to it quickly.'

Danny could feel his heart beating fast in his chest. 'What's this about, Ray?'

'Remember when I spoke about deeds, not words? Well, that time is now. Scroll through those.' Ray handed over a smart phone. Danny took it and started flicking through the images on the screen.

'What you're looking at is the interior of the Muslim Council of Regional Representatives' building in Birmingham. Now, in their ongoing efforts to integrate with British society, the Council has decided to ignore the holidays and hold their annual General Meeting over Christmas. Keep scrolling, Danny.'

He did as he was told, noting the long carpeted hallways, the prayer hall and conference rooms. There were other shots of ceiling vents and pipe works, of maintenance covers and plant equipment.

'The plan is this; on Christmas Eve you'll travel up to Birmingham in the Vauxhall. You'll go to the Council building after nine o'clock that evening, posing as an air con engineer attending a call-out. Don't worry, you'll have all the necessary paperwork. Now, as well as their own guys there'll be a local bobby on the main gate, provided at the taxpayers' expense to provide high-visibility security and kiss the community's collective arse. That's where the passport comes in. Once you're through security you'll head to the plant room on the roof. There you'll find an access hatch near the main condenser. All the plans are right there.'

'But I'm a wanted man,' Danny said.

Ray shook his head. 'They're looking for the fugitive Danny Whelan, not an engineer from Kent. You'll be fine.'

Danny's eyes flicked between Ray and the images on the screen. 'What is it you want me to do at this place? A bit of vandalism? Flood the building?' He hoped—prayed— it was nothing more.

'Vandalism?' Ray glanced at Joe. 'Is he having a laugh?' The smile slipped from his face like melted wax. 'You think I'd go to all this trouble just to break a couple of fucking windows? No, this is bigger, Danny. More your style. Take a look at this.'

He snapped open the black case on the workbench. Inside was a plastic container nestled in foam. On its uppermost surface, fixed into position with blue electrical tape, was a small digital timer.

Danny took a step back, his bearded face draining of colour.

'Jesus.'

'Relax, it's not armed.'

'Is that what I think it is?'

'Not quite. It does possess some explosive properties but essentially it's just a plastic container. It's what's inside it that matters.'

'Inside?'

'The ingredients, Danny. The cocktail.'

Danny's face was a blank canvas. 'What?'

'For fucks sake, I thought you'd be used to all this,' Ray bristled. 'It's a bio-weapon.'

Danny said nothing, just stared at the device as his mind struggled to process what he was hearing. Beside him Ray filled in the blanks.

'Technically it's an organophosphate pesticide derivative, but you don't need to know that. All you need to do is place the device behind the correct inspection hatch, remove a few filters and set the timer. Twelve hours later, in the middle of the Council's scheduled meeting, this little baby will go off with a quiet pop and start working her magic. The ventilation system will do the rest. I'm told the nerve agent will fully disperse around the main conference chamber within an hour. With luck, if it doesn't dilute too quickly, it'll claim a few more lives around the rest of the building. We're talking about a hundred casualties, maybe a hundred and fifty.'

Danny said nothing for a long time, his stomach churning, his heart beating loud in his chest. Several times his mouth moved to form words, but no sound made it past his bloodless lips.

'Now, I don't want you to worry,' Ray urged, easing the phone from Danny's frozen fingers. 'We're going to spend the next couple of days going over the details. I've rigged up a dummy inspection hatch too, so you can familiarise yourself with the positioning of the weapon. It'll be a doddle. And you'll have the gun, of course, as a last resort.'

'Nerve agent?' Danny finally managed to say.

Ray smiled. 'Now you're getting it. Improvised, but very effective. Am I right Joe?'

The ex-soldier nodded eagerly. 'That's right. Early symptoms are breathlessness, fatigue, bronchial problems. Later they'll begin vomiting, then bleeding from every fucking orifice in their bodies. It's a slow, nasty way to die. Untreatable too. Bonus.'

Danny had never seen Joe so animated. His eyes burned brightly, his cheeks flushed with hatred. Ray smiled along with Joe like some sick father and son double act.

'It's a first-strike weapon,' Ray added, snapping the case shut. 'This goes under the bonnet of the Vauxhall.' He unwrapped the firearm and handed it to Danny. 'That's an Accu-Tek semi-automatic. Go on, get a feel for it, son.'

'Point three-two calibre, twelve round mag,' Joe explained. 'Designed more for concealment than firepower, but it'll do the job if you run into trouble.'

'Ideally, you'll come back with all twelve rounds,' Ray said. 'Keep it with you from now on, alright?'

Danny stared at the pistol in his hand, dumbfounded.

Ray laughed and threw an arm around his shoulders. 'Look at him. Cool as a bloody cucumber this one, eh Joe?' His eyes bored into Danny's, his fingers strong through the material of his jacket. When he spoke it was with a passion that Danny found unnerving. Frightening.

'There'll be other jobs after this one, son. With Hooper offing himself and that Paki bastard stepping into his shoes, the time has come to make our voice heard.' Ray screwed up his face. 'Tariq Saeed, I ask you; what sort of name is that for a British Prime Minister?'

'Fucking disgrace,' Joe grumbled.

'Everything's ready, Danny, the money, the technical support, the weapons. This country is about to witness a campaign of terror the like of which has never been seen before.'

'What do you mean?' Danny managed to stutter.

'I mean violence, Danny. Riots, street battles, pitching community against community, igniting the tensions that people pretend don't exist. And you'll be right at the heart of it, a new name, a new face for every operation. By the time I've finished, the inner-cities will burn and the streets will run with blood.'

Ray took a moment, clearly savouring the images of violence in his mind. Then he smiled and spread his arms wide.

'And then, when things can't get any worse, Raymond Carver will rise like a phoenix from the ashes, stepping into the light to lead a new party, one that will banish Britain's multicultural experiment to the dustbin of history. I'll promise peace and prosperity, a reboot of British power and influence, a government free from the iron grip of Brussels. And people will flock to us, yes they will, because they'll want to see an end to the violence, to unbridled immigration and the rape of our laws and customs. The people of this land deserve something better, and I'm going to give it to them.'

Ray grasped Danny's hands, the light shining in his eyes. 'I can't tell you how proud I am of you, Danny, for Luton, for Downing Street. You're doing God's work, son. We're about to embark on a Crusade, and the Lord has looked down from on high and sent me a true Christian soldier.'

The rain pummelled the roof, the wind whistling through the cracks and gaps. Danny looked at the shock-proof case, at the gun in his hand, at Joe's cruel grin. Finally he looked at Ray. 'But you don't even go to church.'

The big man frowned, then let go of Danny's hands. 'What's that got to do with anything?'

Danny shook his head. 'I told you before, Ray. I had nothing to do with Luton *or* Downing Street.'

'It's alright, son, you can drop the act. You're amongst friends here.'

'You're not listening to me, Ray.'

The older man gripped his arms, his cold eyes searching Danny's face.

'I get it, Danny. Trust takes a long time to nurture before it can really take root. You came here, to me, when your support network crumbled in the wake of the bombs. You trusted me to keep you out of harm's way, to feed you, put clothes on your back. I saw that as a test, Danny, a test of my own resolve, my own commitment to the cause. I've never once asked you about Luton or Downing Street, because I wasn't privy to the details of those operations. Who was it, by the way? Who were the principals?'

'The what?'

'Who organised those jobs, funded them? Whoever it

was they'd be proud of you, son, keeping your mouth shut like this. But it's time to move on, continue the struggle they started.'

Danny shrugged himself out of Ray's hands and took another step back. When he spoke he did so slowly, deliberately. 'I need you to listen to me, Ray. I was fitted up over Luton. I thought I was delivering a fridge, that's all. I never knew it was a bomb, and if I did I would've gone straight to the police. As far as Downing Street is concerned, I know absolutely nothing about it. Nothing, do you understand?' He pointed to the shockproof case. 'This mission of yours, I won't do it. I don't care whether they're Muslims or Jedi bloody Knights, I'm not a murderer, Ray. I'm not who you think I am. I'm just a normal geezer. '

Ray stood completely immobile, his tanned face a mask of confusion. After a moment he began shaking his head.

'No, you're wrong. You're one of us.'

Danny held out the pistol. 'Take it, Ray, please. I promise I'll walk out of here now and forget everything I've seen and heard. I'll pack my bag tonight, take my chances on the road. I'll get out of your life for good, Ray, and I promise I'll never mention this place to anyone, ever. All I need is a few quid to—'

'Shut up!' barked Ray. The rain had intensified, hammering the roof in noisy waves. All three men stood in silence. Water dripped from their coats, forming oily pools on the ground. Ray stared at Danny for a long time.

'You did it,' he decided, poking a finger at Danny. 'You've got contacts in the military, drove government vehicles. They found plans for the mosque hidden in your flat.'

'They planted all that!' Danny protested. 'What the fuck do I know about architect drawings or making bombs? I'm nothing, Ray. A nobody.'

Ray didn't say anything. He just stared at Danny, stroking his jaw, breathing heavily, like he'd just walked up a long flight of steps. Joe stood off to one side, the Mossberg now cradled in his arms. He was like a faithful pet, his cold eyes switching between Ray and Danny, between master and trespasser. Danny tried to ignore him, ignore the gun that could cut in him half.

'Let me get this straight, Danny; you *didn't* carry out the Luton operation?'

'Of course not.'

'But you—' Ray stopped himself.

'I didn't do it,' Danny repeated. He saw confusion and disappointment on Ray's face and felt bad for him, as if somehow he'd betrayed him. 'Don't beat yourself up, Ray. The whole country thinks I did it. No one would blame you for thinking the same.'

'Don't be a fucking smart mouth!' He jabbed a thick finger in Danny's chest. 'You don't know anything.'

Danny didn't like the look on Ray's face, nor the way Joe had changed his grip on the shotgun, the barrel slowly turning in his direction. *Just keep your mouth shut, Danny.* But the words were out before he had time to think.

'I know one thing. I know Tess wouldn't like you doing all this.'

The slap caught him full on the face, sending him staggering backwards. The gun left his hand, skidding across the concrete. Ray moved in quickly, pulling Danny towards him, his fists bunching the coat beneath his chin. Danny could feel the strength in Ray's arms, the hatred in his words.

'Remember Seven-Seven, you little prick? Tess was there when that fucker detonated his bomb at Aldgate tube. Lost half her lower intestine, womb destroyed, killed the baby she was carrying, a little boy. My boy. Don't ever mention my wife's name again.' He shoved Danny against the Vauxhall. 'I could've turned you away, thrown you to the wolves, but no. I took you in, treated you like one of my own, all the time believing that you were a fighter, a true patriot.'

'I am,' Danny protested, his face stinging. 'I just can't do what you—'

'We're at war!'

Danny flinched as a crack of thunder split the air overhead, rattling the roof of the garage. Ray moved closer.

'Don't you get it, you ignorant fuck? I need people like the ones who did Luton and Downing Street, committed soldiers, willing to get down into the trenches, get their hands dirty.' He looked Danny up and down, his mouth twisting into a vicious sneer. 'What I don't need is white trash cowards like you, coming into my home, pretending their something they're not, taking the fucking piss out of me.'

'For Christ's sake, it's not like that!'

Ray turned away, his face in his hands. 'Jesus Christ, what a mug I've been. Why didn't I see it? The arse kissing, the little boy lost routine, I thought it was all an act, some sort of test, but it wasn't, was it? You really are innocent.'

Danny pushed himself off the Vauxhall. He felt the toe of his boot make contact with the pistol. 'That's right, I'm innocent. All this is one huge misunderstanding. So I'm begging you, Ray, help us disappear, my dad and me. To New Zealand, like you promised.'

Ray shook his head and sighed. 'There is no New Zealand, Danny, never was.'

Danny felt as if he'd been punched. 'What d'you mean? It was all bullshit?'

Ray tapped the side of his head. 'Think about it, son—container ships stopping in the English Channel? Are you fucking nuts?'

'But why?'

'It's called incentive. To keep you motivated.'

The storm rumbled on outside. Danny felt the panic rising, the walls closing in around him. He saw Joe put a hand on Ray's shoulder, his dead eyes never leaving Danny's.

'Ray, I think me and Danny should take a walk, let things cool down a bit.'

'A walk,' echoed Ray. 'That's not a bad idea. Give me time to think things through.'

'I was thinking of going down to the plantation.'

Danny's blood ran cold.

*The plantation. The hole in the ground...*

Ray stared at Danny for several moments. Then he shook his head and sighed heavily. 'Okay Joe, you and Danny take yourselves down there. I'll join you in a bit. You got your radio?'

Joe shifted the shotgun and patted his pockets.

Danny didn't hesitate.

He knelt down, cocked the pistol and pulled the trigger, the back of Joe's skull exploding in a puff of red mist, his body folding to the ground. Ray roared and charged forward and the pistol barked again. He hit Danny at full speed, their bodies crashing into the Vauxhall, Ray's hands flailing at Danny's face, strong fingers searching for his eyes, his mouth. Danny twisted his head violently and the pistol cracked a third time. Suddenly Ray's hands went limp and Danny rolled across the dented hood, ears ringing from the deafening gunshots. Cordite lingered on the air.

Ray slithered down the bonnet and flopped onto the

cold floor. His hands shook violently and Danny saw a dark streak had followed him down the paintwork of the car. Ray swore, pushing himself up onto his knees and fumbling with the zip of his Barbour. He felt inside his coat, then winced, pulling his hand away and holding it up in the air. It was bright crimson.

'Jesus, look what you've done,' he rasped, his eyes wide with fear.

'I know about the plantation, Ray, about the hole in the ground. I seen it myself.'

The big man held out a bloody hand. 'Help me up, son.'

Danny shoved the pistol into the waistband of his jeans and went to Ray's side, hefting him up under the armpits of his coat. His corduroy trousers were soaked with blood. Ray draped an arm around Danny's shoulders, his other hand clutching his bloodied belly. 'Get me to the house, Danny. Tess'll know what to do.'

They shuffled awkwardly towards the garage door, Danny struggling under Ray's bulk. He glanced over his shoulder, saw the trail of dark blood behind them. So much blood. Ray staggered.

'Need to take a breather,' he gasped. 'Hurts.'

Danny lowered him to the ground and dragged him towards the wall, resting his back against the cold cinderblock. His face was deathly white, his skin beaded with perspiration. His jaw hung open, a thin stream of saliva dangling from his lip.

'Wait there, Ray. I'm going to run to the house, call an ambulance.'

'No,' Ray croaked, his blood-soaked hand grabbing Danny's wrist. 'There's a doctor...in the village. Tess knows.'

Then he fell sideways, his arms flopping uselessly beside him. He lay on the ground, his bloodshot eyes rolling in their sockets, his mouth moving faintly. Danny leaned over him and loosened his collar. His fingers brushed Ray's neck, the skin cold and damp.

'Where's the first aid kit, Ray? Quickly!'

'Tell Tess...' Ray whispered. 'Tell her I'm sorry...'

His throat rattled, an unnatural sound that frightened Danny. Ray took another breath, more like a short gasp, then his eyes glazed over as the life ran out of him across the concrete floor.

Danny scrambled to his feet, his hands and clothes soaked with blood. He was trapped in a nightmare, his mind frozen by sudden death, by the revelation of Ray's insanity. The man had been good to him, sheltered him, made him feel part of something. Now he was lying dead at Danny's feet, killed by Danny himself, preempting his own demise at the hands of his benefactor. They'd been blind to each other. How was that possible? Why didn't he see this coming? Yet deep down he knew something wasn't right. The signs were there but he'd ignored them, like a smoker with a worsening cough. He'd been in denial all this time—and now he had to run.

The Vauxhall's key was in the ignition and he fired up the engine, He rolled back the garage door and dragged Joe's body out of the way, repulsed by the streak of blood and brain matter left on the floor. The bodies lay side-by-side, mouths open, lifeless eyes staring at the roof. Danny steeled himself, grimacing as he robbed the corpses of their valuables.

A few minutes later he pulled the car around the side of the main house. On the seat next to him was a rucksack, crammed with clothes and a few personal possessions, with Ray's gold chain and Rolex, with a thick wad of cash from the man's pocket. He left the car running and barged into the kitchen, grabbing cartons of orange juice and bottled water and stuffing them into a couple of Tess's large shopping bags. Canned goods were next, his hands fumbling with tins of beans, spaghetti, soup—

'Danny? What the hell do you think you're doing?'

Tess stood in the doorway of the kitchen, a pair of oven mitts tucked beneath her arm. It was only then that Danny noticed the joint in the oven, the smell of roasting meat.

'Tess, I—'

'Jesus, look at my floor!'

Tess marched across the kitchen, grabbing a roll of kitchen towel from the marble worktop and unraveling it across the trail of wet footprints. 'You know better than to come in here with filthy boots,' she puffed.

Then she stopped.

She noticed the shopping bags on the counter, the food bulging inside, the open cupboards. She turned to Danny.

'What are you doing?'

Danny dragged the bags from the counter and stood there, one in each hand. He'd never felt more ashamed in his life.

'What's that on your clothes?' She took a few paces towards him. 'Is that blood on your face?' Her eyes suddenly widened. 'What's happened? Where's Ray?'

Danny bit his lip, unwilling to meet Tess's gaze. 'I should've said yes. I could've taken the car, dumped it, gone on the run again—'

Tess yelled. 'Where's Ray!'

Danny raised his head. 'There's been a terrible accident. It wasn't my fault, I—'

He flinched as Tess gripped his arms and shook him. 'What accident? Where's Ray?'

Danny dropped his eyes, his voice shaking. 'He's in the garage, Tess. I'm so sorry.'

Tess's face was a mask of dread. She ran from the kitchen and disappeared into the darkness, the familiar jingle of her bracelets drowned by the thunder and rain.

*Run, Danny!*

He moved quickly, out to the idling Vauxhall. He selected drive and floored the accelerator, raindrops lancing through the headlights, wipers thrashing the windscreen. At the main gates he stamped on the brakes and leapt out, searching for the control box in the bushes. He located it quickly, cold rain running down his face and neck, his bloodstained fingers fumbling with the controls.

The gates hummed into life, swinging inwards.

Danny pulled the gun from his waistband, wiped it clean, and stuffed it deep into a bush by the road. He climbed back into the Vauxhall. His heart pounded, his stomach sick with fear and guilt. There was nowhere he could go now, no one he could turn to. But he couldn't stay. He was heading into the unknown, this time with real blood on his hands. He stamped on the accelerator and roared out into the Hertfordshire night.

Behind him, Tess's pitiful scream echoed across the dark estate.

17

---

## ALTON GRANGE

It was the rattling of the key that woke him.

Bryce opened his eyes, the blistered paintwork overhead swimming into view. The room was still dark, the sun not yet risen above the surrounding woods. Denied a watch or any other timepiece, Bryce had become used to measuring its passage in other ways. The sun was the simplest method, the main gate too, the ebb and flow of traffic. Both were absent right now, which meant that by any measurement, today's wake-up call was earlier than usual.

He heard nurse Orla's heavy footsteps along the corridor, then the lights blinked into life. The nurse swept into the room, thick winter coat wrapped tightly around her ample frame, a red bobble hat pulled down over her ears. She sniffed loudly as she approached Bryce's bed, wiping her nose with the tissue balled in her hand.

'Time to get up,' she announced, her soft Irish tones jarred by the obvious head cold.

Bryce didn't move, cocooned like a larva inside his thin duvet. 'It's early.'

'Don't I know it,' she complained, setting her bag down

on the end of the bed and rummaging inside. She produced a blister pack of tablets, fat, dark spheres of God knew what.

'That mattress of yours is filthy, that's why you've got bites all over your legs,' she said. 'Sully's going to collect it, bring you a new one. I need you up in the next five minutes. Leave the old mattress at the gate.'

Bryce peered between the folds of his duvet.

'Can't I do it later?'

'No, you can't,' Orla shot back. 'Here, these are for you.' She popped two of the pills into her hand and placed them on Bryce's nightstand. 'Take those after you've moved the mattress. I'm not getting my hands dirty today. I've got a Christmas lunch to go to later.'

'Christmas,' Bryce echoed. He'd already calculated that the holiday period was just around the corner. The guards in the gatehouse had strung up a banner of coloured lights and some of the delivery vans had tinsel wrapped around their wing mirrors. Cairo had been signed in the last week of November and since then, Bryce had scratched the days away on the wood at the back of his bedside table, wondering if each notch would signal his last, if Sully would appear without his breakfast tray, instead pushing the trolley that would take his body to the mortuary.

'Where's Sully?'

'He'll be here shortly,' Orla warned, 'so hurry, out of that bed.'

Bryce threw off the duvet and reached for his dressing gown. On the surface he kept up his sluggish pretence, but inside his nerves jangled. Was this the day? Was the mattress thing a sham? He stood up, faking a loud yawn and stretching his arms over his head. He stepped into his slippers and shuffled around the bed, taking his time to pull the bedding off the mattress.

'Hurry up, for God's sake. You're like a bloody zombie.'

Bryce ignored her, folding his threadbare sheets.

'Right, that's it,' she puffed, snapping on a pair of latex gloves. 'C'mon, step aside.'

'I've got it,' Bryce assured her.

'I told you, I haven't got all day.' She elbowed Bryce aside and hurled the rest of the sheets onto the floor. 'Fold that lot up and leave them by the gate. I'll take care of the mattress.'

'I said I've got it.' Bryce tried to stand it up. Orla grabbed it anyway, pulling it off the bed and heaving it upright.

Something hit the floor.

Bryce froze, the objects caught in his peripheral vision, not one, but two, three, four, rolling across the cracked linoleum. Orla let the mattress fall back onto the bed. She bent down, picking up one of the tablets that had come to a stop between her sturdy shoes. She examined it for a moment then turned on Bryce, her face flushed with anger.

'What the hell's this?' she demanded. 'You've been hiding your medication? Is that it?'

Orla shoved him aside and started inspecting the seam with a practised eye. She found the tear in a matter of moments and stuffed her hand inside, pulling out dozens more tablets that spilled to the floor. Then she found the hypodermic syringe, a green plastic safety cap shielding its needle.

'You crafty bastard,' she breathed, holding the syringe up to the light. She shook it, inspecting the clear liquid inside. 'My God, you're in a world of trouble now—'

Bryce's bony fist caught Orla full in the face, sending her staggering backwards. She lost her footing and hit the ground hard, her head cannoning off a thick radiator pipe with an audible crack. Then she lay still, her legs splayed out before her, her arms spread wide, a pool of dark blood already spreading across the floor.

'No!'

Bryce grabbed a sheet and knelt beside her, balling the material and placing it behind her head. His mind raced, uncertain what to do except stem the flow of blood. Already the warm liquid had reached his knees, soaking his pyjamas. Then her eyes opened, frightened and accusing. She moaned softly, her bloodless lips mouthing unintelligible words. Bryce swept a few strands of auburn hair away from her face.

'What shall I do, Orla? Tell me what to do!'

Her lips moved again and he leaned close, straining to hear the words. Her breathing was laboured, short gasps that rattled between her bloodied teeth. Bryce stood up. His first instinct was to get help, but that would surely hasten his own demise. He perched himself on the corner of the bed, his head swimming. His legs and arms felt like water and his hands shook. He was committed now. Do or die, those were his only choices. If Sully walked in now he wouldn't live to see the day's end, of that he was certain.

He stood, searching the floor for it. There. The syringe was still intact, and he slipped it inside the pocket of his dressing gown. He got down on all fours, herding the tablets together with his hands and scooping them into a pillowcase.

Orla moaned again. Bryce tried to ignore her, found her bag on the floor and rummaged inside until he located the blister pack of tablets. He studied the label: *Flunitrazepam.* Bryce had never heard of it, but it sounded frighteningly exotic. Thank God he'd never taken one. His minders had become complacent during his incarceration, the rudimentary check of his open mouth never discovering the pill wedged up inside the gap between his back teeth, or the torn seam in his mattress where they'd been hidden, hoping somehow he would have the courage and opportunity to—

The security gate opened with its familiar metallic screech.

Bryce froze, heart pounding, the sound of Sully's tuneless whistle echoing down the corridor.

The gate slammed.

Sneakers rasped on the linoleum.

Bryce scuttled behind the padded door, the blood rushing in his ears. He'd only get one shot and it had better be right or Sully would kill him with his bare hands. He lifted the syringe from his pocket and pinched the safety cap with his thumb and forefinger.

It didn't move.

Sully passed the crack in the door. 'Orla, I told you to have that mattress ready,' he moaned as he entered the room. 'Where's—'

Bryce flinched as he heard Sully rack his baton out.

He gripped the safety cap again, tugging with all his might, his fingers burning with pain.

Then it snapped off with an audible click.

The door swung open and Sully stood there, half shielded by the thick padding, the baton raised in his right hand.

'Don't move!' he yelled.

Bryce shrunk away, expecting the ugly black baton to come whipping down on his head and body. He crouched in a defensive ball, one arm shielding his face.

'It was an accident,' he blurted. 'I swear to God!'

Sully eyed him for several moments before lowering the baton and taking a step back. 'Move. On the bed.'

Bryce did as he was told, giving Sully a wide berth, acting as he always did, lifeless eyes and listless limbs, but beneath his skin his heart hammered like a pneumatic drill. He plopped himself on the mattress, his hands in his lap, the syringe hidden in the palm of his hand.

Sully tucked the baton under his arm and gave Orla the once over, careful to avoid the blood spreading across the floor. He winced when he inspected the wound at the back of her skull.

'Not good. Not good at all.' He straightened up. 'What happened?'

'I just wanted some fresh air,' Bryce explained, his head held low, eyes on his slippers. He heard Sully approach, saw his trainers nosing into view. 'We argued, she tried to hit me. She slipped, banged her head.'

'Bullshit,' Sully shot back, 'that's not her style.'

Bryce heard the baton retract, watched Sully slip it into its holster. 'It's the truth,' he murmured, acting like an admonished schoolboy.

'Sure it is,' Sully sighed. 'Well, it seems we have a bit of a predicament.'

Bryce flinched as Sully reached down and tugged the belt from his dressing gown. He crossed the room and leaned over Orla, flipping her onto her front. He slipped the thin cord around her neck, put his foot on the back of her head, then pulled it like a noose. His arms rippled.

Bryce leapt to his feet and screamed.

'What are you doing, Sully? Stop that! Stop!'

'Back on the bed!' Sully yelled. He pulled harder and Orla began to convulse, her feet and hands twitching violently.

Bryce held his head in horror, not wanting to look but unable to stop himself.

Sully kept pulling with murderous effort until Orla's body twitched no more. He strangled her for another few seconds, then let the cord fall across her bloated and bruised face.

'That should do it,' he panted. 'Tough girl, that Orla.'

Bryce turned away, sickened, his hands groping for the bed, his legs like jelly. 'You killed her,' he whispered. 'You didn't have to do that.'

Sully stepped carefully over the pool of blood. 'Why prolong the inevitable? Besides, I just finished what you started.'

Bryce couldn't help himself. He glared at the man across the room. 'You sicken me, Sully. You're a cruel, vicious animal.'

Sully marched towards the bed. He grabbed Bryce by the face, squeezing his cheeks painfully. Between the fingers of his other hand he pinched one of Bryce's tablets.

'Not taking your meds, eh Gabe? Is that what you argued about?' He pushed him back onto the mattress. 'I thought as much.' He cocked his head towards Orla's corpse. 'She was being retired after this anyway. A slip in front of a train, a brutal mugging; the details hadn't been worked out. I can tell you one thing though, it wasn't supposed to be like this.' Sully stared at Bryce.

'Attacked by a deranged inmate. Yeah, that would work.'

Bryce shook his head. 'I didn't kill her. You did.'

'Whatever,' Sully shrugged. 'Calls will have to be made. The Prime Minister informed.'

'Yes, do that,' urged Bryce. 'Nigel should know what's going on.'

'Hooper?' Amusement played behind Sully's eyes. 'Nigel Hooper is dead.'

Bryce felt the wind punched from his lungs. 'Dead?'

'Correct. Took a dive off the high board at Millbank. Pressures of the job, by all accounts. I heard they were scraping him off the walls for days. A real tub of guts.'

'Jesus Christ,' Bryce gasped. 'Then who is—?'

He stopped, the answer to his own question so glaringly obvious. How far Tariq had risen in such a short space of time, from a minister on the verge of disgrace to leader of the nation. And how Bryce had underestimated him.

'Bingo,' Sully smiled, reading Bryce's face.

'Poor Nigel,' Bryce whispered.

Sully laughed. 'It was poor Nigel that had you put in this place.'

'We both know this is Tariq's work.'

Sully waved an admonishing finger. 'Show some respect, Gabe. It's Prime Minister Saeed to the likes of you and me. Anyway, it was Hooper's signature on everything, so he'll take the fall. Literally, as it turns out.'

Sully chuckled at his own joke.

'It's all working out nicely, too. There's barely a mention of you these days. No one wants to hear about sick people, Gabe, not even ex-Prime Ministers. All you are now is a news flash waiting to happen.'

Sully's mirthless chuckle frightened Bryce. His own demise was imminent and he shivered, tugging his dressing gown around him.

'Someone will find out about all this. People have died. It'll get out, sooner or later.'

Sully came and sat on the bed next to him. He spoke softly but his eyes were hard and cruel. 'Really? And who's going to tell them? You? If you walked out of here today who would believe you? Everyone thinks you're a basket case.' He drew a finger in the air. 'Lunatic Bryce wails about conspiracy; that's the headline we'd all see, that and your wild-eyed picture. And to cap it all, you're a murderer now. Bottom line is, you'd end up back here. With me.' Sully patted Bryce's leg and chuckled darkly. 'You're never going to leave this place Gabe. Not on two feet anyway.'

He stood up, waved a hand at the body on the floor. 'Well, we can't sit here chatting all day. This mess needs to be cleaned up.'

Bryce cocked his arm and stabbed the needle into Sully's backside, jamming the plunger to its stop.

Sully yelped and twisted away. He clenched his teeth as he yanked the syringe from his right buttock.

Bryce scuttled around the bed, keeping it between them.

Sully studied the syringe with disbelieving eyes. An empty syringe. He hurled it at Bryce's head, missing him by a fraction.

'What was it?' he screamed, reaching for the baton beneath his tunic. He racked it out, his eyes blazing with a fury that terrified Bryce. He pushed the bed towards the enraged orderly and ran for the door.

Sully staggered after him. 'Bastard!'

The baton swished through the air inches behind Bryce's head. He ducked into the corridor, yanking the door shut behind him, his hand shooting for the heavy dead bolt and slamming it home. He backed away from the door as it shook under the force of Sully's assault, his desperate thumping muffled by the thick padding. The handle rattled violently, the shouts and curses promising a world of violence. Sully was like a wild animal suddenly caged, vicious, deadly, desperate. Bryce held his breath, willing Sully to shut up, terrified the syringe had failed to do its job, that the drug inside had somehow lost its potency.

Then suddenly the blows on the door weakened.

The handle stopped rattling.

He heard his name and crept towards the door.

'Gabe,' the muffled voice rasped. 'Can't breathe...'

Bryce dropped to his knees, peered through the crack under the door. He saw Sully's feet, moving, shifting balance. Then the view was snuffed out as Sully collapsed against the door. He heard the baton clatter across the linoleum, then silence. He reached for the bolt and stopped.

Take a breath. Wait.

He went into the washroom and splashed cold water on his face. He gripped the edge of the sink to stop his hands from shaking. He needed to pull himself together, to think. He began to breathe deeply, filling his lungs and exhaling slowly. Eventually his heart rate slowed, his hands stopped shaking.

He waited in the washroom, perched on a lavatory seat, listening for movement from the bolted room, from the rest of the building. It was quiet, only the sound of dripping water, the distant toot of a vehicle at the main gate. Business as usual.

Fifteen minutes passed, maybe twenty.

Bryce went back to the door, knelt down. Sully's body was motionless. Perhaps it was all a sham, Sully lying with his back to the door, his eyes open, a wicked smile on his face as Bryce unbolted the door. How long could he wait like that? Hours maybe.

But Bryce couldn't afford to wait. His gaolers lay on the other side of the door, one certainly dead, the other most likely out cold. They were cogs in a machine. Someone would come looking.

He crossed the corridor. He watched the main gate from the utility room window. Traffic idled, the red and white barrier sweeping up and down. People came and went through the pedestrian entrance, some arriving for work, the night shift leaving. Bryce took a deep breath.

It was now or never.

Back in the corridor he slipped the deadbolt, heaving against the weight of Sully's body. He peered around the jamb. Sully lay curled at his feet, immobile, his mouth and eyes wide open, his dark features now a sickly grey. He saw the baton near the foot of the bed. He ran for it, scooping it up and spinning around to face the door.

Sully didn't move.

Bryce crept closer.

He rapped Sully's sneakers with the baton.

Nothing.

Closer still. He drove the thick plastic cap into Sully's genitals.

Sully didn't flinch. Couldn't.

He was dead.

Bryce tucked the baton under his arm and grabbed Sully's legs, dragging his body out into the middle of the room. He removed his green tunic and trousers and folded them over the back of the chair. He turned around and took off his dressing gown and pyjamas, unable to meet Sully's lifeless eyes.

He'd decanted the tablets carefully, four a day for over a month, a mixed cocktail of unidentified drugs that had filled the syringe and killed his minder. *Torturer,* Bryce reminded himself. Yet still he kept his back to him. He'd deal with the psychological fallout of his actions later. Right now he had to keep moving. The window of opportunity was already closing.

He changed into Sully's uniform, rolling up the legs and cuffs. It looked too big, so he pulled his own clothes back on to fill himself out. Better, he thought, looking down at himself. He slipped Sully's trainers on his feet, wriggling his toes. Too big. It didn't matter. He had no intention of running anywhere.

He rummaged in Orla's handbag, found her keys and security swipe.

Her mobile phone.

The time: 07:42

The temptation to use it was almost overwhelming, to scream his survival to the outside world, but he stopped himself. Who would he ring? Who could he trust? He shoved it in his pocket. He had to keep moving.

He relieved Sully of his NHS ID lanyard and looped it around his own neck. His mind raced, his eyes swivelling around the room. What else did he need, what else could he take to facilitate his escape? Then he saw the book and it seemed so obvious. He hurried to the nightstand, flicking through the pages until he found it.

He left the room without looking back, bolting the door from the outside.

In the washroom he shaved, removing his stubble and tidying up his sideburns. He washed with soap and cold water, scrubbing a healthier complexion back into his pallid skin. He towelled himself dry and took stock of his appearance. Not too bad. He might pass a cursory inspection, but anything else and he'd be in serious trouble. No matter, he had to keep moving now.

Out in the corridor he used the keys to open the security gate and locked it behind him. He stopped, listening carefully. Nothing, only the muted sounds from outside the building. He took the staircase down, as he had the night of the treaty, but this time he descended all the way to the ground floor where another steel gate blocked his escape.

Through the bars he could see a long, dark corridor that led towards a square rectangle of light.

Daylight.

He slipped Sully's master key into the lock and it swung open on well-oiled hinges. There were several rooms along the corridor. Bryce crept past them, his heart in his mouth, expecting voices, a shout of alarm. The last room looked like it had been recently used. There was a low table littered with magazines, several easy chairs, a narrow kitchen with a kettle and a microwave. And a coat stand.

The blue puffer jacket fit snugly over the bulk of Bryce's padded uniform. Stuffed into one pocket was a beanie hat with the initials NY embroidered on the front. In the other he found a thick leather wallet. He flicked it open. To Bryce's surprise he saw it was Sully's, complete with bankcards and cash. Bryce looked around. There was yesterday's paper and a glossy woman's magazine on the coffee table, a TV in the corner, two mugs in the sink. This was their room, his gaolers. He took the cash, stuffed it in his pocket, and threw the wallet in the bin.

Back in the corridor he approached the main door.

The windows were impregnated with wire, but that was the extent of the security measures. Outside, a path cut across a grassy area towards an access road. People passed by, then a car. Soon the facility would settle down again. He had to go, now. He pulled the hat down over his head.

He used the master in the lock. The key turned smoothly.

He took a deep breath, yanked open the door. He stepped outside.

He was out.

He followed the path, filling his lungs with fresh air, tilting his chin towards the sky as a fine drizzle cooled his face. It was a wonderful feeling, to be free, to feel the rain on his skin, the cold air in his nostrils. The urge to run was strong but he kept his pace casual, shadowing a group of people towards the main gate, coats and umbrellas converging towards the main entrance. He thanked God for the British weather.

At the security building alongside the main gate, cars came and went as the barrier waved up and down. He joined a queue of pedestrian traffic that shuffled through a cage of steel fencing alongside the gatehouse. He studied the people in front of him as they touched their ID cards on an electronic reader. The man in front of him, a large, shaven-headed orderly, touched out and pushed the gate as it buzzed. It slammed shut behind him. Now it was Bryce's turn. He stepped forward, Sully's ID card in his sweating palm. He touched the reader.

Nothing.

He touched it again.

The gate stayed locked.

He heard a mutter of impatience behind him. Cold fear gripped his insides. The card wasn't working.

He felt a hand on his shoulder. Panic choked him. He turned around.

'Other way up, mate. Picture side.' The man's nostrils flared impatiently.

'Sorry,' Bryce blurted.

He spun the card over with slippery fingers, wiped it on his jacket. He touched the reader.

The gaze buzzed.

Bryce shouldered it open. 'Thanks,' he muttered over his shoulder.

He walked along a footpath that led to the main road, the hairs on his neck tingling. From every window he imagined someone watching, pointing, the guards exchanging suspicious looks, a hand poised above the panic button that would trigger the wail of sirens and send the facility into lockdown. But nothing happened. Instead, people and cars came and went, the security gate hummed, and birds chattered in the trees. Normality. Everything as it should be.

Across the road a bus waited in a cutaway, its destination glowing above the driver's window: *BAGSHOT*.

Bryce crossed the road on rubbery legs, queuing as waited to board the bus. He paid his fare and wedged himself into a window seat. The doors hissed shut and the bus pulled away. The sign outside read NHS ALTON GRANGE. Bryce had never heard of it, knowing that he would never forget it. He watched the main gate slip behind them, the bus accelerating past the high fence until all he could see were grey slate roofs in the distance, slick with rain. He wondered which one had been his prison. Soon they were gone too, swallowed by the mist. He'd made it.

His hands began to shake and he thought he might throw up. He took several deep breaths and concentrated on the world outside, the passing fields, the trees and hedgerows. If he wanted to live, escaping the facility was just the first hurdle. He'd taken a giant leap into the unknown, one that could see him back behind bars before the day's end. Or worse.

Looming ahead through the windshield Bryce saw the neon glow of a retail park on the outskirts of Alton. He stood up and joined the throng at the doors as the bus slowed to a stop. He kept his head down, allowing himself to be swept by the tide of shoppers as they scattered towards the various stores. He slowed his pace, watching the bus disappear to the north, Orla's mobile phone, Sully's ID card and security keys, were all stuffed down the back of the seat.

It was a smart move, but one that wouldn't fool them for long. No stone would be left unturned once they discovered his escape. If he wanted to stay one step ahead he had to think out of the box.

He headed for a large B&Q store where he purchased a pair of cheap navy overalls and a fluorescent vest. In a discount clothes store he hung Sully's puffer on a hanger and purchased a cheap black winter coat and dark green baseball cap. In Sainsbury's he bought a pre-paid mobile phone and a map of Hampshire. He used the public toilets to change, stuffing Sully's NY beanie and the phone packaging into the waste bin. He fought the almost irresistible urge to buy food; it was too busy here, too public. He left, and caught another bus to the far side of the town.

He found a coffee shop with *Season's Greetings* sprayed in fake snow across the windows and wandered in. He checked his reflection in the mirror behind the counter. Despite the freshness of his clothes, he was satisfied he could pass as some sort of manual worker. He slipped into a booth near the counter. There were other several patrons dotted around, women with toddlers and a couple of rough-looking labourer types. He noted the odd glance but it was natural curiosity, nothing more. No one would recognise him, not forty pounds lighter with a broken nose and shaven head. Still, he kept the baseball cap on.

He ordered a roast chicken salad sandwich—made with fresh farm produce, the menu promised—and a glass of freshly-squeezed orange juice. He picked up a paper from the counter, feeling like a child about to open his Christmas presents. He devoured its contents. Sully was right, the world had indeed moved on. There was no mention of him at all, and scant mention of Nigel Hooper. Both of them had been removed from power. Bryce seethed; soon the same fate would befall Tariq Saeed.

The food arrived, the plump waitress all smiles. Bryce thanked her and ate, the sandwich probably the finest he'd ever tasted in his life. He ordered a slice of apple pie and ice cream to follow and savoured every single glorious mouthful. He couldn't remember the last time he'd felt so satisfied after such a simple meal. The waitress brought coffee while he pondered his next move.

He unfolded the map and checked his position. He was still too close to Alton Grange. He had to go, get as far away as possible. He reached into his pocket, felt the card there. Once he made the call he would know, either way, how all this would turn out. He checked the map, bought another sandwich, then left the coffee shop.

He walked to Bentworth, a quiet hamlet located three miles to the west of Alton, following narrow lanes and public footpaths that led him through damp fields and dark woods. The Sun Inn was where the map said it would be, set back off a quiet country road, a rural free house with a roof that dipped in the middle and tall chimneys either end. Inside the wood paneling was dark, the beams low, and a fire glowed in the hearth. It was cosy and quiet, just a few seniors scattered around the tables.

He bought a drink at the bar, another orange juice. The barman, a surly youth with shoulder-length hair, cracked open a bottle and dumped it in a glass over ice. Bryce picked his spot carefully, an empty table in a shadowy corner. He slipped out of his coat and settled down, stretching his legs out before him. No one was watching, but he pretended to drop something anyway, plugging the pre-paid mobile phone into the socket beneath his feet. The clock above the bar read three-fifteen and the world outside the window had turned a deeper shade of grey. He wondered if they'd found the bodies yet.

He spent the next hour enjoying the warmth and peace of his surroundings until the lights outside blinked into life. He unplugged the phone, got to his feet and pulled on his coat. It was time.

He approached the bar, making a show of patting his pockets. 'Is there a phone box in the village? I've left my mobile at home.'

Without looking up from his own device, the youth pointed to a dark corridor off the bar. 'Down there. You want change?'

'I'm good, thanks.'

The booth was on the left, just before the men's toilet. Bryce slid the frosted glass door open and settled down on the seat inside. It was snug, almost soundproofed, a battered payphone screwed to the wall, the board behind festooned with flyers for local taxis and rural festivities.

Bryce fished inside his coat for the card, now worn and dog-eared, but still legible. He pulled the mobile from his pocket, inserted the SIM, and dialled the number on the card. His heart began to beat faster as the calling tone reverberated in his ears. Then a click on the line, the connection successfully made.

'Hello.'

The voice was the same confident tone that Bryce remembered so well. He closed his eyes, the memories rushing back, the heat of the flames, the strong hands that never stopped working, tearing at the timbers that held him, setting him free.

'It's good to hear your voice again,' Bryce began, hoping, praying, Mac would recognise his own.

There was a pause on the line. 'Excuse me?'

Bryce willed himself to think. He was well aware of the level of sophistication of the government's monitoring programs, the shifting flag words that initiated remote recording, the men and women who worked in the shadows, listening, tracing...

'I was hoping you might remember me. Some time ago you helped me out of a spot, in London. My leg was injured. You sent me a book, in hospital.'

'A book? I don't—'

Then he stopped talking.

Bryce could hear other voices in the background, laughter echoing around a large empty space.

'Jesus Christ, is that you Prime—?'

'Yes,' Bryce confirmed, cutting Mac off.

He closed his eyes again, the phone clamped to his chest, relief flooding through him. 'Yes, it's me. Contrary to popular belief, I'm still in reasonable shape.'

'I don't understand,' Mac whispered down the line. 'I thought you were—'

'Don't speak. Just listen, let me talk for a moment, okay?'

'Sure.'

Bryce took a deep breath. 'The fact is, I'm in serious trouble. My life is in danger and I need your help. Before you ask, there's no one else I can turn to right now, no one I can trust. I can't go into any detail, only that I need to disappear for a while.'

Bryce paused for a response, but all he could hear was something being hammered in the background.

'Hello?'

'I'm still here. Go on.'

Bryce shifted the phone to his other ear and reached

into his pocket for the map. 'Right now I'm in a pub, near a town called Alton. Do you know it?'

'Yes.'

'When it's dark I'm going to head south, towards the next town. It's called Four Marks, on the A31.' He smoothed the map out on his thigh. 'There's a bus stop to the north of town, just after the dual carriageway ends. I'll wait there until midnight. If I don't see you before then, I'll assume you're not coming and move on. Sometime after that I'll probably be dead. I don't know how the story will break, but whatever it is it won't be the truth, you can believe that. I'm not ill. There was never any stroke.'

He was asking too much, he knew that, but he'd committed himself.

'That's it, that's all I can tell you, but I want you to know something. If you decide to have nothing to do with this, I will respect your decision and never contact you again. You have my word.'

He waited in silence, listening to the chatter in the background, to the sounds of industry echoing around those distant walls.

In the corridor, the toilet door creaked and slammed. A shadow lingered outside the frosted glass, then moved away.

Bryce held his breath, the phone clamped to his ear.

'Get moving,' Mac said, 'and stay off the main roads. I'll be there in two hours.'

The line went dead.

Bryce sat in the booth for several minutes, head in hands, the map on his leg stained with tears.

# 18

## SOUTH LONDON

DANNY DRIFTED BACK TO CONSCIOUSNESS, PALE BARS of wintry sunlight streaming through the windows. Something had disturbed him, something that filtered through the layers of fatigue to penetrate his dreamless sleep. He lay motionless, listening. Then he heard it, a man, whistling an unknown tune as feet crunched across the gravel towards him. It was Ray. But that couldn't be. Ray was dead.

He was still haunted.

And hunted.

Outside, the passerby's whistling faded. He lay on the floor, wrapped inside the questionable warmth of the quilt, and stared at the ceiling. There must be a leak somewhere in the roof, because a wide brown stain had worked its way across the cracked plaster, blistering the paintwork and encircling the light fitting above his head. Maybe that's why the premises were empty, why the business had stopped trading.

He rubbed his eyes and checked his watch. It was almost time. He threw off the quilt. He pulled a roll-neck jumper over his t-shirt, slipped his trainers on, then went next door to the small kitchenette. He splashed cold water over his face and patted his beard dry with a towel. He opened the lifeless fridge and retrieved his supplies, a bottle of water, a couple of bananas and a large bar of chocolate. He stared out through the grime of the window as he ate, watching the bleak housing estate beyond the railway tracks come to life, the commuter trains clattering along the embankment behind the abandoned industrial unit.

He put his rubbish back into the bag, and then he moved to the front of the property, to a derelict office. He settled into a plastic chair near the window and peered through the grimy glass.

The council's temporary accommodation centre across the street was a scruffy building, four storeys of orange brick and peeling paint work. Most of the windows still had their curtains drawn but others showed signs of life, a light snapped on here, a glimpse of a shadow there. Danny had watched the comings and goings for much of the previous day, demoralised by the sheer number of non-Brits and their droves of kids, all now dependent on the British taxpayer. That's when he'd heard Ray's voice in his head, the ranting, the hatred, and remembered that he himself hadn't paid tax for years. He was here for dad. Nothing else mattered.

The voice had faded.

It had been a week since he'd fled Ray's estate. He'd driven east that night, then south, picking up the M25 near Uxbridge. He'd driven towards Heathrow, his mind in turmoil, until exhaustion overcame him. He'd left the motorway and found a large hotel, driving to a shadowy corner of the car park. But sleep was hard to come by, and he never closed his eyes until long after the sun had risen. He'd tuned into a radio news station, fearing the worst but hearing nothing. His name wasn't mentioned, nor the deaths, nor news of a manhunt. For the next few days Danny journeyed aimlessly, driving at night, sleeping by day in busy car parks, just another exhausted travelling salesman.

As each day passed he became more convinced that Tess hadn't reported the deaths of her husband and Joe. She was involved on some level, sure, but Danny felt certain that she didn't know about the car, the passport, or anything else. He'd passed dozens of police cars and ANPR cameras since he took flight and he still hadn't been pulled, which meant that they weren't looking for the car. Yet.

Ray loved Tess, that much was obvious. Danny believed he would've kept her ignorant of his plans in order to protect her. Tess would've discovered the bio-weapon and been frightened. She would've kept her mouth shut.

Instead, Danny imagined a night of frantic phone calls, of Tess begging loyal friends to clean up the mess. He had a mental image of Marcus and others, helping Tess bury the bodies in that dark plantation, escorting the wailing woman back to the house. With Ray gone Marcus would keep his mouth shut too, which meant that, for now, Danny had a clean car and a valid passport. He had a chance to start his life again. He had to take it, while he still could. Which is why he drove to south London.

He'd been holed up in the empty industrial unit for three days now, the Vauxhall safely parked on another, larger estate near the old Power Station. Yesterday he'd seen his father for the first time since he'd abandoned him on the Longhill, and he'd nearly wept. It had only been a couple of months, but already the old man's back seemed a little more curved, the skin a little paler, the grey hair noticeably thinner. Stress and worry, that was Danny's fault too; driven from his home, his terrorist son still at large, his life empty.

The guilt made Danny feel physically sick. He'd wanted to bang on the filthy glass, call out to him, but first he had to be certain the old man wasn't being watched.

Dad was a creature of habit. Danny had followed him from a distance into Battersea Park, trailing him around the perimeter road before watching him settle on a park bench overlooking the river. Dad was a sandwich and a hot thermos man. He used to go out every day back at the Longhill, find somewhere decent to enjoy his food and drink. It would be no different here. Later he followed him back to the hostel.

For Danny, the exercise had proved inconclusive. He hadn't seen any police cars, or people with ear pieces hanging about, but then again he was no expert in counter surveillance. His gut told him that they wouldn't watch his dad forever. Danny had faded from the news, whereabouts unknown, the same old mugshot still in circulation, his physical description a world away from the reflection he now saw in the mirror. No one would recognise him. He was Eduard Zala, if only for a couple more days. Then he'd vanish like a ghost.

The risk was worth it, to see dad for a few minutes, to set up the method of communication. Danny had thought about it long and hard. He'd tell him about the convenience store, the one near the Longhill that offered the anonymous mailing address service, the names they'd use, the coded messages on the postcards. It was primitive, but safe. They'd stay in touch, until the day his dad would come to him. And maybe never go back.

Danny checked his watch again. It was just after ten am, and today's activity was much the same as yesterday. Families came and went, wagon trains of prams and mothers, encircled by running, laughing kids. The postman wheeled his little red trolley up to the door and delivered a thick stack of mail. It wouldn't be long now.

Fifteen minutes passed.

Across the street the door opened and his dad emerged from the hostel. He wore the same clothes as yesterday, a faded navy tracksuit and white trainers, a small rucksack slung across his shoulders, a pale yellow scarf wrapped around his thin neck to combat the sharp December winds. Danny slipped his coat on as he watched his dad head up the street towards the park. He took the stairs two at a time, leaving the building through an old fire exit out back and squeezing through a side alley choked with rubbish. He emerged into bright sunlight, slapping the dirt from his clothes, following his father from a safe distance. He kept his pace casual. He knew where dad was headed.

'Excuse me, sir.'

Danny glanced over his shoulder without breaking stride.

'Yes, you.'

He stopped, heart pounding in his chest. Jogging up behind him was a Police Community Support Officer, his belt equipment rattling as he trotted. Danny called them rent-a-cops, low paid and poorly trained. Mugs, was another word he used, although the truth was, he'd never spoken to one in his life. This one was bigger than Danny, probably around the same age, with thick arms and a shock of bright ginger hair spilling out beneath the band of his cap. He stopped a few feet away, his thumbs tucked into his stab vest, his rugged face bright crimson.

'What's the matter?'

'Do you know why I stopped you?'

Danny shook his head. 'No idea.'

The PCSO clearly didn't believe him, the nostrils of his boxer's nose flaring as he caught his breath.

'What were you doing in that building?'

'I wasn't in the building. I was taking a leak in the alley-way. I got caught short, that's all. I'm not in trouble, am I?' He kept his manner polite, respectful, his face neutral.

'We've had some break-ins in the area, small businesses, shops.'

Danny glanced over the officer's shoulder. 'Oh, I thought that place was abandoned.'

'That may be, but there's still plenty of stuff that can be stolen. Fixtures and fittings, copper wiring. If the kids get in you're looking at vandalism, fires.'

'I didn't think of that. Well, I was just having a whizz, that's all.' He checked the time. 'Look, I'm late. If I'm not in any trouble I'd like to get going.'

'Nice watch,' the PCSO observed. 'Is it yours?'

Danny could've kicked himself. He'd put Ray's Rolex on his wrist, unwilling to leave it in the boot of the Vaux-hall. It was a big, chunky gold affair, and easily worth a few thousand quid to a pawnbroker. That was his plane ticket right there, his living expenses for several months. *Idiot.*

'It was a present,' Danny stuttered. 'Can I go?'

'I'll need to record some details first. You're entitled to a copy when I'm finished.'

'Seriously, I haven't got time.'

'Where are you going?'

'To work?'

'Where do you work?'

'The West End.'

'Doing what?'

'Look, I...' Danny's mind raced. 'I'm going to an inter-view. With an employment agency.'

The PCSO looked him up and down. 'Really? In dirty jeans and trainers?'

*Shit.* This was getting out of hand. 'Please, I'm late.'

'As I said, we've had some anti-social behaviour around here, and I'm not happy with your story. You're not under arrest, but I'll need your details.' The officer had already produced a ticket pad and pen and stared at Danny with unblinking eyes. The pen hovered over the form.

'Let's start from the beginning. Your full name, current address and date of birth, please.'

Danny's shoulders slumped. Everywhere he turned, every path he took, bad luck waited. There was no avoiding it, no matter what he did. He was marked from birth, destined never to rise above his lowly station, never to enjoy a single sliver of good fortune that might improve his existence upon this earth. The anger boiled inside him. And all the time his dad was getting further away.

'Your name.' The PCSO's hand moved towards the radio clipped to his stab vest. 'We can do this at the station if you want.'

'Alright, I wasn't having a piss,' Danny blurted. He took a step closer, lowered his voice. 'You're right, I was looking for copper wiring. I'm skint, my dad's ill. We're desperate. Cut me some slack, eh mate?'

The enforcer's hand lingered near his radio. 'That's trespass, possibly criminal damage too. I'll need those details.'

*Shit!* A car drove by, the occupants staring at them as they cruised past. Across the street, a group of women pushing a brood of wailing brats stopped their buggies to watch. He had to think fast, before the real police showed up.

'You want the truth? Look.' Danny turned his pocket

out, allowed the PCSO to see Ray's fat wedge of fifty-pound notes. 'I found that under the floorboards in one of the upstairs rooms. There's tons of it up there, must be thousands. It's all loose, just lying there. I was going to get a bag, come back. Help me get it out and I'll split it with you.'

The officer hesitated. 'I can't do that. That's illegal. It has to be accounted for.'

Danny fumed. 'What do you earn, mate? Twenty grand a year, for putting yourself at risk every day? There might be ten times that up there. And you want to hand it in? Then what happens to it? Let me tell you, it'll all disappear, back into the government's pockets. And what will you get out of it? A bloody certificate and a handshake, that's all, or maybe your picture in the local rag. *Man finds fortune and hands it in;* they can run it in the joke section.' Danny lowered his voice, tempered his tone. 'Look, chances like this only come along once in our lives, mate. If you don't want any of it, that's fine. You can just turn around and walk away. No one has to know. But I'm begging you, please, don't fuck it up for me. I'm not a criminal, I'm just a bloke who's down on his luck, trying to catch a break. And I caught one, first time in my life. Help me out, bruv. Please.'

The PCSO stared at him for several seconds. Then he said, 'Show me.'

Danny led the way, squeezing through the alleyway and clambering over the rubbish. Behind him the officer's eyes roamed the rear of the building, the broken windows and choking weeds, the sagging brick wall that was slowly crumbling under the weight of the railway embankment. The properties on either side were also derelict, silent and empty.

'This isn't right. I'm going to call it in.' There was doubt in his voice, apprehension.

'Don't be stupid,' Danny pleaded. 'You could walk away with a bagful of cash. It doesn't belong to anyone.' He ducked past him, yanking open the fire escape door. 'Call it in then, if that's what you want. Just give me two minutes to fill my pockets, then I'll be gone.'

He ran upstairs and ducked into an office on the landing. There was a wooden stave in there, thick and heavy. Danny had kept it by his makeshift bed, just in case. He heard the officer stamp inside the building, saw the beam of a torch piercing the gloom.

'Up here!' Danny shouted. 'Jesus, there's loads of it!'

He heard footsteps on the stairs, creaking under heavy black boots. The radio hissed continuously, garbled voices trapped between damp walls. Danny waved him up. 'There's more than I thought. Hurry up.'

The PCSO pushed past Danny.

Danny swung the wooden stave.

It connected with the back of the officer's head with a hollow pop. The PCSO hit the ground hard, face down. He lay there moaning, arms by his side, his legs kicking out like a frog. Danny raced forward, wrenched the handcuffs from his belt. The officer flayed at him with weak fingers, muttering something unintelligible. He snapped the cuff over the man's wrist and dragged him toward the wall. There was a thick pipe that ran floor to ceiling, some sort of plumbing duct. Danny shook it. It was old school, thick, well engineered. Danny ratcheted the other cuff around the pipe.

He went to work on the PCSO's pockets, emptying them. He threw his keys and baton across the room, smashed his radio to pieces with the wooden stave, likewise his mobile phone. He knelt over his victim, panting with effort. The man was semi-conscious. There was no blood, no weird stuff coming out of his ears. He just moaned, his eyes fluttering. Thank God he hadn't killed him. He got to his feet.

'I'm sorry mate. I'll make the call, let 'em know where you are.' Danny had no intention of doing so, not until he was long gone. The guy had a bump on the head and a story to tell. He'll live. And he'll probably get that picture too. Danny left the building on the run. Outside the street was empty.

He headed towards the park.

A short while later he jogged through the gates of Battersea Park and slowed his pace. He strode casually along the tree-lined avenues, hands in his pockets, coat zipped high against the cold. Leaves tumbled along the paths and the air was tinged with the scent of a wood fire somewhere. Mums wandered about with kids, runners puffed and panted, cyclists hummed by. Everyone ignored him.

When he reached the embankment overlooking the Thames his dad was already seated on a park bench, munching on a sandwich as he watched the river drift by. Danny studied him from the shelter of a tree for a few moments, took one last look around, and set off across the open ground. His heart began to beat faster as he closed the distance, circling a boisterous football match and a dog walker wrestling with half a dozen snuffling canines. And then he was there.

Danny slid onto the end of the bench, digging his hands deep into his pockets. He watched the slow-moving river, glancing at the old man who turned to him, smiled, then looked away.

The bovine chewing stopped.

From the corner of his eye Danny saw recognition

register across his father's craggy features. He turned to Danny again, the colour draining from his cheeks.

'Danny?'

'It's me, pops,' murmured Danny, watching the river. 'You alright?'

The old man's eyes searched his son's face. 'I didn't recognise you. You look so different.'

'That's the idea,' he smiled, scratching his thick beard. The smile faded. 'I can't stay long.'

The old man's lower lip started to tremble. 'You shouldn't have come.'

'I had to see you, dad. I never did it, you know. I was fitted up. I don't know by who, or why, but that's the truth.'

'I found your letter, son. I gave it to the police. They didn't believe it, but I did. I know you're innocent.'

Danny's lower lip trembled. 'Thanks, dad. You've no idea what that means to me.' It felt strangely quiet, peaceful. Behind him the footballers were gone, the match abandoned. The dog walker had vanished too.

'I have to leave, dad. There's so much to say, so much I need to explain, but I don't have time. I'm heading abroad, the Far East. Thailand first, then maybe Vietnam. I can get lost there. When the time's right you can join me, stay for a—'

The words caught in his throat. They were moving towards him, black uniforms and ski masks, weapons raised. He turned around. Unmarked vehicles carved across the open spaces, tyres spinning rooster tails of mud and grass. A police helicopter clattered above the treetops and settled into a deafening hover above the river. It happened so fast that Danny didn't have time to think, react. Instead he let out a long breath and closed his eyes.

It was over.

He didn't move, kept his hands on his legs, just in case one of the shooters had a nervous trigger finger. Sirens wailed all around. He heard dad's voice, quivering above the noise.

'They've been waiting for weeks. They said you'd come back, sooner or later. I prayed you wouldn't.'

Danny laid a hand on his father's knee and squeezed it gently. 'That's alright, pops. It's not your fault.'

The cars slewed to a halt, the shouts urgent above the buzz of the helicopter. The uniforms drew closer, red dots swarming across his torso like angry fireflies.

'Never got anything right, did I? Never been any good.'

Fear gripped him then, fear of what was to come. Whatever happened, it was going to end badly. 'I'm sorry, dad. For everything.'

Beside him, the old man smothered a sob with a bony hand. He reached out with the other and squeezed Danny's hand with a strength that belied his advancing years.

# 19

# HAMPSHIRE

Bryce clicked the radio off, puzzled.

It had been four days, and still no official word on his escape. Part of him dreaded hearing his name broadcast across the airwaves, yet the lack of news regarding his violent flight from Alton Grange possessed its own unnerving quality.

He filled the kettle and snapped it on, staring out of the kitchen window. It wasn't much of a view. Six feet behind the warehouse stood a high cobblestone wall crowned with wisteria, its heavy foliage glistening with silvery beads of rainwater. Beyond the wall was a wood. He leaned over the sink and craned his neck. The sky was a dull canvas of grey, traversed by darker clouds that drifted above the swaying treetops beyond the wall. A miserable day perhaps, but he was alive. And free.

Mac's boat moving business was situated inland, a solitary building at the end of a short, gated drive off the main road. It was surrounded by high walls and shielded from view by tall trees. Mac had brought him here the night of his escape, much against his better judgement. His rescuer had suggested the police, the media, but Bryce had argued against it. It was too soon, there were too many unknowns. He had to hide, to think. So Mac had driven him to the warehouse.

The small sign next to the Judas gate said, Maritime Movers. Inside Bryce had been struck by the smell, of salt-water and oil. In the centre of the warehouse stood a small boat with an outboard engine, squatting on metal hull supports like a stuffed whale in a museum. Ropes and wet weather gear hung from hooks around the walls, while nets and boxes were stacked neatly across the concrete floor.

Mac had escorted him to a large, untidy room above the warehouse floor, part office, part kitchen, with nautical charts spread across a battered table and an overstuffed sofa against one wall. Bryce's bed, Mac had explained. He'd also explained that he had a family, a wife and two daughters; he had to go home, act normally. Bryce would be safe, locked inside the warehouse, behind the main gate. Mac would return at first light.

That first night had been a fitful one, wrapped in the borrowed sleeping bag, listening to the sound of the wind moaning through the trees. He started at every noise, dreading a sudden chorus of shouts, the terror of hard-faced men dragging him off into the night, but the new dawn brought fresh hope.

Mac had returned as promised, with food and other supplies, and the news that he had to fly to Jersey for two days on business. Bryce had expressed his anxiety but Mac had assured him that no one would come around. He only had one employee, a part-time bookkeeper who acted as his PA. She wasn't due back for another week, and his boat movers were all contracted on a per job basis. The ware-house was safe and secure.

By day Bryce would watch TV in the small restroom, or read one of the paperbacks that Mac had brought him, but he found it hard to settle. He stared at the telephone on Mac's desk, wondering whom he might call, but it didn't matter anyway. The line was dead. At night he listened to a portable radio, laying with it under the sleeping bag like a furtive child, expecting news of his escape to be broadcast across the airwaves, but hearing nothing. Local music stations jostled for airtime alongside news and shipping forecasts. Everything was so normal it frightened him.

Bryce was relieved when Mac had finally returned. He brought with him more supplies and cooked a meal while Bryce cleared the chart table. They made small talk as they ate, and Bryce saw that Mac's shoulders were bent under the weight of a thousand questions but the man was either too gracious, or too nervous, to ask. He wondered if he had all the answers and realised he didn't. What he did have was a plan, of sorts. The tricky part was persuading a stranger to risk everything to help him.

Plates emptied and bellies full, Mac piled the dishes in the sink. He boiled the kettle, made two mugs of coffee, and sat back down. He offered Bryce a cigarette.

'I could die of worse things,' Bryce observed, clamping it between his lips.

Mac chuckled. 'Very true.'

They lit up in silence, eyeing each other across the table. It was Mac who broke the tension.

'So, what happens now?'

Bryce exhaled a thick cloud of cigarette smoke, coughing as it caught in his lungs. 'Now I know why I quit,' he wheezed. He stubbed out the cigarette and held Mac's gaze. 'The truth is, I don't know. It's out of my hands, you see.'

'What do you mean?'

'I've had time to think, Mac. Perhaps too much time, but I'm seeing things a lot clearer now. Like I told you on the way down here, the Downing Street bomb had nothing to do with any right-wing conspiracy. It was designed to stop me, to wipe out a Cabinet that might have supported me and replace it with another—what we politicians refer to as regime change. Thanks to you I was saved, and that created a new problem for my would-be assassins. So they kept me hospitalised and heavily sedated, ensuring I was unable to retake the reins of office. They created a bomb scare, had me moved to Alton Grange, fed me drugs, kept me locked up in that terrible ward. They lied about my condition; there was no stroke, no mental deterioration. I was simply a prisoner, hidden from public view, until I could be conveniently disposed of, no doubt in a considerably less dramatic fashion than previously planned.'

Mac puffed nervously on his cigarette. 'But this is Britain, not some South American dictatorship. We just don't do that sort of thing.'

'What about Iraq? We now know that it was all based on a lie, yet the people who took us into that war still enjoy huge status and wealth. People forget, Mac. The world moves on and us with it.'

'That was different. It was overseas.'

'British troops died for that lie. What difference does geography make?'

'And you think the Prime Minister is behind this?'

Bryce could see that Mac was still struggling with it. 'I told you, yes. There are others, no doubt.'

'Why?'

'The Treaty of Cairo is incredibly important to a lot of people. An expanding Europe equals greater power invested in its leaders, and that power filters down to individuals in national governments and multinational corporations. You've read the papers, yes? Thanks to Cairo's success, every country north of the Sahara is now exploring potential membership of the EU. If that happens—and God knows there's a minefield of Human Rights hurdles to leap before the Commission even begins to consider it—then eventually the mandarins in Brussels will hold sway over more people, more real estate, than the Roman Empire at its very height. It may take fifty, even a hundred years, but imagine the authority that could be wielded, the visions that could be realised. If a couple of hundred casualties is all that's required to initiate such an agenda, then that is a very small price to pay. Don't you see, Mac? History has been built on such decisions and the blood of innocents.'

Bryce could feel his blood pumping, could see Mac's bewilderment as he tried to process what he was hearing. He paused a moment and leaned back in his chair.

'I don't pretend to know what it all means; expansionism, corporate greed, some other agenda perhaps. Cairo was designed as a catalyst, intended to herald great change. I stood in the way of that, so a decision was made. That led to the atrocities of Downing Street and Luton. I believe that Tariq Saeed is somehow a part of it.'

Mac looked dubious. 'What about the bomber? This Whelan fella?'

'A patsy, probably. They needed a scapegoat, a target to pin their deeds on. Historically, Far Right groups are badly organised and poorly funded. They're emotional, and all too easy to infiltrate and manipulate. Compared to their counterparts across the political divide, they're children.'

Mac ground out his cigarette and finished his coffee. Then he pushed his mobile phone across the table. 'So let's stick with plan A. Tell the media. You must know someone who can help, someone who's not part of this bloody great conspiracy. They can't *all* be involved.'

Bryce stared at the phone. It was tempting of course, but not an option. 'You have a family, Mac. A daughter, right?'

Mac's eyes narrowed 'So?'

'You want to put them in danger?'

'Stupid question.'

'Neither do I. You must understand that the people we're dealing with are utterly ruthless. Our lives—me, you, your girls—are meaningless to them. If I marched into the nearest TV station tonight, do you honestly think they'll just put me on air, let me tell my story?'

Mac shrugged. 'Why wouldn't they?'

Bryce shook his head. 'I know how these things work, Mac. You can forget any notion of an objective, independent media coming to my rescue. The people that run the newspapers, the news channels, they consider themselves part of the same intellectual elite as mainstream politicians. They don't see themselves as public servants; they believe they exist to educate the masses, not inform them. I'm on the outside now. The minute I walk into a TV studio I'd be ushered into a nice quiet room out of the way. A call would be made, a car sent. I'd disappear within the hour. Same story with the police. I'd end up back at Alton Grange or somewhere similar, only this time I'd never get out. I'd be dead within a month.' He levelled his gaze at the man opposite. 'I imagine that would include anyone else with whom I've had contact.'

Now Mac looked nervous. 'Jesus,' he whispered. 'So you're telling me there's no one you can trust? No one who's willing to help?'

Bryce scraped his chair back and got to his feet. He rummaged in his coat pocket for a moment then sat back down. 'There's one person. I've given it plenty of thought. I think I might have a plan.'

Mac raised a hopeful eyebrow. 'You do? That's good.'

'I need to get to Tortola.'

'Tortola? In the Caribbean?'

'The very same. I have a friend there, Oliver Massey. He's very wealthy, has a very secluded villa in the hills. He'll help me.'

'How?'

'Firstly, he'll keep me hidden. He'll arrange for security, the very best medical care and physical therapy, then later, legal counsel. We'll work on a media strategy until such time that I am ready to face the spotlight. Then we'll hold a press conference that will make headlines in every country on the planet. I'm going to bring Tariq down, Mac, and his friends. I won't rest until they're all behind bars.'

'Have you spoken to this friend of yours?'

Bryce shook his head. 'I told you, I've spoken to no one. Oliver came to see me in hospital but I have no recollection of it. After that little bomb scare I suspect he's been kept at arms length like everyone else. He's outside of government, and more importantly, the country. He's my only hope.'

Mac rubbed the dark stubble on his face. 'So how do you plan on getting to Tortola? That's a long way away.'

Bryce pushed a dog-eared business card across the table. 'I know a man, one who carries out boat deliveries. World-wide, it says here.'

Mac picked up his own card. 'You're kidding.'

'Remember what I said when we spoke on the phone, Mac? Well, the same rule still applies. You say the word and I'll walk out that door. And I promise you, when they eventually catch up with me—which they will—I'll do my best to keep your name out of it.'

Mac's face darkened. 'That's not funny.'

'I'm not joking. I gave you a choice, Mac, and you chose to help me. I'm making you aware of the risks, that's all.'

'Thanks a bundle.'

Bryce stood his ground. 'It was you that gave me the idea. The night of the bomb you appeared from nowhere to save me, for which I'll be forever grateful.' He picked up the card. 'Then you sent me this, in the hospital. I kept it close, so I could contact you on my return to the living. Then later, when things turned bad, I saw it as a lifeline, a way out.' He waved a finger between them. 'You and I cannot be connected, we've established that. You didn't make a statement the night of the bomb, and the authorities have never contacted you. No one knows you saved my life but me, and I thank God for your humility. That's why it *has* to be you, Mac. We've made it this far. I'm asking you to take me the rest of the way.'

Mac's eyebrows knitted together. 'The Atlantic's a big ask. We normally only go as far as the Med. Longer trips I farm out to other firms.'

'Have you ever done it?'

'Twice. Last trip was four years ago, on a fifty-footer with a good crew.'

'What about a boat?'

'I'm not saying I'll do it,' Mac warned. 'Sailing the Atlantic involves a lot of preparation. Even if we started today, it'd be weeks before we're ready.'

Bryce paled. 'Weeks?'

Mac drummed his fingers on the table. 'Unless...'

'What?'

'Unless we crew a boat. These firms I sub-contract to,

there's a couple in Spain who ferry boats across the pond all the time. I know the owners. We could sail down there, join a crew.'

Bryce grimaced. 'That sounds risky. I could be recognised.'

'With that haircut?' Mac grinned. 'Jesus, even I didn't recognise you when I picked you up.'

'Fair point.'

'Have you ever sailed before?'

'Many years ago,' Bryce told him, 'thirty-two footers, back and forth across the Channel. It'll come back, don't worry.'

Mac didn't say anything for a while. He sat in silence, swirling coffee dregs around his mug as if searching for an answer there. Eventually he pushed his chair back and stood up. 'I guess I'd better make some calls.'

Bryce stood too. 'You'll do it?' Everything hinged on this moment. Without Mac's help, his choices would be dangerously limited.

Mac shrugged. 'What choice do I have? As you pointed out, I've got a family. I think the sooner you're safely off these shores, the better for all of us.'

Bryce closed his eyes, relief flooding through him. He held out his hand. 'Thank you, Mac.'

The younger man took it briefly. 'Be warned, there's a financial cost involved here. Money will have to be spent, and a lot of it. I'll expect to be well compensated.'

'You'll be covered,' Bryce promised, 'every penny. Just get me to Tortola.'

Mac grunted and spun on his heel. He pulled his coat on and paused at the top of the stairs. 'I'll be gone for the next day or two. I'll have to prep the boat for Spain, buy provisions, equipment, see the girls, and generally get things squared away. Make yourself comfortable. There's plenty to eat and drink. I shouldn't be too long.'

'Thank you, Mac.'

A few moments later the Judas gate banged shut. Bryce slumped onto the sofa, drained. The last few days had been a physical and emotional rollercoaster. He wasn't yet back to his old self, and wouldn't be for a long time. Tortola would go some way to curing that, but the memories would haunt him for the rest of his days.

*Memories.*

A thought suddenly occurred to him. Those experiences, those recollections were vitally important. They were traumatic and deeply personal, and somewhere down the line would form the basis of his legal actions that will blow Tariq Saeed and his friends out of the water. Those memories were evidence.

He stood up and hurried across the room to the laser printer beside Mac's desk. He extracted several sheets of paper and sat down, toying with the pen in his hand. He closed his eyes, allowing his mind to rewind to the very beginning, to that bumpy helicopter ride across west London. He saw the sprawl of the Heathrow Relocation Center, heard the words of Brian Davies, felt the touch of Ella's hand on his sleeve.

*Ella.*

The one person he could reach out to, one of many they'd be watching. He'd devoured every paper, but there was no news of her. He'd asked Mac to look, but his Internet connection was faulty. She was out of her coma, Sully had mentioned it once, but that's all he knew. He missed her desperately, yearned for her touch. He made a decision; once in Tortola he would send for her, a circuitous journey that would see her transported behind the secluded walls of Oliver's villa. He would need her guidance, her companionship. Her love. As he'd learned all too painfully, life was too damned short.

He had the time and the tools. There were pens and paper, and stationary, a busy out tray, a photocopier. He'd record the night of Heathrow, the day of the bomb, and every event afterwards. He'd take his time to think, to record every place he'd been to, every face he saw, every conversation he'd had.

The fight back would begin now, today.

He began to write.

## 20

## WHITEHALL

THE AIDE LEANED IN CLOSE AND SPOKE SOFTLY IN Saeed's ear.

'Ambassador Massri is here, Prime Minister.'

'Show him in.'

Saeed stood up, smoothing his tailored jacket and green silk tie. In addition to his blossoming qualities as a statesman, the British Prime Minister also had a keen eye for bespoke attire, a trait not gone unnoticed by the British press. He was often featured in magazines and newspapers, handsome, elegant, the celebrated blue eyes, dark hair and neatly trimmed beard giving him the aura of a movie star. Gossip columns loved him, men envied him and women wanted to be with him. Privately, Saeed loathed the attention of a media that revered vanity and superficiality above all things, but he encouraged it nonetheless. A stylish suit and a winning smile had more cache than a fundamental change in the law, a state of affairs that Saeed had every intention of exploiting.

He walked around his desk and waited. The office was a temporary one, situated in the Old War Office building in

Whitehall and recently refurbished to accommodate Saeed and his administration whilst planners haggled over the New Downing Street. The room was well-appointed, floor-to-ceiling windows along its length, an ornate central cupola above, Saeed's ministerial-sized desk at one end, a pair of impressively tall period double doors at the other. It was a long and intimidating walk across the white marble floor to the Prime Minister's throne but it sent a subtle message. The British respected power and status, the importance of occasion, the gravitas of ceremony, none of which could be successfully conveyed within the post-modern walls of a Millbank Tower the British public would rather forget.

The Egyptian Ambassador's shoes clicked across the marble. He was a small, rotund man, sporting a slick comb-over. Saeed met him halfway. 'Mohamed, a pleasure as always.'

'Prime Minister.'

They shook hands, fixed their smiles. A camera flashed. Saeed waved the photographer out of the room. He ushered Massri to a circle of chairs arranged around a decorative table. The seated occupants got to their feet. Saeed did the introductions.

'You know Anna Morgan, the Attorney General.'

'Of course.' The Egyptian took her hand, and the hands of the others in the room, Saeed's Permanent Secretary, his Director of Communications, and the EU Commission's representative in London, an ageing Swede named Emerson. They exchanged small talk and pleasantries while refreshments were served. When the staff had retired and the tall doors were sealed, Saeed brought the meeting to order.

'We all know why we're here. The Egyptian government has expressed a strong desire to ensure justice is done in the wake of Whelan's arrest.'

Massri acknowledged Saeed with a nod. 'Indeed, Prime Minister. We're all aware of President Bakari's concerns in regard to this matter, concerns shared not just by Cairo but by the whole of the Muslim world. The crimes carried out on these shores, by your citizens, have left a scar in the hearts of Muslims everywhere.'

The Attorney General nodded sympathetically. 'Britain feels tremendous shame and anger over those terrible events. Thankfully, the Treaty of Cairo has gone some way to calm the fears you speak of. Whelan's arrest and expected conviction will draw a line under the matter. From a judicial perspective, of course,' she added quickly.

'This is true,' Massri said. 'Britain has done much to heal the wounds, yet the feeling is more can be done.'

'Go on,' invited Saeed. He knew what was coming, the deal already done. Today was about window-dressing, the discussion officially recorded. It was essential to follow protocol of course, but it was nothing more than that.

'Are you as familiar with the Qur'an, Ms. Morgan?'

The Attorney General shifted in her chair. 'Sadly, no.'

'Then permit me to impart a small education,' Massri offered, pinching his thumb and forefinger together.

*'And we ordained therein for them, life for life, eye for eye, nose for nose, ear for ear, tooth for tooth and wounds equal for equal.'*

'The language and cadence of Islam's holy words are truly inspiring,' fawned Emerson. A murmur of approval rippled around the table.

'Please forgive me,' Morgan squirmed. 'I'm not quite sure where you're going with this.'

'Daniel Whelan,' Saeed told her.

The Attorney General's eyes swept from Saeed to the Egyptian and back again. 'This is the jurisdiction issue we touched on yesterday?'

Saeed nodded. 'Correct.'

Next to him the Ambassador's face darkened. 'Whelan must be punished appropriately,' he growled, his finger pointed righteously at the ceiling.

'He'll be tried and convicted like any other terrorist,' insisted Morgan.

'Tried here? In a British court? Out of the question.' Massri waved away Morgan's words with a dismissive flick of his wrist. 'Once convicted he will languish in your prisons, watching TV, indulging in drugs and pornography. This would be a profound insult to Muslims everywhere.'

'Whelan has to be afforded his rights under European law. Rights that your own judiciary must now observe and protect.'

'This case is different,' the white-haired Emerson informed her. 'Egypt has recently been welcomed into the European family. Her people have suffered. A consensus has been reached.'

Morgan looked at Saeed. 'What consensus?'

'The trial will be held at the International Criminal Court in the Netherlands.'

The Attorney General took a moment to consider the news. 'Whelan is a British subject, and the crimes took take place on British soil. Does the ICC even have jurisdiction in this case?'

'Judicial amendments have been drafted,' the Foreign Secretary announced. 'We'll need your office to ratify them, Anna.'

'Everyone's in agreement?'

'Justice must be served,' Massri warned. 'Islam demands it.'

Morgan smiled and tilted her head. 'And so it shall be, although I do have one or two small concerns...'

Saeed settled back in his chair as the legal discussion continued around the table. History was being made here, the rule of law in Britain circumvented by a determination to appease more profound laws and sensibilities. Much would be made of it in the press of course, and that would have to be carefully managed, not least by his Communications Director who was furiously making notes.

His aide hovered close by. Saeed leaned back in his chair. The man whispered in his ear.

'One of the survivors is insisting on seeing you, Prime Minister.'

He'd attended a private function earlier, a reception for Whitehall staff who'd survived the Downing Street bomb. Saeed had listened to their stories of survival with genuine fascination, the twists of fate that marked the difference between life and death. Except one. He'd ignored her purposely. Still, he had to ask.

'Who is it?'

'Ella Jackson. Gabriel Bryce's former Chief of Staff.'

Saeed exhaled a breath. 'Very well, have her shown to my private drawing room, would you? I'll be down shortly.'

He got to his feet, made his excuses, and shook hands around the room. He took the stairs down to the lower floor where another aide ushered him into a quiet drawing room. The door closed behind him. Saeed waited patiently, hands folded in front of him, as Ella Jackson whirred across the carpet in her battery-powered wheelchair.

'Hello, Prime Minister.'

'Miss Jackson,' Saeed bowed, holding out his hand. 'It's

good to see you—' He nearly said *on your feet* but quickly shifted gear.

'How are you?'

Jackson shrugged. She was one of the most seriously injured of the Downing Street survivors. The theory was, the heavy bomb-proof door of Number Ten had been blown inward by the bomb, hitting Jackson like a truck on a motorway. It had saved her from the blast itself but the resulting impact had crushed her spine and pulped most of her innards below the waist. The wheelchair, including the discretely hidden waste bags, was to be a permanent fixture for the rest of her life.

'Please, just call me Ella. Like before.'

'Yes,' was all Saeed said. He dropped her hand. This would be short and sweet.

'How are you?'

'Tired of going to funerals.'

'And the treatment?'

'Never ending,' she grimaced.

Saeed could see the pain behind her eyes, magnified by the glasses perched on the end of her nose. He'd never liked her, her irritating tenacity, her brusque manner, the way she'd protected Bryce like a faithful dog. He was pleased to see that that woman was gone. Instead, Bryce's aide was a shadow of her former self, her hair unkempt, her tired face devoid of makeup, the skin pale and lined around the eyes and mouth. Her trademark grey trouser suit and shirt were crumpled and stained, her legs as thin as matchsticks, the shoes on her feet scuffed. The fire was gone from her belly, extinguished by her acceptance of a life bound to the chair she now occupied. Saeed felt a momentary pang of pity. Then it passed.

'You've been very brave,' he told her.

'Brave? Oh, I'm not sure about that. Scared, yes. Angry, definitely. As for self-pity, well, I've wallowed in plenty of that. But no courage, I'm afraid. That's been in short supply.'

'I'm sorry to hear that.'

'Nice picture,' Ella said, looking over his shoulder. Saeed turned. The painting was oil on canvas and covered most of the wall behind him, a camel train snaking across the bleached white sands of the Arabian desert, the dawn sky filled with pink and red hues, the dark fingers of the Sawarat mountains in the background. Saeed had instructed that his present accommodations be decorated with more ethnic art, a refreshing change from the severe white colonialists who followed his every step in other government buildings.

'That one is called *Sunrise over the Western Desert*.'

'It's very you,' she replied.

'Thank you.' He wasn't sure if she was being sarcastic.

'Can we talk about something else?'

Saeed checked his watch. 'I can give you a few minutes.'

'I want to see Gabriel.'

The smile remained frozen across Saeed's face. 'I'm afraid I can't allow that.'

The wheelchair whirred as Ella moved closer. 'I've contacted your office many times. You've trained your gate-keepers well.'

'Perhaps you haven't read the papers. These are busy times.'

'Trust me, that's all I do,' Ella shot back. 'I've read all about the bomb—I missed it you see—and Cairo of course, then poor Nigel.' She tilted her head and stared at him. 'Each of those events appears to have given your career a remarkable boost, wouldn't you say, Tariq?'

Her insolence, was beginning to get under Saeed's skin. 'Is there something you'd like to say, Ella?'

'I'm saying you've been fortunate. Things have worked out well for you. Considering Gabriel was about to fire you.'

'I think you're mistaken. Gabriel never mentioned anything to me.'

Her fingers toyed with the joystick of her chair. Saeed wondered if she was somehow recording the conversation. It wouldn't matter; the room was designed for such eventualities.

'Who told you we'd been to Heathrow that night?'

'I beg your pardon?'

'Rana Hassani knew. Which meant you knew. How?'

'What's you point?'

Ella's eyes blinked furiously behind her glasses. 'My point is this; Gabriel knew about Heathrow, about the deaths and mismanagement, your attempts to cover it all up. He was going to shut the place down and fire your incompetent arse into the bargain. And then that bloody bomb went off. And now look at you, Tariq. You're not fit to carry Gabriel's briefing notes, let alone run a country.'

'The opinion polls would beg to differ.'

'You're an arrogant shit, you know that?'

Saeed was tired of the foul-mouthed cripple. 'I'll have someone take you back to the reception.' He turned to leave.

'I want to see him,' Ella barked. 'I have a right.'

Saeed shook his head. 'You're not a relative.'

'He hasn't any. No one's seen him. Why?'

'He's in good hands. The best.'

'Where is he?'

'I can't say. It's a question of security, and your clearance had expired.'

Ella tugged at the cuffs of her shirt. 'I was his Chief of Staff. I had clearance as high as yours. Nothing's changed.'

'It's out of my hands, I'm afraid.'

'Bullshit. Let me see him, Tariq. Or maybe I should go to the press?'

A smile played around the corners of Saeed's mouth. 'With what, exactly?'

'Heathrow.'

'The relocation centre is to be closed.'

The news caught her off guard. 'When?'

'Soon. The refugees are to be given an amnesty, allowed to settle here. The facility is not fit for purpose, as I've stated in a yet-to-be published report.'

'That won't make any difference,' she blustered. 'People should know about the deaths, your mismanagement.'

'And how will you prove all this, Ella? Where's your evidence?' He moved a little closer. 'Whatever you think happened at Heathrow, it's all in the past now. Go to the press if it makes you feel better, but I can promise you that if you do, the blame will be laid firmly at Gabriel's door. You see, I *do* have evidence. Emails to Gabriel, expressing my concerns.'

'You're lying,' Ella whispered.

He could see the fight was fast leaving her. 'You'll lose, Ella. Don't you think you've lost enough?'

She dropped her gaze, twisted her hands in her lap. Her voice was barely audible. 'I want to see him.'

She was persistent, Saeed had to admit. Maybe there *had* been something there? It was a rumour he'd explored once, looking for a chink in Bryce's armour, a way to exploit the man, but nothing was ever discovered. Yet Jackson had revered Bryce, and clearly still did, in a manner that was more than just professional. It was time to nail this particular coffin shut.

He reached into his pocket, for the photos there. He had a feeling he'd need them today. 'I didn't want to have to do this, Ella, but you've forced my hand. We've kept it out of the media for obvious reasons. They're not pleasant.'

She studied the photos, of a naked, cowering Bryce, the ones taken by Sully and Orla. He saw her eyes widen, her hand cover her open mouth. One by one she went through them, unable to comprehend what she was seeing.

'He's deteriorated significantly since the stroke, both physically and mentally. We're doing all we can but I'm told the breakdown is irreversible. He's being taken care of, but it's only a matter of time now.' He watched the tears fill her eyes, and course down the hollows of her cheeks.

'Oh my God.'

'He didn't want you to see him like this. In his lucid moments he made me promise to keep you away. That lucidity is gone now.'

'I don't care,' Ella sniffed. 'I want to see him.'

'I don't advise it. The man we remember is no longer there.'

'Perhaps if he saw me, perhaps if I...' Her voice trailed away. She stared at the photos in her lap, then scooped them up and handed them back to Saeed.

'All we can do now is prepare ourselves for the inevitable,' he soothed.

Ella broke down, sobbing in her chair. Saeed checked his watch; time was moving on and there was much to do. 'I'm sorry, I really have to go. I'll send someone.'

She looked up at him, the sobs catching in her throat, her eyes brimming with tears. 'He respected you, Tariq. You were friends, once.'

'Yes, we were.'

'No, I don't think you were ever a friend to Gabriel. I think deep down you were jealous of him, of his power and popularity. You used him, betrayed him. You disgust me.'

Saeed snapped. He grabbed the arms of her wheelchair and shook it. 'Who do you think you're talking to? Gabriel Bryce was a fool, a Prime Minister by dint of rich friends, a dead wife and a sympathetic electorate. And you, his faithful lap dog, an adulterer, wielding your master's power as if it were your own. Neither of you are worthy of this office.'

He let go and stood up, forcing himself to calm down. Ella's eyes were wide with shock, her hands trembling. Good. Perhaps now she'll learn some respect. He smoothed his jacket and straightened his tie.

'I suggest we put this unsavoury exchange behind us. You won't be seeing Gabriel, now or anytime in the future. Deal with it. And if you even think of going to the press I will make it my mission to destroy both your reputations, do you understand?'

She did, Saeed was pleased to see. Her hands still shook, the bloodless face had paled further and she nodded silently. Saeed flicked one of Bryce's photographs into her lap.

'A reminder, in case your courage does return. Think wisely, Ella.'

He turned on his heel and left the room. At the top of the sweeping stone staircase he stopped and looked down. Jackson was being escorted from the building, her motor whirring, her tyres squeaking on the highly polished floor. Her head was bowed, her frailty even more pronounced.

She was beaten. He'd get no more trouble from her. He

smiled as he headed towards his office, his thoughts turning to other matters.

It had proved simple in the end. Both Bryce and Hooper had been removed, the path cleared for those who possessed true vision. Men like Saeed. Cairo was an important moment, but history would record its true significance; not the welcoming of a new partner into the bosom of the European family but the key that unlocked the gates of Europe. The continent's Muslim population had risen by another eighty million. More were heading west every day. The Ummah was growing stronger, Saeed could feel it. As a boy he'd been taught that the final conquest would be achieved not with bombs and bullets but by sheer weight of numbers. He knew now that those words would come to fruition.

He closed the door to his private office. There was much work to be done, speeches to prepare, a media to manage in the wake of the forthcoming Whelan announcement. And most importantly, an official visit to Cairo, a gesture of Britain's support for the Egyptian judicial system.

Saeed was looking forward to it.

The outcome even more so.

# 21

# ICC DETENTION CENTRE, NETHERLANDS

Danny sat at the table, a cigarette pinched between his tobacco-stained fingers, exhaustion buzzing inside his head like a faulty bulb.

Something wasn't right. From the moment they'd removed him from his cell at Belmarsh Prison he'd asked the question over and over again; why was he being transferred? Why Holland? So far no one was saying anything, not even his useless solicitor. He hadn't even been charged yet, but he knew something bad was heading his way.

From where he sat now, Britain was a short hop across the North Sea. It might've been a million miles away. He was trapped in an alien environment. Everything was different, the language, the uniforms, the buildings, the smells, and it frightened Danny because he didn't trust foreigners

He used to laugh when he saw people on the news—lefties, mostly—moaning about the injustices of the British legal system. Compared to places like Angola or China, a British courtroom was a shining beacon of justice and impartiality. Which was why Danny was frightened. He wasn't in Britain anymore.

He'd been banged up before, but this was different. He was being kept in solitary, in a high security wing. Every time he left his cell they shackled his wrists and ankles. They always grilled him in the same windowless interview room. When he was alone, like now, the coppers stationed outside took turns to peer at him through a metal flap. They were taking no chances.

They let him smoke though. He brought his hands up to his mouth and sucked deeply on the self-rolled cigarette, exhaling his exhaust in a long, thin plume. He watched it billow toward the ceiling before being drawn out through the humming extractor, the only noise on the dead, insulated air. He'd started smoking again the day he was captured. He'd be an old man if he ever got out.

If.

He stared at the mirror on the opposite wall. His hair was a greasy mess, the beard even worse. The healthy outdoor glow of Hertfordshire was gone, replaced by a familiar pasty pallor. The old Danny was back, the one from the Longhill estate.

He wondered who was behind that mirror, wondered if they were actually *listening* to him.

He'd told the cops a hundred times about Eddie, about the truck in Kings Cross, about the fridge with no power cable. He wasn't sure if they believed him. It was hard to read these Counter Terrorist types. They'd questioned him day and night for four days straight. No one seemed bothered about his Human Rights.

*Start recording.*

*Tell us about this, Danny.*

*Tell us about that, Danny.*

*Stop recording.*

And so it went.

He heard voices outside and stubbed his cigarette out in a metal ashtray. The thick grey door swung open and his two interrogators filed back into the room. They sat opposite in chairs that were bolted to the floor. They licked their thumbs and skimmed the files in front of them. Neither man spoke. The chair next to Danny remained empty.

'Where's my solicitor?'

'He's outside.'

'He should be here.'

The senior officer, Harris, closed his file. He was a Yorkshireman, mid-fifties, with thinning dark hair and a scrawny neck. He wore a creased blue shirt and played with the wedding band on his finger. He seemed like a decent bloke.

'There's been a development.' He traded a look with his younger colleague, Simms.

'What development?'

'Concerning your case,' Simms growled. He was bad cop.

'Look, I've been doing this job a long time,' Harris continued. 'You get a feel for people. It becomes easy to spot a liar—'

'I'm not lying.' Danny was tired of saying that.

'The evidence against you is very persuasive.'

'All bullshit.'

Harris opened a file on the table. He didn't look at it, didn't need to. 'Let's go over it again, one more time. The truck bomb was delivered to the Luton mosque by you, you've admitted that.'

'I didn't know it was a bomb.'

'Architectural drawings of the mosque were found in your father's apartment.'

'Planted.'

'You previously worked for the Government Mail

Service, from where a vehicle was procured and used to detonate the Downing Street bomb.'

'I was sacked ages ago. I don't know anything about that.'

'You knew the driver.'

'We worked in the same department.'

'You had access to ordinance during your army career.'

'I drove an ammo truck a few times. That was my job.'

'You haven't named any accomplices.'

'Because there aren't any.'

'What about this mystery man, Eddie?'

'I told you, he wasn't an accomplice. He fitted me up.'

'There's no record of the person you described being released from Winchester Prison during that time period.'

'The landlord of the Kings Head saw him.'

'His description was vague at best.'

'I'm telling the truth.'

'You're not telling us everything. You've had help along the way. From serious people.'

They always came back to this. Danny shifted on his seat. 'No I haven't'

Simms barked across the table. 'You're lying. You were in possession of a brand new passport when you were arrested. Not a forgery, a duplicate. We've interviewed Eduard Zala. He's a family man, hard working. No criminal record. He's clean, like that passport. Where did you get it?'

'Eddie gave it to me.'

Harris shook his head. 'Eddie, again. We could clear up half the murders in London if we stuck his name up every time. Who gave you the car, Danny?'

'I told you—'

'And the money? Where did you get that?'

'Listen, you need to find this Eddie and—'

Harris held up his hand. 'Alright Danny, that's enough. We're just going in circles here.' He slapped the cover shut and sat a little straighter. 'I'm out of options, lad. If there's anything you want to tell us, anything at all, then now's the time. This is your last chance.'

Danny's mind raced. *Last chance.* Was that a bluff? Maybe. Then again, maybe not. Either way he'd play dumb, blame Eddie for everything, take his chances in court, even if it was foreign. He was innocent. The jury would see the truth.

He folded his arms. 'I've got nothing more to say, Mister Harris.'

'Sure?'

'Just charge me.'

Harris got to his feet. 'Don't say you weren't warned.'

Simms held open the door and several people filed into the room, suits and robes. His solicitor followed them in and took up position next to Danny.

'Stand up,' he whispered.

Danny obeyed. Two men and a woman lined up across the table. They wore black robes and white bibs, which made them look like priests. They hadn't come to forgive him. The one in the middle spoke in heavily accented English.

'Mister Whelan, I'm going to read you a statement,'

'What statement?'

The judge silenced him with a loud clearing of his throat. He read from a sheet of paper in his hand.

'Daniel Whelan, you are indicted by the Prosecutor's Division of the International Criminal Court and the charges against you are that, between the dates specified, in the United Kingdom, you did conspire together and with others, namely the use of explosive devices in the commission of an act of terrorism, in particular the attack on the Luton Central Mosque, Bedfordshire, England—'

'I'm innocent—'

The solicitor nudged him with an elbow.

'And a secondary act of terrorism, namely the intended use of a biological device, and the murders of Raymond Eugene Carver and Joseph Stephens in Hertfordshire, England.'

Danny froze.

*They knew.*

The judge was still talking.

'After legal consultation with the Grand Chamber of the European Court of Justice, it is the decision of the Presidency and the Office of the Prosecutor of the International Criminal Court that trial and sentencing will take place at the Sharia Supreme Court in Maadi, Egypt. Custody is to be transferred to Egyptian authorities forthwith.'

The judges turned as one and marched from the room. The solicitor scuttled out after them.

Danny's legs felt like water. He folded into the chair.

'What's he talking about Egypt for?'

Harris tapped his folder on the desk. 'We ran the serial number of the Rolex in your possession. It was registered to a Raymond Carver, former head of the English Freedom Movement. But you knew that, right Danny?'

He couldn't move, couldn't speak.

'When we got to Carver's address in Hertfordshire we found the bodies in a workshop, as well as that chemical IED. His wife Tess was discovered in a bedroom in the main house. Suicide, as it turns out. She left a note—well, more of a statement really—saying that a man called Eduard Zala, who claimed to be a former member of the English Freedom Movement, arrived in a blue Vauxhall seeking shelter a week before Christmas. Zala gave them a hard luck story and was given temporary lodging in the granny flat above the garage, however when Zala's behaviour became increasingly erratic, Ray Carver asked him to leave. Sometime later, in the estate workshop, Zala produced a gun and shot Carver and Stephens dead. The description Tess Carver gave was yours, Danny. The DNA evidence is irrefutable.'

He was a rabbit, caught in the headlights of a speeding car. It was a moment before he was able to speak. 'That's all bullshit. They welcomed me, kept me hidden. I was there for ages.'

'Are you denying killing Ray Carver and Joe Stephens?'

Danny paled. 'They tried to make me use that bomb thing.'

'It was your device. You tried to coerce them, help you carry out another attack.'

'Don't be be stupid! I'd never do anything like that!'

'You should've told us, Danny.' Harris moved toward the door. 'Eduard, Eddie; it's all a bit convenient, don't you think? Still, it's out of our hands now.'

Danny bolted out of the chair. 'Wait, Mister Harris. Why are they talking about Egypt? I'm British.'

'The Egyptian authorities have requested jurisdiction and it's been granted. You want my advice? Listen to your brief and above all, be respectful. Good luck, lad. Something tells me you're going to need it.'

'I didn't do it!' he shrieked. 'Why won't anyone believe me?'

Harris closed the door behind him.

Danny's mouth was bone dry, his heart beating so loudly in his chest that it threatened to punch through his prison issue sweatshirt.

He hopped around the room to the mirror on the wall, swaying in front of the glass, hands cupped around his face. He couldn't see anything beyond his own desperate reflection. He balled his fists and banged against the smooth surface.

'I didn't do it!' he screamed. 'I'm innocent! You can't do this!

The door flew open.

Danny spun around.

A scrum of black uniforms surged towards him, knocking him to the ground. He lay still, unable to move, paralysed by fear. Black boots circled him. He squeezed his eyes shut. He willed them all to disappear, to wake up from the nightmare and find himself back home on the Longhill, lying in his own bed, listening to the sound of his dad pottering in the kitchen. He'd never wanted anything more in his life.

Strong hands gripped his arms and yanked him to his feet. His eyes snapped open. He was marched from the room, foreign shouts echoing along the dull corridor.

His feet barely touched the ground.

A door flew open.

He blinked into the glare of a floodlit compound. A prison van waited, exhaust smoking on the cold air, flanked by idling police cars and heavily armed cops. Others watched from the shadows, whispering, pointing.

Danny began to tremble.

It wasn't the sight of the convoy that made him shake, or the hard faces, or the salty coastal winds that whipped across the prison.

No.

It was what the wind brought with it.

The voices of hate, snatched by the breeze and hurled

over the prison walls, the fury of the religious mob that had laid siege to the building for days, calling for justice, demanding vengeance. And Danny knew they were going to get it. The guards kept moving, bundling him inside the van, sealing him inside a small transport cubicle.

The engine rumbled into life. Sirens wailed.

The van lurched forward and accelerated out of the prison gates. The screams of the mob filled the air, battling with the sirens for supremacy, assaulting Danny's ears as he sat locked inside his own private hell.

Missiles cannoned off the van.

Danny's pitiful wail was lost in the vengeful roar of the crowd .

# 22

# THE SOUTH COAST

He heard Mac up on deck, his voice calm, confident, issuing instructions to Trevor, his burly crew hand.

Bryce was reluctant but Mac was right. Sailing across the Atlantic wasn't easy, but then again neither was sailing to southern Spain. There was the Bay of Biscay to contend with, unpredictable at the best of times, and the inherent dangers of the international shipping lanes that ran up and down the Portuguese coast. Bryce wasn't that experienced, nor did he feel physically robust enough to take turns to skipper the boat *and* keep watch. And if the weather turned it could go bad very quickly. Trevor was family, Mac explained, his wife's brother and an experienced sailor. The cover story was simple; Bryce was a wealthy businessman about to collect his brand new sixty-footer down at Gibraltar and needed to stretch his sea legs. Good enough, Bryce had agreed.

They'd left early that morning. The empty roads were dark and slick with rain. Mac drove the short distance to the deserted marina in Hamble. Beyond the security gate and the chain-link fence the *Sunflower* waited, a thirty-eight foot Beneteau Oceanis tied alongside a remote pontoon. Trevor had pre-loaded her with everything they'd need. The marina was quiet. They boarded without being seen.

Mac ordered Bryce to remain below until they were underway. He made a large pot of coffee in the galley and listened to the radio as the yacht cruised quietly under engine power along the silent channel of the Hamble River and out into Southampton Water. He felt the chop of the deeper sea as the bow turned south and the engine increased power. He was beginning to drift off on one of the bunks when a shadow loomed in the gangway. It was Trevor.

'Mac says it's okay to come up on deck.'

Bryce tugged his coat on and pulled a woollen hat over his head. Outside the sun had risen, climbing above the gently sloping ground to the east. Mac was stood behind one of the twin steel helms at the stern of the boat and Bryce joined him. They stood in silence for a moment and watched the land slip by, docks and refineries giving way to sheep dotted fields and wooded hills. Bryce was gripped with a sense of liberty he'd never experienced before. He took a deep lungful of salt-tinged air and exhaled noisily.

'I'd forgotten how good this felt.'

'I never get tired of it,' Mac smiled. He was hatless, dressed in a red sailing jacket and trousers, a turtleneck sweater and rubber boots on his feet. His eyes were hidden behind wraparound sunglasses. Trevor was up at the bow, winding ropes.

'Shouldn't I get changed into my wet gear?'

'The forecast is good so you won't need it,' Mac said. 'We'll unpack after supper.'

Bryce ran a hand over the digitised instrumentation

panel. 'Sailing's come a long way since I first got my feet wet.'

'She's something, isn't she? The owner wants her moved to Marbella. Trevor will sail her there and do the hand over after we go ashore at Gib.'

Bryce shielded his eyes. 'What's the traffic like?'

'Reasonably light. A couple of large freighters steaming up from the south towards East Solent, but we'll pass well ahead of them. Here, take these.'

Bryce clamped the binoculars to his eyes. He scanned the water ahead, spotting a huge white cruise ship with a yellow funnel steaming down the channel ahead of them.

'Cold start to their holiday,' Bryce remarked.

'Heading to the Caribbean for some winter sun, I'd imagine. Their crossing will be a bit more comfortable than ours.'

Bryce refocused the binoculars until the huge vessel filled the lens. He could see people crowding around the deck rails, men, women, children, braving the cold weather in their coats and scarves, ribbons of coloured streamers trailing from the superstructure and rippling in the wind.

'Lucky beggars. Still, I'm not complaining.' He watched the ship as it pulled away from them into the Solent. 'I'm sorry I put you through all this, Mac.'

'What's to be sorry for? We made it away clean.'

'I still feel a little guilty.'

'Don't. You've already run up a hefty bill.'

Bryce chuckled. 'Oliver will take good care of you, until my finances are sorted. And who knows, when things have returned to some sort of normality perhaps you'll get something out of this. A book deal, maybe. This is quite a story.'

Mac laughed. 'Maybe they'll make a film. I wonder who'd play me?' He pointed off to starboard, past the bright lights and steaming towers of a large power station. 'See that castle there? That's Calshot Spit. Things can get a little tricky here so we need to pay attention. Fancy a job?'

Bryce nodded. 'Anything.'

'Good. How about a round of coffees?'

'No problem.' He went down to the galley, feeling vaguely disappointed. He boiled the kettle and searched for mugs, finding only two. That might prove inconvenient in the coming days, he imagined. He made some toast and brought the whole lot topside.

Mac attacked the toast first. 'Mmm, nice,' he mumbled between mouthfuls. 'Sea air always gives me an appetite.'

'Me too,' Bryce admitted, chewing on his own slice. He gazed off to starboard, watching a long spit of land curving towards them, like a shingle finger beckoning them to shore. There was someone at the water's edge, a boy with a fishing rod, wrapped up in a green jacket and a red and white football scarf. As the *Sunflower* drifted past he raised his hand and waved. Bryce waved back.

'How are you feeling,' Mac asked.

'Okay. I'm not match fit yet.'

Mac polished off the last of the toast. 'Don't worry, I won't push you. Me and Trevor can take care of things if you need to rest.'

'I want to do my bit,' Bryce insisted.

'Alright, then.' Mac gulped his coffee and threw the dregs overboard. 'You can keep watch on the bow if you're up to it.'

'Sure.'

'Don't forget your safety line.'

Bryce made his way down to the front of the vessel, inching past Trevor who was preparing the sails, until he was close to the bow. He lifted his sunglasses from around his neck and slipped them on. The sun was behind them now, its strong light dappling the surface as Bryce searched for objects in their path. Behind him he heard Trevor hoisting the main sail. He watched it billow once, and again, before the wind caught it and snapped it tight. Bryce held on as the vessel listed a little, then settled in the water. There was nothing quite like it, being on a boat at sea, powered only by the strength of the wind. He no longer felt the steady throb of the engines beneath his feet as wind and tide took over completely. He smiled, exhilarated.

The wind pushed them on, the land crowding the Solent on either side, funnelling the boat through Hurst Spit. Bryce kept himself busy, absorbing the nautical chatter of his sailing companions, familiarising himself with the equipment, the feel of the deck beneath his feet. It was all coming back. The land fell away and the open sea beckoned.

The hours passed.

The winter sun overtook them and began its rapid descent towards the western horizon. Bryce stood watch at the bow, binoculars pressed to his eyes. There was a single vessel, far to the southwest, but that was it. The sea could be a place of terrible desolation, he reminded himself, yet at this moment, with the wind whipping across the deck and the boat carving through the green water, he felt more alive than he'd ever done.

He took a breath and closed his eyes.

He heard the sails snapping, the ropes cracking against the mast, the slap of water on the bow.

He heard the squeak of rubber boots.

Then he heard nothing.

·  ·  ·

BLACKNESS.

He heard voices, vague, muffled. Terror squeezed his heart. He was back in Alton Grange, sedated, imprisoned.

*No.*

He could smell the sea, feel the wind on his face. Dark shapes swam into view. Two figures loomed over him, a huge triangle of white behind them. He was on the *Sunflower,* staring up at the mast. The sun had set, the endless sky a deep blue.

'He's coming round. Sit him up.'

Hands lifted him. His vision blurred, then sharpened again. He heard the waves against the hull, felt the deck bucking beneath him. His tongue tasted of salt and blood.

'Gabriel, can you hear me?'

A crouching Mac swam into focus, snapping his fingers.

'Yes,' Bryce croaked.

'How are you feeling?'

'My head hurts.' His tongue felt thick, his speech slurred.

Mac and Trevor hauled him up until his back rested against the curve of the cabin superstructure.

Bryce felt something wet on his neck. He reached up to touch it.

His arms didn't move.

He dropped his chin. He was wrapped in his sleeping bag. No, that wasn't right. He was *trapped* in his sleeping bag.

Swathes of black tape had been wound around his body, spiralling up towards his neck. He couldn't move his legs, his arms, anything. He struggled violently to no avail.

His eyes swam.

'Trevor cracked you good and proper,' Mac chuckled, his teeth white in the gloom. 'I thought he'd killed you.'

'I barely touched him,' Trevor complained. The big man leaned over, grunting with effort as he ran another few loops of tape around the sleeping bag. Bryce felt he was being mummified.

'Stop it, please.'

Trevor responded by shifting position, kneeling across Bryce's right leg. Bryce yelped in pain. Trevor finished off the roll of tape and stood up.

'There, that should do it.' He tossed the empty cardboard roll over the side.

'Get the chains,' Mac said.

*Chains?*

Bryce's stomach lurched. 'For God's sake what are you doing, Mac?'

'My job,' he shrugged. Trevor returned, dropping several coils of rusted chains at Bryce's feet.

'What do you mean, your job?'

'I'm finishing what the Minister started.'

'What Minister?'

Mac smiled. 'Minister Saeed, of course.'

They lifted his body, passing the thick shackles underneath him, wrapping them around his legs, his torso, securing the links with heavy padlocks. They rattled and tugged, satisfied Bryce was safely cocooned. The chains smelt of rusted metal and salt. He looked down at his body. He looked like Houdini.

'You're scaring me, Mac. Please, get me out of this.' He registered the faint note of hysteria in his voice.

'Can't do that.'

'Mac! Please!' He rocked his body across the deck, the padlocks digging painfully into his flesh.

Mac shook his head. 'As I said, I've got a job to finish.'

'What bloody job!' He yelled the words, hysteria

unleashed.

'Normally I'd tell you to keep the noise down, but out here...' Mac let the words trail away. 'Look, you were supposed to die in Downing Street, but you didn't stick to the script. They sent me in after the bomb, only that bloody helicopter lit us up and that was that. The best laid plans, as the Minister often says. Anyway, it was felt that should things slip out of our control again, a mechanism ought be out in place, one that would steer you back to us. It was all worked out on a psychological level, profiling, all that stuff.'

'Clever bastards,' Trevor grinned in the half-light.

'What do you mean, *us*?' Bryce was confused, terrified.

'Minister Saeed. And others.'

'What others?'

'Powerful people, here and abroad.' Mac squatted down on his haunches. 'The sailing trips in university, the painting in your office; for you, boats and water symbolise freedom. That's why they sent you the book and the business card. They were planting a seed, showing you a way out in case things didn't go our way. Subliminal suggestion, they called it. It worked a treat too. I've got to say, that day you rang me I was genuinely shocked. So shocked in fact, I nearly forgot to disconnect the warehouse phone lines.'

Bryce was struggling, physically and mentally. 'The boat business is real?'

'Sure. We use it as cover to move things. People, mainly.' He stood up. 'Nice job on Sully and Orla, by the way. I think the Minister was quietly impressed when I told him.'

'How did—'

'I never went to Jersey. After I picked you up I had to go back to Alton Grange and clean up your mess. Give me a hand, Trevor.'

They grabbed the chains and dragged Bryce towards

the port bow. Inside the sleeping bag he kicked and bucked but his limbs were squeezed tight. He heard the water, loud in his ears, smacking against the hull. Mac and Trevor were shadows now, silhouetted against the deep blue sky. He tried to focus on Mac's face, make eye contact. The art of persuasion; he'd been good at it all his adult life. Now that life depended on it.

'Don't do this, Mac. I'm begging you. There must be another way.'

'Orders are orders.'

'Think of your daughter. You think she'd be proud of you? Of this?'

Trevor laughed. 'Daughter?'

'And a fake wife too,' Mac told him.

'Just get me to Tortola, please Mac. You do that and I'll make sure you both leave the island very rich men.'

Trevor shook his head. 'Typical politician. If all else fails, bung 'em a bribe.'

'None of this is about money,' Mac told him. 'It's about loyalty, about getting the job done. Plus I get to meet some really interesting people on the way. Like Danny Whelan.'

Bryce frowned. 'Whelan?'

'Correct. Met him right at the start, in that shithole pub of his. He was stupid and greedy, like the rest of his breed. He's served his purpose. So have you.'

Bryce shook his head violently. 'No, Mac, please, you don't know what you're doing. There's so much more at stake here, you couldn't even begin to understand—'

Mac gave him a sharp kick. Bryce rolled onto his side, winded.

'Don't patronise me, prick. Besides, I couldn't give a shit about politics.' He unclipped a section of the wire rail. 'Minister Saeed was right about you, though. You're so full of your own self-importance you don't realise how redundant you've become.'

'Tariq Saeed is a bloody murderer!'

'He's the future of this country.'

'I thought you didn't care about politics.'

Mac gave him another kick, and Bryce felt something snap in his left arm. He howled in pain.

'You were beaten by the better man,' Mac snarled. 'You were outthought and outmanoeuvred. He played you like a piano. You can take that thought to your grave.'

Bryce opened his mouth to say something then stopped. He ceased his wriggling, swallowed the sob of fear in his throat. It was pointless. Better to summon whatever courage he possessed and let things run their course. There would be no stay of execution here, no deal to be done. It was over. Mac was right; he should've died in Downing Street, like he was supposed to.

The wind was cold on his face and he shivered. A terrible, lonely end awaited. He looked above him, to the bright swathe of stars that littered the night sky, and prayed it would be quick.

'Stand him up.'

Strong hands gripped the chains and he was hauled to his feet, his back to the sea. They held him there a moment, the boat rising and falling with the swell. Mac smiled in the darkness.

'Don't try and fight it, just let yourself go. It's supposed to be like falling asleep.'

'I doubt that.'

'Well, you're about to find out.'

They dragged him to the edge of the boat, his broken arm shooting pain across his body. Death was moments away.

He heard a screech and looked up. A black-tipped gull drifted out of the darkness and circled the mast overhead, an impassive witness to his imminent demise. The sight gave Bryce some comfort, a winged angel, sent to watch over him during his last moments. It was strange what went through a person's mind so close to the end.

'Hey.'

Mac shook him, the neck of the sleeping bag bunched in his fists.

'Just for the record, Gabriel, I kind of liked you. You amused me, thinking all this was your idea. Like a Turkey inventing Christmas.' Trevor laughed in the dark, a cold cackle. 'Seriously though, you did well to get out of the Grange. You fooled Sully and Orla, fought back. No one expected that.'

'Go to hell.'

'After you,' he grinned.

Mac let go.

Bryce felt himself falling. He hit the water and plunged beneath the surface, the icy cold snatching his breath away, an explosion of bubbles, the water roaring in his ears, his nose. He twisted and turned, sinking fast, the pressure building in his chest, his head. He closed his eyes. He was already deep, way too deep.

He stopped struggling, let himself fall.

Feet first, down into the blackest of hells.

He lifted his head, craned his neck, his eyes burning, searching for the light of the surface and seeing nothing. He fell like a stone.

His lungs were empty. He opened his mouth to take a breath.

The nightmare ended.

## 23

---

## LONDON

Ella sat by her first floor window and stared at the distant Shard, reaching high into the sky above the city of London. She wasn't a particular fan of modern architecture but she felt the building possessed a certain elegance, the way its tapered frame of glass and steel swept up towards that strangely unfinished summit. She wished she lived there, a thousand feet above the streets of London Bridge, because it would be so convenient when she finally summoned the courage to end her life.

She'd thought about other means and methods. Pills were unthinkable, her gag reflex precluding the consumption of anything more than three or four tablets at a time. Besides, statistics proved it rarely worked. Trains and motorways were out; in a wheelchair it would look comical and pathetic, and may even result in death or injury to someone else. She'd considered a gun—her father had one at the house in Sussex—but it was messy, and they would find her on the floor, and Basil the spaniel would be licking her brains off the wall, and she wouldn't put mum and dad through that.

That's why she had to jump.

She'd often played it out in her head, leaving that accursed chair for the last time, crawling to a ledge or a window, dragging herself up and then letting go, the sensation of falling, of moving without the aid of her motorised prison in which she was to serve out her life sentence. She would be free, albeit for a few seconds, and then it would be over.

The resolve to end her life had become much stronger since Gabe's death. A will had been found, his estate bequeathed to the Party, the funeral a private affair. There was no mention of Ella, and that hurt her deeply, but she buried her pain and went to the church in Burnham-on-Sea, close to Gabe's childhood home. Lizzie's sister had made the trip from Guilford to pay her respects, the only family member who did, and the other mourners were those that knew Gabe as friends and colleagues. The turn out was pitiful for a former Prime Minister, and that made Ella especially angry. A photographer took pictures and left before he was challenged. The vicar spread the word, a last minute invite to locals to fill out the pews. It never made much difference. Tariq didn't attend, and Ella was glad of it. She hoped never to set eyes on him again.

At the crematorium on the edge of town, Gabriel's ashes were scattered in the garden of remembrance. Ella had cried; how little they knew him, the women who stood there shedding fake tears, the men wearing solemn frowns as they furtively checked their phones and watches. His ashes should have gone with her, to be cast on the coastal winds or scattered at a spot of breathtaking beauty. Gabe loved a view, loved the magnificence of nature. That would've been more fitting.

At the wake she'd got very drunk, and said some very

rude things to some very embarrassed people. She was ushered out into the rain, where she sobbed beneath an umbrella for half and hour before a taxi with a power ramp was able to collect her. She'd cried the next morning, ashamed of her undignified behaviour, knowing that Gabe would've scolded her for it. She'd cried for days.

She would give anything to see him again.

Being a dead somebody helped. The internet was filled with pictures of Gabriel Bryce. The ones where they'd both been pictured together held a special place in her heart. She'd printed those out and pinned them around her sterile new flat with the extra wide doors and the drive-in shower and the industrial sized lift and the concrete ramps that led to the street. Everywhere she turned she saw him, and that gave her some comfort, but it didn't last.

The hours of despair became days, the days, weeks.

The blu-tac hardened. The pictures fluttered to the floor. Ella left them there. What was the point? Gabe was dead.

That's when she'd first thought about joining him.

Ella had been a churchgoer in her youth. Her parents had joined a progressive outfit, all guitars and clapping and summer picnics, and it had made her smile. They'd told her that their God was the God of love and compassion.

Ella remembered that God and thought he might understand the pain that was eating her. She thought He might let them be together again, so she remained behind her extra wide front door and stared at the walls and thought of ways she could end it. She started drinking, to put herself to sleep and blot out the long, lonely nights. She stopped eating, and washing her hair. Then she stopped thinking, about anything other than her own grief. It consumed her, and she was glad. She'd welcomed the downward spiral of her life, wallowed in her vast reserves of self-pity, if only to reach her goal of seeing Gabe again. This life held no joy for her, therefore it was imperative to speed its passage toward its inevitable end. Soon she would find the courage to do what was necessary.

She watched the Shard a while longer, the way the sun glinted of its glass and steel, the blue sky reflected on its flanks. The view would be breathtaking. The fall, a blessed relief.

Yet today was different. The resolve was there even if the courage was still lacking, but she didn't feel quite as fatalistic as she normally did. It puzzled her. The morning was cold but the sky was clear and blue. The street below was long and narrow and always busy and she watched it come to life. She saw commuters heading towards nearby Angel tube station, she saw cyclists and cars, mums and buggies, school kids and boisterous workmen. She watched a woman pass by below, thirties, wearing expensive shoes and a smart tan coat. Her heels clicked a busy tattoo and she barked into a mobile phone, issuing instructions, exerting authority. A smile played at the corners of Ella's thin lips. *You go, girl.* The woman clicked around the corner and disappeared.

Hunger gnawed at her. She toggled the chair controls with practised ease. She whirred past the TV and flicked it on. She plucked a tin of spaghetti hoops from a specially lowered cupboard and microwaved them. She ate three mouthfuls and left the bowl on the side. She made a coffee, an espresso. She'd bought a special machine, because a friend once told her that overconsumption can trigger a heart attack. So far it hadn't, despite her best efforts. Her friend didn't come around anymore. No one invited her out.

Cripples in restaurants were so inconvenient, and one could never get a decent table.

She watched the news. China was bitching to Taiwan about something or other, a loony bin manager called Parry had been killed in a suspected hit and run and agricultural scientists at a laboratory somewhere had grown some sort of vegetable in a petri dish. Or on a mouse's back. Or something. Ella wasn't really paying attention. She saw Tariq Saeed trotting down the steps of a plane and snapped the TV off.

The espresso was kicking in. She felt unusually restless.

She thought about cleaning the flat and wondered why she would think of that. She hadn't cleaned it in weeks. She barely cleaned herself. She hadn't been out of the flat in nearly a month.

Somebody rang her doorbell and it startled her. It wasn't a bell, more of a buzzer, a very loud one. She should have it disconnected, because no one ever stopped by.

Except Milo.

She whirred into her extra wide hallway and checked the intercom. Milo's face filled the small video screen. She buzzed him in and went back to the kitchen. She fired up the machine. She'd make him a coffee, promise to take better care of herself and then he would leave. It had become a ritual. But at least he came.

She heard the key in the lock, heard Milo swear, heard the door being shoved open, the scrape of paper. He huffed and puffed in the hallway for a minute then poked his mop of dark curly hair around the door.

'Ah, there she is.'

'Hello, Milo.'

He kissed her on the head, wrinkled his nose. 'Nice perfume.'

'It's French. Au-de-mind your own business.'

Milo laughed. He was used to her rudeness. She thought he liked it, enjoyed the banter. Their relationship was so different now, compared to when they were married. They'd fancied each other back then, a whirlwind romance, a quick wedding in the Caribbean. He'd doted on her and she knew it, came to resent it. She'd had an affair and Milo had found out. He was devastated and Ella was ashamed. They'd divorced, and Ella made it her mission to repair the damage, because beneath that tough, journalistic exterior, Milo Kellerman was a kind, decent human being. She found him a girlfriend, an old school chum whom she thought might suit. She did, and they got married. Ella was godmother to their first child.

Somewhere, on some level, Milo still loved her. That's why he came around, when he could, which wasn't often. Milo had a better excuse than most; he ran a national newspaper.

'I could barely get past the door for the post.'

She whirred around. Still tall, dark and handsome, a touch of grey on the sideburns, scruffy chic in designer jeans and a leather jacket, and one of the youngest men ever to run the *Observer*. He gave Ella a lot of credit for that, for dumping him, for forcing him to focus on his career. His arms were stacked with mail.

'Where d'you want this lot?'

Ella pointed to the dining table near the window. 'I wasn't expecting you.'

'Sophie's taken the girls to the country,' he told her. He dumped the mail and began to sort it, fast food menus and junk on one side, letters on the other. Milo was like that, fussily efficient. Mister OCD. 'I've got some stuff to do at the office, then I'm following them down there. You want to join? The girls would love to see you.' He meant it, as he always did.

'You're sweet, but no thanks.'

'The offer's always there.' He held up a glossy flyer. 'You know, you're missing out on some great deals here. Dominoes are doing two for one Tuesday through Thursday. Tempting.'

'Yummy.'

She made him coffee. He stood, leaning against the kitchen counter.

'It's bloody freezing in here.'

'I like it. Did you bring any cigarettes?'

He fished in his pocket, pulled out a pack of Marlboro. He lit two and gave her one.

'Thanks,' she puffed.

He picked up an empty wine bottle, one of several huddled on the counter. 'Where are we this month? South America?'

'France,' she told him. 'I'm working my way through the last decade. They've produced some good stuff, a few quirky whites, a couple of surprising reds. The interesting nights are when I mix the two.'

'Classy.' He pulled on his cigarette and stared at her. 'You're drinking too much.'

'My bags can cope.'

'You have to let him go, Ella.'

She glared and blew smoke. 'Fuck off, Milo.'

She whirred past him and run her cigarette under the cold tap, leaving the butt in the sink. It was strange how life did that, how the passing years can reshuffle the cards. Back then Ella had been the stronger one, an alpha-female bereft of the biological need to marry and procreate. After the split Milo had begged and cried, but she never went back. Then along came the emotional juggernaut that was Gabriel Bryce, and then it was Milo's turn to offer support.

Yet despite what had passed between them, Milo held no bitterness, had never judged her. True love is a bullet most people unwittingly dodge, but Ella took one straight through the heart. Milo saw that, and was there for her. Life was strange, and tragic, and a bloody millstone around her neck.

'This place is a pigsty.'

'You know where the door is.'

'Let me get my cleaner in, please.'

'For the hundredth time, no. I don't want help.'

He pulled his jacket off, ran his cigarette butt under the cold tap too. 'I'll give it a quick once over, while I'm here.'

'Just leave it, please Milo.'

'I promised Sophie I'd help out.' He grabbed the handles of her chair. 'Let's move you over there for a bit.'

'Don't—'

'It won't take long.'

'I don't need your fucking help!'

She was shouting, the words bouncing around the bare walls. Milo let go, went back to the counter. She took a deep breath, offered him a weak smile. 'I'm sorry. I could blame that on my period but we both know that would be a big fat lie.'

He shrugged, pretended he wasn't hurt. 'Hey, don't worry about it. After all you've been through you're entitled to go ballistic now and then.'

She cuffed a moist eye. 'I'm such a bloody coward.'

He crouched down in front of her. He took her hands and squeezed them. 'You're nothing of the sort. You're brave and beautiful and so very, very strong. I think I might've done myself in by now.'

'Plans are afoot,' she sniffed.

Milo searched her eyes. 'That's a joke, right?'

'Of course, silly.'

She whirred around him, parked herself by the dining table. 'You know me, I can't resist a wind-up.' Milo didn't look convinced.

The post was neatly stacked, flyers to the left, correspondence to the right. She put her arm in the middle and swept the flyers into the bin.

Milo smiled and reached under the sink, found a box of cleaning products. He dumped them on the side and ran the hot tap. Steam billowed beneath the easy-access cupboards.

'Have you thought any more about coming back, Ella? The *Observer* would love to have you. I'd love to have you.'

'You're married.'

'You know what I mean.'

She imagined herself working at a desk, at a big daily, and something stirred inside her. She frowned, confused. The new painkillers were screwing with her mind. She started leafing through the mail.

A gas bill, a letter from the council.

'I'd need a ramp built. I don't want to be stuck on the ground floor with the perverts in the mail room.'

Milo laughed, a hopeful stutter. 'The paper is fully compliant with current workplace legislation.'

Ella cursed herself. She shouldn't do that. That part of her life was over now. In fact, it was all over. Everyone would see that soon enough, when her courage finally returned. Even Milo.

For the first time she wondered how he would take the news. Badly, she knew. He would blame himself, for not doing more. She shook off the thought. Milo was a big boy and it was her life, to do with as she pleased. Still, his likely pain troubled her.

She refocused.

A letter from her credit card company this time, offering her a low interest loan. She should accept it, blow the lot, then tell them to whistle. She ripped it in two.

'You're eating something, at least.' Milo scraped spaghetti hoops into the bin, piled empty wine bottles into recycling bags. 'How are you sleeping?'

'On and off,' Ella replied.

A cheap broadband deal; she tore it up and moved on to the next.

'Actually I had quite a good night, last night. Woke up early, though. There was a bloody great seagull, perched on the window ledge, screeching...'

She frowned. The next letter had been hand written, the address covered with a Royal Mail redirect sticker. It had been franked in a post office, probably addressed to her old flat, the Victorian conversion in Stoke Newington with the steep, narrow staircase she used to moan about. The letter had been stamped several times, and redirected, and returned to the sorting office.

'Something interesting?' Milo hovered, recycling bags dangling from his hands.

'Probably not.'

'I'm taking these downstairs.'

'Hmm? Okay.'

He clinked out of the flat.

She turned the envelope over.

On the back, a slick graphic of a yacht. She opened the envelope, extracted the sheets of paper within. Handwritten, the whole thing. Who had the time these days? She was intrigued.

She smoothed it out and turned it over.

*My dearest Ella...*

Her heart stopped.

The world stopped.

All she could hear was her own heartbeat. Her hands shook. She realised she wasn't breathing and exhaled.

She whirred backwards, away from the table. She was suddenly frightened, of the letter, of what lay within. It flapped in the draft, the open window teasing the pages. She heard Milo downstairs, his deep voice in conversation with a neighbour. She closed her eyes and took a deep breath.

*Gabriel.*

He'd written to her, a missive that ran to several neat pages. What did he want to tell her that took such time, such effort? Her heart was torn, the desire to devour his words tempered by the fact that they were from beyond the grave. She'd seen him cremated, had watched in despair as his ashes had been scattered aimlessly. To hear his voice, to read his words of hope, of the chance of a life together, would be too much to bear. But read it she must, because she loved him, as he had once loved her.

She toggled the lever, positioned herself back at the table. She studied the envelope again, the date stamps, the logo; a marine company in Hamble. Ella had never heard of it, had never heard Gabe mention it either. He'd mentioned sailing though, countless times. She put the envelope down, her eyes fixed on the wall across the room. She was stalling, frightened of what lay ahead. The letter constituted his final words to her. He'd suffered a stroke; the text would probably be garbled, meaningless, and unintentionally hurtful. But they were from him, to her. The very least she could do was read it.

She steeled herself, took a breath.

She began to read…

She never heard Milo come back upstairs. She never heard him close the door, or boil the kettle or do any of the things he must've done in the time it took her to read every lucid, dreadful word, every terrible sentence and heart-breaking paragraph. She sat in silence for a long time, numb to the world around her. It had all been a sham; the bomb threat, the stroke, even the funeral. She wondered whose ashes had been scattered in that soulless garden.

He'd told her he loved her, and that was enough. He was dead, she knew that too. The letter was months old. The call had never come, not from Gabriel, nor Oliver's people, and that broke her heart. He'd almost made it, but somewhere between Hamble and Tortola, Gabriel Bryce had met his end. And that made her angry.

The letter hadn't broken her. It was Gabriel's unwitting, parting gift to her.

He'd given her something to live for.

She gathered the pages together and dropped them into her lap. She whirred across the room. Milo was leaning over the kitchen counter, tapping out a text while he smoked a cigarette. She stopped in front of him.

'Hang on,' he said, still tapping. She heard his phone make a *whoosh* sound. He turned around and smiled. 'All done.'

He stopped smiling.

She felt her eyes brimming with tears and she blinked them away.

'Ella, what on earth's the matter?'

'Read this.' She handed him the pages.

Milo looked at her, bemused. 'What is it?' he asked, his eyes scanning the letter. The last page.

'Jesus Christ.'

Ella said nothing as Milo took a seat at the kitchen table and burned through another cigarette as he read and re-read the letter several times. Finally he looked at her.

'I'm so sorry, Ella.'

'Is it enough?'

Milo raised an eyebrow. 'For what?'

'To bury him. Saeed, I mean.'

Milo scanned the letter again. 'Well, it's pretty bloody detailed, I'll say that. Meticulous, in fact. Names, places, dates. It'll need verification of course, and I'll have to speak to legal—'

'Will it be enough?' Ella pressed.

Milo looked at her for a moment. 'For a story, absolutely. As for possible charges against Saeed, a legal case, I can't say, but questions will have to be answered.' He laid a hand on the letter. 'This is a bombshell, Ella. There's enough here to bring down half of Whitehall.'

'I don't care about the rest of them, only him. I want him destroyed, Milo. As he has destroyed my life, and the lives of so many others. You'll do that for me, won't you?'

Milo took her hands in his own and squeezed them as the tears rolled down Ella's face.

'For you, anything.'

Ella could feel her heart beating fast, the embers of a familiar fire glowing, burning inside her once more.

'Good. So let's bury the bastard.'

# EPILOGUE

DANNY BRUSHED ASIDE THE TENT FLAP AND STEPPED outside, shielding his eyes against the low sun.

He took a moment to stretch his aching limbs then headed off, trudging between the rows of white canvas tents that stretched across the flat, sun-baked desert.

He walked slowly, conserving his energy in the oppressive heat. The surrounding terrain was featureless in all directions, except for a thin ridge of hills to the southwest. Beyond those hills were the mines where most of the others worked. Danny hadn't seen them yet, and he thanked God for that particular blessing.

Out there, across the arid desert, hundreds of prisoners toiled night and day, carving out a network of tunnels in search of precious rocks and minerals. It was dangerous, crippling work and many had died. Danny had no intention of joining them.

The mines and the victims they claimed were regular topics of discussion around the evening cooking fires; the nature of the accidents, the injuries sustained, which seams were the most dangerous. They talked of ways to improve their chances of survival, and then they stumbled back to their tents for a few hours rest. Others slept where they lay, wrapped in thin blankets beside the fires. Some never woke again. Workload, poor diet, disease; they all took their toll.

That was where Danny came in. The dead were keeping him alive.

Sometimes Danny longed to join them. Their spirits were free to roam the desert, to travel on the winds, to leave this place far behind—wherever this place was. Someone said it was the southern Egyptian desert, probably near the Sudanese border. Wherever they were, they were a long way from civilisation.

The details of his trial were fading now, only the terrifying aftermath still etched into his memory. They'd dragged him from the court in Maadi and transported him to the notorious Burg-al-Arab prison outside Alexandria.

The beatings and rapes were so bad that Danny had to be hospitalised twice, the doctors using the opportunity to chemically burn the tattoos from his arm and neck. His screams had filled the prison. He'd written to his dad for a while, until one day a guard had brought his letters back to him. Pointless, he'd explained in broken English; his father was dead. He'd laughed, and Danny had broken his jaw. That earned him another round of beatings and solitary.

They came for him just after his first year. No one had visited him, no one had written, so they assumed no one would care.

He was removed from his cell and transported to a military airfield to the west of the city. He was shackled to the floor of a cargo plane with dozens of other prisoners, most of them non-Egyptians, all criminals. They wouldn't be missed either. The flight took two hours and headed due south, to the farthest frontier of the new European empire. Maybe even further.

They deplaned and the aircraft took flight. The dust settled.

Danny saw the camp for the first time.

Row after row of canvas tents stretched away into the distance, shimmering in the heat haze. There were no fences, no watchtowers or patrolling guards, just the tents, the flat desert and the unrelenting sun. They were herded into a fenced off compound and ordered to strip. They were given prison uniforms of black cotton smocks and baggy pants. They were also told that escape was impossible; only death waited beyond the endless horizon.

The first six months in the desert were the worst of Danny's life. The beatings continued, because of his white skin and the reputation that preceded him. He contracted dysentery yet clung to life while hundreds died. Eventually his fever had broken, the stomach pains and the chronic diarrhoea gone. His fear had left with them. He'd looked death in the face and lived to tell the tale. It just didn't scare him anymore.

The word spread quickly. The hand of God had touched the Infidel Whelan. The other inmates left him alone.

He'd watch the sun rise and hear the call to prayer echo across the empty desert. He'd watch the inmates gather in the dusty square where the huge stone Qibla rose out of the desert floor to point towards the Holy City of Mecca. He craved the peace and comfort their worship brought them. He learned Arabic and took the testimony of faith, the *Shahada*.

He entered the fold of Islam.

Things were different after that.

He shaved his head but kept the beard, the sun turning his skin a dark brown. He'd become one of them, the very thing he'd once detested, and the irony brought a toothless smile. Some nights, as he lay on his cot, his thoughts turned to the King's Head and wondered what they would make of him now.

One of the guards offered him work as a gravedigger in exchange for English lessons, and Danny said yes. It was hard work, gruesome at times, but it was infinitely better than working the mine. If a man died in there, and many did, the body was hurled down a disused shaft. If they died in camp, Danny would be called on to transport the corpse to the graveyard across the desert and bury it according to custom.

And business boomed, Danny discovered. Men met their deaths in a variety of different ways; disease, heat stroke, religious punishments. The dawn brought fresh corpses, the circumstances of their deaths never investigated. This was a prison after all, one never visited by officials from Cairo or Brussels. Danny doubted they even knew it existed.

At the end of each day, after supper, Danny would sit on the dune overlooking the camp. He would watch the fires glowing in the dark and think of home. There was no way of knowing what was going on beyond the horizon other than the gossip of the new arrivals. He'd heard rumours, chiefly that Prime Minister Saeed was no more, but most of the inmates were illiterate criminals from Africa and the Middle East, uninterested in anything beyond their own miserable experiences. Danny thought it better not to know, anyway.

The years passed and the graveyard got bigger. It was only a matter of time before Danny ended up buried beneath its shifting sands. After everything that had happened to him, it was the very best he could hope for.

At least, that's what the old Danny Whelan would've believed.


THE HOT SUN dipped towards the horizon.

The empty desert opened up before him. Half a mile away the burial ground shimmered like liquid in the distance. He took a disciplined nip from a water bottle, wiped the sweat from the grey stubble of his head, then climbed aboard the wooden cart. He gave the listless donkey a gentle slap of the reins and set off across the desert floor.

By the time he reached the cemetery the shadows were beginning to lengthen, grave markers stretching across the sand like dark fingers. He brought the cart to a halt and jumped down. Only three bodies since noon, and a pair of grinning Somali gravediggers gave him a hand to unload the white-shrouded corpses. The cemetery was kept neat and tidy in accordance with custom. And it was deserted.

The freshly dug graves bordered the empty desert. Danny likened it to standing on a shoreline, an unchartered sea stretching away before him. They lay the bodies next to the open graves and waited. It wouldn't be long now.

Time passed.

The sun sank lower, the sky to the east turning a deeper shade of blue. One of the Somalis, Zayd, pointed to the dust cloud on the horizon, the sound of the distant engine carried on the still air. The jeep circled the cemetery, bumping and swaying before coming to a halt a few yards away, the engine rattling noisily as it died. The door was kicked open and a pair of booted feet swung to the ground.

The sergeant's name was Haji. He complained a lot,

about his meagre salary, his overweight wife back in Port Said. He spoke English because Danny had taught him, and he was well aware of the commercial opportunities the dead occasionally presented.

He beamed when he saw the bodies.

'Three today? Perfect.'

He looked to Danny for approval of his growing vocabulary. Zayd leaned on his shovel and smiled.

Danny wiped the sweat from his brow. 'Two of them have gold,' he announced in flawless Arabic. That was the trade off. Haji spoke English, Danny, Arabic.

The soldier grinned. 'Let's see.'

He produced a pair of pliers from his pocket and knelt down next to the first corpse. He pulled the shroud away, exposing the dead man's face. He poked his fingers inside the mouth and dragged the jaw open, twisting the head roughly from side to side, peering inside the cavity. He lapsed back into Arabic.

'Ah! This one's practically a gold mine.'

He rammed the pliers home, jiggling them around until he found purchase. Then he tugged and twisted, grunting with effort until the tooth came free. He held it up to the light, inspecting the mess of metal, blood and tissue. 'Not bad. Let's see what else this poor bastard has to offer.'

He leaned over.

Zayd swung the shovel.

He caught Haji on the back of the head with a loud *clang*, knocking him to the ground. The sergeant reacted faster than Danny expected. He rolled over then scrambled to his feet, clutching his bleeding head.

'Fucking...pig...'

His words were slurred, his neck caked with blood and sand. He tottered like a newborn foal. The Somalis grabbed his arms. Danny moved in quickly. He snatched the Beretta pistol from Haji's belt, cocked it, and shot Haji in the head. The donkey brayed, startled. The sound was a hollow pop in the vastness of the desert.

They stripped the corpse and Danny changed into Haji's uniform. Like Danny, Haji was thin, of average height and shoe size. The uniform wasn't a perfect fit but it was good enough. It looked lived in, sweat stained and faded by the sun. With his dark skin, shaved head and thick beard, the Somalis agreed Danny would pass muster. They buried the bodies in the graves and filled them in, slapping the dirt with their shovels.

Danny gave the vehicle the once over: it was a soft-skinned Humvee, one he'd driven many times in Afghanistan. Inside Danny found water, a spare jerry can full of diesel, Haji's mobile telephone, and a Tupperware container with several falafels inside. He split the food and the water with the Somalis and hugged them goodbye. They took the cart and set off into the desert.

He flicked the ignition, checked the gauge: just over half full. Including the spare fuel he was good for maybe two hundred miles. There was something else too, something that made Danny's heart race faster, stuffed in a compartment in the driver's door—a map. He spread it out on the bonnet, absorbing the detail, building a picture, the well-used tracks that criss-crossed the desert, the wadis, the villages and border crossings. He saw a major road that stretched the length of the country. It was definitely less than two hundred miles away.

He threw the map onto the passenger seat. This was it, there was no turning back now. The enormity of what lay ahead overwhelmed him, but his spirits soared on the freshening desert winds. He had a chance now, a real one.

He estimated he'd spent four years in captivity. Time and age were working against him. Inevitably, the job would soon go to someone younger, stronger. And when it did, his life would end in the black hell of the mines. He had to run, and run now.

How long it would be before Haji was missed was hard to say: maybe a couple of hours, maybe overnight if he was really lucky. Worst case he could be fifty miles away before anyone realised. And if Danny could make it to a town or a city, then he had a shot at getting home. His Arabic was fluent, his appearance and familiarity with Islamic custom more than passable. All he needed were clothes and money, and that's when the Beretta would come in useful. After that he'd pay his way onto a ferry and get to mainland Europe. He would head for Britain, and arrive like any other asylum seeker, demanding the right to a better life while claiming all manner of travesties against him. He would wait to be processed, he would bide his time. And then, like so many others, he would simply disappear.

He waited until the sun had finally dipped below the horizon. He climbed into the Humvee and took a rough bearing from the dashboard compass, his finger tracing the map until he found a distant track that headed due east. It led to a highway, just over eighty miles away. With luck on his side he could make it before midnight.

He crunched the jeep into gear and hit the accelerator. He struggled with the euphoria of being free, fighting the urge to drive away as fast as possible. Instead he gripped the wheel and kept his speed below thirty, his dust trail to a minimum. Ahead, the empty desert stretched before him, the sky darkening, the cloak of night eager to embrace him.

He reached up and adjusted the rear view mirror. The sprawling encampment was slowly fading into the distance, its myriad of cooking fires shimmering in the dying light like stars in the heavens.

Danny floored the accelerator.

When he looked again, it was gone.

### **End**

# THANKS

Thanks for taking the time to read ***The Horse at the Gates***. I hope you enjoyed it.

If you did, please review a short review on Amazon. That would be most helpful.

And why not join my **VIP Reader Team** to receive **book news**, **bonus content** and **new releases discounts**?

Just visit:

www.dcalden.com

**Something to say about *The Horse at the Gates*?**

My social media door is always open, so come on in and join the conversation!

## THE ANGOLA DECEPTION

**The world's population is spiralling out of control. It's time to cull the herd.**

They call it the Angola virus, a lethal pathogen born not in the squalor of an African prison but in the sterile laboratories controlled by The Committee, a powerful group of global elites hell-bent on enslaving humanity and replacing nation states with a ruthless One World Government.

**Unless former US Navy Seal Frank Marshall can stop them.**

But Frank is a broken man, haunted by his involvement in the Nine-Eleven attacks, his hands stained with the blood of innocents. Washing it off won't be easy, but Frank has to try because his very soul depends on it.

And that means embarking on his most dangerous mission yet, one that will take him from the mean streets of Harlem to a tough estate in south London, from the baking deserts of Iraq to the frozen peaks of the Swiss Alps.

And Frank will have to move fast, use every military skill he's ever learned if he is to stay alive and save humanity from decimation.

Because speed is everything. And the clock is already ticking.

**Start reading now!**

# THE ANGOLA DECEPTION

*"It would have been impossible for us to develop our plan for
the world if we had been subject to the bright lights of
publicity."*

**David Rockefeller**
**Address to the Trilateral Commission**

# PROLOGUE

"This is it? This is everything?"

Engle blinked behind the lenses of his horned-rimmed glasses as he appraised the government flunkey before him. The younger man was dark-haired and square-jawed, with shoulders that strained at his cheap suit. He looked more like an athlete than a bag carrier for Special Advisor Marshall, and his manner, well, to say it was abrupt was an understatement. The guy was just plain rude.

At sixty-seven years old, and Director for Special Projects at the United States Geological Survey, Professor Bruce Engle was unused to being dictated to. Keyes, on the other hand, was a low-level bureaucrat, yet he seemed indifferent to Engle's status, or indeed the importance of any of the VIPs sitting around the conference table. Engle glanced at the others, his own indignation mirrored on their faces.

"That's all of it?" Keyes repeated. "Including backups?"

Engle waved a liver-spotted hand at the piles of folders, tapes and CD-ROM discs stacked at the end of the table. "It's all there, as requested. And why isn't Marshall here? He should be here."

"You spoke to him this morning."

"He called me at five am. I was barely conscious, for Chrissakes. I don't appreciate these sudden changes. Of arrangements or personnel."

"Mister Marshall has authorised me to act on his behalf."

"This is unacceptable," the professor grumbled.

Frank Marshall was a National Security Special Assistant at the White House, and Engle's only point of contact since the data had been confirmed. He'd ordered Engle to make a list of names of those who knew the whole picture: the security guys from the International Energy Agency, the whistle-blowers from Saudi Aramco, Gazprom and ExxonMobil, and two of Engle's trusted colleagues at the USGS in Virginia. Twenty-three men and women in all, the only people on the planet who knew the terrifying truth, now gathered around a grimy conference table in a disused office in Manhattan. Marshall had impressed upon them the need for secrecy. Disinformation was to be positively encouraged, at least for the foreseeable future. They'd all agreed, especially Engle; lately his nightmares of crumbling cities and starving populations were keeping him awake at night.

Keyes produced a plastic tray and pushed it across the table.

"I'll need all your identification, please."

"Is this really necessary?"

"The Secret Service will need to record your personal details."

Engle tossed his wallet into the tray. Keyes took a moment to examine the driving licences and social security cards, the corporate IDs and passports, then handed the tray to someone waiting outside the room.

Two more men appeared, both young and fit like Keyes, wearing the same cheap suits and each pushing a small cart. They began clearing the table, dumping documents and CDs into the carts. One of them dropped a folder, the computer printouts within spilling across the floor.

"Goddamit!" Engle swore, clambering to his feet. With considerable effort, he knelt down and retrieved the documents. "This is sensitive data," he grumbled. "Be careful."

He pulled his cell phone from his pocket and speed-dialled Marshall's number. No signal. He approached Keyes, who waited by the open door. He seemed oblivious to Engle's presence, his gaze fixed on his watch, his index finger resting on the lobe of his left ear. That's when Engle noticed the small, flesh-coloured receiver nestled inside. *Odd*, he thought. Perhaps he had a hearing impediment. He cleared his throat.

"Mister Keyes?"

The government man looked up, and Engle saw there was something wrong. Keyes was sweating, his eyes darting over the professor's shoulder, towards the men clearing the table behind him.

"Are you all right?"

"Me? Sure."

Engle held his cell phone aloft. "I can't raise Marshall."

"He's on his way. Step aside, please."

The men with carts squeezed past him and rumbled outside. His precious data – all of their data – was now in the hands of someone else.

"He's coming here?"

The distant chime of an elevator seemed to startle Keyes. He reached for Engle's hand and shook it. It was clammy, hurried.

"Take a seat. Help yourself to coffee. Mister Marshall will be with you shortly."

Then he was gone, the door swinging closed behind him.

Engle turned to his colleagues and shrugged. "That's it, then. I guess we wait."

"They seemed to be in a real hurry," observed one of the guys from the International Energy Agency.

"I think they call that indecent haste," Engle agreed.

He flopped into his chair, fatigue compounding his irritation. He understood the need for secrecy but a decrepit office was taking things too far. The furniture was dated, the walls yellowed with age, the brown carpet almost threadbare in places. This office hadn't been used in years. Overhead, a bank of strip lights buzzed and flickered. Engle slipped his glasses off and loosened his tie. He pinched the bridge of his nose as a painful drum began to beat behind his eyes.

He checked his watch and cursed. Where the hell was Marshall? He reached for his cell again.

*No Service.*

"Does anyone have a signal?"

Heads shook around the table. Engle got to his feet, swatting the dust from the seat of his pants. He snatched at a nearby wall phone and jiggled the switch. Dead. He slammed the phone down and marched toward the door.

The Head of Operations from Saudi Aramco got to his feet.

"Bruce, where are you going?"

"To complain," Engle growled. He grabbed the door handle and twisted. It didn't move. He frowned, tried again. He turned to the Aramco executive.

"Ahmed, help me please."

Engle stepped back as the younger Saudi grappled with the brass knob. The door shook but didn't open.

"It's locked," Ahmed said, looking at the others.

Several of the men got to their feet. Engle moved aside, anger boiling in his veins. *What in hell's name was going on here?* He watched the others yanking the handle, working their fingers into the gaps around the door, important people, all experts in their fields, now sweating with effort, forced to vandalise the fixtures and fittings. Disgraceful. Suddenly the lock gave way with a loud crack, sending two of his colleagues tumbling across the carpet. Engle hurried over and helped them to their feet. He buttoned the front of his sports jacket and marched towards the open door.

"Wait here. I'm going to find out what the hell is going on."

Outside, the floor was open-plan, dark, empty. Engle hurried towards the lobby, busy with office workers moving back and forth between the elevators and some kind of brokerage firm.

There was no sign of Marshall.

He passed a stairwell. He heard a shout from behind the door, then the sound of rapid footsteps quickly fading to nothing. Engle pushed it open. Footprints stamped dusty trails on the concrete steps. A door slammed somewhere above, echoing down the vastness of the chamber. He grabbed the handrail and began a slow climb to the floor above. Puffing hard on the landing, he yanked open the door and stepped inside.

"Hello?"

His voice echoed across the empty space. There were no offices up here, no desks or chairs, no bathrooms, no light fittings, no wall partitioning, not even carpet. It was just an empty space, silent, devoid of life, stripped back to its industrial skeleton. Like a construction site. So where were all the workers?

Curiosity got the better of him. There was an air of recent industry about the place. The dust was much thicker here, but not from neglect. The toe of his shoe caught something and he looked down. A heavy black cable snaked across the concrete floor, one of several dozen that trailed away towards the building's massive central supporting columns. He wandered over towards them. The columns were huge, lancing from floor to ceiling like giant redwoods, partially boxed in by large sheets of timber. There were more building materials here, saws and benches, with sandbags piled high against the fresh lumber, the cables disappearing somewhere inside. He saw chalk marks on the wood, seemingly random numbers and roughly drawn crosses and arrows. Nearby, powerful-looking drills and jackhammers lay discarded in an untidy heap on the floor, as if their operators had abandoned them in a hurry. Engle shook his head in disgust; not even nine am and already on a break. Goddam unions.

A sudden wave of dread gripped him.

Maybe they'd been duped. Maybe Keyes wasn't who he said he was, the meeting a ruse to steal their precious data. The Russians, perhaps? Or the Chinese? Both were masters at commercial espionage. Maybe that was why the man was so nervous. Why they'd been locked in.

He had to speak to Marshall.

He fumbled inside his jacket for his cell phone; still no goddam signal. He swore and strode across the room to the window. Finally, the signal bar crept upwards. He punched Marshall's number and waited, relieved to hear a crackling ringtone. He thrust a hand into his trouser pocket and rocked on his heels as he waited for Marshall to pick up.

He glanced out of the window, and for a brief moment forgot about the call.

Engle never missed an opportunity to marvel at the sheer beauty of the world around him, the wondrous legacy of its violent creation, the land masses and eco-systems that had, against all the odds, fused together over millennia to form a life-sustaining environment that most people barely appreciated. This was just such an opportunity.

Beyond the thick glass, the sky was a glorious blue, the view breath-taking, the horizon, endless. In all of his visits to New York, Engle had never set foot inside the World Trade Centre, and here, near the top of the North Tower, he could see all the way out to—

The morning sun caught a reflection, light bouncing off metal.

Then he saw it, growing larger by the second as it hurtled across the Manhattan skyline, the rising, screaming whine of jet engines that rattled the windows and shook the floor beneath his feet. For a moment, Engle's higher brain functions refused to process the scene he was witnessing.

The airliner filled the window.

His eyes widened in horror, the scream trapped in his throat.

The phone slipped from his hand and clattered to the floor.


The cell in his pocket stopped ringing.

From his vantage point in Jersey City, Frank Marshall swallowed hard as he watched a huge ball of flame engulf the top of the North Tower. Moments later a muffled boom rippled across the Hudson River. All around him, people began to gather along the boardwalk. He registered the gasps of horror, the frantic phone calls, the shock and fear. Then he made a call of his own using an encrypted satellite phone.

"Go ahead," ordered a distant voice after a single ring.

"I'm in Jersey. Are you watching this?"

"It just made CNN. Where's our party?"

"Inside."

Frank watched a young Latina staring open-mouthed at the smoking tower across the water. Tears rolled down her cheeks, her hands cupped around her face, as she swayed in denim shorts and roller blades.

"You're sure?"

"Remote camera showed them still there at eight forty-three. They broke the door and Engle moved out of shot. Probably went snooping."

"Any possibility he took the elevator back down?"

"Doubtful."

"And you have the data?"

"I just spoke to Keyes. We got everything, even a detailed index. It's all there."

"Good work."

"What's the plan?"

Frank was eager to get going before the next plane reached Manhattan. He glanced over his shoulder, towards a dark blue Chevy Suburban parked a short distance away. Inside, two of his security team were watching the drama unfold. He circled a finger at the driver and heard the engine start.

"The jet's at Teterboro," the voice on the line told him. "Our guys at NORAD can't keep this thing shut down for much longer. Pretty soon the FAA will initiate a ground stop, so get a shake on. We'll see you back in DC."

"Roger that."

Frank slid into the back seat of the Chevy.

"Let's go."

"What about the other plane?" asked the driver, searching the sky through the windshield. "D'you wanna wait?"

Frank glared at the back of his head. "Sure, good idea. Go grab some hotdogs and a six-pack. We'll make a day of it, you sick fuck."

The driver took the hint and shifted the SUV into gear.

Frank stared out of the window as the Chevy circled the lot and headed for the exit. Hundreds of people were now descending on the Jersey shoreline. They gathered along the boardwalk, their expressions a mixture of horror and disbelief. Some were openly crying, just like the Latina. There'd be plenty more tears by day's end. Frank knew that much.

As they headed west on Second he forced himself to take one final look. He'd always believed the operation was necessary, but now it was underway he wasn't so sure. For the first time in his professional life, doubt troubled him. If what they'd done turned out to be a mistake, they'd all burn in hell for eternity. Frank's skin suddenly tingled, the hairs on the back of his neck rising.

*Hell.*

He hadn't thought about that concept since he was a boy.

He turned away and focused on the road ahead, folding his arms to stop the sudden, inexplicable shaking of his hands.

Behind him, across the river, a thick plume of black smoke belched from the shattered summit of the North Tower, an ugly stain across the sky on what was an otherwise beautiful September morning in New York City.

## CHAPTER 1

THE NIGHTMARE WAS ALWAYS THE SAME.

He was a boy again, lost in the middle of a vast corn-field. He heard his brother laughing, glimpsed a flash of colour, Jimmy's orange T-shirt bright amongst the towering stalks. Roy surged after him, thrashing through the corn, thick rubbery leaves whipping his face.

"Jimmy!"

Only the wind answered, a low hiss that stirred the corn around him. Dark clouds blotted out the sun. He heard his dead parents calling, their voices laced with a shrill note of warning. The corn towered above him in silent, menacing ranks, pressing in on him, seeking to trap him.

*Devour him.*

Roy charged onwards, his sandals slapping the dirt as he ran, the cornfield morphing into a dark, ancient wood. He heard a telephone ringing, its urgent trilling echoing through the gnarled and twisted trees. He crept deeper into the woods where the shadows were darkest, where the air was still, drawn by the insistent ringing.

The clearing lay ahead, the phone box at its heart, its

red paintwork cracked and peeling. Weeds sprouted around its base, its watery luminance dappling the clearing. Roy inched forward and reached for the door handle. He tugged, and the naked figure floating inside jerked wildly.

"Jimmy, it's me. Please come out."

Jimmy cocked his head, no longer a boy but a man, the gold St Christopher pendant and chain around his neck glinting inside the cloudy waters of the phone box. Roy banged on the glass and his brother's bloodless body twisted like an eel to face him.

His eyes snapped open. He screamed soundlessly in an explosion of bubbles.

Roy screamed too...

HE JERKED AWAKE, heart thumping like a hammer in his chest. *Bloody dream,* he cursed, fingering the sleep from his eyes. Spooked him every time.

He stared at the ceiling, the back of his skull thumping steadily. He was hungover, yet he struggled to remember the events of the previous evening. He'd been drinking, possibly in The Duke, but he couldn't be sure. He recalled flashing lights and heavy music, a half-naked girl, a couple of tattooed lumps crowding him in a dark booth. His head pounded and his mouth tasted awful. He didn't even remember getting home.

He took a shower and dried off, taking stock in the mirror. He wasn't in great shape for thirty-eight. His short blond hair was rapidly thinning, his body a little more soft and baggy. Vicky once told him that he looked like the actor Jason Statham, but Roy didn't see it. The truth was he'd grown lazy over the years. *A bag of shite*, he heard Jimmy laugh.

He brushed his teeth and cracked the bathroom window. It was quiet outside.

Roy liked this time of day. Most people had gone to work, the kids to school, and the rest of the estate was a long way from surfacing. It was a sliver of tranquillity, but Roy knew it wouldn't last. Soon the muffled drone of a TV would filter through the wall on one side, later the jack-hammer thump of a sound system on the other, rattling the family photographs in the sitting room. Right now they were still, arranged in a collection of neat frames above the wonky shelf and the fake electric log fire; Roy and Jimmy as children, Mum and Dad standing behind, beaming faces and ice cream cones. Teenage Jimmy in full parachute gear, grinning as he waited to jump from an aircraft ramp. Jimmy again, older this time, unshaven in dust-caked civvies, an assault rifle slung across his chest, a wide smile across a face burned brown by the Afghan sun. And Roy's favourite, the black and white ten-by-eight of Jimmy and Max, the toddler suspended in mid-air, his chubby face a mask of delight, Jimmy's strong arms held aloft to catch the boy. Irrepressible Jimmy, Max's forgotten uncle, Roy's rock, gone.

And no one knew where to, or why.

He got dressed in jeans, T-shirt and a navy blue jacket and left the flat. On the balcony outside he heard his neighbour hurling a mouthful of abuse at her brood of fatherless kids. He ducked into the stairwell and vowed for the umpteenth time to get his act together and get as far away from the Fitzroy Estate as possible. He crossed the road and entered the park opposite, a cold wind whipping at his clothing as he headed for Kingston town centre.

An hour later Roy was trudging up Whitehall, past the long lines of police vans that stretched towards Trafalgar

Square. Nelson's famous column loomed ahead and soon he was swept along with a steady stream of protesters.

The demo was a big one, maybe a hundred thousand crammed into the square, a living organism that ebbed and swayed before a huge platform erected in front of the National Gallery. Thousands of flags and banners fluttered in the breeze, and a police helicopter clattered overhead. Roy made his way towards the media stand erected in front of Canada House, pushing and shoving through the throng until he found himself directly beneath the rows of TV cameras, guarded by steel barriers and thick black lines of riot police.

He opened his jacket and produced his folded cardboard sign. It felt flimsy and insignificant, but he was close enough to the cameras to be noticed. He unfolded it and held it above his head, hoping the news crews might catch the large, block capital words in thick black ink:

*Justice for Jimmy Sullivan. Inquiry Now!*

He looked towards the stage as the crowd suddenly roared, the noise deafening.

"Here we go," an ageing protester next to him grinned, rubbing his hands together. The man wore a sheepskin coat with a peace badge pinned to the lapel. He was fired up for the occasion and Roy felt it too, although he was certainly not political. All he cared about was his homemade sign and the hope that someone, somewhere, might ask, *who is Jimmy Sullivan?*

Onstage, the diminutive figure of Anna Reynolds, the formidable Member of Parliament for Selly Oak, took up position behind a bloom of microphones. Roy craned his neck as the cheering crowd pressed forward and Reynolds' booming voice cut through the chill air. "It warms my heart to see so many decent, hardworking people here today..."

The crowd roared. She was a pro, Roy had to admit, a bridge across the social divide, privately schooled yet a champion of the working classes, her provocative words and dramatic timing stirring the crowd's emotions. As the minutes ticked by her voice began to rise in pitch and she began stabbing the air towards Whitehall, where police vans had formed a blockade across the road. Even Roy found himself jeering.

"Our world is changing," Reynolds boomed from the stage. "Today, less than twenty giant corporations now dominate more than half of the world's economic activity. One of this government's biggest sponsors is TDL Global, a corporate entity richer than Italy, Portugal and Greece combined, yet the hardworking families of this country are forced to struggle against a tide of rising prices and failing local services. Let them go there," she cried, "let them talk to the beleaguered communities, let them try and explain to a pensioner living in a tower block that the lifts don't work because of crippling cuts, greedy banks and government inaction! This cannot, must not, be allowed to happen!"

The crowd thundered its approval, a wall of noise that made the hair on the back of Roy's neck stand on end. Reynolds was in full flow, a modern-day Boadicea, rallying her fighters, preparing them for battle. Flags and banners waved manically, and the crowd surged back and forth. His sign still held aloft, Roy's arms were beginning to ache.

It was just after the second speaker had left the stage, when the dark clouds had drifted overhead and the first drops of rain began to spatter the crowd, that Roy noticed them. They were forty strong, maybe more, masks and bandanas covering their faces, moving as one through the crowd. They congregated a short distance from the stage, close to Roy and the glaring eye of the news crews.

*Trouble*, was Roy's immediate thought.

The third speaker took to the stage, a little-known environmentalist. Gone was the inflammatory rhetoric of Reynolds, replaced instead by the dull tones and measured arguments of a stuffy academic plunged into the spotlight. Roy sensed a change of atmosphere, the mood of rebellion unexpectedly tempered, replaced by a tide of impatience that rippled through the throng.

The catcalls started a few minutes into the speech, whistles and jeers competing with the amplified drone from the stage. Someone barged past him, a whip of fair hair, followed by a man with a camera perched on his shoulder. TV people, hungry for good footage, pressing into the crowd. As rain began to slice across Trafalgar Square, Roy's eyes were drawn to the speaker onstage. He felt sorry for the man, his thin hair plastered to his head by the sudden squall, the pages of his speech clutched like a wet rag in his hand. Poor bastard.

"Shut up, will you? We can't hear him!" shouted the man in the sheepskin coat.

A dreadlocked anarchist twisted around, lashing Roy's face with his dreads. He snarled something unintelligible, then shoved Roy hard in the chest, causing a ripple through the crowd. Roy felt himself pushed forwards, and before he could recover his balance the fists began to fly.

He heard a woman shout, saw the TV reporter being assaulted by a masked anarchist. Roy lunged forward and punched him in the face. The man went down hard and Roy grabbed the woman around the waist, pulling her back through the melee until they were swept up against a barrier.

Missiles arced through the air, a barrage of bottles, stones and paint bombs. People were getting hit, some dazed and bleeding, many more covered in pink and green paint. The riot cops surged forward, unleashing a fusillade of baton blows on the closest demonstrators. Roy clutched the reporter's hand and shoved his way through the throng until they found a break in the barriers. He ducked through and led her beneath the safety of the scaffold stand as the missiles continued to fly. Breathless, Roy sank to his knees.

"Close one," gasped the reporter.

She was mid-thirties, slim, with a bob of mousy hair. Her nose was a little bloodied, her shirt ripped at the neck, her face paled by the proximity of violence. Still, she seemed pretty together despite her close call. Roy watched her cameraman squeeze through the gap and join them beneath the stand.

"Thanks, buddy."

"No worries," Roy muttered, getting to his feet. The woman held out her hand. "I'm Kelly Summers, MSNBC. You kinda saved me back there."

The cameraman winked at Roy. "A three-week stint in Kabul and she thinks she's invincible."

Summers smiled sweetly. "Fuck you, Art."

"Classy," Art chuckled, checking his camera.

Summers asked, "What brings you here today?"

It took a moment for Roy to realise the opportunity that had presented itself. He produced his placard and launched into his story until Summers held up her hand.

"Wait. Let's do this right."

Summers positioned Roy in front of Art's camera and smoothed her hair down. "You've got ninety seconds. Take a breath, think before you speak, and be concise. Okay, here we go..."

Summers launched into her piece to camera and Roy did his best to tell Jimmy's story. As Summers wound up the segment a firework exploded overhead, a huge bang that rained a brilliant shower of sparks onto the crowd below. They panicked like a herd of cattle, and a phalanx of riot police charged into them, armour-plated Robocops swinging their batons mercilessly, their visored faces contorted with state-sanctioned rage. The noise was deafening, the chaos complete, the air ripe with body odour and fear.

A barrier gave way and the mob spilled into the media pen, scattering in all directions. Roy found himself swept away on the human tide, clutching and clawing at those around him, desperate to stay on his feet. The historic square had become a coliseum of mayhem.

"Come here, you!"

Roy yelped as a cop's gloved hand yanked his collar. He struggled free, plunging into a gap between two outside broadcast vehicles, the familiar dome of the National Gallery looming above him. He burst out of the narrow opening and collided with a trio of yellow-jacketed policemen, sending them tumbling to the ground like fluorescent skittles. They were on him in seconds, his arms wrenched and twisted into painful locks, stiff handcuffs ratcheted over his wrists.

"You're under arrest, violent disorder," puffed an overweight plod as he frogmarched Roy toward a waiting van.

His protests fell on deaf ears. He was searched and shoved into the van, squeezed up against a catch of grumbling detainees. He leaned his head against the mesh-covered window, bumping and swaying with the motion of the van as they headed along Pall Mall. His little interview, his one real chance of telling Jimmy's story, would be swallowed up by the riot, the mayhem played out again and again on every TV and news channel across the country.

Who'd care now about a missing Brit in Iraq? The opportunity had passed. He wouldn't get another one like that.

The van raced along the Mall and turned hard right into Horse Guards Avenue, passing the famous parade square, the Cabinet War Rooms, the bronze soldiers on their granite plinths. His thoughts turned to Jimmy and the dream, the pain it represented. When his parents had died their loss had been heart-breaking, yet he'd got over that eventually.

With Jimmy it was different. Despite the passage of time, there was no coming to terms with his disappearance, no peace to be found. His brother haunted him, and Roy was scared.

He peered out through the grimy Perspex window as the van howled through the busy streets of Victoria. He watched the crowds, saw their anxious faces, their nervous flight towards bus stops and train stations, escaping the city before the violence spread. Roy felt their fear too, a sense of trepidation that plagued his dreams, a growing apprehension that made his mouth dry and his heart beat fast inside his chest.

Something was coming.

Something dark and terrifying.

## CHAPTER 2

Reverend Clarence Hays was halfway through his sermon when he noticed the man with the red ponytail seated in the rear pew.

He'd seen him before, several times in fact, but he stood out simply because he was white, and it was unusual for a white man to be a part of the congregation at the Calvary Southern Baptist church on West 131st Street.

Not that Hays minded of course; all were welcome in God's House, even here in Harlem, where white folk were scarce and usually only seen behind the windshields of police cruisers.

Yet the man intrigued him. Hays recalled the first time he'd walked in, midway through a Wednesday evening service. He'd loitered at the back of the church, hands in the pockets of a black winter coat, baggy pants gathered around a pair of scuffed shoes, a few days of carroty growth on his face. Hays presumed he was homeless, seeking temporary shelter from the winter storms, but lately he'd re-evaluated that assessment. The stranger didn't possess that beat down quality that bent the backs of most unfortunates. He had a presence.

Hays finished his sermon and the first notes of the piano began to echo around the hall. Soon the swaying choir were in full voice, the achingly sweet sound of James Pullin's *He's Faithful* filling the room. Hays watched the white man bringing his hands together and mumbling the song's words. There was a strange intensity about him, his lips playing catch-up with the lyrics, his clapping hands trying and failing to keep the simple rhythm, the expression on his face far removed from the beaming joy of his fellow worshippers. Hays had seen that look before, in the faces of the sick and the dying, the death row inmates back in Kentucky. It was a look of desperation.

He knew he didn't have long.

As the hymn filled the rafters, Hays slipped out into the corridor at the back of the church. He grabbed a hat and overcoat from his office then threw the bolt on the rear door. Out in the alleyway, he popped the collar of his coat up against the chill and made his way to the street, a thin crust of frozen snow crunching under his shoes.

As he reached the end of the alleyway, he saw the white man trotting down the steps of the church, stopping beneath the red neon cross to zip up his jacket and tug a Yankees beanie over his head. The street was empty, silent, the temperature hovering somewhere just above zero, crystals of snow drifting through the light of the street lamps.

They were alone.

Hays wasn't a big man, or especially courageous, but behind his lectern, doing God's work, he felt as big as a mountain. He felt that same strength now. He held up a hand as the man headed towards him.

"Excuse me, sir."

Immediately the man veered to his right, large hands whipping from his pockets. He moved out into the street, watching Hays but saying nothing.

"I don't mean you any harm. I'm Reverend Hays, from the church."

Hays smiled and raised his homburg, allowing the light to reveal his ebony face. The man hesitated. A distant siren wailed on the cold night air.

"What do you want?"

Hays smile widened. "I have everything I need. It's what *you* want that I'm interested in. Can we talk?"

THE CHURCH WAS EMPTY, the congregation long gone.

Settled in the warmth of his cramped office, Hays poured two coffees into chipped black mugs emblazoned with *Christ is Lord* in swirly gold lettering. The stranger sat in the shadows, out of the glow of the gooseneck lamp on Hays' desk.

The reverend eased himself into his creaking chair and studied the stranger as he sipped his coffee. He was a big man, over six feet, wide-shouldered, and there was some meat on those bones too, though not as much as there should be. He was thinning on top, a dusting of freckles on his scalp, his remaining red hair tied into a thin ponytail that dangled past the frayed collar of his shirt. Those deep-set eyes missed nothing, Hays was sure of that. They roamed the walls, the floor, the dusty bookshelves, the ancient laptop that whirred quietly on his desk. Most of all they studied Hays, his face, and especially his hands. The stranger tracked them as Hays moved, as he scratched the grey curls of his beard and drank his coffee. The man was stretched tighter than a snare drum. Maybe he was a fugitive from the law, although on second thoughts Hays doubted it. White men didn't exactly blend in around Harlem.

"It's just us," he soothed. "Please, try to relax."

"I'm fine."

His voice was deep, resonant. There was authority there, but Hays couldn't place the accent.

"My name is Clarence Hays. What do I call you?"

"Frank."

"Okay," Hays smiled, rising from his chair. "Well, Frank, let me officially welcome you to our humble church."

His guest hesitated, then took the offered hand. He had a strong grip, and clean fingernails too, unusual for a man on the streets. Frank retreated back into the shadows.

"Without sounding like a bad movie, I'm guessing you're not from around these parts."

Frank twisted the beanie in his lap with those big hands. "I like the singing," he said. "Reminds me of when I was a boy."

*He's from Boston.*

"Yes sir, we sure like to sing around here," Hays chuckled. "Prayers are mighty fine of course, but I truly believe that people connect with the Lord on a different level when they sing. Uplifts the soul, wouldn't you agree, Frank?" His guest said nothing. Instead, he slurped the dregs of his coffee.

"You want another?"

"Got anything stronger?"

Hays shook his head. "I'm not in the business of feeding a man's vices, Frank."

The man smiled for the first time.

"I'm no alcoholic, Reverend, though for a time I tried my best to become one."

He had good teeth, Hays noticed, clean, even, and the eyes were unclouded by the ravages of liquor or drugs. This was no bum.

"Too much coffee makes me edgy," Frank explained. "I tend to smooth it out with the occasional drink."

Hays believed him. He reached into the bottom drawer of a battered filing cabinet and produced a bottle of Old Crow Reserve and two glasses.

"Made in my home state of Kentucky. Not the finest, but not too shabby either."

He poured a couple of shots and watched Frank take his glass without lifting it to his lips. Hays' instincts were right. Frank had a story, one of pain and loss that would be as desperate as the thousands he'd heard over the thirty-five years he'd been a minister. All Frank needed was someone to tell it to.

Hays leaned back in his chair and sipped his own liquor. The computer hummed faintly, the alleyway outside deserted, silent.

"It's not just the singing, am I right, Frank? There's another reason why you came to us."

The big man nodded, staring into the untouched contents of his glass as he swirled it around in small circles. When he spoke he did so quietly, eloquently, without hesitation.

"I grew up in a children's home in Southie, a Catholic one. I remember taking confession as a boy, and I'd sit there in the dark and the priest would promise me all kinds of eternal tortures if I didn't stop my sinning. I was ten years old, for Chrissakes. Back then the most sinful thing I ever did was use a curse word or two, but those images of damnation kept me awake most nights."

Hays watched him take a small sip of bourbon. He'd

had ex-Catholics through his doors before, most burdened from a young age with institutional guilt, their spirits cowed by the withering gaze of a spiteful God who was quick to judge and relished the punishment of sin. That certainly wasn't the Lord that Hays knew and loved, no sir. Frank would come to see that.

"That priest told me it was a sin to take your own life," Frank continued, "but God has to understand that sometimes people just can't live with themselves anymore."

"Is that how you feel, Frank?"

"I used to. There was a time when I'd wake up and promise myself I'd seen my last sunrise. I've stood on top of buildings and bridges, I've waited on subway platforms and closed my eyes when I've felt the rush of an oncoming train..."

Frank's voice trailed away. He tipped the rest of the bourbon down his throat.

Hays said nothing, allowing the poison to flow, the layers of guilt to peel away and reveal the pain beneath. Across the room, Frank hung his head, the beanie wrung like a rag in those strong hands. When he looked up his eyes were moist, his voice a whisper.

"But I couldn't do it because dying would be the easy way out. I have to live, to be reminded of the pain I've caused, the families I've destroyed. Men, women, even children, God help me. I have to suffer."

Frank crushed his face into his beanie.

Hays got to his feet. He was troubled, and not just for the man's soul. It was clear Frank had blood on his hands, and two scenarios sprang to mind; either Frank was a murderer, in which case Hays would have to somehow steer him towards the authorities. Or he was a veteran.

Hays had met plenty in his time, men haunted by their

experiences on the battlefield, those battles continuing long after the homecoming bands had packed up and gone home. He'd have to tread carefully here.

He walked around the desk and crouched down in front of Frank. The tears flowed freely, coursing down Frank's hollow cheekbones, catching in the red growth on his chin. Hays took his hands in his own.

"We've all made mistakes, Frank, each and every one of us. You carry this burden with you like Atlas with the world on his shoulders, but it's time to let go. Jesus brought you to me, I can see that now, and together we'll—"

Out in the corridor, the back door rattled violently.

Frank shoved Hays to the carpet and sprang from his chair, sweeping the lamp onto the floor. Hays lay frozen, watching the gun in Frank's hand. He heard a muffled curse from the alley outside, saw shadows flash by the barred and frosted glass, the sound of laughter and running feet. Then silence.

Hays' voice soothed in the darkness. "It's just kids, Frank, fooling around. Happens all the time."

He picked himself up, retrieved the lamp from the floor, tinkered with the bulb. A soft light flickered, glowed. Frank was in shadow, his face ashen, the gun gripped in both hands and pointed towards the window. Hays moved closer.

"It's okay. Please, put down the gun."

He raised his hand, laid it on the sleeve of Frank's coat, felt the limb beneath, rigid, like rock, He applied a little pressure, felt no resistance, saw the barrel of that big, ugly automatic tilt towards the worn carpet.

"This is God's house, Frank. There's no danger here, only refuge." Frank lowered the gun. He stood in silence, his ashen face hovering like a ghost in the shadows.

"We want to help you," Hays whispered. "Me and Jesus, we've got your back, Frank."

"I've done terrible things—"

"We'll get to that, son. Right now it's what's in your heart that matters."

He reached down, took Frank's free hand in both of his own.

"I believe Jesus has brought us together this night. He guided you to me, and He did it for a reason, Frank—salvation. Yes sir, salvation lies right here in this church. Let me help you, son. Please."

The gun clattered to the floor. Frank sunk to his knees, wrapped his arms around Hays and held on tight, sobbing like a baby.

As Hays comforted the troubled soul he whispered a quiet prayer of thanks, for the abundance of God's love, and for the strength to guide this broken man along the path to redemption. As he breathed that quiet litany Clarence Hays felt another, deeper rush of emotion, of compassion, of joy, and realised that God was with them both, right there in the room.

FRANK WOKE FROM A DEEP, dreamless sleep.

Above him, the ceiling was adorned with heavenly clouds and a flock of multiracial cherubs. He shifted beneath the thick eiderdown, the small cot creaking beneath his body. He felt safe here, as Reverend Hays had promised he would. Memories of that first night came flooding back.

He'd gone to pieces.

Yet it was here, in a rundown church in Harlem, that Frank learned that the guilt that ate him like a cancer was nothing more than the affirmation of his own humanity, the spiritual declaration of a good soul determined to right a wrong. Frank Marshall wasn't a good man, he knew that, but he no longer felt the desperation he'd felt that first night.

He kicked off the eiderdown and stood, working the blood back into his muscles. He retrieved the Beretta from under the cot, checked it, then slipped it into the back of his trousers. Outside, the morning sun barely penetrated the alleyway. The air was heavy and silent, muffled by an overnight snowfall. He let the curtain drop back into place. He reached for his gun and held it low behind him as the floorboards creaked outside his room.

Someone knocked on the door.

"Yeah?"

Hays poked his head around the frame. "Morning, Frank. You decent?"

Frank tucked the pistol away. "Sure. Come on in."

Hays carried two mugs of steaming coffee over to a battered table in front of the equally battered sofa. "Here you go. Black, no sugar." He straightened up, pulled his Mets sweatshirt down over his large belly. "You sleep okay?"

"I did, thanks."

Frank sat on the battered sofa, cradling the coffee in his hands. "I thought I might start on the hallway today. Paint-work's a little tired, and you've got a few loose boards out there." He'd fix them all in due course, except the ones outside his room.

"The work isn't compulsory, Frank. You can stay as long as you like."

"I gotta earn my keep. I've been here nearly two weeks."

"And the church is better for it," Hays admitted, his eyes wandering around the recently painted walls. "Oh, I have something for you." He reached into his back pocket and held out a crumpled leaflet.

"What's this?"

"A support group, run by veterans, right across the river in Brooklyn."

Frank smoothed out the leaflet and gave it the once-over. A soldier on the cover, his head in his hands, silhouetted against the Stars and Stripes, the letters PTSD liberally sprinkled throughout the text inside. It was close enough to the truth.

"Thanks," Frank said, and he meant it.

Hays got to his feet. "I'll leave you be."

"I'll see about that hallway if it's all the same."

Hays smiled and closed the door behind him. Frank stood there in silence, the air stuffy and heavy. He felt restless, uneasy. He snapped on the TV, the screen flicking into life as he pulled on socks and sneakers. On the screen, a MSNBC anchor stared earnestly into the camera as he ran through the headlines at the top of the hour.

As usual, it wasn't good news: the economy was back in the toilet, there was civil unrest in Europe, and a massive cyclone in Bangladesh had made tens of thousands of people homeless. The stark images reminded Frank of the early seminars, where the speakers had likened humanity to a plague of locusts, multiplying, devouring, laying waste. He fingered the faint scar on his right shoulder, a natural reaction whenever he thought about *them*.

He ran the hot tap in the bathroom and shaved. Raised voices drifted in from the TV, the muted roar of a large crowd, a reporter's breathless monologue, then another voice, the dull, nasal tones of a blue-collar Brit.

"—Working for TDL Global in Iraq. Officially my

*brother went missing in Baghdad but the Iraqi authorities claim they have no knowledge of the incident in question—"*

Frank's hand gripped the edge of the sink, the razor frozen in mid-air.

*"That was three years ago, and my brother has been conveniently forgotten by everyone, the British government, his employers, even my local MP. How can a man, working for a giant corporation like TDL, simply disappear without trace? And why won't anyone hold an inquiry?"*

Frank stepped out into the room, chin lathered with foam.

*TDL Global.* A huge building block in the pyramid of power. Frank had run black ops under the banner of their Security Division for years. Including the Iraqi operation.

*"What is it you hope to achieve by coming here today?"*

The reporter thrust her mike beneath the guy's mouth. The man with the homemade sign looked tired, beaten. He watched him turn away from the reporter and stare into the camera.

Into Frank's eyes.

*"If there's anyone out there who knows what happened in Iraq, please come forward. My brother's name is Jimmy Sullivan—"*

Frank jolted as if he'd been Tasered.

He reached for the medallion around his neck, felt the smooth metal between his fingers, remembered that young face frozen in death.

*Jimmy Sullivan.*

He found the TiVo remote and rewound the segment. There was desperation in the Brit's words. He was seeking the truth, swimming against a tsunami of bureaucracy, lies and disinformation. He paused the segment, the Brit's face frozen on the screen. The man had no idea what he was up against. The evil that had taken his brother was unchallenged, unstoppable—

Frank's legs felt weak and he sagged onto the sofa. It was so clear now, like sunlight bursting through the clouds.

This wasn't a coincidence.

And right there on the TV screen, was a man adrift, battling against an unseen evil, his desperate plea a last throw of the dice. And his brother Jimmy, the seed, the genesis of it all.

Frank grabbed a pencil and paper from the table and scribbled some hurried notes. Then he gathered his things.

FRANK STOOD in the doorway of Hays' office, hands in his coat pocket.

The reverend was sat behind his desk, punching numbers into a calculator and scribbling on a pad. He looked up.

"I think I've found a way," Frank announced.

Hays leaned back in his chair. "You're leaving?"

"Yes, sir."

"That's a mighty quick decision, Frank."

"It's hard to explain. There's a man I can help. He doesn't know it yet but I can ease his suffering."

"You know this person?"

"No, but we're connected. I need to find him. Give him some peace."

"I understand you need to right some wrongs, Frank, but this is kinda sudden, don't you think?"

Frank shook his head. "It feels right. I have to do this."

"The path to salvation can be a long and difficult one. Evil is out there, watching and waiting, looking to foul things up for righteous men."

"I know all about evil, reverend. We go way back." He pulled the Beretta from his coat pocket and laid it on Hays' desk. "Could you take care of this for me? For the record, I've never used it. I took it from a kid in Phoenix one night. A desperate kid."

Hays hesitated. "Sure," he said, wrapping his handkerchief over it and placing it in a desk drawer. "You need money? I don't have much but—"

"Thanks, I'm good."

Frank pulled his beanie hat over his ears, tucking his ponytail up inside.

Hays walked around his desk. "You sure about this, Frank?"

"Certain."

The Reverend held out his hand. "Then good luck to you, son. Never forget that Jesus will be with you every step of your journey. And we'll be praying for you too, right here in Harlem."

"I appreciate that."

"Wait a sec."

Hays walked over to the coat stand in the corner. "I want you to have this. It's my personal travel Bible. I've had it since I was a young preacher."

Frank turned over the small, leather-bound book in his hands. "I can't take this. It's too personal."

"Nonsense. It'll be there for you on your journey, like it was on mine. My card's in there too, in case you need to talk. Call me anytime, day or night."

"Thank you." Emotion squeezed Frank's throat.

"Come back to us, when you're ready to start your life again."

Frank nodded. "Sure."

He stepped forward and gave the pastor a warm hug. "Goodbye, reverend. And thank you."

He left without another word, through the back door and out into the alley. The cold air felt good on his skin, the sound of fresh snow crunching underfoot as he reached the street. The crippling remorse, the fear and panic that had plagued him for years, was gone. He paused for a moment, watching the pavements, the roads, the sky above. Then he took a deep breath and set off, heading south, towards Manhattan.

Frank Marshall was back from the dead.

And back on the grid.

# CHAPTER 3

He woke in a cell inside Belgravia police station.

He swung his legs off the mattress and stood up, blinking beneath the harsh strip light. The chaos of the previous day was a distant memory, the slamming of doors, the stomp of standard-issue boots, the shouts. All he heard now was the drip of the stainless steel toilet pan in his cell, the faint rumble of early morning traffic out in the street.

And the jangle of keys outside his cell. The inspection flap scraped open.

"Take a step back, chum."

Roy did as he was told. The door swung inwards. "Duty sergeant wants a word," said an overweight gaoler. He pointed to Roy's feet. "You can put your trainers on."

A few moments later Roy was standing in front of the custody desk, his personal possessions sealed in a clear plastic bag in front of him.

"It's your lucky day," the sergeant said, pushing the bag across the counter. "You're being released without charge."

"That's because I didn't do anything."

"You say so. I'll need your autograph."

Roy signed the paperwork, slipped his belt on, and was escorted off the premises.

He was glad to be out in the fresh air. He found a coffee shop near Victoria Station, bought a latte and a newspaper, the first few pages splashed with lurid pictures of yesterday's riot. He pointed to the TV in the corner and asked the waitress if they had MSNBC. She shrugged her shoulders. He finished his coffee and headed for the station.

Roy was back on the Fitzroy by mid-morning. He dropped his clothes in the washing basket and stepped into the shower, soaping away the memory of his overnight accommodations. He changed into sweatpants and a T-shirt and fired up his laptop. He scoured the internet for his segment but found nothing. He collapsed onto his bed, frustrated.

He read his paper.

He dozed.

The musical chime of a text message woke him from a deep slumber.

*In future, don't make promises you can't keep.*

Roy rolled off the bed. Shit. Max's football match.

He hurried into the hallway, hopping into his trainers and tugging on a jacket. He was out of the door in less than a minute, wheeling his decrepit racing bike down the stairs and pedalling for the main road.

The school was a private one, a couple of miles to the west of Kingston town. It had walled grounds and impressive spires, and a boating club with private moorings along the Thames. Roy whizzed through the wrought-iron gates and headed towards the green chessboard of sports pitches at the rear of the school. He bounced onto the grass, skirting the half-dozen rugby matches in progress, and headed for the soccer pitch at the far edge of the playing fields.

He propped his bike beneath the branches of a large oak tree and took a moment to catch his breath.

Two teams of energetic kids chased a football up and down the pitch while a group of well-heeled adults shouted encouragement from the touchline. Roy spotted Max almost immediately, and not because he was on the pitch impressing the others with his skills: instead he played alone, clumsily kicking a ball around behind the grown-ups, his small body swamped in oversized shorts and shirt, his mind lost in a world of its own.

Roy hesitated.

No one had seen him yet. He could turn around and head home, send a text, make some sort of excuse. As he wrestled with his options he saw Vicky peel away from the touchline and march across the grass.

*Busted.*

She came to a halt in front of him, her pretty face furrowed in anger.

"You made a promise."

"I know, I—"

"He's six years old. What's wrong with you?"

"Nothing."

She looked great. Dark brown hair expensively cut, tanned skin and perfect teeth, a smart black overcoat with a silver faux fur collar, black knee-length suede boots. A long way from the cute graduate he'd met way back when. He felt long-buried emotions stirring, then reminded himself that Vicky wasn't that same person anymore.

"A real father wouldn't desert his son like this."

"Here we go."

"It's not Max's fault."

"How many time have I told you, it's not about Max."

"Liar."

The wind ruffled the collar of her coat in tiny silver waves. "It doesn't have to be this way, you know."

Roy raised an eyebrow. "Meaning?"

Vicky stared at her designer boots. "Nothing. Doesn't matter."

"Where's whatsisname?"

"Nate's working."

"Nate," Roy muttered. "Stupid name."

"Grow up, Roy. Go say hello to your son."

He watched her stamp off towards a clutch of well-groomed women, their cold eyes appraising Roy's rusted bike, his mud-speckled sweatpants and tatty combat jacket. He could read it in their faces; he was *that* Roy, Vicky's mistake, poor Max's indifferent father. The loser. He gave them a sarcastic wave.

Max was toe-poking the ball around, floppy brown hair bouncing as he ran. His movements were clumsy, his tongue protruding between his lips as he focused on kicking the ball at his feet.

"Hey, Max!"

Roy squatted down and spread his arms wide. The ball ran past him, quickly followed by an oblivious Max who puffed after it. Roy caught his arm and scooped him off the ground. He held him in a gentle embrace.

"Sorry for being late, Max," he whispered in the boy's ear. Daddy had a bit of trouble."

The child responded with a faint whine of protest. He was a rag doll in Roy's arms. Defeated, Roy let him down. "Go and play, then."

He heard the rustle of dry leaves behind him, heavy footfalls beating the ground.

A flash of grey hair swept by, coat tails flapping, the ball scooped from under Max's feet then dribbled around him with enviable speed and dexterity. Max squealed with delight.

"Come on, son, show us what you got!"

The man turned this way and that, running proverbial rings around Max who chased him with unbridled joy. Then he took a big swing and hoofed the ball into the distance. Max's little legs pumped after it.

"That's it, son, go get it!"

Roy's stomach lurched.

Sammy French smiled, watching Max chase the ball across the grass. "Look at him go. Like shit off a shovel." He turned back to Roy. "You ever watch them Paralympics? I saw a mongoloid kid bench-press six hundred pounds once. Fucking amazing."

He shoved his hands in his pockets.

"Been a long time, eh Roy? I'd say you look well, but I'd be lying."

Sammy French was six years older and four inches taller than Roy, with long grey hair that swept back from his suntanned forehead and nestled in gelled curls over the collar of his coat. He had ice-blue eyes and a sharp, angular face that men thought dangerous and women ruggedly handsome. His smile was Hollywood white, his athletic build always wrapped in expensive clothes. Even today, on a windswept playing field, Sammy French looked like he'd stepped out of the pages of an Armani winter catalogue, uber-cool in a fawn trench coat, designer jeans and brown suede shoes. He had the looks, the money, a big property portfolio, and a dangerous reputation. He was everything Roy wasn't. No wonder some of Vicky's friends eyed him from the touchline.

Sammy cocked a thumb over his shoulder. "How old's the boy?"

"Six."

"A spastic from birth, eh? Must be tough."

Roy bristled. "He's got a few learning difficulties, that's all. Development issues. He's getting treatment. We don't say spastic anymore."

Sammy's face darkened. "You trying to tell me how to speak, Roy?"

"No, I—"

"That's what I thought. Hang on, it's coming back."

Max puffed towards them, chasing after his ball. Sammy brightened.

"Give it here, twinkle toes." He trapped the ball beneath his shoe then kicked it into the distance again. Max spun around and chased after it.

Roy cringed as Sammy moved closer and laid a hand on his shoulder. "I was sorry to hear about your brother."

"Thanks."

"A gobby little fucker as I remember. Shame what happened to him."

"No one knows what happened. Officially he's still missing."

"So's Lord Lucan, and he ain't coming back either. I'll say one thing about him, Jimmy had bottle. I could've used someone like him, ex-Para and all that. Went missing in Baghdad, right?"

"He wasn't in Baghdad. The official story is bullshit."

"Poor bastard. That's one place you don't want to go walkabout." He turned his collar up against a fine mist of rain that swept in across the playing fields. "Anyway, it's you I need to speak to."

"Me?"

"Correct. I need a favour."

"A favour?"

Roy paled. It'd been years since they'd spoken, although Sammy was a local face around Kingston, flitting between his many businesses in a white convertible Bentley. Sammy French lived in another universe compared to Roy, so what the hell could he want from him? Whatever it was, Roy had a feeling it wouldn't be legal.

"It's a bad time at the moment, Sammy. I've got a lot on my plate."

"Haven't we all."

The final whistle shrilled, signalling the end of the match. Roy watched the mud-caked boys on the pitch shake hands, a signal for the parents to hurry en masse for the car park as the fine mist strengthened into a steady rain. He saw Vicky pop up a Burberry umbrella and call to Max.

"I've got to go," Roy said, backing away from Sammy's glare. "Sorry I couldn't help."

Vicky was tugging a sweatshirt over Max's head. Roy smoothed the boy's hair down.

"Hey, Max, you did really good today."

Vicky sheltered them both with the brolly. "He's soaking. I have to get him to the car." She glanced over Roy's shoulder. "Who's that?"

Roy saw Sammy waiting a short distance away, oblivious to the rain.

"No one. An old friend."

"He looks upset."

"He was born that way." Roy leaned over and kissed Max on his head. "I'll see you soon, Max, I promise."

Vicky forced a smile. "We won't hold our breath, will we, Max? Say bye-bye to Daddy."

He watched her hurry away.

Between him and his pushbike, Sammy stood immobile, hands thrust into his pockets, shoulders damp from the rain.

As Roy approached Sammy produced his mobile and speed-dialled a number. "Start the car, Tank. I'll be there in five."

Roy swallowed hard. Sammy wasn't going to let it go. They faced off in silence, in the rain, until the playing fields were empty. Then Sammy closed the gap between them.

"That was a bit naughty, walking off like that. You didn't even hear me out."

"Listen, Sammy, I don't—"

The punch landed just below the rib cage, expelling the air from Roy's lungs and dumping him on the wet grass. Roy flinched as Sammy grabbed the collar of his combat jacket and dragged him beneath the shadow of the tree. He yanked him up and kicked him hard, sending him careering into the pushbike. Roy fell to the ground in a painful heap, bike wheels spinning on top of him. Sammy grabbed it and threw it to one side. He wasn't out of breath, his face showed no signs of anger; this was Sammy French, taking care of business. He slapped the dirt from his hands.

"I don't like being disrespected, Roy."

"Jesus Christ, take it easy, Sammy."

Roy touched his lower lip, muddy fingers red with blood.

Sammy loomed over him. "Like I said, I need a favour. It's not a request."

He squatted down and pulled a hankie from his pocket. He handed it to Roy, who pressed it to his lips. Blood blossomed. Sammy spoke.

"I might've moved up to the big house, but I like to keep my ear to the ground, find out what the old Fitzroy faces are up to, who's been banged up, who's dead. Who's working, what they do."

*Oh shit.*

"You work at Heathrow, right Roy? Borders Agency, Terminal Three?"

Roy shook his head. "I won't do anything dodgy—"

Sammy whipped his arm back and cracked Roy around the face with an open-handed slap. He grabbed him by the collar and twisted the material in his large fist. "You'll do as you're told, you little cunt. Understand?"

Roy nodded, withering before Sammy's icy glare. The big man suddenly thawed, veneers like pearls in the gloom.

"In the meantime don't do anything stupid, like change your job or go on holiday. Business as usual, got it?"

Roy nodded again.

"Good boy. I'll be in touch."

Roy watched him duck under the branches and head across the playing fields in long, loping strides. He pulled himself up, swatting the wet grass and mud from his clothes. His lip stung and his hand shook when he dabbed his mouth. He never imagined he'd cross paths with Sammy French again.

And he was frightened.

He wheeled his bike from under the tree and headed across the grass towards the distant gates. His legs felt too weak to pedal. When Sammy wanted something, he got it. Roy's immediate thought was drugs; Sammy must be sending a mule through customs, and Roy would have to turn a blind eye. What else could it be? And what if it went wrong? Arrest, a lengthy prison sentence, his security clearance gone, which meant no job and no future worth thinking about. He'd be trapped on the Fitzroy forever, scraping by on benefits.

He thought of Jimmy then, longed for the comfort of his brother's company, his wise counsel. But Jimmy was gone. Roy had no one to turn to.

The wind picked up, rain lancing across the playing fields in cold, silver sheets. He mounted his bike and pedalled out through the main gates. He barely noticed the weather, the passing traffic, the clouds of cold, fine spray. As he neared Kingston town centre the traffic began to snarl, brake lights blooming, windscreen wipers beating off the rain. Roy weaved through it at speed; with any luck someone would jump the lights and hit him, or maybe he'd slide on a manhole cover and break a leg. No Roy, no favour.

Then he thought about the pain he'd have to suffer, the potential for serious injury, disability, or even death, and that scared him even more.

Roy kept moving, heading for the grimy cluster of tower blocks that loomed in the distance.

CHAPTER 4

Located thirty miles east of Denver, the Golden Gate Canyon State Park is an area of breathtaking natural beauty, comprising rugged mountains, pine forests and lush meadows covering over twelve thousand acres of pristine real estate.

For the average visitor there's plenty on offer: hunting, fishing, trekking, and when the snows sweep down from Canada in late November, a whole host of winter sports, triggering the seasonal stampede to the Rocky Mountains.

Just over half a mile northeast of the park's visitor centre, a hard-packed dirt road intersects a gentle curve on the Crawford Gulch Road. Staked out with *Private Property, No Trespassing* signs, the road runs straight for a hundred yards then bends right into a narrow, steep-sided and densely wooded valley.

Josh Keyes knew that from the moment he turned off the blacktop and onto that road his approach was being monitored. As he powered the Grand Cherokee Jeep up the first mile he knew he'd already passed at least a dozen cameras. He also knew that the mountain he was driving towards was sown with motion sensor systems, thermal imaging cameras, pressure pads, optical beams and ground radar. To back up the technology, security teams of private military contractors were on standby to ward off any trespassers.

But it hadn't always been like that.

As he rounded another bend high above the valley, Josh recalled the first and only breach, back when they were still breaking ground.

A moderately influential conspiracy blogger had turned his spotlight on the curious project underway at Blue Grouse Peak. He'd encouraged his followers to ask questions, apply pressure, to find out why the FAA had issued a Prohibited Airspace order above the area. The blogger himself had hiked up through the forests and went to work with his video camera for two days before a security team rumbled him. His body was eventually discovered sixty miles away, at the foot of a popular mountain trail. An autopsy found traces of cocaine and marijuana in his bloodstream. A search of his home computer uncovered hundreds of pornographic images of children. The story soon died.

The Committee didn't screw around.

But the episode had unnerved them. That's why security was paramount, why they kept the legend of Bohemian Grove alive, the annual frat party in the Californian woods that attracted the attention of every conspiracy nut in the country, and drew attention away from Blue Grouse Peak. Smoke and mirrors, Josh smiled. The Committee were masters at it.

He rounded another bend, and then the plateau opened up before him, a wide, snowy meadow dotted with Scots pines that sloped up toward the magnificent lodge built beneath the jagged bluffs. Josh was always impressed, not just by the architecture or the way the facility blended in with the surrounding landscape. No, it was what lay behind those thick granite walls that impressed him most.

He followed the road until it dipped beneath the building into a huge underground parking lot. It was almost empty and would remain so until closer to the Transition. That's when they would come, to escape the death and anarchy of the cities. He parked the Jeep, swiped and scanned his way through the security cage, and took an elevator to the complex above.

The lobby of The Eyrie reminded Josh of the Park Hyatt in Chicago, all polished floors and thick rugs, expensive furniture, discerning artworks, and long-drop light clusters hanging from the cathedral-like ceiling. One wall was all glass, offering a spectacular view of a snow-dusted valley. And that was just the lobby.

The Eyrie boasted a hundred lavish suites, three restaurants, two bars, a cinema, gymnasium and health spa, and a host of other luxuries. There was a state of the art communications centre, conference rooms, a barracks for the security force and two, all-weather helipads. It was more than a luxury retreat; it was a redoubt, a command and control hub, one of several dotted across the globe, built by the Elites, for the Elites. Or it would be, once the Transition began. Right now, it was pretty empty.

As he cut across the lobby Josh recognised a couple of faces: the current Defence Secretary, the Chinese wife of a billionaire computer mogul, a Nobel Prize-winning geneticist, a British blue blood. No one paid Josh any attention, except for the uniformed clerk behind the sweeping reception desk.

"Good afternoon, Mister Keyes. They're expecting you in conference room three."

"Thanks."

He took the elevator back down a couple of levels. He checked his reflection in the elevator doors, smoothed his neatly trimmed black hair, a legacy of his Navajo ancestry. That, and his hunting skills of course.

The doors swished open. He walked along a polished granite corridor to conference room three. He paused outside the door and cleared his throat.

A man and a woman waited for him inside, both middle-aged and suited, trusted advisors of the most senior Committee members. And both very pissed off.

No words were exchanged as Josh took a seat. He produced a memory stick and inserted it into the tablet waiting for him on the table. The lights in the room dimmed. CCTV footage began to play on the room's huge projection wall.

"These are the latest images of Frank Marshall," Josh began.

On the wall Frank was seen from several different camera angles entering a bank, crossing the lobby, speaking to an employee.

"Where was this taken?" Freya Lund inquired in her lilting Swedish accent. She was a severe-looking broad, snow white hair swept back off a thin, tanned face, wrinkled neck protruding from a starched white shirt beneath a black suit jacket. She reminded Josh of a Quaker. Probably hadn't been laid in decades.

"Yesterday, nine-oh-two am, Bank of America, Manhattan. He accessed a personal deposit box in the vault."

"Why didn't we know about it?" the man next to her barked.

His name was Beeton. His boss was once a blue-collar guy too, his construction business growing from a single mall in Cincinnati to one of the world's largest commercial construction empires. It was the billionaire's company that had built The Eyrie, and Beeton was his consigliere. With his gnarled hands, shaved head and flattened nose, Beeton was a man not unfamiliar with physical violence, a Teamster leg-breaker in his younger days. Or so the rumours went.

"I guess he never declared it," Josh said.

Lund tutted. "This is a clear breach of policy."

"Yes, ma'am."

"How did we detect him?"

"He used a fingerprint reader to gain access to the vault. The bank's entry-point system is interfaced with the Homeland Security network and we got a hit. A security team was scrambled, but Frank was back on the street and gone in less than ninety seconds."

Lund scribbled notes on a yellow legal pad. "Do we know what was in the box?"

Josh shrugged. "Hard to say."

"Humour us," Beeton growled.

He reminded Josh of a city detective, tie askew, sleeves rolled up, thick forearms folded in front of him. The sort of guy who would enjoy beating out a confession.

"Knowing Frank, I'd say cash, credit cards, a passport or two. Rainy day stuff."

"The box is not the problem," Lund said. "It's Marshall himself. He's been on the ground since TWA eight hundred. He has intimate knowledge of our organisation and its operations. Especially Messina."

Beeton slapped a gnarly hand on the table. "Why in God's name haven't we picked this maniac up yet?"

*Because Frank Marshall is a smart guy*, Josh didn't say.

He glanced at the footage looping on the screen, saw

Frank push his way through the bank's revolving doors out onto the street, a large black holdall slung over his shoulder. The sidewalks are packed with commuters, a sea of umbrellas tilted against a heavy rainstorm. Frank pulls on a cap, unfurls a plain umbrella and plunges into the human tide. Within seconds he's lost. Smart. His former boss looked pale and thin, and Josh found the ponytail faintly amusing, but looks could be deceptive. Frank Marshall was one of the best, totally ruthless.

Or had been.

"What about the city's surveillance network? The MTA systems?"

Josh shook his head. "Nothing yet."

Beeton ran a hand over his shaved head. "Help me understand this, Keyes. One of our most senior security guys bolts from a highly sensitive installation, flies back to the States, disappears in Texas, then stages his own suicide. A few years later he waltzes into a downtown bank, helps himself to the contents of an undeclared strongbox, then disappears like a ghost. Again." He held up a couple of thick fingers. "I got two questions; how did he stay off the grid that long, and why is he back?"

"I've no idea."

"That's real helpful."

Lund said, "Tell us about Marshall's suicide."

"Three days after Frank landed at San Antonio, his clothes, wallet and driving licence were found on the shores of the Amistad Reservoir. His RFID implant went cold about the same time. He was presumed dead after the subsequent investigation."

"You failed to notify your superiors that Marshall had absconded from his post in Iraq. Why?" Lund tapped her pen on the table like a schoolmistress. "His seniority and deep involvement with Messina should have prompted your immediate action."

Josh shifted in his chair. "Like I told the inquiry, Frank was deeply upset. I figured he'd calm down, call me from Kuwait. It was a mistake."

Lund brought the lights back up and scribbled a few more notes on her pad. Then she leaned back in her seat and fixed Josh with cold grey eyes.

"I'm finding it difficult to understand how we got here, Mister Keyes. Specifically, how you were unaware of Marshall's mental state prior to his disappearance."

Josh glanced at the wall, at the frozen image of Frank Marshall. The compound at Al-Basrah was the last place he'd seen Frank, alone in his office, mumbling incoherently, cuffing tears from his eyes. While Josh had wrestled with his conscience, Frank had left Iraq without warning.

"I worked closely with Frank Marshall for many years. In all that time his conduct and behaviour never gave me any reason to doubt his mental health. In my view, he was a highly professional, dedicated and respected leader. I trusted him completely."

Lund arched a pale eyebrow. "A misguided trust, it would seem. Perhaps you were too close."

Josh recalled the impossibly blue sky, his pale reflection in the elevator doors as it transported him far above the streets of Manhattan.

"I was twenty-four years old when I was assigned to the New York office. My second op put me in the North Tower on the morning of Nine-Eleven. I was in a washroom on the hundred and seventh floor when we got word the planes had gone dark. The truth? I was terrified. Every fibre of my being screamed at me to get the hell out of that building. But Frank was in my ear, coached me all the way. He got me through that morning, and every operation after that. Do I feel a sense of loyalty towards Frank Marshall? Sure I do. Does that loyalty extend to covering the ass of a man who has betrayed me? Who has undermined The Committee's confidence in me? No, ma'am, it does not."

Lund made a *hmmm* sound. "Is there anything else about Marshall you can tell us? His motivations, intentions, anything?"

Josh shook his head. "No, ma'am. If Frank Marshall had secrets, he didn't share them with me."

Lund put down her pen and leaned into Beeton's ear for several moments. Beeton, his eyes never leaving Josh's, nodded in agreement.

"Marshall's intimate knowledge of Messina poses a considerable risk," Lund announced.

"I doubt Frank would do anything to expose us, ma'am. In my estimation—"

Beeton rapped his knuckles on the table. "This isn't a debate, Keyes. We're not asking for your opinion here."

"Understood, but with all due respect, Frank can't stop the Transition."

Lund shook her head, as if explaining to a child.

"You're missing the point, Mister Keyes. Before or after the Transition, it doesn't matter. What troubles our leaders is the message that Marshall's continued liberty sends to others in our organisation. Word has spread; a senior figure has abandoned the cause, a man who has intentionally deceived us, and who has managed to avoid detection and capture for some time, despite our efforts and considerable resources. He has challenged our authority, made us appear impotent. This is unacceptable. Do you understand?"

Josh nodded. "Absolutely, ma'am."

"This is a critical period for our organisation," Lund

continued. "As the Transition approaches, some of our people may begin to question their faith in Messina, their role in its implementation, or indeed their very humanity. These are natural reactions, but doubt and uncertainty can do us great damage. What we need now is stability and, more importantly, an unswerving conviction in the path our leaders have chosen. We must be as one, Mister Keyes. Marshall's continued autonomy jeopardises that."

Josh sat in silence as Lund swiped at a message on her phone. She folded her arms, gave Josh a cold stare. "You are to track Marshall down and return him to us for evaluation."

Josh raised his eyebrows. "You want him alive? All due respect, I don't think—"

Lund silenced him with a raised hand. "Marshall's capture will send a strong message. Fears will be calmed, faith restored." She tapped her notes on the table. "A replacement has been found, and your FEMA workload reassigned..."

*No!*

"A field team, plus any additional resources, will be made available to you. Is this understood, Mister Keyes?"

Beneath the table, Josh balled his fists. This was a demotion, plain and simple. He was out of the loop. He wanted to punch the walls. Instead, he remained poker-faced.

"Of course."

Beeton leaned forward in his chair. "You know the sonofabitch best, Keyes. We don't care what you have to do, just find him. Right now Marshall's a goddam tumour that needs cutting out. Quickly."

"I'll take care of it," Josh assured them.

"Do that. And after he's been wrung dry, you can drop the bastard back into that goddam lake. Is that clear?"

"Crystal."

"Good. The clock's ticking. Any more fuck ups and it's on you."

Lund picked up a telephone, signalling the end of the meeting.

Josh got to his feet and headed straight for the car park. He had to swallow his anger, focus.

Outside the sun had set, the eastern slopes shrouded in a cold grey blanket. Josh steered the Grand Cherokee down the twisting dirt road, headlamps slicing through the mist. Did they really think Frank would be picked up that easily, confess his crimes and cheerfully place a noose around his own neck? The Committee wasn't stupid, no sir, but they had to know that an experienced field operative like Frank would be an extremely hard target to hit. And where to begin? Like all operators, Frank's real identity had long been erased: birth certificate, medical records, even his social security number. Frank Marshall did not exist, period.

In fact, there was never any Frank Marshall in the first place.

Nor a Josh Keyes.

What was real - and very dangerous - were the lies he'd told to Lund and Beeton.

He'd not only respected Frank Marshall, he'd felt a deep sense of loyalty to the man. Frank had taken him under his wing from the very beginning, fast-tracking his career, promoting him to trusted lieutenant, anointing Josh with authority, responsibility, praising him to others in the organisation. He owed Frank everything.

Later, when the anxiety attacks began, the secret boozing and erratic behaviour, Josh had covered his boss' ass as much as he could. He'd pleaded with Frank to get help, got him prescription drugs, cleaned up his puke, dry-cleaned his suits, stood in for him at meetings. Yet even in his darkest moments, Frank had never confided in him, not once. Josh figured it was some kind of delayed post-traumatic stress. Whatever it was, it had turned his former mentor from a stone-cold killer into a pussy-ass cry-baby. If Josh delivered him to Lund and Beeton in one piece, Frank would probably spill his guts about his breakdown. They would discover the extent of the lies and cover-ups that Josh had committed to save Frank's drunken ass. If that happened, Josh was finished. The Committee demanded loyalty from its people. Anything else was simply unacceptable. And unforgivable.

And there was something else too, something that Frank was keeping from everyone, something that made them all nervous.

He recalled the surveillance footage, the field-craft that had fooled the cameras, that familiar posture, the loping stride, the resolve in those watchful eyes. Whatever mental hellhole Frank had descended into, he'd managed to claw his way out, and now Frank was back.

More than that, Frank was on a mission.

Before Josh killed him, he would find out what it was.

# CHAPTER 5

"Sit down," Roy mouthed through the glass partition.

"Please, boss, my brother, he wait for me in Arrivals. Give him message, yes?"

"Not possible. Take a seat. Someone will see you shortly."

He waved the man away and flopped down into a chair. Beyond the security glass, the holding room was populated with seventy or so new arrivals seeking refuge in Britain. Roy knew that most would now be rehearsing stories of torture and persecution for his colleagues in the processing team, but he didn't blame them. He'd probably do anything to escape whatever Third World shithole they'd flown in from, a recent and vocal observation that had earned him a written warning.

The blot on his copybook had worried Roy; there wasn't much work out there, and the irony was if he ever lost his job, he'd probably end up competing for employment with someone on the other side of the glass. He'd done well to get this far, Assistant Immigration Officer. He just had to tread a little more carefully.

He thought of Sammy and checked his messages. Nothing. There'd been no contact since their run-in at Max's school. Maybe there'd been a change of plan. Whatever the reason, Roy was glad. As each day passed he began to relax a little more.

Another new arrival tapped on the security glass.

It was a woman this time, Somali or Sudanese, Roy guessed, wrapped in a red and green silk gown. There was a vague beauty about her, the light brown eyes, the high cheekbones, perfect white teeth. She held a screaming child up to the glass like a trophy.

"Baby sick," she mouthed.

The kid wailed like a banshee. Roy punched the intercom button. "The doctor will be here soon."

"Baby sick," the woman repeated.

"Won't be long," Roy smiled, ending the conversation.

The woman stared at him for a moment then turned away, heaving the child onto her hip. He heard the door behind him click and he sprang out of the chair. His team leader, Yasin, marched in. He raised a suspicious grey eyebrow at Roy.

"Any problems?"

"Possible sick child. The woman in green." Roy pointed through the glass.

"Noted."

Yasin clutched a sheaf of folders to his chest and walked along the row of interview booths, placing one at each station. Roy trailed behind him, eager to please. The stench of his written warning followed him like a bad smell.

"Need a hand, Yaz?"

"No."

Yasin snapped on booth lights as he went, creating a stir on the other side of the glass. He doubled back along the booths, tapping microphones, straightening

chairs. A young Asian man approached the glass. Yasin raised his hand and leaned into a microphone. He spoke rapid-fire in one of his many dialects. The man hesitated, then stepped back. Yasin nodded his thanks. Roy was impressed. That's why Yasin was a team leader: a stickler for the rules and the command of several tongues ensured his rapid rise up the promotion ladder. His appearance helped too, the bald dome and large grey beard a magnet for those of the faith who felt they might get a sympathetic ear. Instead, they got the same rigorous interrogation that everyone else got, regardless of race or religion. Yasin was an equal opportunities bastard, but the man was tough on his troops too. They'd been sort-of friends once, during probation. That hadn't lasted long.

The door opened again and a line of tired-looking immigration officers filed into the room. They took a booth each as Yasin briefed them. Roy's phone chimed an incoming message and he stepped out into the corridor:

*I'm downstairs, in Arrivals. Can we meet?*

Roy frowned; Vicky never texted him unless it was to berate him for something, usually Max. He ducked back into the interview room.

"Yaz, can I take my break early? My ex-wife is here."

The team leader glowered at him. "I told you before, it's Mister Goreja. Remember, you're already on a warning. You want to return to the ramps?"

Roy shook his head. He'd worked airside at Gatwick for several years, loading and unloading baggage in long, back-breaking shifts and in all weathers. He'd hated it.

The older man checked his watch. "Thirty minutes, no more."

Roy mumbled his thanks and tapped out a reply to Vicky. He took a back staircase down to the Arrivals concourse.

The coffee shop was tucked between a newsagent and a currency exchange kiosk. Roy ordered a white coffee. He searched for a table and swore under his breath when he saw another colleague sitting nearby. Colin Furness was in his early sixties, a widower, and a heartbeat away from retirement. Any conversation with the terminally dismal Colin depressed Roy. He didn't want to end up like that, miserable, embittered by his job yet fearing the emptiness of retirement. The older man saw him and waved.

"Hi, Colin."

"Roy. What brings you over to the dark side?"

"Meeting the ex. You?"

"Chemist. Bowels are playing me up something chronic today."

"Sorry to hear that," Roy smiled, moving all the time. "See you later." Colin looked disappointed.

He found a table at the back of the room and sat down. He sipped his brew and watched a gaggle of new arrivals filing past the shop. Many were loaded with luggage and duty-free bags, and almost all of them were woefully under-dressed for the March weather waiting for them.

He saw Vicky approaching and waved. She bought a coffee and weaved through the maze of tables towards him. She wore a navy raincoat belted tightly around her waist, her dark hair heaped stylishly upon her head, a pair of expensive-looking sunglasses clamping it all in position.

"Are you sure you don't want to sit in the storeroom?"

Vicky chided, dropping breathlessly into the chair opposite Roy.

Roy bristled. Even her accent had changed, far more cultured than it used to be.

"I'm on a break and I don't want to get hassled. What are you doing at Heathrow?"

Vicky looped her laptop bag over the back of her chair and swiped a few stray hairs off her forehead. "I'm doing a human-interest piece, a working mum who happens to be a pilot."

Roy smirked. "Not exactly investigative journalism, is it? Still, I guess it's the best you can hope for at that rag of yours."

"*The West London Herald* has a circulation of over a hundred thousand. That's hardly a rag, Roy."

"Whatever."

Roy simmered. Unlike him, Vicky was ambitious, determined. She'd just got her degree in journalism when they'd first met, during that distant, hot summer. A year later and they were married, with Max already on the way. Roy was happy. Vicky, on the other hand, had begun to regret her recklessness. Five years on and his ex-wife had her Masters, a good job, and a smart flat close to the River Thames. They were worlds apart, always had been. Roy knew that from the moment he'd met her. He was still in love with her, he knew that too, but her success intimidated him. And when Roy felt worthless he usually went on the attack.

"I thought you were a senior reporter? Isn't that the sort of fluff they give to a work-experience kid?"

"Everyone mucks in at the Herald. George needs copy for the online edition. I said I'd cover it."

"Hardly the big break you're looking for, is it? Must be killing you."

Vicky sipped her coffee, wiping lipstick marks off the rim of her mug. "It'll come. One has to be patient, that's all."

"One does," Roy mocked. "Then again there's always Jimmy. There's a story, right there."

Vicky frowned. "Please, not again."

"That's it, just keep ignoring it. It never goes away for me."

She glared at him across the table. "I don't need reminding, Roy. It's what broke us, remember?"

"I don't get you. It's an important story, with local interest. Right up the Herald's street."

"It would smack of a personal crusade."

"It is."

"Yes, for you." Vicky sighed, nursed her coffee. "Maybe you should face the truth. Jimmy's been gone for three years. No one comes back alive after that, especially in Baghdad."

"How many fucking times do I have to say it? He wasn't in Baghdad. You heard his voicemail." He took a breath, swallowed his frustration. "Jimmy was working at some installation near the coast when he went missing. The only thing I can find on the Internet is the ABOT, the Al-Basrah Oil Terminal, where they load the big tankers. It's a story, Vicky, an important one. You could speak to George, get the Herald to demand answers. No one's talking to me anymore."

"Lots of people go missing in Iraq, Roy. Not just westerners."

"So use that angle then."

Vicky didn't answer. Instead, she finished her coffee and scraped the cup to one side. "I need to talk to you about something else, Roy. Something important."

"More important than Jimmy?"

She gave him a hard stare. "At this moment in time, yes."

Roy bit his tongue, checked his watch. "Make it quick. I've got to go soon."

Vicky cleared her throat. "Well, as you know things between Nate and me are going well. We're serious about each other. And he cares about Max, too."

Roy boiled with jealousy. Nate Anderson, a big-shot hedge fund manager, son of a wealthy New York financier. Roy had taken an instant dislike to the man, not just because he was sleeping with his estranged wife, but also because he was taller, better looking and infinitely more successful. He had lots of money, a nice car, and a pent-house apartment that overlooked Hyde Park. Vicky had once said the view was magnificent. Roy had remarked that the view she was probably more familiar with was that of Nate's bedroom ceiling.

*He's better at that too,* Vicky had smiled.

Touché, bitch.

The truth was, the American hailed from a different universe and Vicky had been drawn into his orbit. In a short time, they'd gravitated towards each other like two shining celestial bodies, their compatibility written in the stars. By comparison, Roy felt like an insignificant lump of moon rock. No, more like an alien turd on a lump of moon rock.

Vicky's words pulled him back to the table. "Things have changed, Roy. Nate's been offered a position, a senior one."

Roy responded with a sarcastic handclap. "Congratulations. Remind him to take the silver spoon out of his arse before he sits on his new throne."

"It's in New York. He wants Max and me to join him."

Roy's face dropped. "Say again?"

"He wants us all to go to New York. His family is very influential, so visas and employment won't be a problem. Max would be taken care of too—"

"He's asked you to marry him," Roy realised.

Across the table, Vicky took a breath. "Yes. Once things are settled between us."

"Settled? That's cold."

"It's a wonderful opportunity, Roy. There's a special school for Max in Connecticut. We're talking the very best in care and facilities." She reached into her laptop bag. "Here, I printed out their prospectus. That's for you, to keep."

Roy skimmed the pages. It was all ivy-covered buildings and state-of-the-art amenities under a cloudless Connecticut sky.

"You could come and visit whenever you like," he heard Vicky say. "We'll pay your airfare of course."

Roy swiped the prospectus to one side. Damp rings of coffee soaked through the paper. "That's all well and good, but as you rightly pointed out, we're still married. I'm Max's father. I have rights."

Vicky plucked a tissue from her pocket and blotted the prospectus. She avoided Roy's sullen gaze. "We wouldn't do anything without your permission, Roy. Nate has a family lawyer. This could all be done with the minimum of fuss and at no expense to you. You can meet him if you want. I really think—"

"On what grounds? The divorce, I mean."

"We've been apart for two years, so a no-fault separation would work. I'm not interested in blame."

"Sounds like the paperwork's already been drawn up."

"Nate is taking up his position at the end of next month. He wants us to travel together. As a family."

Roy sat in silence for a while. She'd wounded him, but in doing so she'd also handed him a little power. And he intended to use it. He checked his watch again. "I've got to get back. I'm late already."

Vicky reached across the table. "Please, Roy, we need to discuss this."

He shook her hand off his arm. "I don't have to do anything." He stood up and leaned over the table. Cold coffee slopped across the prestigious Connecticut school. "You've got some nerve, Vicky. You were never there for me, so why should I help you? As for divorce, well, a courtroom might be a good place to get everything out in the open. Like a missing brother-in-law. Someone might actually sit up and take a bit of notice."

Vicky shot out of her chair. He could see the pain in her eyes, the angry twist to her mouth.

"Don't do this, Roy—"

"Tough shit. Max stays here. You don't like it, I'll see you in court."

He dodged between the tables, flushed by his rare victory. He swerved towards the counter and ordered a coffee to go. He heard Vicky's heels clicking angrily from the coffee shop, and the satisfaction of his triumph quickly faded. Vicky wanted a new life, that was all, but Roy still found it difficult to forgive her. In the early days, she'd been sympathetic about Jimmy while Roy had chased shadows. They'd talked, and argued, then fought, long and hard. Bitterness had turned to poison. Vicky had left, taking Max with her. She'd joined the Herald, but shied away from the story for fear of getting burned by her personal involvement. Roy hated her for it, but deep down he knew she was right. Jimmy was gone. A newspaper story, if there was one, wouldn't bring him back. Vicky had broken his heart, twice.

All he wanted now was revenge, and she'd given him the opportunity to exact it. Yet surprisingly, it didn't make him feel any better. At that moment he wasn't sure whom he disliked more, himself or Vicky.

Out on the concourse, he took a detour to the men's toilet. He threw his half-finished coffee into a waste bin. He urinated then washed his hands. He dried them on a fistful of paper towels that followed the coffee into the bin.

The radio on his hip crackled.

He left the toilet. Not once did he look in the mirror.

At that exact moment, a hundred feet away, Frank Marshall was moving through the Arrivals hall towards the exit.

He'd passed through customs without incident, using one of the passports taken from his personal strongbox in Manhattan. In this case it was a Belgian one, in the name of Doug LeBreton, and although Frank's face had changed since the original photo was taken, it hadn't changed that much. Gone were the ponytail and the scruffy clothes; now Frank wore a grey suit and blue tie, a black raincoat draped over one arm, a leather carry-on in his hand. He looked like a businessman, not the first-class type but more of a travelling salesman, an eighty-hour-a-week guy who lived for commission and would travel anywhere to get it. Generic. Forgettable. Like the rest of his fellow passengers on the American Airlines red-eye flight, he looked a little beat, having endured a bumpy ride east in the grip of a fast-moving jet stream. The aircraft had landed on time, and now he had a thirty-minute window, maybe less, to get clear of the airport.

Overhead signs pointed him to subways and bus stops.

Frank kept moving towards the cab rank beyond the terminal doors. Outside the air was cold and damp, the grey sky already darkening, the roar of distant aircraft competing with the black snake of taxicabs rattling in front of the terminal. He spied the cameras overhead, the faces of the crowd around him, the cars that loitered nearby. He had fifteen minutes now, maybe less. Soon the phones would be ringing in a dozen agencies across Europe, Doug LeBreton's mugshot broadcast to police, security services, Interpol and others. He kept his head low and shuffled forward to the head of the line. A black cab squealed to a stop and Frank ducked inside.

"Where to, mate?"

"London. The West End."

The cab pulled away. Frank spun around in his seat, swiping the condensation from the rear window. He watched the traffic behind them, saw no wild movements, no sudden acceleration or changes of direction. They joined the freeway into the city. As the driver answered a personal phone call, Frank shoved the now-useless Belgian passport deep behind his seat.

Just before they reached the sprawl of Hammersmith, Frank ordered the driver to pull over. He paid the man in cash and disappeared into the darkness of a nearby park, emerging onto a busy high street on the other side.

He checked a route map and mingled with a group of shoppers clustered beneath the shelter of a bus stop. He waited ten minutes and boarded a bus towards southwest London.

An hour later he checked into a modest hotel on Richmond Hill. The lobby was empty when he arrived and he paid cash, in advance, for two weeks. For an extra hundred, the manager was persuaded to overlook the formalities and

Frank was given his key. The room was clean and comfortable, and the view beyond the window provided a glimpse of the River Thames at the bottom of the hill.

He took a long shower, switched the lights off, and stretched out on the bed.

For the first time in forty-eight hours, he could relax a little. As his breathing slowed and sleep beckoned, Frank clutched the dog-eared travel Bible to his chest and thought about the path of redemption he'd chosen. He was a way down that path now, his sights set on another who was lost, who mourned a loved one and sought closure.

Frank would deliver that closure, and more, before the demons, both real and imagined, caught up with him again.

And when they did, Frank would destroy them all.

## CHAPTER 6

THE BUS RUMBLED TO A STOP OUTSIDE THE FITZROY Estate.

Roy shuffled off with a dozen others and trudged beneath the concrete archway, a fine mist falling through the yellow wash of street lamps. On nights like these the estate reminded Roy of a prison, dull grey concrete blocks surrounding the exercise yard, the long balconies stacked on top of each other like tiers of cells. Only this prison had no guards, no watchtowers or lockdown. There were no bars or fences either, but Roy felt trapped within its walls just the same.

Two men loitered on the first floor landing. They were draped over the balcony, the pungent smell of cannabis drifting in the air. Roy recognised one of them, his neighbour's latest boyfriend. Dwayne, or something. He seemed oblivious to the cold, wearing only jeans and a white vest. A comb with a black fist handle poked out of his unkempt afro. The other man was better dressed for the weather, a New York baseball cap pulled low over his brow, a black hoodie over that, black jeans and trainers. The street robber's uniform of choice. They stopped talking as Roy approached.

"Evening," Roy muttered, fiddling with his key.

They didn't answer, and neither did Roy expect them to. This was the Fitzroy, after all.

He shut the front door behind him.

He kicked his shoes off and made a cup of tea in the kitchen. He used the rest of the water to stir up a curry-flavoured Pot Noodle and retired to the living room. He slumped onto the couch in front of the TV. He ate. He channel surfed. He was bored and tired, but not enough to go to bed. He toyed with his phone, considered texting an apology to Vicky. He decided against it. She was probably with Nate.

He stretched out on the sofa, found a late night movie on the TV, one about a kid who could jump through time and space just by using the power of thought. He wished he could do that too.

He fell asleep.

The phone trembled on the coffee table.

Roy bolted upright, startled. He cuffed saliva from the corner of his mouth and fumbled for the remote. The time-jumper was gone, replaced by a man and woman kissing in soft, black and white focus and speaking in posh voices. He snapped the TV off. He scooped up his phone: almost one in the morning. He didn't recognise the number. He thought it might be Vicky, a new phone maybe, but calling him wasn't her style. She was a texter, her messages always sharp, disapproving.

"Hello?"

"Open the door, Roy."

*Oh shit.*

"Sammy?"

"Open the door. Leave the lights off."

The phone went dead. Roy sprang off the couch. He dropped the bolt on the front door, eased it open, peered along the landing. Deserted, the prison silent, slumbering like a dormant volcano. Then he heard movement in the stairwell, footsteps, the rustle of clothing. He retreated back down the hallway. A familiar shadow loomed in the doorway; Tank, Sammy's minder.

"In the sitting room," she commanded.

Tank's voice growled like a man's. She was a former cage fighter, and used to work the door at one of Sammy's nightspots. She was tall, just over six feet, and had one of those dreadlock Mohawks that was woven into a thick clump across her head. She was the butchest, most intimidating woman Roy had ever met. He slapped the light off.

"Pull the curtains."

Roy scraped them together.

He heard the front door close, the bolt slide into place. His legs felt hollow.

Two men entered the sitting room. The light came back on. Sammy's face was shrouded in an expensive designer hoodie.

"Jesus Christ, Sammy, you scared me to death."

Roy cursed himself for uttering the word. He didn't want to put ideas in anyone's head.

Sammy flicked his hood off and smoothed his grey mane. "Shut up."

Roy complied. Then glanced at the other man in the room, the one dwarfed between Sammy and Tank, a little older, fifties, carrying a black sports bag and wearing a dark coat and jeans. His balding grey hair was shaved close, his broken nose spread wide across his deeply lined face. He sat down on the couch and kicked his trainers off. He produced a packet of cigarettes from his coat pocket and lit one. Sammy broke the difficult silence.

"Roy, this is Derek. He's going to be staying here for a bit."

"He's what?"

Derek nailed him with a malignant stare. "Put the kettle on, son. I'm dying for a cuppa."

He was a Scot, his accent thick and harsh. Roy's feet were rooted to the carpet. "Say again?" he stammered.

Derek glanced at Sammy. "Forrest fucking Gump, this one." He sniggered, but the humour never made it to his cold grey eyes. "Tea. Now."

Roy willed his legs to move and headed for the kitchen. He filled the kettle, grabbed a mug from an overhead cupboard. Sammy trailed in behind him.

"What's going on, Sammy?"

"Derek needs to lay low for a while."

"He can't stay here."

"Yes he can. You live alone, rarely go out, no girlfriend— wait a minute, you're not a poof, are you, Roy?"

"Course not."

Sammy smiled. "Just checking. Like I say, you live alone, no regular visitors. You and Derek are a good fit."

Roy's mind raced. "There's no room."

"Really? Far as I can tell you've got two bedrooms in this shoebox."

"Yeah, mine and Max's."

Sammy's smile disappeared. "Don't lie to me. That kid hasn't stayed here for over a year. The mums down at the school, they like to gossip. Seems you're not pulling your weight as a dad, ignoring the kid. Still, I can see why; when the fruit of your loins turns out to be a window-licker, I guess it's hard to connect on an emotional level. And your ex, she thinks you're a loser. The word is, she wouldn't let him come within a thousand yards of this shithole. Smart girl."

He took a step closer, looming over Roy. "Derek stays. And a word of advice; him and me go back a long way, so I recommend you pay him the appropriate level of respect.

"Course," Roy mumbled, pulling open a drawer and fishing for a spoon. There was no point in arguing. His life had just gone up a few notches on the shit-o-meter. Or down. Whatever. "How long will he be here?"

"A few weeks. Six, tops."

Roy's eyes widened. "Six weeks? Jesus Christ, I've got a life here, Sammy."

"All evidence to the contrary."

Sammy produced a thick roll of fifty-pound notes from his pocket and peeled several off. "That's for Derek's keep. He likes a drink, but he's a punchy drunk, so stay out of his way when he's on one." He slapped the wad onto the counter.

Roy stared at the money, more cash than he'd held in his wallet for longer than he could remember. He had a sudden mental image of himself at the airport, boarding a plane, squeezing into a window seat, flying off to the sun, Sammy's cash stuffed into his pocket. Never coming back.

The image melted away as a cold sweat prickled Roy's skin. "This is about my job, right, Sammy?"

"Bingo."

"I can't do anything illegal. They don't just sack you, they prosecute."

"You'd better be careful then."

Roy felt a rush of panic. He wanted to charge past Sammy, out through the front door, run until his lungs burst. Coarse laughter drifted in from the room next door.

"Don't make me do this," Roy whispered. "You know I'm straight, always have been. I just want a quiet life. I can't afford to get mixed up in—"

Sammy grabbed Roy around the throat and slammed his head against a kitchen unit. Pain flashed and crockery rattled. Sammy's strong fingers dug into his neck. Roy wheezed.

"Sammy, please—"

The kettle whistled, filling the kitchen with steam.

Sammy grabbed it with his free hand.

"You ever watch the History Channel Roy? I saw this programme once, about the Roman Empire. Back then they used to pour molten lead into people's mouths as a form of execution. Cruel fuckers, eh?"

He held the kettle close. Roy could feel the heat on his cheek.

"We can work things out a couple of ways, Roy. Tank wanted me to use violence. She gets off on it, crazy fucking bitch."

He lowered the kettle and dropped his hand. Roy coughed and spluttered.

"I said no. I told her, I've known Roy Sullivan since he was a kid. Violence would work, sure, but I'm going to cut him some slack, for old time's sake. No rough stuff, just these." Sammy handed over his mobile. "Scroll through them. Some good ones there."

Roy took the phone. He jolted as if he'd been stung. The picture on the screen was of him, seated in a booth in an unfamiliar night spot, a drink in one hand, giving the camera the finger with the other, a stupid grin plastered across his chops. He swiped the screen: a topless girl straddled across his lap, platinum-blond hair falling down her back, voluminous breasts thrust in Roy's face. *What the hell?*

"Keep going," Sammy urged.

Roy did as he was told. With each image the mood darkened; clinking glasses with two hard-looking men, one shaven-headed, the other lank-haired, both suited, both tattooed, dead eyes and expensive wristwatches. A serious Roy, in deep conversation with same. Roy doing a line of coke.

The last picture was the worst; the lap dancer again, staring into the camera, her face ashen, eyes blackened, a deep cut across the bridge of her nose. Dried blood caked her hairline, her lips. Sammy snatched the phone from Roy's trembling hand.

"That's Tank's handiwork. Sofia didn't mind too much, though. You know what Polish birds are like, hard as nails. She got well paid too. In any case, she'd swear in court that it was you who did that."

"Me?"

Roy was suffering from system overload. It looked like him in the photos, but he didn't remember any of it. He must have a double—

"Yes, you," confirmed Sammy. "You made it easy, leaving your glass on the bar while you popped to the Ladies. I bet you don't even remember leaving The Duke."

"The Duke?"

"Thought so. Anyway, I don't think a night on the gear with a couple of jailbirds would go down too well at work. As for the sexual assault on poor little Sofia—"

"I didn't touch her. I've never seen her before in my life."

"The camera never lies, Roy. Your fingerprints are all over her arse." Sammy flicked through the images again.

"Seriously, there're some cracking shots there. Oh, she reported the assault to the police, by the way. Made a statement, gave a description, of you, in fact. Not an accurate one, not enough to get you lifted, but she'll pick you out of a line-up if she has to. You see where all this is going, Roy? You're at a crossroads, and you've got two options."

He waved his phone in Roy's face.

"Option one; you fuck things up for me and this little photo shoot will find its way into the hands of the law. Then, after you've done your bird and you're rebuilding your shitty little life, I'll be there to remind you how you fucked things up. And that'll never stop, Roy. Ever."

Sammy leaned against the counter, folded his arms.

"Judging by the look on your face, I'm guessing you're going for option two."

"What do you want?" Roy finally managed to croak.

"Derek's going to catch a plane. I'll let you know which one when the time comes. All you have to do is get him onto that plane, avoiding the usual formalities. You know, stuff like customs and security checks. Walk him through the terminal unmolested and get him to the gate. That's it."

In any other situation, Roy would've laughed. Smuggle someone onto a plane? In this day and age? Then he realised Sammy was still talking.

"All the time Derek is here you mustn't have a single visitor. Not one. No one comes through that front door unless it's Tank or me. I don't care who it is; gas man, electricity, Jehovah's fucking Witness. No one gets in. No one sees him. Got it?"

"I got it."

"Good." Roy flinched as Sammy patted his cheek. "Now fix him his tea."

Sammy disappeared into the sitting room.

Roy held onto the counter. He wanted to urinate but was afraid to move. He was in deep with Sammy now, deep enough to have serious, life-threatening consequences. He heard the front door close, saw two shadows pass by the window.

He was alone with Derek.

He forced himself to focus.

He made tea and carried it into the sitting room. Derek was stretched out on the sofa, a cushion behind his head. He kicked his legs off, produced a small bottle of Scotch from his sports bag, and poured a stiff measure into his tea. He sparked up another cigarette, the smoke swirling around the room. Roy moved to open a window.

"Leave it," Derek ordered.

"I had bronchitis as a kid. I can't be around cigarette smoke."

"You'll get used to it."

Roy let the curtain drop back into place. "I'll go make up the bed."

"You do that. And I like a cooked breakfast."

"I've got to work in the morning."

"Well, you'd better set your alarm then." Derek took a deep pull of his cigarette and exhaled in Roy's direction. The Scot's hard eyes bored into him. "What time do you finish?"

"I should be back by half-seven."

Derek waved at the DVD's stacked beneath the TV. "Your movie collection is shite. You got Sky?"

Roy shook his head.

"Netflix? Amazon?"

Another shake. "Can't afford any of that. It's just Freeview."

"Fuck sake," Derek swore. "Get some more movies. And

pick me up a paperback or two. I like to read. Crime, murder, that type of thing."

"Sure."

Derek stretched out and reached for the TV remote. "Fucking Freeview," he muttered.

Roy excused himself, made up the spare bed and retreated to his bedroom. Then he dragged a chest of drawers inch by silent inch across the carpet until it blocked the door.

He climbed into bed and lay beneath the quilt for a long time, staring up at the bars of light that stretched across the bedroom ceiling. He listened in the darkness, to the sound of the TV across the hall, to the pad of feet on the carpet outside, to the echo of Derek urinating in the toilet; and much later, the sound of the spare room door closing. A short while after that, Derek's snores filtered through the wall between them. They were long and loud, and seemingly never-ending.

Red digits hovered in the darkness: 03:19. An early rise meant less than three hours sleep. A black cloud of despair settled over him. His flat, his private sanctuary, had been invaded by another, a man in hiding, belligerent, dangerous. Hiding from who was anyone's guess, but Roy assumed it was the law.

Six weeks, Sammy said. All he had to do was tough it out until then, after which he'd probably be arrested for trying to smuggle Derek onto a flight. And even if he got away with it, would Sammy ever let him go? Would he use this whole episode as blackmail, demand favour after illegal favour, until one day the police kicked his door in? Of course he would. And when Roy finally outlived his useful-ness, he'd have boiling water poured down his throat. Or something. Roy shivered in the darkness.

He'd managed to avoid the displeasure of Sammy French for most of his life. As kids, both he and Jimmy had been tolerated, allowed to hang around the playground while Sammy and his gang ruled from their fortress of monkey bars.

As the years went by, Jimmy joined the army, mum and dad passed away, and Roy was left alone, a permanent fixture on the estate where new gangs had taken over the playground. Sammy had gone too, the law finally catching up with him.

He'd resurfaced a few years later, a different man. Gone was the wildness of youth, replaced by a ruthless ambition for legitimacy. But for those who knew his past, the stench of gangland hovered around Sammy like a cloud of flies. Despite the nightclubs and restaurants, and the big house that overlooked Richmond Park, those who knew him were convinced. Sammy French was, and always would be, a dangerous criminal.

And now Roy was fixed on his radar.

For the first time in his life he considered running. He could pack a bag, grab his passport, empty his paltry savings account and get the hell out. But where would he go?

So the problem remained, and now he lay ten feet from a psycho stranger. He was trapped, the walls of his bedroom pressing inwards. The hours passed. Panic ebbed and flowed. The bars across the ceiling faded and the sky outside paled.

He thought of Jimmy and realised what the dream meant. It was a warning, an omen of bad things to come, now personified by Sammy and Derek, brutal prophets of doom about to ruin his life.

Roy snuck out of bed and rummaged at the bottom of his cupboard. He found Jimmy's old army day-sack, retrieved the Gerber combat knife from inside, and wedged it beneath his mattress. He climbed back into bed, his fingers finding the tough black plastic of the hilt, reassured by its proximity.

But sleep evaded him, and his thoughts turned to the airport, to the task that lay ahead. As the sun crept above the horizon, Roy realised that he was about to face the most dangerous challenge of his life.

The next few weeks would decide if he made it through to the other side.

## CHAPTER 7

Josh tugged his seatbelt a little tighter as the Gulfstream G650 dipped her nose towards the distant lights of RAF Northolt. He felt the undercarriage lock home with a solid thump and watched the rise and fall of the port wing as the aircraft levelled for landing.

Beyond the wingtip, patchwork fields surrendered to the grey urban sprawl of outer London. Josh was a native of Arizona, born and raised beneath the warmth of its eternal sunshine. By contrast, the view outside looked cold, damp and miserable. Despite this being his first trip to the UK, Josh decided it was another reason not to stay a minute longer than necessary. The plane would be kept on standby. The hunter team would do their job.

They were scattered around the cabin now, six former Special Forces guys and two Marines from Force Recon, all of them with extensive operational experience in a wide variety of countries. The Marines were communications specialists who'd served with the JSOC Signals Team. They would be juiced into a myriad of global surveillance systems, acting as Josh's eyes and ears. Like the rest of the guys, they were primed and ready to get the job done.

The Gulfstream returned to earth with a gentle bump and a muffled roar of reverse thrust. It taxied around the apron and veered inside a private hangar where it jerked to a stop and shut down its engines.

Josh was out of the aircraft first. Two men waited at the bottom of the steps. He didn't recognise either of them.

"Mister Keyes?" said the well-groomed collegiate type wrapped in a smart overcoat and scarf. "Mister Beeton sent me. My name is Fisher. I'm from the embassy."

They shook hands and Fisher reached inside his coat.

"These are your temporary passports, all bearing official stamps of entry. I'll need those back before you leave the country."

Fisher was younger than Josh, well-scrubbed and impeccably dressed, probably a rising State Department star, cutting his diplomatic teeth at the Court of St James. He was confident, authoritative, and brandished Beeton's name like a baseball bat.

Josh fanned the Canadian passports like a hand of cards. He saw stamps and mugshots and pseudonyms. He nodded his approval and pocketed them.

The man standing next to Fisher was older and taller, forties, with big shoulders and receding grey hair that was cut short to a scalp that sported several pale scars. His had a lined face around sharp eyes, and a strong jaw that sprouted a couple of days of grey growth. He was dressed casually, jeans and a roll-neck jumper, a black North Face coat. He greeted Josh with a rough, calloused hand.

"Dave Villiers."

His voice was deep, the accent London, heavy.

"Mister Villiers is SIS," Fisher announced, "but his loyalty is to us. He'll act as your local point man."

"Good to meet you. Where are we headed?"

"Mister Beeton has arranged for the use of a house in Chelsea," Fisher said.

"Then let's go."

Three vehicles waited nearby, black Audi Q7's, doors and tailgates open. Villiers slipped behind the wheel of the nearest one, and Josh got in back. Fisher rode shotgun next to Villiers. The hunter team squeezed themselves and their gear into the other two. They left the airport in a tight convoy and headed into central London.

Josh didn't talk as Fisher tapped away on his mobile. Villiers remained silent too, steering the big Audi through the heavy traffic. Josh checked his phone; nothing from Beeton or Lund. All of his FEMA responsibilities had been handed over to someone else, his own inbox empty, except for a reminder, a National Advisory Council meeting at the end of April. Not the whole council of course, just the key players already selected for the continuation process. Josh cursed under his breath; another crucial meeting he would miss because of this goddam reassignment.

Fifty minutes later the Audis turned into a quiet street in Chelsea. Expensive properties crowded the narrow road on either side. Villiers swung the wheel into an open driveway that dipped beneath a luxurious period house into an underground parking lot.

Fisher led them inside and up to the first-floor reception room. The heavy drapes had been drawn, the giant wall-mounted TV muted. Pots of coffee and plates of sandwiches waited on a long sideboard. The hunter team ignored the refreshments, piling their gear against the wall and waiting in silence for instructions. Josh and Villiers sat down on the large sofas grouped around a glass coffee table. When everyone had settled, Fisher addressed the room.

"So, welcome to London, gentlemen. This house will be your main base of operations while you're here in the UK. No doubt you'll have questions, many of which will be answered by the briefing packets left in your rooms. Please familiarise yourselves with them, and the details of your Canadian passports too, should you fall foul of local law enforcement. Bear in mind I know nothing of your operation, and neither do I need to know. Deniability, gentlemen, is essential. Remember that when you're outside these walls. Understood?"

Josh nodded. He guessed Fisher was a product of The Committee's covert executive programme, its secretive alumni liberally sprinkled across every branch of government. While people like Josh and his hunter team got their hands dirty, Fisher and his kind fought a different and infinitely more complex war, in the chambers of Senate and Congress, in front of TV cameras and microphones. Everyone had a role to play, even those who were oblivious to what was happening around them.

He was reminded of George W. Bush's visit to the elementary school on the morning of Nine Eleven. He recalled the President's face, the bewilderment, the incomprehension when he'd heard about the hit on the Trade Centre. He'd been rooted to his chair, dumbstruck. Frightened. That shit couldn't be faked.

The conspiracy theorists were all over it, though; Bush was complicit, the good ol' boy routine masking a sinister, Machiavellian personality. They couldn't have been more wrong. Some of his administration, sure, but Bush? Not a chance. Every president after Eisenhower had been vetted, groomed and selected. Most had no clue about the power that existed behind the throne. The truth was, it didn't matter who was president. The Committee held true power because they controlled the global media. They'd fought a secret war for decades, to sanitise and trivialise the news, to disengage the population from the ideas and principles of freedom and democracy, to shift focus from the dull grey world of politics to the shining lights of a celebrity culture that dazzled and entertained.

*Four Americans butchered in Benghazi? The White House complicit? Screw that! Kim Kardashian is trashing her sister's boyfriend on Twitter, y'all!*

The Committee's war on reality was almost complete. It was a twenty-four-hour news cycle now. Scandalous headlines, salacious gossip, reality TV, the ethnic cleansing of morals, values, traditions, culture, all clearing the way for the Transition, when everything would be wiped clean. Humanity, reprogrammed and rebooted.

Josh couldn't wait. But killing Frank Marshall came first. He heard Fisher talking, and refocused his thoughts.

"—is a highly secure, mission-capable facility with a secure command suite situated in the basement. Where are the comms guys?"

Josh's Eyes and Ears held up their hands.

"We have hard-wired, piggy-back feeds routed via the embassy into all major stateside intel hubs," Fisher explained, "plus encrypted voice and data access to TDL Corporate and our Executive and Legislative sponsors in DC. I suggest you familiarise yourselves with the equipment as soon as possible."

Eyes and Ears looked at Josh. He nodded, and the men grabbed their shockproof cases and left the room.

"That's it," Fisher said."Any questions?"

Josh shook his head.

"Okay, your confidential briefing package has been pre-loaded on to the AV system. I have to get back to the embassy. My number's there." He snapped a business card onto the glass table and left the room.

Josh worked the controls of the huge LED TV. Two blown-up images of Frank Marshall filled the screen, one in front of the bank in Manhattan; the other a much clearer shot from the immigration desk at Heathrow.

"This is the target," he told the room. "His name is Frank Marshall, a former TDL executive in Security Division. Marshall is an extremely dangerous individual with extensive knowledge of our organisation and its objectives, and now he's gone rogue. The Committee wants him located and terminated fast."

Josh swallowed, conscious of the lie. There was no going back now.

"Twenty-one hours ago, Marshall passed through Heathrow using a Belgian passport in the name of Doug LeBreton. The last confirmed CCTV shot we got of Marshall was outside the terminal waiting for a cab. Dave?"

Villiers drained the dregs of his coffee and got to his feet. The screen divided into multiple frames, the Heathrow taxi rank, stills from the Met police's ANPR system, street maps of west London.

"CCTV shows Marshall boarding a taxi outside Terminal Three. The driver was detained, the taxi searched, and the passport recovered. He confirmed Marshall was dropped off in a lay-by near Hammersmith."

Villiers blew up the street map to full-screen.

"He entered this park at eight-oh-seven pm yesterday evening. The only other exit is directly across the park, which empties onto Chiswick high street. We've gone over the footage from there with a fine tooth-comb, but we've failed to get a hit. We think we know why. Directly adjacent to the park entrance is a row of sheltered bus stops with limited camera coverage. The routes are varied, mostly heading west or southwest. My guess is that Marshall crossed the park and boarded a bus here, out of view of the CCTV. There are several bus companies that operate from that location and we've pulled last night's footage from their vehicles, but reviewing it will take some time. There are a lot of routes, a lot of stops." He turned to Josh. "Any ideas where Marshall could be headed?"

"None. His record shows he's visited the UK before, but only on a layover. He's never been to London. We need that footage."

"We're working as fast as possible."

"Good. Tell me about your set up."

"The investigation is being run out of Vauxhall under the banner Operation Talon. A confidential FBI file has been generated at your end, and that's been picked up by Interpol and fed to SIS and Scotland Yard. Marshall is wanted on international warrants for illegal banking practices and money laundering. We've also thrown in connections to terrorist organisations in Europe and Pakistan to beef up inter-agency cooperation. Frank's profile has been circulated on the Met's intelligence briefing system as a wanted individual, and I've got two mobile surveillance teams on standby for the legwork."

"Sounds good."

"Can I make a suggestion? Marshall will want to remain anonymous, keep his head down. That means frequenting less affluent areas of the city."

"If he's still in town."

"True, but until we've established otherwise, we have to assume he is. So he'll be staying in cheap accommodation, paying cash for everything. A man like that will stand out, especially an American. Once we've established his destination, I'd recommend distributing his profile to local hotels and B&B's. The tactic has worked for us worked before."

Josh hesitated. "Frank knows he's being hunted. If he gets a sniff of the dogs, he'll bolt. We may never find him."

"He has to stay somewhere, and low-rent establishments like cash payers."

Josh considered it for less than two seconds. "Okay, do it. Anything else?" Villiers shook his head. "In that case, we'll wrap it up for now."

Josh got to his feet and approached the contractors. "Get prepped and ready to deploy. When you're done, hit the racks. Unless we get any hard intel, the next briefing will be at seven am." They filed out of the room.

"Heavy-looking team," Villiers observed. "I was told this would be a bag job. A rendition."

"The situation has changed."

*Another lie.*

He handed Villiers a file. "Frank has an extensive background, both military and as an ops commander with TDL. If he wants to bring it, he will." Josh helped himself to another coffee, stirred in cream and sugar. "There's no room for complacency on this one, Dave. I'll coordinate the intel, authorise whatever assets we need, but locally I'll need you to keep things tight. We locate him, box him in, then take him down clean. I can't afford a single fuck up on this one."

"Understood."

Villiers fingered the intelligence packet, withdrew the black and white of Frank leaving the bank in Manhattan.

"I'm guessing you two know each other. Can you tell me something about him? Something personal?"

"He's a former Navy Seal, smart, resourceful, and highly dangerous. If he sniffs you out, he'll end you. That's all you need to know."

"What's he done?"

"That's not important. What's important is finding him."

Villiers got the message, got to his feet. "I'll crack the whip. Anything comes through, I'll be in touch."

The Brit left the room, and Josh drained his coffee. He was tired and edgy, the last seventy-two frantic hours taking their toll. He needed sleep, but it was a race against time now, and the clock was ticking.

He crossed the room and peered through the heavy drapes. The street below was devoid of life, no cars or pedestrians, just empty roads and sidewalks. Even though they were in the heart of London, it felt as if the Transition had already passed. What would it be like, he wondered, after the clean-up, after the regeneration?

The thought had consumed him when he'd attended his first orientation seminar at Turner's private ranch in New Mexico. Those first few nights were troublesome ones, the enormity of what lay ahead denying him sleep, the knowledge that the civilised world had no choice, and had to take action.

Now the only thing keeping him up at nights was Frank Marshall. But why England? Why now? So many goddam questions.

Josh let the curtain drop back into place. He had to file a report to Beeton, the first of his daily dispatches to Denver. One a day, until Frank was caught and rendered unto Caesar.

He headed down into the basement. Despite the pressure he was under, part of him was looking forward to the hunt. Frank had to be flushed from his bolthole, and once he was out in the open, Josh would unleash his dogs.

And when that happened, Frank Marshall wouldn't have a chance.

## THE HUNT BEGINS

Can Josh locate and kill Frank before the Transition begins?
Will Roy escape Sammy's clutches? And what exactly does
The Committee have in store for humanity?

Get ***The Angola Deception*** and discover the horrifying
truth behind the world's deadliest conspiracy.

**Order your copy of *The Angola Deception* now!**

ALSO BY DC ALDEN

*Invasion*

*Invasion - The Lost Chapters*

*The Angola Deception*

*Fortress*

**Discover more at:**

**www.dcalden.com**

44651916R00254

Printed in Poland
by Amazon Fulfillment
Poland Sp. z o.o., Wrocław